Love Letters at  a Bookshop

Kiley Dunbar is Scottish and lives in England with her husband, two kids and Amos the Bedlington Terrier. She writes around her work at a University in the North of England where she lectures in English Literature and creative writing. She is proud to be a member of the Romantic Novelists' Association and a graduate of their New Writers' Scheme.

Also by Kiley Dunbar

Christmas at Frozen Falls

Kelsey Anderson

One Summer's Night
One Winter's Night

Port Willow Bay

Summer at the Highland Coral Beach
Matchmaking at Port Willow

The Borrow a Bookshop

The Borrow a Bookshop Holiday
Christmas at the Borrow a Bookshop
Something New at the Borrow a Bookshop
Love Letters at the Borrow a Bookshop

KILEY DUNBAR

Love Letters
at the
Borrow *a*
Bookshop

hera

First published in the United Kingdom in 2024 by

Hera Books
Unit 9 (Canelo), 5th Floor
Cargo Works, 1-2 Hatfields
London SE1 9PG
United Kingdom

A CIP catalogue record for this book is available from the British Library.

Print ISBN 978 1 80436 463 5
Ebook ISBN 978 1 80436 462 8

Look for more great books at www.herabooks.com

Printed and bound in Great Britain by Clays Ltd, Elcograf S.p.A.

I

This book commemorates meeting Michael at the top of the Waverley Steps, and that huge bouquet of blue cornflowers. I'll never forget x

Advertisement: A Novel Holiday Idea

Borrow-A-Bookshop invites you to live out your dreams of running your very own bookshop in a historic Devonshire harbour village… for a fortnight.

Spend your days talking about books with customers in your own charming bookshop and serving up delicious food in your cosy cafe nook. Get to know our wonderful volunteers (all locals), always ready to offer a helping hand.

After shutting up shop, climb the spiral staircase to your bedroom with picture window seat and settle down to admire the Atlantic views. When your holiday's over, simply hand the keys to the next holidaymaker-bookseller.

Request your booking early. Currently, there is a thirty-two-month waiting list.

Includes full use of cafe kitchen, courtyard seating/catering area, one double bedroom upstairs, one single downstairs, plus small bathroom and private lawned back yard.

All bookshop and cafe takings retained by the Borrow-A-Bookshop Community Charity, Treasurer: Ms Jude Crawley, MA

Apply by email

£400 charge per let for 14 days

Chapter One

The Borrow-A-Bookshop stands – actually, it sort of slumps in its relaxed, four-hundred-year-old seaside cottage kind of way – in a quiet cobbled square just off Clove Lore's main thoroughfare, an alarmingly steep slope that the locals call Down-along when approaching the village from above and Up-along when standing on the harbourside and contemplating the long, sweaty trudge all the way up to the visitor centre.

Up at the top of Clove Lore's slope there are endless Atlantic views and the sense of standing Gulliver-like over the higgledy-piggledy slate rooftops below. Less picturesque, but unavoidable in a three-times winner of the 'Most Instagrammable Village in Devon' award, you'll also find extortionate fudge concessions, a massive car park, and no end of coach drivers lined up on the promontory's benches, drinking from thermoses and waiting for their holiday parties to return from paddling and pint-sipping Down-along.

At the foot of the slope, you won't be able to miss the delicious aroma coming from the Siren's Tail pub on the harbour wall, or the tinkling music of the cliff waterfall over the beach. Its waters plunge down onto green boulders before vanishing inside narrow caverns and

3

crevices, carried out of sight nobody knows how far under the sand.

At high tide your eyes will be delighted by the few colourful little boats bumping together on their ropes below the ancient stone harbour cob. When the waters retreat, the seabirds drop in, picking through the rock pools. On July afternoons like this one, the crests of gentle waves glint with stars, like someone's scattered sequins in the Atlantic.

Austen Archer's story, however, begins neither Down-along or Up-along, but rather in the middle of the slope, where today you can't get moving for tourists regretting their slippy summer sandals, all clinging to gateposts for dear life as they pass gingerly up and down the wide, cobbled footpath that forms the village's spine, snapping precarious selfies outside the charming old cottages that line both sides, their front gardens a-froth with flowers and spiked with breeze-blown palm trees.

Here in the middle is where the hardy ones cling; a few tenacious locals refusing to give up their homes to the holiday rental market, as tough as the opportunistic buddleia bushes that have taken root in Clove Lore's gutters and gullies.

Midway is where visitors stop, glad of the rest, to buy a choc-chip tub at Mrs Crocombe's Ice Cream Cottage and to browse the shelves at the Borrow-A-Bookshop and cafe where, if you're very lucky, the latest tenant is a dab hand at Devonshire cream teas and frothy coffees, or if you're bang out of luck they're only doing cans of cash-and-carry pop and multipack crisps.

You see, once a fortnight the Borrow-A-Bookshop changes hands and its new tenants (known locally as 'the Borrowers') arrive, drawn here by dreams of holidaymaking and bookselling. Most of them rock up thinking themselves the luckiest devils in England. Many leave with immediate plans to get themselves back on the waiting list for another stay.

Some, the luckiest of them all, never leave, and they get to call Clove Lore their home forever. These folk are the hardiest of all the middle-of-the-slope clingers-on; open-hearted enough to recognise they've fallen for the place, and brave enough to commit to it.

Jowan, the bookshop's owner, has come to recognise the susceptible ones; the ones for whom a fortnight's holiday can never be enough, though he hasn't yet made up his mind about Austen. She's only just shouldered her (brand new) hiker's rucksack plus a bulging book tote into the little square not a second past her prearranged five o'clock arrival time.

Jowan doesn't know it, but she's been rattling around the visitor centre for ages, killing time in the souvenir shops, driven by her anxious determination to never arrive early or late for anything.

Her hands had shaken so much, Jowan had to key in the shop door's passcode for her, while Aldous, his elderly Bedlington terrier, stood by his side, sniffing the air, hoping this Borrower would be the type to sneak him treats. (This one, Aldous noted, smelled disappointingly of coffee and something minty. Neither of those pongs was of any interest to him. The person had, however, given him a good fuss out on the cobbled courtyard and called him 'cute', so he had generously cocked his head to let her scratch behind his ear too, not a favour he granted to just anyone.)

'Here y'ar, then. She's all yours,' Jowan said, in his piratey way, his single pearl drop earring tapping against his bristled jaw, as he pushed open the sky-blue door of the Borrow-A-Bookshop, allowing Austen to step carefully inside.

'Oh my days!' she gasped, steadying herself with a hand on the sales desk by the door, where the pay point and laptop waited to spring into life come tomorrow morning. These recent additions, however, looked to be the only modern things in the building.

Years of experience with bookshop holiday orientations told Jowan to hang back on the mat to allow this one to adjust to the sensations no doubt bombarding her now.

They looked younger and younger every summer, Jowan thought, watching her with a patient smile, while their clothing grew more elaborate. Austen, who the ledger had informed him was indeed one of their youngest bookseller guests at only twenty-five, seemed to be wearing some kind of cityfied wellington boots in spotlessly clean, clumpy white plastic, and she looked comfy in loose black dungarees with a notebook in the pouch-pocket and some sort of complicated strappy grey thing underneath with holes at the shoulders where feathery lines of delicate black ink tattoos peeped out. Silver earrings dangled in slender threads from multiple holes in her left lobe, while the other was unadorned save for one tiny hoop. Her canvas tote bag asserted 'The Book Was Better' in loopy cinema-reel writing.

She looked like she was making up her mind whether to cry with happiness or faint in terror. Jowan folded his arms and let her explore.

Slipping her backpack carefully to the floor, Austen pushed the oversized clear acrylic frames of her glasses back up the freckled bridge of her nose. She allowed her

6

eyes to voyage around the room, which smelled stuffy and papery in the nicest way, having been shut up since the cleaner left the place spotless at noon.

A fizzing feeling of warmth bloomed in her chest at the sight of the floor-to-ceiling shelves packed tight with books; some brand new, most pre-loved, and a fair few antiquarian, all extremely tempting and touchable.

She wasn't really thinking anything, more feeling the place out, gently creeping fingertips along the first rows of spines within reach. Poetry books. Hundreds of them.

She turned to smile in appreciation, to show Jowan she was still with him, even though she was dizzy with the excitement as she took in every detail: peaceful reading nooks hidden away between the stacks; rugs, both oriental and raggy, overlapping on warped old floorboards that had been polished to a nutty sheen; colourful ceramic vases dotted here and there, spilling over with dried flowers; and on the exposed stone wall above the shop's fireplace, a frame crowded with photographs of grinning Borrowers going way back – so many holiday dreams already come true.

And there stood the shiny black cast-iron spiral of stairs that featured heavily in the pictures she'd seen in the online reviews and magazines and had thought looked dreamy, especially with the little hearthside nook beneath them where the children's section blazoned its rainbow cover art – a riot of irresistible reads.

Patchwork beanbags were positioned next to a rather nice old leather armchair where Austen could already see herself curled up with a cup of green tea and a favourite volume of poems.

A sign above the fireplace read, 'Children's Storytime, Friday 4–4:30 p.m.'

'Who does the storytime?' she asked, whipping her head round to face Jowan, who gave her a straight-lipped smile.

'Oh, I see. Me, then?'

'Yep, 'fraid so. Radia's idea.'

'Radia?'

'You'll soon meet her, don't you worry,' he said with a chuckle. 'Go oan, don't be shy, have a proper look about. That's the small bedroom. Big un's upstairs.'

Austen took a few tentative steps towards the bedroom door at the foot of the staircase. This room was brighter than the shop, thanks to its ocean-facing window letting the sun flood onto a white bed. Cheerful red dahlias bobbed in the window box on the sill outside. Austen could just catch the tiniest glimpse of shimmering water and blue horizon between the white cottage backs, slate roofs, and raggedy palm crowns zigzagging and staggered down the hill to the water's edge.

Had she been alone, she'd have thrown herself onto the bed and napped in the sun like a cat; it had been a long journey from Manchester, but she was aware Jowan was expecting some kind of reaction.

'It's even prettier than I pictured,' she said, closing the door behind her. 'It's the light, I think.' She'd noticed the change in the cab on her way from the station. As they'd drawn closer to the coast the sky had taken on a dreamy bluey-pink glow like she'd never seen before.

'Artists' light, they call it,' Jowan informed her proudly. 'Folks been comin' to Clove Lore with their easels and paints since Victorian times, tryin' to capture the light. You a painter?'

'No, definitely not a painter,' she said, her hand travelling reflexively to the notebook in the pocket on her front. 'I'm not arty.'

'Creative, though, I'm reckonin',' Jowan put in.

She shook her head, a little panicked. 'I love to read,' she said with a shrug, in case Jowan was getting the wrong idea about her and thinking she was going to do clever, creative things while she was here. Was there an expectation she'd do more than basic bookselling and baking? Apart from, apparently, hosting a children's storytelling session? That was bad enough. Was she also required to be dynamic and extroverted when she'd always been at her best working away behind the scenes, unnoticed?

The idea she was expected to be something more than that, and while on holiday too, made her suddenly hot and flustered. She wanted to lift her messy, permed waves from the back of her neck to cool herself, but she held it together by blowing out a slow breath and keeping her face turned away from Jowan.

Mercifully, he'd already decided to change the topic. 'Your kitchen is, of course, the bookshop's cafe kitchen. Just store your food in there 'longside your cafe ingredients, should you have any.' He gestured all the way across the shop towards a low door. 'Be sure to let us know if there's extra bits an' bobs you need.'

Austen felt she'd better inspect the cafe; Jowan clearly wasn't going to leave until she had, and she'd be mortified if he found her rude.

On her way, she let her fingertips graze the neat rows to her right: Biography, Gardening, Lifestyle, Cookery, Architecture – she'd have to map out and memorise all these sections, she was realising – until she reached the entrance to the shop's cafe.

Lowering her head, she to passed into the white room – light and bright like the little bedroom – with lace at the windows and red gingham tablecloths contrasting with the modern gloss and chrome of the food prep area. There was another till on the countertop next to empty glass domes for displaying cakes.

These, and the sight of the blank blackboard with the word 'menu' in swirly white chalk, set her nerves buzzing even more.

She was expected to fill that board with specialities when all she knew was her mum's vegan and gluten-free chocolate granola bars and her dad's lemon-lime meringue pie (both of which she'd practised many times at home before setting off on her adventure). She hoped that would be enough to satisfy hungry book-buying customers.

'Everything shipshape?' Jowan enquired once she emerged back onto the shop floor, a little paler than before.

'It's a bit overwhelming,' Austen confessed. 'Amazing, but overwhelming.'

Jowan only smiled. He was used to this kind of thing. 'You'll soon get the hang of it. Just make yourself at home.'

She couldn't help grinning at this. Her own bookshop as a home, and for two whole weeks.

'I'm going to,' she said, passing back towards the till point, past the long wall of General Fiction on her right.

'Now, here's sommit else you need to know.' Jowan gestured to a round table by the door, all set out with slim volumes of literary fiction in smart jackets and prizewinners in shiny hardback.

'Every guest changes this display on their last day to reflect their own readin' taste,' he told her. 'An' you must leave it for the next bookseller to keep in place during their fortnight – a legacy of your stay.'

Austen eyed the books as he spoke, her gaze falling on one in particular. If Jowan noticed the way she froze at the sight of it, he didn't show it.

'Fletcher and Rosemary before you picked these out,' he carried on. 'Eclectic tastes, eh? Couple of English teachers, they were.'

Jowan was smiling, waiting for a response.

'Oh, yes?' Austen flustered, still fixed on the copy of Callista Flyte's *Chosen*, the author's name blazoned in blood red.

The austere black jacket with its grainy photograph of high-heel footprints in concrete declared it 'a masterpiece'. Austen knew that was no exaggeration.

She should be used to encountering her old employer's books by now. They were, after all, everywhere she went. Train station billboards lauded Callista Flyte's 'tense, thrilling storytelling', and 'devastating psychological insight'.

Her importance was debated on Austen's favourite bookish podcasts. She was serialised on Radio 4 and dramatised on BBC One; her talks sold out at book festivals nationwide; and Austen couldn't pass a 'little free library' in a city phone box or country village beehive without seeing Flyte's name sing out from glossy spines.

The Book Programme had Callista on as a regular guest reviewer, where she was always quick-thinking and charming, as well as witty enough to get away with being occasionally caustic, and all of this ensured her latest releases comfortably occupied the top of the bestseller lists, picking up prizes all around the world, where readers devoured her gripping explorations of the human condition in twenty-three languages, no less.

Flyte's influence was everywhere, and nowhere more so than inside Austen's brain, where she was insinuated into every fold and pathway.

'Read that 'un, have you?'

Jowan's enquiry made her muscles seize.

'I… I know her, actually,' Austen said, before realising what she was doing. It was an old habit she couldn't seem to stop, even though she really should have by now. It had been ages since it all came to an end. A whole year, in fact.

'You know Callista Flyte?' Jowan echoed.

'M-hm.' Austen nodded, still, she noticed, enjoying the faint glow of pride it gave her to tell people her claim to literary fame. It was only a shame that the pride was mixed in with the familiar (and growing) sense of indignity that she was *still* boasting about this. 'I was her assistant,' she added, and immediately wanted to kick herself.

Jowan looked impressed, and somehow that worsened the wincing feeling. She had vowed not to lay claim to Callista Flyte again, and especially not here. This holiday was supposed to be all for herself and nothing to do with Callista. Even though she had booked it in the first place with her old boss in mind, originally requesting a spot on the waiting list for the two of them.

It must be two, no, almost three, years ago now, when she'd made the booking, picturing Callista writing all day by the sea and resting at night. It would have been the perfect mix of writing retreat and a break away from London, and Austen would be free to potter a little in the bookshop and fill the windows with her boss's backlist.

She'd thought she might invite the press down for double-page weekend features. 'Flyte takes Flight to a Devonshire Bookshop Hideaway', the headline might have read, and there'd be shots of the author in her trademark black-rimmed glasses, her comfy white linen, the year-round black sandals, and her prematurely white corkscrew hair. Austen remembered fondly that it took Callista's stylist half the morning to tame those spirals ahead of a TV network meeting or an award show.

When asked by interviewers how on earth she managed it all, Callista would be effusive in her praise for Austen, her 'clever assistant, truly the best, don't know what I've done to deserve her'. She'd heard Callista say it a thousand times.

'Not her assistant no more, then?' Jowan asked, with a hint of caution in his voice.

Maybe he'd noticed her shrinking? Maybe he was remembering how the booking request had originally been for two people?

'Uh...' Austen replied. 'No. Not anymore.' She pulled a hidden-lipped smile that hopefully struck the right balance between 'and that's fine by me', and 'please don't ask any more about it'.

'Well, good,' Jowan told her, brightly. 'Glad to have someone who knows what they're doin' with book industry things. Reckon you're the right person to have around for the Borrow-A-Bookshop events programme.'

'The... the what?'

'No need to worry, 'tis only a few nights you'll need to open late, maybe help set out the chairs. We've a volunteer helping with it all, wine on order from the Siren's Tail, an' tickets already sold out. All you needs do is stay open, work the till, then lock up again. Here you are.' Jowan handed her a leaflet from a pile on the counter. She read it under her breath.

> Your favourite bookshop is now hosting your favourite authors.
>
> Tickets include an autographed book and refreshments.
>
> Sunday 14 July, 4 p.m: Meet Polly-Jo Gates, author of the bestselling 'Panda in a Puddle' series for children.
>
> Saturday 20 July 7 p.m: Winner of The Coffee House Book Prize, Simon Graeme Bloom talking about his novel, '*The Fallen Proud*'.

This drew her up short. Bloom shared a literary agent with Callista. See, there she was again! Inescapable. Austen inhaled through her nose and read on.

> Friday 26 July 7 p.m.–late: Take the spotlight in our open mic poetry evening where you are the star, hosted by Devon's own poet laureate Meg Rawlings reading from her new collection, '*Not Averse to Love*'.

'Everything all right?' Jowan asked.

'Yes, fine,' Austen lied. 'I didn't know there'd be bookshop events happening while I was here. Sounds… *fun?*' Her voice turned squeaky at this stretch. It didn't sound fun. It sounded exhausting, and an awful lot like her old job, and look how that ended.

Jowan stooped to lift Aldous. 'Patti has all the event stuff in hand, don't worry. And there's the volunteers to help whenever they're needed, whole band of 'em, you'll see. Just remember, it's your bookshop to do as you like with. Having fun's what it's all about.'

He gave her one last look, waiting for her to agree, before he turned to leave. 'Number's by the till should you need us, an' we can be found up at the Big House; looks like a big old sandcastle on the hill. Come up any time. OK?'

'Got it,' she said, relieved he was stepping out into the sunshine once more.

'I'll let you get yourself 'climatised, then.' He made Aldous wave a paw, which the little mutt didn't look very pleased about. 'Say goodbye, Aldous.'

She gave the dog one last scratch on his curly beige head before they set off, out through the little courtyard and onto the slope, turning left and Up-along, and out of her hair.

There'd been such a lot of *peopling* since her five a.m. start from Manchester Piccadilly; lots of crowd-jostling and small talk with taxi drivers, and then there'd been all that waiting and asking for directions to the bookshop, but now she could finally relax. She'd made it.

Pushing the door closed with a satisfying click of the latch, she took in her big, peaceful bookshop and, after checking no one was watching through the windows, she screamed for sheer relief and happiness, quietly at first but then louder, her voice dampened by the walls of paperbacks. 'My own bookshop!'

With a cackle, she ran right up the spiral staircase, making it clang and rattle. At the top she was greeted by low ceilings, a bathroom, small and clean, and, finally, a big white marshmallowy bed. She dived upon it, still celebrating, and dancing her legs.

'Two whole weeks!'

Rolling onto her back, she flopped, breathless, staring up at the white ceiling.

Now what should she do? Unpack? Make some tea? Familiarise herself with the stock? Check if there was a cash float in the till? She should have asked Jowan about that.

'Later,' she told herself, scrambling onto her knees and over the low headboard, slipping into the broad window seat cut into the thick stone wall and softened with plump cushions. Once settled, she unlatched one of the panes, letting in the sweet sea air and distant gulls' cries.

The cornflower-blue sky, alive with Jowan's special artists' light, drew her gaze. She stared out for a long, silent time while the few gauzy clouds drifted high over Clove Lore.

Her whole body softened. This was when she was most at ease; when nobody was watching.

Someone, Jowan she assumed, had left binoculars on the window seat and she lifted them now, adjusting the sharpness, scanning the wide horizon.

From up here she could make out the corner edge of the harbour wall pub and, beyond it, the glittering ocean where a fishing boat was making for the open sea, just a little tub of a thing, heading out where the sunfish flapped their wings above the surface, making strangers to Clove Lore, unused to such sights – including Austen – think for a second they were seeing dolphins playing.

'This,' she told herself with a sigh, all alone and unobserved, and with nobody asking anything of her whatsoever, 'is perfect.'

Chapter Two

'What the heck is *that*?'

'Radia!' the little girl's aunt Patti chastened, peering into the fishing net at the writhing thing on the hook, screwing up her nose. 'So... what the heck is it?'

'That,' said Monty Bickleigh proudly, 'is *Anarhichas lupus*. First one I've seen in years.'

Aunt and niece stared back blankly as the *Peter's Bounty* bobbed on the millpond stillness of the fine July afternoon just off Clove Lore in what Monty assured them was the best sea angling spot he knew. They'd been on the water for ages and this was their first interesting bite.

'Also known as the Atlantic catfish,' the fisherman added, still as much of a sea creature encyclopedia as he'd always been. Fishing was his family business going back generations, although nowadays Monty only took his brother's boat out to hook a few specials for his flourishing seafood barbecue business, Bickleigh's Harbourside Bites.

'It doesn't look like a cat,' Radia informed him, after giving it a long look. In fact, the grey blob looked more like an eel than anything feline.

Monty joined her in appraising the thing, doubtfully. 'Put it back?'

'Yeah, and quick.'

Yet Monty had some last nuggets of fishy information for his guests. 'Bit of a sad, solitary creature this one, forever scouring the depths of the North Atlantic. Not many fishermen want them in their nets.' He released it from his hook and examined the thing, eye to eye. 'It's one of those clever fish that make their own antifreeze so they can survive in icy water.'

'Clever and *ugly-bugly*,' Radia confirmed.

Monty gently plopped the thing back under the blue surface.

'Your mum will be almost done with her call,' said Monty, looking up at the sky and not the fancy mariner's watch on his wrist.

'Nearly pyjama time,' Patti agreed.

The sun was now a melting semi-circle on the fiery horizon.

'Aww,' Radia protested. Now that she'd officially completed her reception year at the local primary school, she felt herself far too old for early bedtimes, and it was hard to argue when the sky was still ablaze like this.

Patti Foley had lived here by the shore for eleven months now and the Devonshire sunset was still enough to strike her silent with wide-eyed wonder. Some evenings this summer she'd watched as the whole western sky turned the colour of Peach Melba sorbet streaked with raspberry sauce.

'Mrs Crocombe's Ice Cream Cottage will still be open if we hurry,' said Patti, struck with inspiration.

'Ice cream for supper?' asked Monty, though any objections he might have were drowned out with Radia's celebrations.

'Let's haul anchor, Cap'n,' Patti told him, and the three were soon puttering their way back towards the protective harbour mouth of Clove Lore, Radia stifling her yawns in case the promise of a cone was withdrawn and they whisked her straight to bath and bed instead.

Alongside keeping Radia busy while her mum, Joy, had her fortnightly phone call with her expensive (and priceless) counsellor, Patti also shared bedtime story duties in their little cottage for four, another of her 'cool auntie' privileges.

Radia had told her she 'did the best voices' of the three grown-ups, and that fact alone made up for any socialising Patti might be missing out on because she was needed at home, splitting the childcare load with her older sister.

The fact she'd had zero social life to speak of until eleven months ago – even when she'd been living in central London and could have had her pick of amazing women in amazing bars, had she actually gone to any – didn't enter her mind. In London, after diving into the scene for a while, going on a year-long run of dates with friends of friends in town for the weekend or spending the night with incredible women she'd met through apps, she'd eventually found herself all dated out and wondering why she was still girlfriendless.

After that, she'd clung to the lie that she was enjoying her event planning job so thoroughly that she simply didn't have time for going out on her nights off anymore, and there was no time for dating, or even chatting with the cute women she regularly bumped into through work. You can't avoid meeting single people at weddings. They're even marked out as single, designated to sit at what often turns out to be the most fun table at the reception. But as the organiser, guests were off limits to Patti anyway.

So, she'd started keeping herself to herself, and that was fine by her. But when the opportunity arose last summer to leave it all behind and join Joy and Radia in Clove Lore, she hadn't even had to think about it.

Now that she was here, she had an even better excuse, no, a *perfectly legitimate reason*, to stay home of an evening. She was making up for all that family time lost when her sister was living her nomadic IT consultant life and dragging Radia all over the globe with her. Now they were all settled together, and everything was perfect.

Sure, sometimes Patti read to Radia for an extra-long time at night to avoid gooseberrying in Monty and Joy's loved-up zone in front of the TV (where more often than not, Monty was dozing after a long afternoon's seafood grilling on the quayside), and she didn't want to disturb them, especially not when their relationship was still relatively new; getting on for a year next month.

Still, that wasn't enough to bring Patti down. In fact, she was happier than she'd been in ages. She had her sister – now, mercifully, contented and safe with Monty – and her six-year-old niece back in her life. Plus, there was plenty of wedding planning work up at the Big House, so she had no problem paying her share of the bills and feeding her houseplant-hunting habit, even if her new boss – Araminta Clove-Congreve, lady of Clove Lore's manor house and estate, and Jowan's wife – could be a teensy bit micromanaging.

'Mine's a double raspberry ripple with sprinkles,' she grinned, nudging her niece's arm as Monty brought the boat safely home again, cutting the engine by the harbour steps.

'And of course a flake,' Radia added wisely.

'Obviously,' she agreed, hugging her.

Yes, life for Patti Foley was full and busy, punctuated by beautiful sunsets, long walks, rest and reading, and she didn't need a thing to change. She was, at last, settled, and not in any way wistfully wondering if she'd ever find a forever kind of love the way her big sister had with Monty.

Chapter Three

Austen wasn't the only new arrival in Clove Lore. Up at the Big House, Araminta Clove-Congreve was wringing her hands at the sight of the removal lorries reversing to a halt outside the grand lobby, making the driveway gravel crunch in the otherwise quiet evening.

'Jowan! Come and look,' she called from her spot behind the glass. 'Those vans are twice as large as the unit they've bought. They can't be full, can they?'

Jowan joined his wife at the floor-to-ceiling arched windows of the entrance hall of the three-hundred-year-old house, where the upper floors had only recently been converted into apartments for private occupation.

Selling off the lion's share of the family manor had been a drastic solution to her money problems, but it was the only way Minty could stay on in the building that her spendthrift grandfather had built at the heart of his once-sprawling headland estate. The pretty gardens remained today, but the model dairy, estate cottages and the old chapel were long gone, leaving Minty, Jowan and little Aldous only one small bedroom behind the kitchens, a ballroom (from where Minty conducted her wedding business) and the impressive lobby where they stood now in the summer twilight.

'This is none of our concern, is it, Mint?' Jowan urged softly, knowing that once piqued, his wife's desire to intervene could not be diminished. Once the lady of the manor, always the lady of the manor.

A driver climbed down from the first van and walked round to the back to open its doors. Lights automatically came on inside, illuminating several very large framed portraits, packed for transport as though they'd come on loan from a gallery for an exhibition.

'See, it's only paintings, hardly any furniture,' Jowan tried, knowing this wasn't any kind of a salve. Even if the newcomers had arrived with only a Bag for Life between them, Minty would have something to say about the inconvenience.

The man was joined by the driver of the second van and they fixed a ramp in place.

'It's a little late for unloading, isn't it? They'll wake the whole house,' Minty complained.

Jowan thought it best not to remind his wife they were the only residents, apart from Leonid and Izaak (Minty's estate staff, a pair of loved-up husbands) who occupied the apartment immediately above their heads, who by now would be crashed in front of Netflix for the evening.

'Good grief!' Minty cried at the sight of rail upon rail of clothes coming down the ramp, all in garment bags, *vintage Louis Vuitton* garment bags, if she wasn't mistaken, which she rarely was when it came to such things, being a waspish English landowner of long standing.

'But there's only one fitted wardrobe in Apartment One!' Minty protested.

'Let them worry about that, eh? They're not *your* tenants. Come on, let's finish supper and catch up with *The Archers*.'

Minty wouldn't be diverted and stood fast, peering out. 'Those frames won't fit along the old servants' corridors, will they?'

Even Jowan fell into quiet observation at what happened next. He'd been ready to suggest it wouldn't hurt if the new tenant's belongings were ferried through the main entrance and up the grand staircase to the service doors that led to all the new apartments – Izaak, as the new building caretaker, held the keys. But now a black London cab pulled in behind the removal vans, its headlights shining in the rapidly falling darkness.

For a moment after the engine was cut and the interior light came on, there was no movement, and the cabby, with a puzzled look on his face, suddenly jolted into movement as though realising his passenger had no intention of opening their own door. He hopped out and hauled it open like a chauffeur.

A head of long, luxurious chestnut hair came first. The glamorous woman, in head-to-toe black Nineties Gucci, stepped graciously out into the night, drawing off black shades (which made Minty tut and mutter about what sort of silly woman wore sunglasses after sunset, honestly! A pretentious one, that's what). She looked to be in her late fifties, despite the fact that she was clearly no stranger to scalpels and syringes.

The Clove-Congreves watched the cabby receive a roll of notes drawn directly from the woman's handbag with its handle of oversized pearls.

Obviously feeling he ought to bow or something, the driver attempted an awkward sort of hat tip before fetching a large, round vanity case from the boot and delivering it up to its owner.

Minty, overtaken by her nosiness (and a sense of feudalistic duty that would run through her no matter how small her estate shrank), slipped outside, making Jowan follow reluctantly behind, more motivated by morbid curiosity about how this interaction would pan out than a desire to meet the new residents of Number One, Upper Apartments, Clove Lore Big House.

'Welcome to the village,' Minty said fulsomely. 'I'm Araminta, owner of this estate and founder of the Clove Lore Wedding Company.'

'Be a dear, and hold this for a sec,' the woman replied, handing over her vanity case while she rummaged in her handbag for a ringing phone.

Minty only looked at the case, her face like thunder.

For an awful moment Jowan didn't know what to do before hastily deciding to take the luggage from the younger woman himself.

'*Antoine?* Is that you?' the woman crowed into the phone. 'Thank goodness, where *are* you, darling?' She walked away from Minty and Jowan, still standing stiffly at the foot of the steps. 'Yes! It's worse than I feared. The absolute middle of nowhere.'

Minty gave Jowan a look so severe he immediately set the case down at his feet. She'd have had plenty to say about manners being of the utmost importance *even in the middle of nowhere* had a young man not stepped out of the taxi – very young, definitely not the woman's husband. He shouldered a racket bag over a thin black sweater that set off his handsome, glossy blondness.

'Uh, good evening,' he said, approaching quickly so he could lift the case from the gravel. 'She's, uh, had a long journey.'

At least someone in the family had the decency to feel embarrassed. 'Hmm.' Minty raised an eyebrow that said tiredness was no excuse, so her husband stepped in.

'Pleased to meet you, son. I'm Jowan, and this is Araminta. We live here in the main house. Well, what's left of it.'

The young man let this sink in before jumping to respond. 'Ah, of course. How do you do.'

He held out a hand for Minty to shake, again appeasing her sense of propriety. 'I'm Jasper, and...' he nodded to the woman now loudly conversing in lavish French over by the rhododendrons, 'that's Estée, my mother.'

'You'll need tea after your drive from... London?' Minty gestured to the retreating cab.

'Oh, uh... thanks, but I'd better get Mum settled. She's not great after eight p.m.'

'How so?' Minty cocked her head, glancing towards the woman once more.

'She's had a little in-cab cocktail hour. After her Zolpidem and whatever was in the hip flask, she won't be feeling very... sociable.' He attempted a laugh, but Minty remained unmoved. 'I'm kidding, of course,' Jasper said, stiffening, but with an uneasy look that confirmed the sleeping tablets and booze thing was nevertheless true.

'We was wonderin',' Jowan began. 'Did your mother actually see your apartment, before buying it?'

'Or, at least, read the measurements?' Minty added, as another rail of clothes was trundled down the ramp.

Jasper's eyes flicked between the pair, his neck length-ening like startled hares in the meadow when Aldous thought he was sneaking up on them undetected.

'You've bought an apartment of four hundred and fifty square foot,' Minty explained. 'Yet you seem to have brought the Royal Academy's entire summer exhibition with you.'

'Where'd you want these, then?' one of the cockney removal men interrupted, having eased a ten-foot gilt rococo frame from the van.

'Family portrait, is it?' Jowan said, tipping his head to admire what could be seen of the painting through the wrapping, where a schoolboyish version of Jasper, dressed in cricket flannels, was effetely holding a bat and looking pained, while a broad, handsome man in a dark suit stood unsmilingly behind the slender, seated figure of Jasper's mother in a slinky silver evening gown. She appeared illuminated all around by a golden glow, very much the focus of the painting.

Jowan peered closer, his eyes narrowing. 'Hold on,' he said. He glanced across the gravel to where the woman was ending her call with a loud, 'Kiss, kiss.' 'Do I recognise your mother from somewhere?'

'I don't think so,' said Jasper quickly, while Minty looked between the two men.

'Jasper?' Estée called from a distance away, holding a keycard in the air. 'Do the honours, darling.'

Jasper jumped into action. 'Excuse us. It was nice to meet you, Mr and Mrs, uh...'

'Clove-Congreve,' Minty tolled.

'Jowan and Minty,' her husband corrected, trying to guide the exasperated Minty back inside, while the new arrivals crunched their way round to the side of the vast property to their own private entrance door.

'Mum? Have you measured the place at all?' they heard Jasper enquire, before Jowan closed the doors upon the pair.

'Now Mint,' Jowan pre-empted, following his wife back to their spot in the flagstone-floored kitchen where they'd been drinking bedtime cocoa by the Aga and feeding Aldous their toast crusts. 'They're perfectly nice.'

'I know *nice* when I see it, Jowan.'

'Well, the lad's all right.'

'But the mother, Jowan! Did you see those heels? Teetering around, shouting in terrible French about redecorating, as if the apartment wasn't brand new and ready for them to move into.'

'That's what she was on about, was it?' Jowan was impressed. Minty knew a little of a lot of languages.

'I know the type,' she said, ominously, sitting again in front of *The Times*.

'I never had my wife fixed as a snob,' Jowan chuckled gently, as he took his seat and Aldous scrambled up his owner's outstretched legs to the cosy spot on his lap once more.

'I'm no such thing, Jowan de Marisco!'

He knew to tread gently if she was using his old name from before their marriage two summers ago, after which he'd taken the terribly modern step of adopting her ancient family surname.

Jowan gave her a level look and shook out his own newspaper (he preferred the local rag to the broadsheets).

'It's not that she's… loud and clearly out of place,' Minty went on, confessionally. 'But, really! It's… it's…'

'Good for Clove Lore to have new people,' he said. 'And good for us to have new neighbours.'

Minty screwed up her lips and suppressed an eye roll.

'My love, we've the opportunity of making new friends now the apartments are finally selling. Let's welcome them. That's the job of the landowner, is it not?' He reached a hand across the kitchen table where once upon a time a cook, valet, kitchenmaid, chambermaid and coachman had eaten their meals.

Minty took his hand in her own with a thin, accepting smile. 'I suppose so,' she said, letting her better nature overrule the stubborn part of her that resisted change, something she'd seen so much of in her nearly sixty-nine years as her family's funds dwindled away to nothing and the estate fell into near bankruptcy. She'd saved it by agreeing to the sale, but now she was wondering at what cost to her newly-wed privacy and peace?

The pair jumped at the sound of a knock at their kitchen door, sending Aldous into a barking frenzy.

'What on earth! Have they let themselves in?' Minty shrieked, as the door pushed open to reveal the shame-faced removal men, supporting between them a towering ceramic figure of a leopard with emerald eyes, frozen in a pouncing pose, its incisors fiercely bared.

'There's a back door to the apartments, i'n't there?' enquired the braver of the two men. 'Can't get these round those narrow corridors to her majesty's flat.'

Minty sighed wearily and, with a withering glance at their mucky boots, signalled that the men get on with it, if they must.

'I'll ask Izaak for the service entrance key,' Jowan volunteered, leaving the room as the men informed him there was a second leopard out on the driveway.

'Come as a pair, mate,' one of them laughed.

'Must 'ave been a BOGOF,' quipped the other.

Minty only groaned and sank her head into her hands.

It had taken all evening, but Austen had settled into the bookshop. First, she'd memorised the layout of the shop, making a map for herself to keep by the till so when people requested particular books, she had a good chance of directing them to the correct shelves.

She'd spent a little too long poring over the poetry titles, and had pulled a few books to put aside for herself, trying not to be too greedy, remembering that she wasn't getting paid for this working holiday: all the profits would end up in the till, not her wallet. She'd made do with an Audre Lorde, a Mary Oliver and a Lucille Clifton, all poets she admired.

She'd got to grips with the cafe kitchen too, getting stuck into the first batch of her mum's chocolate granola bars, since she'd brought the ingredients from home. The whole time she was prepping them, she'd reassured herself out loud, recounting each step of the recipe in her note-book. 'OK, that's the almond flour folded in.' 'Now the coconut oil and maple syrup.' 'Looking good, Austen.'

She'd always talked to herself. Her mum frequently told her, even as a pre-schooler, that it was down to Austen being an only child, but if she *only knew* the toll child-bearing took on a pelvic floor she'd understand why there were no Archer siblings for her to talk to.

Her mum was one of those 'let's talk about our feelings' kind of mums who didn't believe in taboo subjects, and even though that had its advantages (Austen's school friends all thought she was so lucky, having a mum who was a friend), as a teenager, Austen had often thought with cringing regret that a mum can be *too open* about stuff.

Once the vanilla-pod-scented, glossy slab of granola was setting in the fridge, she'd moved on to practising using the coffee machine. Again, she'd talked her way through it, like she was two people: one a nervous wreck of a child needing direction; the other, a kindly, competent adult.

'This doesn't look right,' she'd said, peering doubtfully into the frothed milk. 'Hmm, maybe it's because it's cow's milk? Keep going,' the more level-headed side of herself encouraged. She'd persevered until she had a silky froth right up to the top of the jug. 'That's better. Now the espresso.'

She practised and sampled and criticised and celebrated until she had a fairly decent mocha and a flat white under her belt (minus the pretty leaf shape on the foam; latte art was beyond her skill set and she'd made peace with that fact).

The sun had long since melted below the horizon when she realised she'd forgotten to eat, so she'd taken a fruit tea and a slice of granola up to bed, along with the Mary Oliver book, and she'd slept surprisingly soundly until morning, dreaming of how she'd soon be floating around the stacks, tidying and advising, ringing up books at the till, keeping busy and being helpful. Nothing obtrusive or showy required; just the easy, quiet life of a seaside bookseller.

Chapter Four

Someone had beaten Austen to the opening time she'd been so looking forward to.

A man, tall and thin, and a little older than her, she reckoned, tapped gently on the other side of the glass of the still-locked door a little before nine.

He smiled when he saw her approaching, so she must have managed to hide her disappointment that she wasn't going to have the inaugural sign-turning moment she'd been planning to film for her 133 followers on TikTok.

Hastily flipping the sign to 'open', she unbolted the door and let the man, and the sweet morning sea air, inside.

'Did I rush you?' he asked, a gap showing in his dimpled smile.

'No worries, come in,' Austen said, hoping her voice didn't sound as shaky to him as it did to her.

'I am one of the volunteers,' he told her in an accent she was registering as softly Polish, as he stepped onto the mat. 'I'm Izaak.' His hand, when he offered it, was more of a reassuring clasp than a shake. 'Do you have everything you need?'

'I think so.' Internally, Austen was praying this volunteer hadn't been assigned to help her run the shop. She wanted to do it by herself.

'Good, good.' His eyes briefly danced around the interior. 'I have a holiday-warming present for you.' He handed over a bundle wrapped in brown paper. 'Honey cake. You can sell it in the cafe, if you want to.'

The aroma had already hit her. Freshly baked and lightly spiced. 'You made this?'

He nodded his assent.

'I will, thanks. After I've had a slice for my breakfast.' Her stomach constricted at the scent − a reminder that she'd barely eaten since she arrived in Clove Lore.

'I do need some stuff, actually. Ingredients,' she said, realising she might be in a bit of a bind if she had to get the shop open *and* deal with the food situation.

'OK,' Izaak encouraged.

'Eggs, lots of them, and more milk. I used up the cow's milk that was in the fridge, practising the coffees. And oat milk. Almond too, if you can get it. Is the convenience store up at the visitor centre open yet?'

'Eggs, all the milks, what more?' Izaak was already making a note on his phone. Was he volunteering to do her shopping for her?

'Oh, uh, lemons? Limes too. And… sugar.' Her brain struggled to dredge up her ingredients list. She wasn't great at shifting focus when forced, and doing more book-shop cafe baking hadn't been at the front of her mind this morning.

'What about you?' Izaak said, meeting her eyes.

'What about me?'

'Lunch? Dinner? Did you bring groceries?'

'Oh! Uh… I can get stuff, don't worry…'

'We have a kitchen garden up at the estate where I work,' he interrupted. 'The Big House?'

'Where Jowan lives?'

33

'That's it. There's hothouse tomatoes and salad. And hens for your eggs. Also onions? Potatoes?' Izaak held his finger poised over his phone screen.

'Well, yes, please. The cupboards are empty, actually.'

He nodded. 'I'll bring your food later today. There's a surplus of courgettes too. Leonid told me to seriously push the courgettes,' he added with a laugh.

'Leonid?'

'My husband, and the estate's head gardener,' he replied proudly. 'I'm the handyman-caretaker, and I work the ticket booth. That's where I'm going now. The estate gardens open in twenty minutes and there'll be a queue already. So, is this your list?' He showed Austen his phone screen and she nodded, not wanting to trouble him by adding anything further, even though she could have done with some orange juice, ramen, and a big bag of ready-salted crisps. 'I'll come back in my lunch break,' he said.

Austen felt her shoulders drop with the relief. He wasn't sticking around. This reminder of how antisocial she'd become did not pass unnoticed and a pang of guilt hit her.

'Should I give you some money now, or…?'

'Petty cash will cover the groceries. OK. I go.' He slipped his phone into the pocket of his white polo where the embroidered logo read 'Clove Lore Estate and Gardens'.

'No, wait!' she stopped him. 'Let me give you something. Wait there.'

She dashed through the shop and under the low door frame into the cafe where she quickly unwrapped Izaak's golden, ridged honey cake and placed it under one of the glass domes on the countertop before wrapping up two

34

of her chocolate granola slices, one for Izaak, one for his green-fingered husband.

The excitement bubbled up in her once more. This bookselling thing might work, she thought, as she returned to where Izaak waited, especially if this was the extent of the volunteering: friendly people unobtrusively staying put on the doormat and bringing her honey cakes and the offer of homegrown veggies.

'Here you go,' she announced on her return.

But as Izaak turned to her, clasping a book in his hand, a little of the excitement was shaken from her body.

'I'll take this, please,' he said, showing her Callista Flyte's *Chosen*. 'It's better to turn up with it, even if I haven't finished it, right?'

The look on her face must have told him she was drawing a total blank.

He went on to explain, 'For the book club, at the Siren's Tail. They've all read this in preparation for the discussion. Or they'll pretend to. It's more a social thing than a reading club. Minty wanted to try something a bit more highbrow than our usual murders.'

Izaak, misreading her awkwardness, offered to help her ring it up on the till. 'I'll show you how it works, don't worry.'

He typed in the short code written in the book's flyleaf in pencil, which made the title appear on the laptop screen. 'This removes this book from the stock system. OK?'

Austen nodded, watching him type the price into the hand-held card machine. 'Five pounds fifty, yes?' he said, pointing to the pencil marks yet again.

Austen did a convincing job of pretending she hadn't read the point-of-sale instructions booklet from cover to cover this morning, and Izaak just seemed happy to be being helpful.

The whole time that he was paying, Austen had to tell herself *not* to mention the fact that she knew the author of the book he was buying, even though the compulsion to blurt it out was almost overwhelming.

Izaak tapped his card on the machine and a moment later it reeled out his receipt. 'Sold,' he said with a nod.

'Got it, thanks.'

'Will you come? It's Wednesday night. There's a buffet.'

'To your book club? Oh no, I don't think so...' Austen couldn't think of anything worse than being stuck in a room filled with strangers talking about the woman who'd thrown her overboard the moment things got weird. The biggest influence on her life, her boss, her sort-of friend, her...

'No problem, it was just an idea.' Izaak must have noticed her spiralling. 'You can come if you like. But you are on holiday, so no pressure.'

'It's just, uh, I prefer poetry,' she said, hoping that would be enough for him to drop the subject.

'We're more about bestsellers at book club,' he said with a smile. 'And anything with a good murder!'

She wanted to remark that *Chosen* is more about the psychology of obsession than it is a detective story or a CSI sort of thing, but she didn't suppose it was worth it, and certainly not before he'd even read a page.

With one last promise of bringing some of the estate's cucumbers ('big like this,' he showed her, measuring between his hands) he let himself out into the morning sunshine.

Once he was safely crossing the courtyard and making for the slope, Austen silently shut the door.

After a resetting breath and a shake of her still-damp curls, she took out her phone and filmed herself flipping the sign to 'open', slowly pulling the door, her lungs expanding as, at last, she took the time to inhale the lovely warmth of the first morning of her holiday.

'Welcome to the Borrow-A-Bookshop,' she said into the mic before hitting 'upload' and sending her idyllic snapshot of her day out into the inevitable losing battle against indifferent algorithms. She didn't mind this, so long as she was keeping a record of her trip. That's what mattered, documenting it all. She had nobody to please but herself, and any customers who might happen to stumble along.

'Any minute now, book buyers,' she told the empty courtyard, rocking on her heels at the top of the shop steps and peering along the passageway towards the slope, expectantly. 'Whenever you're ready.'

Chapter Five

The thing with bookshops is, it's all or nothing. Customers, much like summertime courgettes, come either in one big glut, or one big nothing.

Austen had dusted, tidied and pottered her way through a whole lot of nothing for most of the morning, wondering if Izaak was going to be her only customer all day long. She sniffed a wry laugh at the thought that, of course, her only sale this entire fortnight was going to be a Callista Flyte book. She was fated – no, *cursed* – to be followed around by the mocking legacy of their relationship. That's what happens, she supposed, when you're the forgotten one, out of the spotlight and left behind.

She was about to cut herself a second slice of the seriously delicious honey cake when a message pinged in the baggy side-pocket of her drapey grey pants – which she'd paired with a black ribbed vest, one of her favourite easy combinations – and she reached for her phone, thinking it would be her dad again, checking in.

She'd already sent home multiple photos of every room in the place and daft selfies messing around pretending to be very busy and important in her bookshop, her glasses perched on the tip of her nose, just to make them smile, but this message wasn't from her parents. It was from a stranger.

Well, sort of.

She'd followed the 'Feint Heart Bookshop, Paris' on TikTok for half a year now, though, apart from one initial post showing a gloved hand placing down a steaming cup of coffee on an antique desk in front of a condensation-streaked, wintry shop window, and then the same person opening a slim volume of Sylvia Plath's poems, they hadn't posted anything else. The scene had been cluttered in a picturesque social media kind of way with piled books, and the whole thing had looked and felt very, very French. Since then, they'd maintained a classy Parisian social media silence.

Except now they had commented on Austen's shop-opening video from this morning; the only person to take the time to word a proper response so far, although plenty of people had 'liked' it and there was a stream of loveheart-eyes emojis.

> @FeintHeart: Bonjour from another bookseller. J'espère que vous vendez beaucoup de livres. Bonne journée!

Austen's French GCSE was finally coming in handy. She got the gist of their message, but she still hit 'translate' just to be sure, before typing her reply.

> @AustenInk: Merci! Happy bookselling to you too! Sell, sell, sell!

For a moment she considered adding a croissant emoji but, in the nick of time, thought better of it. That would be tacky. A Real Deal Parisian Bookseller wasn't likely to be impressed with that at all.

'Good save,' she reassured herself, before hitting 'send' and considering making a second strong coffee to help steel herself for the quiet afternoon ahead, imagining herself reading poems in the sunshine behind the shop counter.

That was when the glut happened.

Coachloads of people, all coconut-scented with sun cream and overburdened with beach bags and picnics, either sweaty and on their way back up from the beach, leaving sand everywhere, or fresh from the visitor centre and on their way downhill with holiday money to spend. They seemed to arrive all at once and there were suddenly questions, lots of them, all being directed at her, only some of them relating to books.

When was the next bus to Barnstaple? Where was the man with the little dog who was here last time they called in? Did she have 'that one by Jane Eyre?' Of course they're sure that's the author's name; do they *look* stupid? Did she sell stamps as well as postcards? No? Why on earth not? Where were the customer toilets, please?

On and on they went, some wanting to chat about the weather, some who understood the Borrow-A-Bookshop concept and wanted to know how they could get on the waiting list, others remarking, 'Not much of a holiday, is it? Working in a shop!'

Austen smiled and replied as best she could, gripping the counter to steady herself, feeling like she was at sea in a choppy tide, keeping her head above water.

Only, nobody seemed to be buying anything, despite all the customer rummaging, book lifting, blurb reading and reshelving going on.

This made her wince from her vantage point by the till. Why couldn't they put books back in the exact spot they came from? Some just laid the book down flat on top of the stack, not even attempting to replace it, setting Austen even further on edge. She'd have to tidy and re-alphabetise before bed tonight. What a mess they were making.

The worst offenders were the ones coming inside with ice cream cones, sticky-fingering all the spines or flicking their way through the new notebooks and assorted stationery in the racks by the door.

When Izaak appeared with a produce crate loaded with green leafy stuff, eggs, bread and milk, she found herself blinking at him, unrecognising, at first.

'I can jump on the till, if you need a break?' he told her through the fog of her panic.

'Oh, no, I'm OK. Nobody's buying anything, anyway.' She indicated with a subtle nod a young guy in the corner shamelessly waiting for his phone to charge on the shop's socket while absorbedly reading a graphic novel, and then the elderly couple, obviously glad of the shop's cool, shady comfort, sitting in armchairs amongst the stacks quietly reading their newspapers.

'Those two aren't even pretending they want to buy a book,' she whispered.

Izaak looked at the pair, raised an eyebrow like he was busy plotting – making Austen's panic deepen – before slinking over to the woman behind her *Express*.

'Lovely day, isn't it?' Izaak asked her, all casual and light. Austen watched on. 'Can we interest you in a coffee or cake with your reading?'

There'd been some discussion about what kind of cakes were on offer, the gluten-free, vegan granola bars getting a disappointing brush-off (there may have been some unkind speculation over 'what could possibly be in it, then?' which Austen had to fake a smile through). Still, the pair were hastened into the cafe, remarking all the while to a grinning Izaak that a cup of tea and some honey cake did sound nice.

And that was it. The cafe had its first customers, served by Izaak, thank goodness, leaving Austen to tackle the sudden surprising queue that had formed at the till, again all at once, of browsers turned buyers.

This was not a good time to realise there were no bags in the shop, apart from the branded canvas totes that cost a tenner – which almost every customer objected to, but many still bought.

Austen got through it with a combination of reminding herself that she was actually bookselling – a dream come true – combined with a bit of slow, deep breathing and drawing upon her years of book industry gophering, interning and author assisting. She was used to being at the bottom of the pile, so slipping into 'service mode' came back to her like she'd never stopped. She prided herself on being a problem solver. She could do this.

Yet, when Izaak popped back onto the shop floor to announce that he'd better get back to the Big House now that the queue for refreshments had gone down, Austen's heart sank.

'What will I do with the cafe?' she asked over the heads of the queue at her till.

Izaak shrugged and spread his hands. 'Tell them the cafe's closed until it turns quiet? The honey cake's sold out anyway.'

'It is? How did my granola bars do?'

He gave her a thin-lipped look of apology.

'Oh, that good, huh?'

'There'll be another volunteer popping by later. You've got this!' he said encouragingly, his two thumbs up, before bobbing out the door.

'Thanks for the food!' she called after him.

Her next customer shuffled forward in the queue – the young man who'd by now finished charging his phone. He presented Austen with his book bundle: A-level revision texts and YA sci-fi romance mash-ups.

'This is my dream job,' the boy told her, starry-eyed, as she rang them up.

'Mine too,' Austen replied, even if the reality was proving a little different to the fantasy.

–

At last, as four o'clock approached, there was a lull. The torrent of lunchtime customers – which had become a steady afternoon trickle – came to a sudden complete stop. The silence in the shop surprised Austen so much she had to check between the stacks before she could believe she really was alone again.

This was her chance to sort through Izaak's groceries and hopefully make a sandwich or something. So, leaving the shop door open, she made for the cafe.

'Oh!' She staggered to a stop at the sight that greeted her.

The kitchen was no longer a picture of pristine orderliness. There were unwashed cups stacked on the counter, crumbs on the tabletops, and the glass dome that had contained the honey cake was empty and aslant on its dish.

Austen set about a speedy clean-up, clattering the cups into the washer, searching for a fresh cloth, putting away Izaak's gift of milk, eggs and veggies, trying to be quick and efficient, something she was good at.

Such a busy bee. Buzz buzz! she imagined Callista's voice saying in that way she always did, usually while sitting behind her old-fashioned typewriter in her sunny Mayfair loft room, peering through her thick-rimmed specs, barely looking up as Austen worked her way through that day's To Do list. Austen was never completely sure if the bee comments weren't somehow a criticism; like her menial multitasking was disturbing the artist. She'd always make sure to minimise her movements, to silence herself as best she could, so Callista could focus on the important stuff.

The bleep from her pocket told her she had a message. Another notification from the Feint Heart Bookshop. This time a private message, which she might have thought a bit intrusive if they'd sent anything other than book talk.

'I sold one book only. The fault of the rain.'

This was accompanied by a photograph that made her breath catch. A moody greyscale shot taken through a door frame looking out at a rainy street scene where Parisians under dark umbrellas dodged puddles.

She quickly typed her reply. 'But it looks so beautiful!!'

'Did you sell books?' came the reply.

Austen considered her answer. She'd sold lots, but would that come across as bragging to this poor bookseller stuck indoors with no customers on a wet day? What time was it in Paris? They're an hour ahead, aren't they? They must be closing up to go home.

'A few. It was a very pleasant first day.'

'*Je suis si content pour toi.* No… I am *delighted* for you. Delighted is correct, yes? Ah! A customer for me, at last! I will make them take twenty books, croyez-moi! *À bientôt.*'

Austen smiled at the screen. It was a simple interaction with a bookseller hundreds of miles away but it made her feel less alone, like a member of a big network of people who had opened their stores this morning not knowing if they'd sell a single paperback. It was nice to feel part of something.

'I thought you might be hiding out through here,' a very real voice said from the cafe doorway, making Austen jerk her head around, clasping the phone to her heart.

'Jesus!' she yelped.

'You frightened her,' came a second voice, from a little girl peering out from behind the awkwardly smiling woman.

'Oh no, I'm sorry!' said the woman, advancing.

'Have you got any scones?' the little girl asked incongruously, and in such a familiar way, Austen wondered if they'd somehow met before and she'd forgotten about it.

'No scones,' Austen confessed, still standing stiffly, she realised, flattened against the kitchen cabinet behind her.

'You're Austen,' the woman was saying.

'Uh, yes. Hi?' Austen blinked, trying to act normal. She'd have to get used to the disadvantage of everybody knowing who she was in a village full of strangers. 'You're a volunteer?'

'What are those?' the girl interrupted, springing up onto the tall stool in front of the counter, her finger pressed against the glass dome.

'Those are my chocolate granola bars.' Austen was aware of her tone. Apologetic. On the defensive.

'Please can I have my pocket money?' the child asked, turning to the woman, who rolled her eyes and reached into the pocket of her berry-red summer jumpsuit, cropped to reveal delicate gold ankle chains and a deep green ivy vine tattoo on her foot winding its way out of sight.

Austen had to tell herself not to stare. She didn't like the feeling of strange eyes assessing her own tattoos. Well, most of the time she didn't.

The woman handed the child a five-pound note, telling her with an indulgent smile, 'You already owe me for the toffees and that *Beano* yesterday.'

She looked surprised when the girl immediately hopped off the stool. 'You don't have to come with me. Wait here.'

'Where are you going?' the woman asked.

Austen was beginning to feel like she'd been forgotten. She slipped her phone into her pocket.

'Mrs Crocombe's, for a chocolate ice cream.'

'OK, but straight there and straight back, OK? Here, take this.' The woman handed the girl her phone. 'Call the shop if you need to.'

'O-*kay*,' the girl said with a dramatic sigh.

'And tell Mrs C. where I am.'

'OK,' the girl said again, with a groan this time.

'And don't talk to strangers.'

'OK!' She disappeared through the bookshop.

'And bring me one!'

'Raspberry, OK, OK!' the retreating voice called back, making the woman laugh. Then her attention turned back to Austen.

'Sorry about that. Start again?'

Watching this pair's antics had given Austen time to recover from the fright they'd given her. She let her shoudlers fall.

'I'm Patti,' the woman said, with a rainbow arc of a wave. 'And yep, I'm yet another volunteer. Sick of us yet?'

46

'Austen Archer,' she returned. 'I've only met you, and... Izaak, was it? And Jowan, the owner.'

'And Aldous?'

'The dog? Him too.' Austen laughed now, though she wasn't sure why. It had something to do with the greenness of Patti's eyes, she concluded. So green she couldn't fail to notice. Beautiful, really. She took a second to recover from the sight of them before saying, 'Does she normally get to walk about the village on her own?' She pointed in the direction the child had gone.

'Uh, no. *Obviously* I'm going to give her a head start then sneak after her, like I always do.' The woman's lips curled in the wickedest way when she spoke. Austen noticed they were a cherry pink against her summer tan, while her black curly hair was cut in a messy shag style, wild like her own, only longer and naturally curly, not a home perm like hers, done by her mum in her parents' en suite.

'You coming?' Patti bobbed her head towards the doorway, smiling conspiratorially.

Austen automatically laid down her cloth and followed her through into the shop. Still not a single customer was around.

'Should I lock up?' Austen asked, like this wasn't, in fact, her shop. She'd always deferred to others like this. It was her way.

'Nah, let's just peek Down-along. Customers can't get in without coming down the passageway, anyway.' Patti stepped out into the afternoon sun.

Austen closed the door behind her and followed. The air was filled with the scent of salt and seaweed and this woman's peachy sunscreen. Austen took a deep inhale.

'Customers kept you busy?' Patti asked.

47

'Non-stop, since about eleven.'

They made their way between the cafe chairs and tables set out in the cobbled courtyard with the big terracotta pot and palm tree at its centre.

'Did you remember to eat?'

The way Patti said it, so casually, made Austen feel utterly transparent.

'Did my mum tell you to ask me that?' she joked.

'You look the type who forgets to eat when they're focused.'

'Hungry, you mean?' Austen said with a laugh, and Patti smiled back.

'Dedicated.'

'More paper and ink than flesh and blood,' Austen said, blurting words that Callista Flyte had directed at her once and which had pinned her like an arrow.

'What?' Patti scrunched her nose like she wasn't sure if Austen was making a joke. Only, Patti wasn't laughing, not even close. She looked concerned.

'Never mind.' Austen swept a hand, dismissing her unguardedness, wondering why she'd said it in the first place.

They'd passed through the narrow pathway between the two cottages that led on to the slope when Patti slowed to a stop, peering Down-along, exaggeratedly hunching behind a hydrangea bush like a spy.

'She doesn't like me fretting,' Patti directed over her shoulder to where Austen was hanging back, out of sight from the slope.

'How old is she?' Austen said, hoping to hide the fact that she was feeling self-conscious sneaking along behind this stranger, and trying not to look at the smooth, freckled skin exposed by Patti's racer-back top and the way the red straps of her jumpsuit criss-crossed where her shoulder blades had caught the summer sun.

'Six, would you believe? Seven next month,' Patti said, breezy and unaware. 'Sometimes I think she's a teenager in the body of a six-year-old. Other times, I remember she's just a baby.'

'She's independent though.'

'Yeah. She spent the first five years of her life travelling all over the world, so she's kind of grown-up for her age.'

'But you live here now?' Austen asked.

Before she could answer, Patti jerked back into the shade of the passageway, hissing, 'Here she comes. Quick!' With a hand against Austen's arm, she gave her the gentlest push.

The pair scurried back into the cobbled courtyard. All the while Austen was burningly aware of the cool pressure of Patti's fingers where they'd made contact with her flesh. Patti's laughter chimed brightly from behind her as they flew up the steps and into the shop. Austen joined in, laughing too.

By the time the little girl wandered back into the cafe, both Austen and Patti were nonchalantly busying themselves, shuffling chairs under their tables and wiping surfaces as though they hadn't spied on her at all.

'Successful mission?' asked Patti, casually, before throwing a crafty look at Austen.

'Mrs C. gave me *three* ice creams. One's for you.' The child surrendered the tub to a surprised Austen. 'She told me she didn't know what you like but she was making a lucky guess with pineapple and mango.'

'Well,' said Austen, turning the tub in her hands and freeing the little plastic spade. 'Let's see.' She took a small taste. 'Yep, definitely a good guess.'

The girl tasted her own scoop, eyes boring right through Austen. 'What's your name?' she asked, innocently, but still disarmingly blunt.

Patti answered for her. 'Austen, this is Radia. Radia, Austen.' The woman made the introductions like they were at a fancy, grown-up party, and evidently Radia appreciated that.

'Pleased to meet you,' the girl said in a grand way.

Patti chuckled and shook her head, eating her own ice cream. She was used to the child being precocious, Austen figured.

'Can we have some of the granola bar on top of our ice creams? Like, crumbled up?' Radia asked, setting a few coppers and five pences on the countertop by way of payment. 'Mrs C. gave me change.'

'Oh, well, sure.' Austen lifted a slice from under the dome. 'It didn't sell too well today. Maybe Clove Lore isn't a granola kind of place.'

She crushed some of the oaty, nutty bar over Radia's chocolate tub, then offered some for Patti's.

'Could be a new recipe,' Patti said, holding her ice cream out for Austen to decorate.

'You should tell Mrs C.,' added Radia. 'She's always experimenting with new flavours.'

'Who is this Mrs C.?' Austen wanted to know.

'Another of the volunteers,' Patti clarified. 'She owns the Ice Cream Cottage two doors down. Lets the Borrowers use her washer-dryer. Her utility room at the back of the cottage is left off the latch during the day, so you can just walk in. She's… kind of a matchmaker. Beware, is all I'm saying.'

Austen looked between the mock-serious Patti and the grinning Radia, flummoxed. 'A matchmaker?'

'She's got a track record of poking her nose into everybody's business. One of these days she'll get a taste of her own medicine,' Patti said, wickedly.

'I like her, *a lot*,' Radia put in, as though that was an end to it. 'She makes the best ice cream *and* she talks about things.'

'Oh! OK,' Austen said, acceptingly. 'Then, she does sound nice.'

As soon as Radia bowed her head to tackle her granola chocolate dessert, Austen pulled a bemused face for Patti, hoping it would make her smile. She was delighted to witness her new acquaintance smothering a laugh, her green eyes sparkling.

Austen had to force herself to concentrate on her own tub after that. 'Pineapple and mango ice cream with vegan, gluten-free chocolate granola. Who knew? It's the perfect mix.'

'Wait a minute, can you eat that ice cream?' Patti said, alarmed. 'Are you vegan?'

'I'm vegetarian. I make the granola at home for Mum. She only eats plant-based, and she can't have gluten.'

'Got it. I'm veggie too,' Patti replied.

'You stole that chicken nugget off my plate last night,' Radia interrupted, shooting an accusatory look at Patti.

'I didn't say I was the world's most brilliant vegetarian. Sometimes… I lapse.' Patti aimed this at Austen and somehow it sounded like she wasn't talking about foodie habits at all.

Austen's body noticed it first, before her brain did. A tiny burst of elation moving through her system. Was this woman flirting? While her daughter was right there eating ice cream? This was very confusing.

'So, um...' Patti seemed to be shaking off a secret thought too, her eyes moving searchingly across Austen's face. 'Anyway... we need to set up for the author event.'

'Oh my God, that's tonight!' Austen threw a palm to her forehead. 'I'd forgotten, what with all the people and...'

'It's actually...' Patti looked at a non-existent watch. 'Now.'

'*Eee!* I can't wait!' Radia exclaimed, drumming her feet on the rung of the stool and setting her empty tub on the countertop. 'We love *Panda in a Puddle*, don't we?'

'Yes, we do,' Patti agreed, wearily. 'We read it every night. Many, *many* times!' She widened her eyes at Austen. 'If anything, I feel like I know that Panda too well.'

Again, Austen found herself laughing, half dazed, half galvanised by Patti's bright, easy presence. For a moment, all fell still – the strangest little pause – apart from the gulls calling from the rooftops.

It gave Austen enough time to wonder if she was imagining it. Was this woman watching her with something questioning, a soft groove forming between her brows?

'Right! Anyway,' Patti said, setting down her spoon and tub before making a decisive clap with her hands. 'Let's set up. Paper cups are in the cabinet behind you. We'll need a big jug of cold tap water too, for the squash. Sam's supposed to be bringing biscuits. She's another volunteer. Well, more of a conscript really, poor thing. I'll take all these chairs through to the shop, OK?'

Austen, who always responded well to being told what to do, set to work while Patti instructed Radia to go and find the box of *Panda* books to set out by the till.

Austen found the jug and the squash bottle and let the kitchen tap run until the water turned cool against her fingers.

Yep, she'd been imagining things. This was, Austen reminded herself, one of her worst habits. Getting all stuck in her own head – not to mention her feelings – about people who barely registered her existence. Patti, even though she looked about the same age as her, was An Actual Mother. A fully fledged grown-up with a child. Austen had mistaken kindness for something more before. From then on she'd known to nip any stupid misconceptions in the bud.

This was good, she told herself, as she filled the jug. She was learning, at last, how to protect herself from her own overactive imagination. This was growth.

So, with a pleasant ice cream sugar buzz coursing through her bloodstream, and her first day in the bookshop firmly under her belt, Austen forced herself to be sensible. There was a book event to sort out. A kids' book event, of all things. But, with help – not something she'd been used to having in her working life – how hard could it be?

Chapter Six

A queue of families was forming in the courtyard already but Polly-Jo Gates, VIP children's author, wasn't flustered. She was an author very much used to this sort of thing. She'd arrived with her own pre-signed bookplates – always a bonus – and what must have been the world's most obliging husband, six foot tall and wearing a panda suit.

He hadn't said much, only asking for a straw so he could drink his strawberry squash through the Panda's smiling mouth and whether he could trouble Austen for some ice.

Austen assured him nobody would mind if he took off his panda head until the kids arrived, but he insisted on maintaining the illusion that he was indeed *the* Panda in the Puddle, just in case the early arrivals spotted him headless through the glass door.

This had made Patti whisper, 'Panda in a puddle of sweat,' as she wafted by, setting out the last few chairs in front of the children's area. She'd been so close to Austen's ear, the new Borrower had felt the soft waves of Patti's hair graze her cheek. She'd failed to keep her composure and laughed a loud '*Hah!*'

Luckily, neither Panda nor the author noticed, but Austen could feel Radia's eyes narrowing upon her from behind the till where, apparently, the little girl was going to handle book sales.

'Mum installed this till,' she told Austen – who'd turned to pouring the rest of the squash into cups. 'That's how I know how it works. We lived in the bookshop last summer. That's when Mum met Monty and they *fell in love.*' This last part was pronounced in the most emphatic way.

Austen managed an impressed, 'Wow, that's… very cool.' She observed the tiny disappointed feeling smouldering then burning out like the carelessly dropped ash from one of her dad's cigarettes on the fabric of his shabby tweeds.

'Yeah, we were digital nomads,' Radia told her, carefully sounding out every syllable. 'But now we live Downalong in the cottage with the sunflowers.'

'Oh really? I love sunflowers,' Austen replied, a little absently, straightening to survey the shop now that the chairs were set out in curved rows for the grown-ups and the rugs were arranged for little ones to huddle at the foot of the leather armchair in the kids' section. Patti, with one hand resting on a hip, was doing the same from the other side of the shop, Austen noticed.

'I think we're ready?' Austen checked with Radia, who gave her an assured nod. The panda took it upon himself to open the door, making some of the guests scream in delight while a few of the babies wailed in terror.

'Ready, Auntie Patti?' Radia called across the shop floor, and the words echoed around the stacks, reverberating through Austen.

'Auntie?' she couldn't help repeating.

When Austen spun on her heel to look to Patti for confirmation, she was met by the most astonishing, wide-eyed look of surprise she'd ever felt penetrating her.

'Of course she's my auntie. Who did you think she was?' Radia was bellowing over the growing rabble.

As the families filed inside, Polly-Jo greeted them enthusiastically, an old hand at this kind of thing, but Austen felt herself rooted to the same spot.

The parents claimed their seats, lifted babies from over-engineered slings, dished out tissues and breadsticks and rice cakes from nappy bag pockets, and all the while, Patti was grinning back at Austen from across the shop.

It all suddenly made sense. Patti was the cool aunt, shelling out for ice cream and sweets, and keeping her devoted niece entertained. That explained Patti's easy manner and how she didn't fuss over the child.

Austen didn't go so far as to tell herself this answered her other questions about whether Patti had in fact been flirting with her. Now it seemed like a real possibility, the idea scared the life out of her, so she shut it down without examining it. But why was Patti just standing there now, still smiling at her across the bustle of the room?

Again, Austen didn't want to think too hard about it all. She knew what happened when she got these buzzing, excited feelings about someone. She was invariably wrong about them and she'd be left stewing in a one-sided situationship until it got so weird she scared them away. And yet, Patti wasn't breaking her gaze, and that made the whole thing even more exhilaratingly terrifying.

At that moment, a gang of ecstatic tots, who had been scaling the stoical, puffing panda like a cliff face, succeeded in taking him down in a great clattering landslide of picture books and strawberry squash. Austen jumped into full consciousness once more and dashed for a mop.

'And *now* it feels like a book event,' Patti said, grinning, setting about saving the bear, hauling him to his feet just seconds before his wobbling head could come off and shatter the children's illusions.

'So, who wants to hear my new story?' Polly-Jo Gates called out in a jolly way, not minding the chaos, and the happy cry that followed scared the gulls from the rooftops.

–

Samantha Capstan arrived late for the event, making the bell over the Borrow-A-Bookshop's door chime right in the middle of a delightful lull when all the little ones were sitting in rapt amusement listening to Polly-Jo's latest tale.

In this episode of his adventures, the Panda, who, it turned out, was devoted to all things aquatic, was graduating from his puddle to an Olympic-sized pool and learning the art of synchronised swimming, only there were no other pandas to join his team, so what was he to do?

Austen was almost as absorbed as Radia, who hadn't left her spot behind the till, but was hanging on Polly-Jo's every word. They barely registered the breathless fair-haired girl of twenty slipping through the door and tiptoeing towards Patti at the back of the crowd.

'Sorry I'm late,' Sam whispered. 'Minty wanted to go over the details for the summer meadows thing.'

'And you were too scared to tell her you were expected down here?' Patti whispered back, with a knowing eyebrow quirked.

She and Samantha shared Minty Clove-Congreve as a boss at Big House Weddings and had often consoled and commiserated with each other in stolen moments hiding in the manor house's cloakroom, where Izaak could also be found whenever Minty was on the event-planning rampage.

'It was her idea I come and help at the bookshop events in the first place,' Sam complained.

'She's getting good at delegating, that's for sure,' Patti joked, but seeing the frazzled way Sam was rubbing at her forehead, leaving a pink mark, she added, 'I won't tell her if you want to just go home and get some rest.'

The look of relief in Sam's eyes was extinguished almost immediately by the realisation that this wasn't an option.

'Minty's paying me for helping out tonight, and I...'

'Got it,' Patti cut in, saving her having to say it. Sam needed the money. In fact, she needed every penny she could get, never mind the fact that she'd already put in a shift up at the Big House running catering inventory in the kitchens, and Patti knew she'd arrived at the Big House straight from the laundry her Mum had run single-handed until the accident.

Poor Mrs Capstan had tripped on Clove Lore's cobbled slope while hauling bedding – belonging to the holiday rental cottages – on her 'laundry sled' to her van at the top of the village. A horribly shattered cheekbone had meant a race to A&E, followed by an operation, and Sam stepping in for her mother with immediate effect rather than risking her mum's business going under. The summer season was the laundry service's busiest time, and that, combined with a shortage of workers across the region, meant that Clove Lore's holiday property landlords would simply switch to another laundry, and if they did, they were unlikely to go through the palaver of switching back.

After only four days of juggling multiple jobs, Sam was feeling the strain.

'How's your mum doing?' Patti asked.

'Doctor reckons it'll be another four to six weeks before she can do any of the heavy stuff.'

'Laundry isn't for sissies,' Patti said, then wished she hadn't said anything. 'You know what I mean. Your mum's always grafting.'

'Hmm,' Sam hummed her agreement. 'She was.'

'And the apple hasn't fallen far from the tree. She must be really proud of you,' Patti encouraged.

Samantha would have wept if she wasn't so sleepy. People being nice to her was the last thing she needed.

'I've got it all covered here,' Patti said in an insistent whisper. 'Here, head up the slope and surprise your mum with these.' She led the yawning Sam to the cafe where she placed the last of the chocolate granola bars in a white paper bag, slipping a ten-pound note into the cafe till.

Turning Sam by the shoulders, Patti marched her out through the shop, past the giggling children hearing all about the panda recruiting other creatures (a Friesian cow, a zebra, a raccoon and a badger) to join his synchronised swimming troupe.

Once outside, she walked the girl to the end of the passageway.

'But what about Minty?' Sam said, stepping onto the slope.

'You were here, weren't you?'

'Yeah, but I didn't do any work.'

'How much was she going to give you?'

'Five pounds for the hour.'

Patti scoffed, but seeing Sam's earnestness, she hid her outrage. 'Well, I won't say anything if you don't.'

Sam nodded and turned wearily for home. The slope looked a lot steeper than it had this morning when she'd made the laundry run.

Of course, she would have to confess to Minty that she'd not been needed at the book event. It wouldn't be right to take the money if she hadn't helped out. All this internal struggle to earn another fiver! But only she knew about the bills in the drawer at home. The ones her mum hid, unpaid. Green reminders and red final demands. If they knew where her dad was, they might have taken the humiliating step of asking him for the money, but he'd been long gone for years and the two women had fought to keep everything together, Sam foregoing college for any work she could find. And there were jobs, what with the Devonshire tourist industry growing all the time, only they were all minimum wage, and after tax, it barely made a dent in the mortgage payments.

She trudged slowly uphill, chewing absently on one of the granola bars from Patti's bag. She was calculating her day's earnings so far, before remembering the laundry van needed filling with petrol in the morning and that would wipe most of her profits out again. This had to be rock bottom.

Up she climbed, her white trainers getting dustier as they scuffed against the dry cobbles. The late-afternoon sun blazed over the headland and every flower in the cottage gardens lining the slope released its perfume.

Hot and red-faced, Sam reached the top of the slope where the path split off for the lush, hoverfly-haven greenness of the headland footpath to the left and the lane to the visitor centre car park, where she'd left the van, to the right.

The branded white laundry dress with the words 'The Clove Lore Laundress' on the pocket that she'd worn all day, even while on duty up at the Big House, had been tight around the armholes and was leaving a nasty red mark on her skin the sweatier she got.

Her mum had thought she'd better wear it. The land-lords expected it, not that any of them lived in Clove Lore, but occasionally they'd do the rounds of their rental properties. This morning one of them happened to be Down-along and had greeted Sam at the door of one of the many cottages in his holiday rental portfolio. This one used to be old Mr Acaster's place down near the lifeboat launch; now it was anybody's who could afford two grand for a fortnight's stay. It was changeover day, and the land-lord was overseeing a visit from the electrician. Sam had hefted the bagged, unwashed sheets from the doorstep and handed him a freshly pressed pile from her sled.

'Thank you, Caroline,' he'd said. And Sam had been too dumbfounded to tell him Caroline was her mum. How could he mistake her for her mother? Granted, he'd barely looked at her, nobody had, as she'd scurried from door to door, picking up and dropping off. It had given her a sharp sense of how invisible her mum must feel.

She'd have brooded on this all the way back to the van if there hadn't been someone blocking the lane to the visitor centre, made all the narrower by the overgrown ancient hedgerows that lined the route. Another tourist, no doubt. Only, this one didn't have his eyes fixed on the sea views that opened out from the end of the lane, nor was he snapping holiday selfies. He was looking at a handwritten sign taped to a lamp-post sticking out of the hedgerow: the sign Sam had stuck there only this morning.

In black marker it read: *Wanted, morning laundry assistant, short-term, immediate start, no experience necessary. 6 a.m.–11 a.m. Sled provided.*

She slowed to look at him, all sleek blond hair and designer gear. He didn't look local and he didn't look short of cash, but something about the way he was staring at the notice told her he was thinking deeply about it.

'You interested?' she said from a few feet away.

'What?' he startled, snapping grey eyes towards her blue ones. He looked horrified, disgusted even. Sam felt it in her soul.

'No, I don't mean… I'm talking about the job.' She pointed to her sign. 'You seemed interested.'

'God, no! I was just… Do I look like a laundry worker?'

'Do *I*?' she bit back, feeling her cheeks redden horribly. She hated confrontation, but he was asking for it. That was when she realised she shouldn't have said anything because his pale eyes ran down her body like quicksilver.

'Well, yes, you do. *Aren't* you?'

She felt herself shrink under his examination, growing aware of the moisture along her hairline that she knew for sure was making her baby hairs clump and spike. She'd have felt ridiculous if she wasn't so indignant.

'There's nothing wrong with laundry work.' She straightened her back, curling her fists by her sides, seriously endangering the granola slices. 'And even if you *were* interested, I doubt you'd be able to hack it.'

'I didn't say I was interested.'

'What's that then?' she snapped, pointing to his elegant hand where he clutched one of the torn-off strips from the advert. Her mobile number.

He quickly crumpled it. 'Uh, I…' He collected himself. 'I was a runner at the Saatchi, and before that I interned on set for Obsidian Cruz. I am *not* washing other people's underwear in this godforsaken tourist trap.'

Now it was his turn to blush. He looked furious with himself for having lost his composure.

'Well, I don't know who *Sachet* is, or Obsidian *Cruise*.' She tried to get as much sarcasm into her pronunciation as possible. 'But I do know there's no shame in actual hard work. Besides,' she added, looking over his baggy black summer jumper, oddly tight trousers and ridiculously bulky trainers by a designer so painfully obscure she couldn't recognise them, 'you hardly look like you need a summer job. Why don't you intern somewhere super exclusive and posh for free?'

'Interning? Here?' he scoffed. 'I just saw a sign for a donkey sanctuary. I hardly think they're looking for someone like me.'

'What exactly are you?' she pushed.

'I'm... well, I'm obviously better than...' He indicated first Sam's home-made sign, then the entire Clove Lore panorama. 'This.' He gulped and stood even straighter.

Sam only nodded, her anger getting the better of her. She had to fix her eyes on the path as she strode past him. 'Donkey Sanctuary wouldn't want you either,' she said as she drew level with him, holding her nerve and telling her feet not to stumble now.

She could feel his eyes on her as she passed by, keeping her head down all the way to the end of the lane, wondering what had come over her. Arguing with a strange man? And with nobody around? He could have been a serial killer for all she knew, hunting down menial workers and beating them to death with one of his ridiculous sneakers.

Her mum would be horrified if she knew her daughter had been so rash, putting herself at risk. Except that guy hadn't looked dangerous, now that she was replaying the whole thing in her mind. He'd looked kind of drippy, and more mortified than angry, and – the thing that had made it seem safe to unload at him – he'd looked kind of… sad, actually.

'No,' she told herself as she pressed the key fob in her dress pocket and let herself slump into the driver's seat of the laundry van. 'I'm not going to feel bad about that pillock. *Too good* for Clove Lore and laundry!' She slammed the door and started the lazy engine, sending a big plume of grey fumes into the air. 'Rude grockle! What's he even doing here if it's not good enough?' she muttered, clunking into first gear and moving away.

She complained all the way along the headland, past Elliot the vet and his wife Jude, who were turning into their cottage gate with their two rescue greyhounds on leads, along past the primary school and into the drive of her home where her mum would be waiting for her, apologetically offering to order takeaway, which Sam would refuse, knowing how tight money was. All evening, as she sorted their dinner, she'd brood about the stranger who'd made her feel an inch tall and worthless, too confounded even to mention the encounter to her mum, and wishing for his sake that she never laid eyes on him again as long as she lived.

Chapter Seven

There was time, Austen promised herself, to take a quick look at the sea before opening Borrow-A-Bookshop. Nobody was likely to be knocking her door down, desperate to get their hands on a paperback this early on a Monday morning, not when the holidaymakers were probably just ordering their full English breakfasts in the coastal B&Bs, and the locals were still setting off for work.

Plus, the baking was all done. This time, two freshly made lemon-lime meringue pies were waiting under glass on the cafe counter.

She'd filled a takeaway cup with what passed as a reasonable-ish oat milk latte, laced her boots, and set off Down-along to get a glimpse at what generations of holidaymakers came here for.

Standing now at the end of the harbour's long wall by the glass lantern, which she supposed worked as a kind of mini lighthouse, Austen understood what all the fuss was about.

This little spot of coastline, sheltered from the Atlantic breakers by its curving cove and high rocks, was absolutely breathtaking, even more so because at just before eight o'clock nobody was about. A fisherman had waved to her from his boat, the *Peter's Bounty*, as they came back in with the morning's catch, but mercifully nobody else had their eyes on her.

A bubbling bank of vast white clouds along the horizon line separated the dark blue sea and blue-pink sky, but otherwise the morning was clear and sunny. Even at this time of day she had to raise a shielding hand as she looked directly above her to where the gulls took their time circling in the warm thermals having picked the shore clean of their breakfast hours ago.

She'd drawn her notepad from the back pocket of her baggy black shorts, worn today with a matching boxy shirt and cropped vest underneath, and she poised her pen at the top of the first page.

She'd write something, she thought, to capture this feeling in words. The feeling of being a tiny thing in a great big bubble of beautiful blue, with only the *shush-shush* of the waves and the clanking of boat chains and bobbing buoys in the harbour to distract her.

There had to be some words out here waiting for her, somewhere amongst all this lovely scenery and peacefulness?

But the pen didn't move. The words stayed away.

'What is it you want to *say*?' she asked herself. 'Something about this place. Old stones underfoot... sea salt, and books.'

Still, she didn't write a scratch, telling herself instead to really look around her.

'The poet's eye,' she said under her breath, 'is specially trained to notice things unseen by others.'

They weren't her words, but her dad's, from his lecture on the Romantics. 'The Big Five', he called them. Keats, Byron, Shelley, Wordsworth and Coleridge. Every autumn term, he'd dust off the same old lecture and say the same old things about them to his fresh new undergraduates.

Austen knew these poets as well as her dad did; she'd grown up with them. The Archers' was a house of poetry. For a long time, Austen had thought she had rhyme running through her, and for years she couldn't do anything to stop the flow of words that popped into her brain without even trying. 'The divine muse rising unbidden from her slumber,' she'd heard her dad call it.

'Where are you now then, divine muse?' Austen asked.

She hadn't written anything in two years. She'd begun to feel a fraud, carrying around her blank notebook in case inspiration struck.

She let the book lie still on her lap.

'It happens to everyone,' she told herself, loosening her grip on the impotent pen. 'Just breathe, and look at the scenery.'

She took a deep inhale and a long exhale. 'Smell the flowers and blow out the birthday candle,' her mum would always tell her. A slow yoga breath. The scenery around her emerged from the blur once more. She'd overfocused. Tried too hard. That was always her problem; trying to force things.

The light had changed again overhead, the glare turning a glowing soft blue. Devon really was putting on a summer show for her.

She'd holidayed with her parents in St Ives and Sennen Cove, way down in the depths of Cornwall, when she was younger, and they'd toured the Cornish galleries and craft workshops, scoured its arts and literary festivals, but they'd never strayed into Devon. Austen wondered why. Her parents would love it here in the peace and quiet, although, Austen thought wickedly, they'd suffer with-drawal symptoms if they weren't within touching distance of an artist's open studio or a world music stage, especially her mum – though her father was just as art and culture hungry, only he was wry and witty and a little more urbane, whereas her mum was softer and barefoot, and would happily spend the rest of her life looking after her rescued wildfowl down on her allotment, so long as she got to go to WOMAD and Hay-on-Wye once a year.

They were well suited, her parents. Loved-up and happy, and Austen knew, ever so slightly worried about her. She'd never really made it off their comfortable, incense-scented and book-scattered launchpad. Various bookish jobs around Manchester, followed by being Callista Flyte's assistant in London, had looked like the beginning of her career, but she'd ended up back in her old bedroom in the family's bohemian two-storey flat in leafy Levenshulme after her twenty-four-month long immersion in literary circles.

But, Austen consoled herself, she wasn't at home now. She was in Clove Lore, and all by herself on a fully fledged solo adventure, albeit a cosy one, not exactly out of her comfort zone. She always knew where she stood with paper and ink.

There it was again. Callista's voice, calling her out, not unkindly, more matter-of-fact. *You're more paper and ink than flesh and blood*. It might not have seared itself quite so indelibly into her memory if she hadn't said those words moments after an awful, failed, clumsy response to Callista's perfectly innocent friendly kiss.

Austen groaned at the reminder of how she must have appeared in that moment to her boss. A moment she'd replayed and analysed so often it had lost all sense of reality. Now it was a cringing, hideous, abstracted thing, over-examined, a thing she saw from two viewpoints, neither agreeing with the other.

She could see herself, pink-cheeked and champagne-confident after Callista's big book launch party at Foyles bookshop. Austen had the job of carrying the boxes of promo materials – and Callista's bag and coat – that evening, and she'd been delighted when, once she'd checked off the VIP list, Callista had told her to 'take the night off, enjoy the party'. Then she'd asked if Austen had anyone she wanted to call, a 'special friend' who she might want to keep her company, 'away from all of us old bores'.

There'd been a searching, wistful look in the author's eyes, followed by a gleam of something hopeful, or at least, that's what she thought she'd seen, when Austen had told her there was 'no one special' she wanted to invite.

Then there'd been glass after glass of bubbly, and then... *ugh!* She couldn't bear to unpick it all again. But, of course, she was going to.

And there it was, happening once more before her eyes. The lingering embrace, the whispered, effusive, 'Thank you, Austen dear, I'd be nowhere without you.' Then there was a second's hesitation, followed by the quick press of Callista's lips to hers, then another, slower kiss, again initiated by her boss – which Austen, in the months that followed, had convinced herself she must have misinterpreted. Yet Austen had still gone and lunged at her like a lovesick teenager. *Ugh!*

To fight off the sickening, shrinking feeling she had every time she thought of that night, she forced open her notebook once more and poised her pen nib hard at the centre of the page, making a black indentation. She scrawled some letters.

words!

The sound of her heart beating in her ears overtook everything. She pressed harder still.

words

she wrote again.

She'd scratched the next 'w' into the page as she heard, no *felt*, the presence of someone standing over her shoulder. Snapping the book shut, she twisted round to see who was disturbing her.

'Jowan said you looked like a writer,' Patti hazarded, though Austen was giving her such a look, she quickly wiped the smile from her face. 'Sorry, I keep sneaking up on you.'

Trying to hide the book and pen away inside her shirt pocket wasn't going well for the agitated Austen, so she slid them beneath her thigh and immediately felt ridiculous for doing so. 'I'm not a writer,' she said.

Patti's eyes flashed from Austen's face to where the book was hidden and swiftly dropped the subject.

'I hope you didn't mind me sending Samantha Capstan away last night. I know you could have used her help with closing up.'

Patti had left shortly after the kids cleared out and the poor panda had been allowed out of his suit and been revived with one of Austen's iced coffees (another item to add to her cafe repertoire today). Radia had turned suddenly tired and ready for bedtime stories, and Austen, wishing for a return to the quiet solitude of the evening before, had insisted she'd be fine putting the chairs away by herself. So they'd gone and, alone again, she'd locked the door, pulled down the blind and leaned against it, catching her breath, her mind buzzing with thoughts.

'It was fine, honestly,' Austen said now. 'It took thirty minutes to reset the shop and I was asleep by nine.'

The part about sleeping was a barefaced lie. She hoped Patti couldn't tell. The way she was looking at her with that easy smile and those clever green eyes worried her. She seemed to be able to see into her – or right through her. Last night Austen had, in fact, sat inside the bedroom window seat until way past midnight, batting away intrusive thoughts about Patti. Her eyes. Her lips. The winding ivy tattoo she'd glimpsed once and then been too afraid to look at again. She forced herself to not look now.

Austen reached for something to say. 'Did Radia enjoy it?'

'Oh my God, she loved it! Couldn't you tell?'

Austen couldn't help the laugh that escaped her.

'I mean, she made that poor woman read the book twice,' Patti added.

'She was pretty insistent,' Austen agreed.

'It's best to give in, I find, when Radia wants something that's easy enough to give.'

'She's not with you today, then?'

'She's with her mum. My sister. I mean, obviously, her mum's my sister. I...'

Was Patti getting flustered? Was she thinking about the misunderstanding last night, and how Austen had been utterly unable to hide her relief when she found out Patti was in fact *Auntie* Patti? She'd definitely been astounded and gaping-mouthed when she realised she had jumped to the wrong conclusion. She'd been over the top, in fact. Too much.

In her embarrassment, Austen willed her body to transform itself into a boneless puddle so she could slide out of sight over the harbour wall, plopping into the sea never to have to face Patti's incredulous delight again. How she wished she could avoid the amused, wide-eyed stare she was giving her now. What a relief that would be. But no, Austen was still just sitting there, hard stone against her bottom, fixed by Patti's gaze and the laughter around her lovely mouth.

'I'm sorry I was weird last night, I...' Austen blurted, but Patti was speaking over her.

'Listen,' she was saying. 'I was wondering...' Patti rubbed the toe of her chunky sandal on the stones like she was about to risk asking something. Then she stopped herself with another laugh. 'Sorry, you go first.'

Fresh alarm had hit Austen like a tidal wave, and she found herself springing to her feet like a jack-in-the-box. 'I was about to say... I'd better open the bookshop. It's after nine,' she blurted.

And there it was. The look on Patti's face that told her she was *definitely* being weird again. She'd seen it from Callista too, that night. *Ugh!*

She turned away and set off at a pace.

'Wait,' Patti called just as Austen was almost free and practically running for the slope. 'You forgot this.'

In her hand was the notebook, held by the cover and flapping open, showing Austen's scrawled attempts at kick-starting inspiration only moments before.

Austen swiftly took it back, making the pen tucked inside the pages fly into the harbour. Patti's eyes followed it into the water.

Austen didn't hang around, turning to go again. 'OK, thanks!' Austen held the book up in a goofy kind of salute as she raced away, her cheeks burning with embarrassment. 'Bye, then!' Had Patti seen the pages and her pathetic attempt at wringing words from herself?

She stomped along the harbour wall past the Siren's Tail where the tourists were spilling outside after breakfast, some gripping crabbing nets and buckets, others making determinedly Up-along towards the visitor centre.

The perfectly well-adjusted Patti would be standing there still, watching Austen bolting and wondering what on earth was wrong with her.

Patti couldn't know, of course, that Austen wasn't at all how she appeared. She might have, at first, seemed to her like the kind of happy-go-lucky independent woman who borrows bookshops miles from home and everything's easy-breezy, but the truth was that she was a mess.

She was the sort of woman who spoiled her boss's book party by lunging at her, having apparently misread the signals all evening long. She was the sort of woman who mistook collegiality or friendship for something else and wound up recoiling from hideous blunders.

She tapped the edge of the notebook to her temple as though it could tap the memory right out of her head. Picking up her pace, the morning sun heated the back of her neck as she strode up the slope. Far better to run from confusing situations than risk feeling the way she had back then.

It struck her that she'd left her coffee cup down on the harbour wall. Patti would be picking it up round about now and binning it for her, thinking she was crazy, or rude. Probably both.

Austen clenched her hand around her phone in her shorts pocket, climbing on past the cottage near the foot of the slope with the sunflowers by the door. The one that was surely the house Patti shared with her sister and niece.

Austen didn't let herself look in at the windows, telling herself instead to concentrate on the mortifying feelings of what she'd done that night a year ago.

A small part of Austen was convinced Callista *had* kissed her back, and hard. A residual memory persisted of how all the good stuff had been there: hitched breaths, two smiles touching, eyes open then closed, one hard heartbeat, two hearts together, and then… the author had pulled away, astonished, accusing, wiping her mouth with the back of her hand and fixing her glasses.

'What are you doing?' she'd said, stepping even further back, her voice a hiss. 'I'm not… we're not… you know I'm married!'

Austen had never even seen the guy, but yes, Callista had a husband living on some Colorado ranch with the horses, cattle and dogs that she paid for. He'd call now and again, but there didn't seem to be anything like a marriage going on between them. She'd assumed it was some kind of tax arrangement, or something to do with green cards.

That part of her boss's life was surrounded by a silent mystique she'd never dared pry into – nobody would, not even the *Vanity Fair* interviewer who'd trailed and flattered and cajoled Callista for a fortnight while writing their career-charting cover story about her. Callista protected her private life.

And yet, that kiss had been building between them for so long, and when it happened, it had felt like a seismic shift bringing them closer together. For all of thirty seconds.

After she'd broken away, Callista's eyes had jumped around the stacks. She'd turned to check no one had seen, then – with her hands held out as if in self-defence – she'd said, 'Austen! We can't do this! I… I don't think of you in that way. You must know that?' Austen could recall seeing her hands shaking. 'You're… you're…' Austen knew something bad was coming and, looking back, she should have run for the door there and then, but there'd been a tiny glimmer of hope that Callista was going to see the hurt in her eyes and falter, and that she'd break down and admit the feelings that had been simmering between them for weeks. 'You're more paper and ink than flesh and blood to me. You understand?'

Even though she'd felt the words penetrate like an arrow, Austen had been the one apologising for overstepping, telling herself she must have been way out of line and that poor Callista was indeed the innocent, injured party in all this.

Callista had brushed her hands over her trademark white linen like she was brushing off Austen's touch, and she'd left with her writer friends to continue the party elsewhere, somewhere Austen wasn't invited.

The next morning, Callista's email arrived on her phone asking her to place the ad for her own replacement. She was fired.

She'd had enough pride not to undertake this final task for her boss, but had packed her things and left London that day knowing she'd made herself ridiculous and unemployable in the same misguided instant the night before. The book world is a small, whispering one, and she knew that if anyone had glimpsed them through the shelves at Foyles, word would be spreading already. She knew how she'd come across in those stories, too: like the author-obsessed Annie Wilkes in *Misery*.

I'm your number one fan, Callista, she could imagine Kathy Bates saying dementedly.

Stephen King hadn't got it far wrong, based on the reality of their codependent two years together. Sure, nobody had done any kidnapping or anything, but right until the last second Austen had believed it could end in a Happy Ever After for them. Talk about deluded!

She'd fled home to Manchester and hadn't so much as considered kissing anyone else ever since.

At least, not until last night, sitting under the stars at her window with the vision of Patti's smiling green eyes and the memory of her fingers grazing her bare arm in that millisecond that had ignited something dangerous within her, ensuring that kissing Patti was *all* she'd been able to think about, and that simply was not a safe headspace to be in.

Chapter Eight

Minty thought that nine a.m. was a perfectly reasonable time to knock on the door of Apartment One. Any countrywoman with an ounce of respectability would be up and about her day already, especially a woman with a thousand cartons and crates to unpack and a bulging wardrobe to organise.

No one answered her knock, so she called through the door.

'I took the liberty of bringing your mail. It's been arriving in your letter box for days. You'll need this key to collect it yourselves.'

She listened against the oak panels that had once led to her grandparents' first-floor bedroom with its impressive views over the estate's picturesque 'model' farm buildings and the herd of Longhorn cattle that had won every show in the South West; all frittered away by her wasteful grand-father and wildly reckless father.

She was sure she could hear feet dragging close to the door, but still no one touched the latch.

'Well,' she said, affronted. 'I'll post them through. Good morning to you.'

—

Jasper stood stiffly on the other side of the door in the dark apartment so crowded with boxes he'd been unable to reach his own bedroom, and had resorted to sleeping on the sofa under his favourite black Moncler coat, now reduced to a makeshift duvet.

He watched the letters drop onto the cream carpet. He'd seen red bills before, of course. There'd been plenty of them since his dad upgraded to his new, happier family with a beautiful Croatian socialite – who he'd lured away from a top-seed tennis ace – and she was currently pregnant with their first baby. All this information he'd picked up from family friends – the news was yet to hit the sidebar headlines. The thought of everyone in the world knowing soon – and it was only a matter of time – made him feel queasy.

He rubbed a thumb at his temple. How had the bills followed them so quickly from London? He'd hoped there'd be at least a few weeks' reprieve, and the most naive part of him thought they might somehow cease altogether and they really would be starting afresh.

A stirring sound from the open door of the master bedroom just off the open-plan kitchen-lounge made him flinch.

He'd have to hide these letters, and quick. He couldn't risk his mother seeing them before she'd had her first espresso and Percocet of the day.

Where even was the espresso machine?

'Mona! Coffee!' Estée called groggily.

Good. She was still out of it. He had time. Reality wouldn't dawn for his mother for a while yet if she was still under the sleepy illusion that Mona, their housekeeper, was going to magically appear with her usual silver tray of stimulants and morning skincare supplies.

What he wouldn't give to see her now. Funny how Jasper was only just stopping to spare a thought for what had become of Mona since his father abruptly stopped paying her salary and turfed her out last week.

'Go back to sleep,' Jasper hissed towards the darkened doorway as he sneaked towards the couch to pull the calf-length puffa coat over his pristine white pyjamas.

He replaced the black silk sleep mask perched on top of his perfect blond hair with a pair of dark shades. He and his mother interchangeably wore each other's. In their old place there were always umpteen pairs lying around discarded. Today he'd have to make do with her Nineties Chanel. God knows where the others had got to. A pair of black summer slip-ons completed the look. He reached for his wallet and tiptoed through the door in search of a dark roast San Salvador.

Slipping through the Big House's grounds, Jasper barely registered the freshness of the air or the clear blue sky up above; he was too set on his mission to avoid a maternal morning meltdown. He paid no attention to the eyes upon him: tourists wondering if he was a movie star or young celebrity chef holidaying incognito, or the locals appraising him, stony-faced and resolutely unimpressed, shaking their heads and muttering about incomers and grockles.

He bounded on past the visitor centre, aghast that their coffee shop wasn't open yet. How did the people around here *cope*? The baristas in his favourite haunts seemed always to be behind their counters no matter what time of the morning he rolled home. Why did everything in Devon have to be so inconvenient?

His finely attuned nose picked up a whiff on the breeze: something strong and black brewing somewhere down the slope towards the harbour – which he hadn't even contemplated walking down last night. It looked far too steep to be safe. Yet the thought of his mother dragging herself out of bed and coming face to face with that wall of boxes and the maze of clothing rails, her hair sticking up frightfully and her make-up smeared, drove him onward. Life was so stressful when there was nobody to take care of the little things for you.

'*Hufft!*' No sooner had his soft soles hit the twenty-degree gradient of the cobbled slope than they slipped from beneath him, leaving him clinging, dry-mouthed and irrecoverably ruffled, from a garden railing. His wallet had sprung from his coat pocket and was tumbling down the slope. He watched helplessly as the last of his notes came loose and flitted this way and that.

'No, no, *no*,' he warned them, scrabbling on hands and knees to catch them, wanting to groan at the memory of charging Platinum cards all day long, never once thinking about the accounts (his father's) that absorbed his daily expenses. Those cards, as he'd discovered when trying to Deliveroo his favourite sashimi on Saturday night, had all been blocked. He, like his mother, had been cut off.

He hadn't fully processed the enormity of possessing only fifty quid in notes (the last of his money in the world) until they were fluttering about on a sea breeze. Would they somehow dematerialise too? Like everything else he'd been familiar with?

He dived for a ten-pound note lodged in a dense fuchsia bush by a cottage gate only to be met with a pair of white pumps and bare ankles. He raised his eyes to find the hem of a starched white, dowdy dress, his brain convincing him for a second that it must be smart, efficient Mona in her maid's livery come to rescue him. Had Dad relented? Did he have a heart after all?

'What are you doing?' asked Samantha Capstan, coolly.

He grabbed the note and sprang to his feet, almost slipping again.

Instinctively, she shot a hand out to steady him but he acted like he hadn't noticed and she hastily tucked it away again.

'I'm doing a coffee run,' he told her, fixing his shades.

'Course you are. Well, you're in my way.' She turned her head to indicate the sled behind her, loaded with bundles of white bed linen strapped in place with bungee cords.

He stepped gingerly aside to let her pass. There was something different about her since last night. Her hair was knotted up high on her crown and loose bits floated round her face. He might not have noticed if it wasn't for the burst of blue by her temple. A small flower. She didn't seem the type to go slipping flowers behind her ear.

Her hand reached for the spot and she gently touched a fingertip to the frilly petals as she moved by, letting him know she could feel him staring and it was making her self-conscious.

She seemed cross. That hadn't changed.

Jasper hadn't forgotten the way she'd shouted at him. Was everyone in Clove Lore like this? How he longed for the easy anonymity of Chelsea and Knightsbridge.

'I...' he began, and Sam stopped hauling, letting the sled come to a halt again. She flicked her eyes to him impatiently.

'I don't know where to get coffee,' he said, unaware it sounded so pleading.

With a deep sigh, Sam pointed down the slope. 'First right. See? Between those cottages? The bookshop along that passageway sells coffee, if they're open yet.'

'Great,' he said.

She was still looking at him, he noticed. He wasn't sure what she could be waiting for. A ten-pound note caught his eye fluttering gently between a rusty drainpipe and the painted stone of a cottage's porch. He refused to chase it while she was present.

For a second longer, Sam held still, glaring at him expectantly, before shaking her head and dragging the sled on up the slope, the effort requiring her to lean forward and dig deep.

Jasper was sure he heard her muttering something but had no idea it was an irritated, 'Would a *thank you* kill him?'

As soon as she was a safe distance away, unlikely to glance back, he lunged for the last of his notes before making his way down the slope in search of his mother's caffeine.

Chapter Nine

The box had been waiting for Austen on the steps of the Borrow-A-Bookshop when she arrived back from her mortifying encounter down at the harbour. For a long moment she only looked at it, before hefting it through the door and onto the counter.

'What are these in aid of?' she asked the box, sorting through its contents and finding some shiny new hardbacks, some well-thumbed ex-library books, most of them Mills & Boon, and a couple of cheap millionth-edition Dickens' novels from the early twentieth century that had lost their dust jackets.

Underneath she found the note.

> *I've had a very successful book rummage around the charity shops, as you can see. These need shelving after pricing up and adding to the stock system (pretty straightforward, and the instructions are in the guest info book – just shout if you need help). We heard the kiddies' author (and panda) visit made a big splash! Well done indeed. Jowan*

'Pricing up?' she asked herself. 'The instruction book didn't say anything about how to price books.' She turned a foxed copy of *A Tale of Two Cities* in her hands. 'Do I just make up a price? Is there a database with second-hand book guide prices?'

This felt like something she should know, having been in the book industry (or, at least, industry adjacent for a while), but she was drawing a blank.

Reprieve came in the form of a young, oddly dressed guy, bursting in the door and demanding, 'Is this the coffee place?'

He ignored Austen's invitation to browse the shelves while she made his six shots of espresso in the same cup.

'Extra hot,' he'd asserted, and she'd worked the machine as fast as possible, aware he was shifting his weight from foot to foot on the other side of the counter.

'Any lemon-lime meringue pie with your enormous coffee?' she asked, hoping to bring some calm to the flustered boy.

He only glanced at the impressively green pies beneath their domes before dismissing the idea with a curt 'refined sugar', as though that explained everything.

He'd pocketed his change without checking it, thanked her, and beat a hasty retreat, leaving the shop door open behind him. Austen watched him go in quiet astonishment.

'Don't mind him,' she told the pies. 'I think you're pretty, even if you are a bit sugary.'

She pulled her phone from her shorts pocket and filmed herself lifting the glass lid and pulling a 'wow' expression, before posting the film without any editing other than the caption, 'Home baking with your books and coffee? #lemonlime'.

In the time it took to return to the book box on the shop counter, she heard the ping of notifications.

Borrowing this bookshop was doing wonders for her follows.

The very first comment on her video made her forget the bookshop altogether.

'I would like some pie please. Send to the Feint Heart, in the Fifth, next to the statue of Voltaire. I will be waiting.'

'Fifth dimension?'

'Arrondissement.'

Austen chastised herself. She didn't want this nice person thinking she wasn't smart and cultured. She switched to private messaging and typed her reply.

'I was joking. You'll just have to come here for a slice, I'm afraid. Waiting times at the Tunnel being what they are. How are things at the Feint Heart today?'

'Quiet. It is too early to sell books. *Plutôt* I... what is the word in English? I *balaye*.'

Austen hit 'translate' on the message and typed back, 'Sweep?'

'Yes! I sweep. Did you sweep? My day, I think, is a lot of sweep and clean.'

Austen sniffed a delighted laugh. She loved this person's way with words. Person. A reminder she had no idea who she was talking to. She didn't have a mind to ask, however. It didn't feel like it mattered that much. Not when she was being treated like a fellow bookseller, so she typed.

'There's sand on the floor. I really should vacuum.' It took her two goes to spell the word 'vacuum' and it still didn't look right. 'Maybe I should take up sweeping. I know how to spell that without googling it.'

The Parisian's next message overlapped with her own.

'Every day I have a challenge. I will sell such and such before sunset. Today I have *Prufrock and other Observations*.

85

First edition, 1917. You know "The Love Song of J. Alfred Prufrock?"'

'Yes! "Do I dare to eat a peach?" T. S. Eliot. I love that poem! So, what do you win if you sell it before sunset?'

'Win?'

'What is your reward for selling it?'

'Ah! I will close early and read.'

'Sounds perfect.'

'Only if I sell the book. What do you do today?'

'She looked at the box of unpriced books.'

'Actually, I have a job to do. Maybe you can help me, please?'

'*Bien sûr!* Tell me.'

And so they chatted, and the Parisian bookseller explained how Austen could search for the same titles in the box in comparable condition at any of the big online second-hand retailers like Alibris or BookFinder. It sounded time-consuming, Austen replied, and they'd gone on to say she could simply pick a price based on instinct, which Austen approved wholeheartedly.

'So there's no database with guide prices?' she asked.

The bookseller mustn't have seen this as they replied instead with a question.

'Can you look at the shelves for tired books?'

'Tired? As in, tatty?'

'Swap some of these new titles with the tattiest and place the worst in a box close to the door. A courtesy gift for your customers.'

'Free books? Is that what you do?'

'Non.'

'Why are you telling me to do it then?'

They came straight back with a laugh emoji. So, whoever this person was, they weren't above a smiley face after all. Still, she was glad she'd stopped herself sending the croissant emoji the other day.

'You know? I think I'll set up a swap box. A bring-a-book/take-a-book kind of thing. They're really popular in England. And the bookshop owner told me I can do whatever I like with my shop.'

'Do you look after everything alone?' the Parisian asked. 'The keys, the stock, the money?'

'Everything. Amazed they let me.'

'*Chut!* You are *complètement compétente*.'

'Glad one of us feels that way.'

The Feint Heart bookseller signed off with a brisk bout of *tsk-tsk*ing at her lack of confidence and a final '*bonne chance*', and Austen, feeling suddenly giddy, dashed to the poetry shelves on the hunt for a book she felt sure she'd seen there.

'Aha! Got it!' she pulled the book free, and carried it to the desk where she wrote on a sticky note the words, 'Do I dare to eat a peach? Book of the Day, £10' and, standing the *Prufrock* on a perspex display stand, she snapped a photo.

'Challenge accepted. Who will sell theirs before sunset?!'

Smiling, she sent the message all the way to her intriguing new acquaintance in the Fifth Arrondissement.

Chapter Ten

By Monday afternoon, it was clear that Austen had discovered her bookselling mojo. It hadn't been difficult once she'd tapped into the junior version of herself – the girl who'd completed the local library's 'summer reading challenge' within the first week of the holidays every year and had proudly taken the certificate to show everyone back at school come September. Her classmates hadn't been anything like as impressed as the teachers were, and that had been her first clue that she was uniquely cut out for a bookish life.

Then, thinking of that little girl, word-hungry and probably a bit precocious, and very much always feeling like an awkward outsider, she'd curated a special display of picture books and chapter books that she would have loved to pick up in a bookstore when she was small, only there hadn't been anything like as much diversity in kids' stories then as there was now.

There'd been a few wistful tears as Austen pulled out books from the shelves with Queer representation at their heart: books showing loving, supportive families who were human beings above and before their 'non-traditional' set-ups; books about hiding away, and books about coming out; books about joyful acceptance, and books about found family; books about childhood mental health and well-being, self-knowledge and kindness.

When they were finally set out in their display, the covers made up a joyful rainbow of colour.

That's when she determined to move on to creating a pre-teen and then a young adult display, too, made up with books with the same messages: *you are enough as you are, you can drop your mask, let yourself live and love just as you want to, it gets easier with time and with the right people around you.*

When she'd spotted big gaps in the stock, she'd even taken it upon herself to ring Jowan to ask if there was a budget for ordering books in, and he'd replied that of course there was. It wasn't big, but there was credit on the account and a request form on the POS's stock system where she could simply buy whatever she wanted directly from the supplier.

'Overnight delivery, it is, on new stock,' he'd told her. 'Reckon any of these titles'll get folks' backs up?'

'Possibly,' she'd replied, choosing to trust Jowan. He'd looked like a peaced-out old hippy, so now was his chance to prove that's what he really was. 'But they're not the readers these books need to be found by, so they don't really matter.'

'Good-o,' Jowan had replied with a chuckle. 'Crack on then, you know best what the young uns want.'

There are stories for everyone, if you look hard enough, so that's what Austen did, ordering in books featuring young disabled characters, children of colour, honouring a variety of cultures, bodies and genders, preferences and pronouns; books celebrating neurodiversity and embracing facial and physical differences.

She made sure to cater to kids that had been called 'reluctant readers' who might actually fancy a really cool graphic novel over a thumping great school library hardback. Or maybe they just hadn't been tempted by the blandness of the celebrity bestsellers that everyone pushed upon them.

The whole project was exhilarating.

The boxes arrived on Tuesday just as she'd dealt with the mid-morning rush on coffees and cake. It hadn't taken long to unpack and finish her displays: a snaking spectrum of sunshiny books positioned all across the fireplace, the wall racks, windowsills, and in prime position behind the till point.

Austen posted videos of the shop transformation to her social media, and she let herself feel glad for all the wonderful young people who'd pick up these stories and see themselves reflected back, possibly for the first time ever, hearing a message loud and clear that nobody, not at any age, can hear too often: *it is absolutely OK to be your truest wonderful self.*

The whole thing had felt like a great big karmic offering to the universe, righting some of the wrong-headed, blundering things she'd done in the past, and it had been the perfect way to stop herself remembering how ridiculously she'd behaved in front of Patti on Monday at the harbourside.

It was soothing and healing in the best way, until two things happened, both at the same time on that first Tuesday afternoon in her shop, when all her restocking and displaying was finished, and both threatened to shake the new foundation of competent adulting that she'd managed to build for herself.

Firstly, there'd come the phone call from home.

'Hi Mum.' Austen knew it wouldn't be her dad ringing from the landline for the simple fact that he'd never done it before, not even when she was living in London. He much preferred the ease of texting, and for a modern man living and working in the liberal arts, he left much of the keeping in touch and family-wrangling to his wife.

'Aussie! How are you, darling? I saw your lovely films from the bookshop. We're so proud of you.'

'Thanks. Is everything OK?' Austen checked the time on the till display. 'You're not down the allotment?'

'I had to ring you first, to let you know,' she began ominously. 'Now I don't want you worrying…'

'Oh God, what's happened?'

'I drew your cards this morning.'

'Oh.' Austen's shoulders slumped. 'Go on then.' She tried to keep the weariness out of her voice. Her dad was sceptical enough for the both of them about these things, and it hurt her mum's feelings when he made fun of her interests. Knowing how deflated it made her, Austen had promised herself she wouldn't join in.

'I've drawn them every day since you left, you know…'

'Just in case,' they both said at the same time.

'I know,' Austen added. 'So what did I get today?'

'The Lovers.'

'Oh, OK!' Austen didn't mind that card at all.

'Inverted.'

'Hmm?'

'I drew the card reversed.'

'And that's… bad?'

'Well, you could interpret it as a kind of portent, yes. Especially since that's what I drew on Sunday *and* Monday. That's three times, Austen. You can't ignore the universe when she's insistent like that! It's a warning about false love. If you were here, I'd do your tea, to get some clarity on it. You see why I had to call.'

Austen was agreeing and thanking her mother (and hoping it didn't sound half-hearted) when she heard her dad's voice in the background. His university had broken up for the summer and she could already picture him haunting his study, researching and writing, trying to finish his long-awaited book on Georgian poetry and political intrigue. He'd been writing it for six years.

'Ask if she's given any thought to the master's degree,' he called, sounding very much like he was on his way back from the fridge with something in his mouth.

'Can you not drop crumbs, Jerms,' her mum retorted. Jerms was her nickname for him since they met at a rally in the Nineties and fallen in love instantly, when Jeremy and Bernice had become 'Jerms and Berns' forevermore.

'What was that?' Austen asked.

'Nothing, you know what he's like, muttering and mumbling around the house.'

'He still thinks I should do another degree?'

'Well, it's one option, isn't it?'

They'd had these conversations before, awkwardly at the dinner table, when her dad tried hard to hide his disappointment about his daughter's return from London.

'I'll find something,' Austen promised, feeling her heart sink. 'It's just not that easy.'

'I know, love. Maybe there'll be a nice bookshop job for you when you get back? Now you've got all this experience?'

Austen didn't want to tell her mum that she'd already applied to all the bookstores in the North West this month and not heard a word back from any of them.

'Bookselling's harder to get into than you might think. People stay in those jobs forever. It's like, a vocation, not a casual thing.'

'I know,' her mum soothed again. 'He worries about you, that's all. Listen, I'm helping Fawn with the bean harvest at two, got to go. You will remember what the cards said, won't you? Three lovers, all turned on their heads. It's a warning of some kind.'

Austen only laughed. Three lovers? Three warnings? Hardly accurate when she'd been bustling around in her bookshop for the last couple of days, all by herself – well, with her customers to keep her company, and the Parisian always at the end of their chat thread.

That reminded her, she ought to check in and see what they were up to. They'd got to the 'what are you having for lunch?' stage in their acquaintance and she wouldn't want to miss telling the stranger that she'd had sliced tomatoes with basil and bread. This was vital information.

'You don't need to worry about me, OK? I'm doing great. Honestly.'

And her mum had, reluctantly, hung up, after a lot of I Love Yous, partly because she absolutely meant it, and partly because Bernice Archer had read a study that said children who were told every day that they were loved were ninety-six per cent more likely to form successful relationships in later life. Bernice had told her upward of fifty times a day, just to be on the safe side.

On hanging up, Austen hadn't had time to check her phone for foodie updates from her friend over the Channel, because Radia came through the door bringing a peal of laughter.

'Hi Radia!' Austen greeted her, looking out into the square for Patti following behind.

'You're not on your own, are you?' Her voice had a definite wobble to it, Austen knew. Thank goodness only the child heard it. She had, probably, a full five seconds to compose herself before the girl's aunt bounded in and Austen could make her apologies for being daft the other morning, and maybe they'd all chat and browse her new book displays, and maybe that'd turn into coffee, or maybe more ice creams, who knows?

'Hi!' Someone stepped into the shop using Patti's voice, and smiling with Patti's mouth, but this was definitely not Patti. 'I'm Joy. Radia's mum?'

From her tone, Austen knew she must have been gawking at her in confusion. She fixed her face into a grin. 'Great! Hi! Nice to meet you, sorry I was…'

Joy nodded like she knew how that sentence would have ended, and her sleek black bob shifted about. It was uncanny, really, how similar the sisters were, even without Patti's wild waves, and the resemblance set off all kinds of strange, nervy feelings inside Austen.

'We brought you a pen,' Radia announced, holding up a black Sharpie.

'Oh, uh, OK. Thank you.'

'It's from Patti. She said you chucked your other one in the sea. And she felt bad for sneaking up on you.'

'Oh, she shouldn't have…' Austen took the pen, her eyes flitting to the open door and the blazing sunshine beyond.

'Patti's busy, with work, or she'd have come herself, probably,' Joy said, a little shakily.

'Well, thank you. You can never have too many pens,' Austen told the little girl, resolving to be sensible and not disappointed. Patti had thought about her enough to send these two to the shop, hadn't she? That was nice.

'Ooh!' Radia's eyes lit up as she spotted the new book displays and she dashed into the kids' nook under the stairs to investigate, leaving the grown-ups standing in silence.

'How, um, how is Patti?' asked Austen, as casually as possible.

'You know, busy,' Joy told her, and a fresh silence bloomed. 'I worked here,' she added after a pained moment. 'Last summer. Not bookselling. Tech installation.'

'Ah!' Austen pointed to the till and laptop. 'It's uh, all working lovely.'

They exchanged polite hidden-lipped smiles. Joy rocked on her flat soles. Austen was sure she could hear the cafe clock ticking.

What she wanted to say was that she'd love to see Patti if she was passing, and that she hadn't meant to run off like a lunatic on Monday, and that Patti had just happened upon her at a tricky moment when she'd been trying to wring some words out of her cortisol-soaked brain, and she regretted not staying to talk. But Austen didn't dare say any of that.

'Can I have this one?' Radia bounded out from the kids' section with a large picture book about crayons making up a colourful community celebrating their differences, the sort of book that made some people tut and call for a ban.

It was paid for with a quick flash of Joy's credit card and the pair had stepped outside into the sun again before Austen had blurted anything she might regret, like, *will you give Patti my number, maybe?*

'Thanks for the pen,' she called weakly after them, but they were away, leaving her alone in the cool of the shop, not quite knowing why she felt so thwarted and like she possibly wasn't doing as well as she thought she was.

The notification pinged on her phone, and she grabbed for it, smiling already.

'Cheese is enough for lunch, yes? Only cheese?' it read.

'I'd say so,' she began typing, and with that she let herself ignore the feelings of being jolted out of her cosy bookshop comfort zone by her mum's tarot cards and her dad's disappointment, and the fact that she'd really wanted to see Patti walk through the door but she'd sent her sister in her stead.

Austen drifted off into the low-demand, low-stakes world of conversation with her Parisian friend, where, unlike in the here-and-now of Austen's real life, everything was simple and easy.

Chapter Eleven

Jasper, who'd had more than enough of packing crates and impossible-to-fit artefacts from his old family life and nowhere near enough cupboard space or hangers, found he had to get out of the apartment by Wednesday evening. He ended up by the quayside, his stomach rumbling, drawn by the aroma of langoustines and sardines cooked in lemon herb butter drifting out from the grill-stand of Bickleigh's Harbourside Bites.

The smell put him in mind of the marina restaurants of Port Vauban or Malta's Grand Harbour where they'd summered on his father's yacht when he was a kid. What he wouldn't give to be back there now with a full belly and not a care in the world.

The chalkboard propped by the sizzling grill told him a portion of seafood with sauce and salad started at ten quid.

He'd have to take *something* back to the apartment for his mother, though he knew perfectly well she could survive on little more than cigarettes and air – a trick she'd learned setting out as a teen model back in the Eighties.

In recent years she'd subsisted on The Ivy's signature grilled vegetable salad (her absolute favourite), handfuls of almonds, diet pills and cocktail olives, but nowadays she looked underfed and exhausted. Plus, there was no money to send her to the clinic where they'd pump her full of collagen and proper food all summer long, restoring her glow. Dad wouldn't be interested in funding her little 'holiday' anymore.

He pulled out his phone to ring his mother and beg her to join him down at the harbour for something to eat, but before he could find her in his contacts, the message onscreen told him SERVICE DISCON-NECTED. CONTACT PROVIDER.

'Contact the provider?' he said wryly.

Dad had been the provider of everything. It seems he was taking his promise (or his threat) to 'make a man' of him at twenty-one very seriously indeed. It was only a few weeks since he'd been blowing out the candles on his birthday cake on the rooftop bar of The Mondrian over-looking the lights of the city, surrounded by a guffawing, high-spirited guest list limited to eighty of his closest friends (and a few paid B-listers), none of whom he'd had the courage to contact since all this happened, and none of whom had reached out to see where he'd disappeared to.

The last thing he expected to happen next was for a laugh to burst from somewhere within him, but neverthe-less that's what happened; a big, blurting, out-of-control laugh, which felt dangerously close to morphing into hysterical tears, but the sight of that laundry girl marching by stopped him immediately. He composed his face, trying to pretend he'd read something amusing on his useless phone.

Only she didn't even glance his way. Instead, she was waving to the man barbecuing fish and asking how someone called Joy was doing, before she disappeared inside the pub.

He felt for the two five-pound notes in a pocket of his Balenciaga cargos, pulling one free and examining it for a long time, stopping to squint now and then at the propped-open pub doors.

This was the last money he had in the world. The rest he'd rolled up and slipped into his mum's purse in the hope she'd discover it and think it was spare change forgotten from long ago. He didn't want her to know that it was all he had left and he'd given it to her. She still had her pride, though in her current state as a moping, semiconscious lump under the bedsheets, it was harder to see.

Dare he go inside the Siren's Tail and risk not having enough money for some takeaway food and a drink? Could he handle the embarrassment?

It hit him that he had no idea how much his favourite cocktails cost individually, only knowing the totals he'd sign off on his credit card at the end of the night, more often than not in the region of two or three hundred quid. Was five pounds enough for a drink in a seaside pub? Since when did five-pound notes have Winston Churchill on the back? He'd never held one long enough to notice before. Maybe they'd let him run up a tab? The hysterical crying feeling came back in a horrible panicky rush.

That was when he became aware that he was being watched, and by a curiously squat, red-faced fellow wearing a Barbour jacket that had seen better days.

The man was leaning on the wall of the lifeboat launch, chewing what appeared to be a neon plastic ice cream spoon like he was a cowboy turning a matchstick in his mouth in some old movie.

'Can I help you?' Jasper called out, defensive, with no intention of helping anyone, least of all a staring yokel.

'You're the boy from the Big 'Ouse,' the red-faced man informed him, making his way across the cobbles to where he stood.

'Who are you?'

'Bovis is the name.' He thumbed his chest. 'I 'appen to have worked up at the Big 'Ouse back in the days before it was split into flats. I was the Mistress's groundsman and gamekeeper. I hear you've met the Mistress. I mean, Mrs Clove-Congreve.'

'You've heard a lot.'

'That's what I do. Listening. Lookin'. I'm always watching the comings and goings round Clove Lore. Lookin' out for trouble.'

Between the fastenings on Bovis's open Barbour, Jasper clocked an unpleasantly tight pastel t-shirt with some embroidery on the pocket.

'Your t-shirt says you're from the Ice Cream Cottage. Is that your cover?'

'*Hmph!*' Bovis zipped his jacket with a brisk tug.

'I won't detain you if you have important security detail to see to.'

'We've got a smart one 'ere,' Bovis remarked, turning to address a merry white-haired woman hobbling down the slope towards them.

'I hope you're being polite to the young gentleman,' the woman called back. 'He'll be having a time of it, adjusting to a new home and all.'

Bovis at least looked humbled, but really, thought Jasper, did everyone around here already know his business?

'How's your mum?' the woman asked. 'Word has it she's not left that apartment since you got 'ere. Not ill, I hope?'

Seeing his face fall, the woman cajoled, 'Oh, don't mind us. We're a friendly lot. You'll get used to it. One thing's for sure, you can't keep yourself to yourself in Clove Lore.'

Jasper fought hard to suppress a shudder. Yet, there was something vaguely familiar about the woman, who was now introducing herself as 'Letitia Crocombe, of Crocombe's Ices' and telling him he must 'pop in for a cone' when he's passing.

'Pleased to meet you,' he said, examining her pale, podgy cheeks and twinkling eyes. That's it! She looked like Nanny Cliff. The kindly woman who'd spend her days with him in the nursery before he was sent away to prep school and was thereafter subjected to various hopeless au pairs every summer or half holidays when he went back down to London.

'I've got a nice courgette and banana bread ice cream I'm trying out,' she was saying with a smile. 'You can be the first to sample it, if you're quick.'

Jasper didn't know what to say, but the woman was taking him by the arm and directing him towards the pub doors where the laundry girl had just entered.

'I'm ever so glad you've decided to join us for book club. That shows proper community spirit, does it not, Mr Bovis?'

The man only grunted and followed on.

'Sorry, I don't...' Jasper began.

Mrs Crocombe patted his hand, her voice melting even softer. 'There's sarnidges, you know? And you don't *have* to 'ave read the book.'

'I never do,' Bovis put in. 'I just sits and listens.'

By now they were through the pub door and in a big bar room with good foody smells – fried stuff that made him weaken and gulp – and lots of tourists in bright high-street fashions chatting in family groups, the kids scrolling on phones.

'I try not to eat bread… usually,' he said.

Mrs Crocombe tutted this away.

At that moment, the landlady, Bella, in a strawberry-print dress, her long hair bouncing behind her, pushed through the swing doors from the function room revealing a vast buffet set out on long tables.

'I do, uh, however, have a fondness for… literature,' Jasper said, his eyes fixed on the inviting spread until the doors swung shut again. 'I'd be glad to… listen along with you, if no one objects?'

Bovis slapped him on the shoulder approvingly and led him through the doors. 'It's Bella's Scotch eggs bring me to club, being honest. Best set an example and make a start ourselves?' Approaching the table, Bovis handed the hungry boy a plate.

Jasper wanted the ground to swallow him, taking him to anywhere but this weird back room with the oars and fishing nets arranged along the walls above long banks of cushioned seating. There were chairs set out in a circle in the centre of the polished dancefloor for the book club discussion. How awful! But then his stomach won out.

With his heart cracking a little at what he'd been reduced to, and with deliberate reserve, he helped himself to some cherry tomatoes and cucumber sticks, while Bovis shook his head and added to his plate crustless cheese and pickle sandwiches and various beige things in breadcrumbs which all smelled so tasty Jasper feared he might cry.

He couldn't feel the eyes upon him from across the room, but he made out the voice of a girl with a

Devonshire accent as thick as clotted cream, saying, 'What is *he* doing here?' and it was irritating enough for him to know precisely who it was without having to turn around.

–

Samantha Capstan was supposed to be enjoying a rare night off, but it didn't feel like it when Minty, her boss from the Big House, was in for book club as well and had perched beside her, reeling off a list of tasks for tomorrow's wedding party.

'What's the young man doing here?' Minty parroted Sam's exasperated question. 'I expect he's making an effort to get to know his community.'

'His community? He's a tourist, isn't he?' Sam said, her eyes still fixed on his back.

'No. He's from the Big House apartments. His name is Jasper Gold.'

Sam repeated the name under her breath. Why did it sound familiar? 'And he lives at the Big House. Alone?'

'Alone with his mother. She's permanently indisposed. Won't leave her rooms, or answer the door. Strange woman.'

'That tracks,' said Sam. 'He's strange too. And rude.'

'I've found him perfectly genial. And he's here, isn't he? That shows a modicum of civic responsibility. His mother, on the other hand…'

As Minty droned on about how the woman was haunting the Big House like the ghost of a jilted Victorian bride, Sam was remembering the way this Jasper person had made her feel up on the coastal path when he'd told her he was too good for her seconds after laying eyes on her. 'I guess he's polite to you because you're…'

Sam had been about to say 'old', but gulped the word down. Minty raised an enquiring eyebrow and waited.

'Because you're lady of the manor,' Sam blurted hurriedly, saving herself.

She always seemed to be blundering in front of Minty. If her boss wasn't so intimidating it would be easier, but Sam found her terrifying.

Mrs Crocombe saved her from further consternation by taking a seat next to them with a mug of tea and a big plate of cake and biscuits all for herself, as though the sneaked scoops of her own ice creams all day long wasn't enough sweetness for her. She had her copy of tonight's book ready under her arm.

'How's your mum?' Mrs Crocombe asked in her usual kindly way.

'Resting at home, thanks,' Sam answered. 'The bruising's really coming out now. Looks horrible and yellow.'

Mrs Crocombe sucked air between her teeth. 'Poor woman. I'll send her round a tub of peaches and cream tomorrow. That's her favourite, isn't it?' Mrs Crocombe was of the opinion there wasn't a problem in the world that couldn't be fixed with ice cream.

Sam told her it was. 'How do you remember that?'

'I never forgets a favourite,' she winked. 'Loved it since she was your age. And you're getting on for twenty-one now? Goodness me. The time flies away from us.'

'Birthday's in December,' Sam said with a nod.

'Not long now. Plannin' a big party, are you?'

Sam hurriedly shook her head before Minty, who was listening closely, could get her hooks in and start booking out the ballroom for a lavish do. That was exactly the kind of thing she'd barge her way into, never thinking of the expense to Sam and her mum. 'We might go away for my twenty-first,' she lied.

'Oh yes?' Mrs Crocombe wheedled.

'London. West End maybe. Mum's always wanted to see a big show,' Sam rambled in panic. The show part was true but the chance would be a fine thing. Musical tickets cost a bomb, and that's before trains and hotels and dinners.

'Young Jasper could help you out there,' Minty crowed over the room.

Jasper dutifully made his way towards them and took a seat, leaving a chair on either side of him, presumably, thought Sam, for his massive ego.

'What can I help with?' he asked, the picture of politeness.

'Young Samantha's planning a big birthday trip to London. You must know all the best places,' Mrs Crocombe said encouragingly, and all eyes turned expectantly to Jasper.

'Uh, yes, of course. I can give you some recommendations.' He addressed this to Sam, but quickly dropped his eyes to where Bovis was forcing a half-pint glass upon him and patting his shoulder.

'Bitter shandy,' Bovis said, before shuffling round the chairs to take a seat behind Mrs Crocombe who was smiling her thanks at him, as though it had been her idea to fetch the newcomer a proper drink from the bar.

'For me?' Jasper said, a little eagerly, Sam thought, watching him as he lifted the glass in toast to Bovis before taking a sip. Everyone had fallen back to chattering now, but Sam sat silently watching the new arrival taste his drink in a slow, curious way that suggested he'd never had a shandy before. She saw his pupils dilate sharply at the first taste, and his irises bloom the most shocking silver grey before he tipped his head back and finished half of it.

As he examined the glass in his hand afterwards, oddly dazed, Sam found herself having to look away. Why was she so fascinated by this ridiculous person and his snooty fish-out-of-water ways? Why was she feeling this stupid pang of pity for him like he was one of the scruffy, half-starved foster kittens her mum was forever bringing home from the rescue place down the main road?

She tried to listen to Minty and Mrs Crocombe's chatter now, but nothing sank in, and all the while the infuriating, rude Jasper sat opposite her in the circle speaking to no one and toying with his food.

She couldn't know it, but Jasper was well aware of her gaze upon him and was using his last reserves of decorum to hold himself back from devouring in seconds the food that his empty stomach craved so badly, especially not in front of the laundry girl who, maddeningly, seemed to be every place he went and was always looking down on him in that judgemental way that left him feeling positively skinless.

He raised a cherry tomato to his lips. Mercifully, Samantha, her cheeks blooming an arresting shade of pink, shifted in her seat, turning her shoulders against him so he could at last eat unobserved. A tiny part of him missed the heavy weight of her blue eyes upon him but he was too hungry to entertain the feeling for long.

Chapter Twelve

Patti had saved the seat next to her at book club (handily, Izaak had offloaded a box of courgettes on her, begging her to take them or he'd be forced to pitch this lot over the harbourside). So, she'd waited for as long as she could, the veggies marking out the spot she hoped Austen would fill, but as Bella, the pub landlady, said they'd be starting in two minutes, Patti gave up hope and set the box on the floor.

The last time she'd seen Austen, at the harbour lantern on Monday morning, the Borrower couldn't have got away faster. It didn't make much sense to Patti when she'd been as welcoming as possible.

Maybe that was the problem? Austen was people-shy, or maybe she was just Patti-shy. Still, all she'd been about to suggest was a tour of the Big House grounds and maybe something to eat, to get her out of the shop for a while. It was like Austen had sensed what was coming and bolted.

Patti had read this as the great big red flag that it was and had stayed away since then. And yet, when she saw Jowan making for the chair beside her, Aldous dancing round his feet, excited by the possibility of a cheese and pickle sandwich, her mood sank.

'How do?' said Jowan as he lowered himself into the seat by her side, Aldous immediately taking the opportunity to sniff out the untouched food on Patti's plate.

She quickly slipped the dog a cheddar cube and he (knowing it would be forbidden by Elliot, the spoilsport vet) delightedly swallowed it whole.

'Hey, Jowan,' said Patti. 'Are you looking for someone?'

He was scanning the faces of the book lovers all seated in a round, then checking the thin crowd by the buffet where Bovis was making short work of a second plate of Bella's mini Scotch eggs.

'Aye,' he began. 'I was hoping young Austen would drop by. Brought her these.' He lifted a carrier bag filled with paperbacks onto his lap. 'She had this idea of a giveaways box. You know, books that are too bashed about to take any money for?'

'That's a nice idea.'

'I thought so. I told her I'd be bringing these to the Siren at seven, but…'

'You tried to rope her into book club?'

'You make it sound underhand.' Jowan's sandy, grizzled jaw quirked as he grinned. 'Perhaps I did. But 'tis a shame, her hiding up at the bookshop all day and night.'

'Have you called in to see her?' Patti tried to sound casual.

'This afternoon. Chock-a-block, it was. She had customers queued up at the till, and the cafe room closed up, making them take their coffees out in the courtyard where she could better keep an eye on them from the shop.'

'That sounds smart. Since she's on her own.' Patti slipped Aldous a sausage roll, which he accepted, but in such a way that made it clear he'd have much preferred the mini scone with strawberry jam and clotted cream on the side of her plate. 'I don't mind volunteering to help out more, if she's run off her feet?'

'Seemed happy enough. If not a little distracted by her phone.'

'Oh?' She didn't try to hide the feelings this set off in her. Patti wasn't the hiding things type.

'I only stayed an hour to help clear the queues. I knows when I'm not wanted. But the girl's phone was beep-beeping and ring-dinging like a fair. Messages,' he clarified.

'She must be missing her friends,' Patti said.

Or there's someone waiting at home for her? She'd heard from Jude Crawley, the bookshop's treasurer and bookings manager – and a one-time Borrower herself – that Austen's original holiday reservation had been made for two.

'Ah, speak of the devil!' Jowan interrupted Patti's thoughts.

There in the doorway was Austen Archer, looking like a woman only just realising she'd been duped.

'Over here,' Jowan summoned her, with pirate-like joviality. 'Here's a spare chair.'

'No, no, allow me,' said someone else from across the circle, already on his feet. The new guy, Jasper, looking like this was his chance to escape. 'Please, take my chair.'

By now the chat had fallen to a murmur and everyone was watching the Borrower, wondering what she would do.

'Oh, I'm not... I wasn't planning on staying,' she was spluttering, eyes darting between Jasper, Jowan and Patti with a look of desperation.

Patti bounced up onto her feet, lifting the bag of books from Jowan's lap. She glided across the room, fully aware of Mrs Crocombe watching her.

In a whisper, Patti told Austen, 'If you make a dash for the door now, they won't be able to stop you. Here. These are the books Jowan mentioned.'

Austen, still thunderstruck, gazed at the bag for a moment before taking it. 'This is book club, isn't it?' she said.

A little buzz of conversation began again in the circle. Minty was telling Samantha to 'be a good girl and collect the subs money', handing her a lockbox. Samantha dutifully lifted herself from her chair and managed to hide her eye roll from everyone but Patti – and possibly Austen – who were glancing back at the crowd cautiously.

'You don't have to stay,' Patti said again in a whisper.

Austen's eyes had fallen only for the briefest second onto the plate of food still in Patti's hand, but it had been enough to make Patti suspect she likely hadn't eaten again.

'Unless you want to grab a quick bite?' Patti added. 'It won't start for another couple of minutes, and everyone's already gassing away again.' Patti shifted a little so Austen had a full view of the room.

Everyone was talking and eating once more. Mrs Crocombe appeared to have a great deal to say all of a sudden. That set a little alarm bell ringing in Patti's head, remembering how determinedly Mrs C. had tried to set her sister up with Monty last summer. That woman could sniff out a match between the Clove Lore residents and visitors the way one of the Big House Bridezillas could spot a mismatched floral centrepiece in a wedding marquee.

'The food does look nice,' said Austen, eyeing the snacks, oblivious to Mrs C.'s whispers. 'I've been living off Izaak's salad stuff.'

'Come on,' Patti tipped her head towards the buffet, and led Austen towards it, putting a plate in her hands. 'You need some carbs.' To encourage her, Patti topped up her own plate before dipping a carrot stick into some hummus and taking a crunchy bite.

Austen followed her lead, keeping her back turned to the room.

'How are things at the bookshop?' Patti ventured. 'Jowan says you've been run off your feet.'

'I have. It's been fun actually, but a *lot*, you know?'

Patti resisted the urge to volunteer to help out during her lunch breaks from Big House Weddings. Softly softly was the only way with Austen, who clearly didn't like people interfering.

Austen was already halfway through a spicy chickpea sandwich, and Patti tried to smother all the questions she wanted to ask this woman by filling her own mouth too. She shoved a breaded mushroom in and chomped, meeting Austen's eyes for a second, making them both sniff an awkward laugh.

'This is so good,' said Austen. 'I've barely stopped today.'

'You can't sell books on lettuce alone.'

Another smile from Austen before she took another bite.

'Listen, about the other morning,' Patti began. 'I hope you don't think I was being pushy. I just wanted to make sure you weren't lonely or anything…'

Austen seemed to force down the mouthful, already shaking her head. 'Mm, no,' she gulped hurriedly. 'No, I just had to get back to the shop…'

'Sure, it's OK. I understand.' Patti had reached out to touch Austen before she realised what she was doing, whipping her hand back down to her side just millimetres before making contact.

Seeing Austen's eyes widen, Patti garbled, 'God, sorry. I… I'm usually much more chill than this.' Patti couldn't help smiling, however, as she rolled her eyes at her own awkwardness. This wasn't like her at all. When she had met cute women in the past she had no trouble acting human in front of them. What the hell was all this? Thankfully, Austen was smiling too.

'You seem fine to me,' Austen said, before fixing her eyes on her food once more.

Something inside Patti softened at the sight of Austen eating. She took a step away, hoping she'd read this as a sign that she wasn't going to crowd her or ask anything of her. She just wanted Austen to feel comfortable.

No sooner had she widened the distance between them than Jasper inserted himself. He set his empty plate on the table. 'Uh, if you would like to take my place at book club, I won't mind at all,' he said, addressing Austen. 'I should get going anyway…'

'You're the six-espressos-in-one-cup guy,' Austen said, brightening.

'Wow!' Patti added. 'You must really love your coffee!'

Jasper didn't respond, only pressing his point by glancing back at the crowd, now drawing their books from bags and pockets and turning to business. 'I wasn't going to stay, you see?'

'Subs, please,' came a small voice from behind Jasper, and all three turned to see Sam Capstan, standing with the cash box open.

Patti immediately handed over five pounds in coins. 'I read the book ages ago, probably won't remember half of it,' she confessed.

'I didn't even have time to finish it,' Sam replied with a shrug. 'Only got to chapter ten. Kept falling asleep.'

'I'm not staying,' blurted Jasper.

'What's that, then?' Sam pointed to his empty paper plate on the buffet table. 'You eat, you pay.'

'I, uh, I…' His shoulders dropped. 'Of course.' Jasper reluctantly placed a five-pound note in the box while Sam glowered at him.

'Oh no, I've only got a card!' Austen interrupted the tension simmering between the pair. 'And I've been completely stuffing my face. Sorry!'

'Don't worry,' Sam told her. 'It doesn't matter.'

'But it matters for me?' Jasper put in, indignant.

'I didn't bring any more cash,' Patti said, not entirely sure why Sam seemed to have one rule for the Borrower and one for this new Clove Lore resident, though she had her suspicions this wasn't their first meeting and that something was definitely up with these two. Whatever he'd done, Patti was glad she wasn't on the receiving end of tiny Samantha's glowering fury.

'Can I drop mine into the pub tomorrow morning?' Austen asked Sam. 'I've got cash at the shop.'

Jasper, who had been staring down at another five-pound note in his hand, spoke at last.

'Allow me, please,' he said, falteringly, and – growing paler by the second – he held the note out to Sam.

All three women watched as Sam tried to pull it from his grip. It took a few painful seconds, but with a tug, she freed it.

'I owe you,' Austen told him. 'Thanks.'

'She could do you another quadruple coffee,' Patti put in, hoping to break the hostility radiating from Sam towards this helpful – if uptight – guy.

'That's not what you call a six-shot,' Austen said, turning to her, seeming to forget the weirdness. 'It's like a sextuple shot or something, isn't it?'

'I don't know,' Patti beamed back, enjoying this. 'Single, double, triple,' she counted on her fingers, 'quadruple, fivetuple…'

Austen blurted a laugh. 'That's not a word.'

'What is it then?'

She hesitated, seeming to think very hard indeed. 'No idea. And here's me with an English degree.'

Patti barely registered Sam huffily retreating, or Jasper taking the opportunity to fill his plate, this time with sliced melon and strawberries, before he too returned to his seat. They were alone by the buffet once more.

Patti had the strongest urge to say to the Borrower *let's make a run for it now*, but Austen was still reeling off nonsense words.

'Sextet? No, that's not right either. Sextuplets is when there's six babies, right? I guess you could just say three double shots, couldn't you?'

Patti wanted to stand there all day and listen to Austen jabbering, but her ears picked up the conversation at her back where Izaak had sidled over to Mrs Crocombe.

'Those two look cute together, Mrs C.,' he was saying.

Keeping her back turned to him, Patti at first assumed he meant Sam and Jasper, but deep down she kind of wanted it to be her and Austen under discussion.

'That's nice, dear,' she heard Mrs. C. reply, uninterested.

'That's all?' Jowan put in jovially. 'No *who is she? Where's she from? What's her marital status?*'

'You've changed, Mrs C.' said Izaak. 'You've changed.'

They really were talking about Austen! Patti tried hard to split her focus between Austen telling her about her book swap box idea and making sure she followed wherever the conversation over her shoulder was going.

'My matchmaking days are behind me,' Mrs C. was saying sadly.

'No more betting book?' Izaak said, much too loudly if he was trying to be furtive.

'Better let love run its natural course,' the old Cupid replied.

'What's all this?' Even Minty was getting involved now. 'Letitia Crocombe, done with meddling in affairs of the heart?'

'I think…' she defended herself in a pointed way, 'after last summer season, we'd all be better off minding our own business.'

At this, Patti twisted to catch a quick glimpse of the little gang huddled in one half of the circle. Mrs Crocombe was holding a stoical, dignified posture, her lips pursed. She'd clearly said her last word on the subject.

Everyone who'd been around last summer understood why Mrs Crocombe was no longer interested in these things. She'd had her own heart hurt, so pairing up the strays of Clove Lore had understandably lost its appeal for her. They all remembered the dark day her silver fox sea captain boyfriend (for all of two weeks) had set sail without saying goodbye, leaving her abashed and bewildered and doubting his motives. There had been the prospect of a small windfall coming her way at the time, and there'd been much gossip around the village ever since about whether he'd somehow caught wind of it and dropped anchor with a view to nicking her cash.

Bovis, who had been there to pick up the pieces and was just as devoted a lapdog as ever there was, caught Patti's eye now and gave her a surprisingly soft smile.

Izaak suddenly seemed to notice that Patti was listening in and tried to change the subject. 'Here again, Bovis?' he said. 'You were never one for book club?'

'Eyes and ears of Clove Lore, I am,' Bovis assured everyone. "Sides, Letitia will need seein' home safely.'

'Like she needs it. It's light till gone ten,' teased Jude Crawley, who had only just arrived and was pulling up a chair, widening the circle.

'Shall we begin?' Mrs Crocombe said, flustered.

But Jowan was still one topic behind. 'I dunno,' he said, shaking his head. 'Clove Lore without it's love matchin' is like... is like... well, me without my Mint.'

The 'aww' that went up in the circle drew Austen's attention.

Patti wished she could tell what she was thinking about this place and these people. She hoped Austen felt welcome and useful in the village the way she did these days.

'Now we've collected the subs, let's get started,' Bella was saying, pushing up the sleeves on her strawberry print dress. 'How about we go around the room and you can all tell us if this is your first Callista Flyte novel.'

The transformation in Austen was instantaneous. Patti watched it happen. Her whole body seemed to tense up. Without a word or another glance at Patti, Austen had abandoned her plate and was making for the door.

'Someone here can tell us *all about* Callista Flyte,' Jowan was announcing proudly.

Austen froze, her back to the room. Patti didn't understand what was going on, but she knew it wasn't good. She watched Austen turning slowly on the heel of her boot, her eyes huge and appealing, and with the smallest shake of her head she silently begged Jowan not to say any more. Only Patti noticed. The rest of the book club members were peering at Jowan, wondering what he was on about.

'Oh! My mistake. I, uh… sorry,' he said.

'My husband's had too much sun,' Minty joked, hiding her concern, and soon the little moment of panic was over. 'Come and sit down, you two,' Minty commanded. 'Plenty room. Bovis, bring another chair.'

Patti and Austen were powerless against Minty's insistence. The pair filed slowly into the circle and even though Patti tried directing Bovis to place the spare chair next to where she and Jowan had been seated, he annoyingly put it right at the other side of the circle between Izaak and Jasper.

So, without being able to exchange another word with Austen, book club began, and Patti, Austen, Samantha and Jasper were trapped for the evening.

Chapter Thirteen

'What did we think this book was about?' Bella asked the group.

Austen squirmed in her chair. There'd already been the excruciating 'icebreaker' where there'd been some loud coos of admiration from the group when she'd confessed to having read all of Flyte's books.

'Got a fan, 'ave we?' Bovis had remarked.

Jowan, obviously sensing something wasn't quite right, had stopped any further prying by telling the room that Austen was a 'mad keen reader – read everything, she has'.

In the past, it had felt like a flex telling people she'd read the books even *before* they were published.

Sometimes Callista would call her in the middle of the night to read aloud excerpts, asking Austen's opinion, and more often than not, as soon as she tried to frame a response, not too gushing, not too underwhelmed, her boss would speak over her, full of new enthusiasm for her work in progress, having simply talked it out a little.

'You've been *so* helpful, Austen, can't thank you enough! I'm going to crack on,' Callista would say, and she'd be gone again. Sometimes she wouldn't even bother hanging up, so Austen could hear the sound of typewriter keys clacking through the night, and she would listen to her boss working while she dozed. It had been soothing, knowing they were in it together, sharing in the writing process. Just knowing that she was contributing a tiny part to Callista's success had made Austen proud, and the interrupted sleep and crazy hours had felt worth it. Even now, they still felt worth it.

'Well, it's a high-falutin' thriller, isn't it?' Jowan was saying now. 'It's about what pushes someone to do out-of-character things.'

'In this case, murder,' Mrs Crocombe put in.

'It's a psychological study of the mind of a person driven to their very limits by a predator,' added Minty.

'Well, a stalker,' said Jowan.

'She's not just stalking though, is she?' said Bovis. 'They're breaking in, moving his stuff around, playing mind games, wrecking his relationships. Scary stuff.'

This seemed to surprise everyone.

'*Wot?*' he puffed, glancing around. 'Letitia told me the plot, an' read me some pages over dinner.' He indicated the well-thumbed book in Mrs Crocombe's hands.

'You and Mrs C. are having dinners together?' Izaak enquired wickedly, risking throwing the reading circle way off topic. Austen would have liked that. If they could abandon the book altogether and chat about these two old folks fancying each other, which, Austen thought, they evidently did, she'd be very grateful.

'We works together, don't we?' Bovis was protesting. 'It ain't all selling ices and moppin' up, you know!'

Mrs Crocombe was markedly silent on this topic.

Landlady Bella quickly got things back on track, asking, 'But was the killer justified? Is that what the author is saying?'

'The woman didn't deserve what happened to her, even if she was wrecking his life,' put in the young Scottish woman who'd come in last (taking their numbers to twelve book clubbers, if you counted Aldous, which everyone did). She'd introduced herself to the newcomers as Jude Crawley, the bookshop's treasurer and bookings manager.

'Shovin' her out a window,' exclaimed Bovis. 'I reckon she 'ad that coming to her. How he'd lost his job an' everything because of her meddlin'.'

'And his marriage broke down,' added Bella.

'He should have informed the police,' said Minty.

'She *was* the police though, wasn't she?' Sam threw in, looking like she was enjoying the opportunity to correct her boss.

'Someone higher up than her bosses could have stopped her nonsense, had he made a report,' insisted Minty.

'I think he was ashamed of having let himself be manipulated by her in the first place,' said Patti, and just hearing her voice made Austen sit a little straighter. 'He didn't feel he could tell anyone. That and the fact he'd been flirting online with this woman who wasn't his wife. He's a cheater, or as near as can be, and if he'd reported her weirdness, all of that would have come out.'

It felt strange somehow; Patti knowing Callista's work like a regular stranger. Austen couldn't put her finger on why that felt different to all these other people having opinions on her books.

'His cheating and secrets came out anyways, didn't they?' Bovis said. 'I liked the detective bits myself. How he tried to solve the mystery of this woman knowing so much about his life, things nobody else knew, not even his wife.'

'How much of the book have you read, Bovis?' Jude asked, eyes glinting at Izaak, who was smirking back. 'You don't have to pretend to us you're not a reader.'

'I only caught a few bits 'ere and there,' he said, blushing.

'Seems to me this author doesn't like women much,' said Mrs Crocombe, saving him. 'They're either corrupt, or crazed, or fickle. Look how his wife walks out as soon as she thinks her husband's having an affair. Doesn't even question it.'

'The evidence the stalker planted was so convincing though,' argued Jude. 'The lipstick, the underwear, the texts! I'd have my doubts too.'

'No, you wouldn't,' countered Izaak, knowingly. 'Not with Elliot. You'd see it was a set-up.'

'Not with Elliot, obviously,' Jude agreed. 'But with this guy, I would. He was kind of... seedy.'

'He was a creep,' said Mrs Crocombe. 'I don't know why we're supposed to care about him. In fact, I don't reckon the author likes men that much, neither. There isn't a single character in the book you'd give houseroom to.'

'Houseroom?' Patti was asking.

'You know...' Mrs Crocombe replied. 'Houseroom... folks you'd allow near you, or in your home. But this lot were all awful, even the police!'

'Exactly,' Austen heard herself saying, and since the word was out and all eyes had turned upon her, she had to go on. 'The, um, the author creates an environment where nobody can be trusted, right? And if everyone has deep flaws, isn't she really asking who amongst us has the right to determine what's considered moral or amoral? It's kind of clever... isn't it?' She heard her own voice losing its initial enthusiasm under Minty's silent scrutiny across the circle.

Bovis and Mrs Crocombe exchanged confused glances, and Jowan placed a hand over his wife's, as if pre-empting what was about to come.

'I doubt very much the author believes humanity can run amuck,' Minty began. Jowan resignedly withdrew his hand. 'Stalking and manipulating? Taking the law into their own hands? Lying? Killing? The author cannot be justifying any of those things, or comparing them to everyday, ordinary people's flaws? Not unless the author themselves is a complete psychopath.'

'Invasion of privacy has to be the cruellest crime of all,' croaked Jasper, as though he'd suddenly awakened from a silent nap.

Everyone looked at him in surprise, except Austen. An indignant little flame had ignited within her and she was trying to muster a response to Minty's rudeness. Callista was a genius. Why couldn't they see it?

'I think there's worse things,' Samantha was answering Jasper. 'Exploitation, for one. Indifference to people's struggles? Believing you're superior to the little people? Letting folks go hungry or cold and never helping? Happens right under our noses and nobody notices. *That's* criminal.'

'Well said, Sam, thank you,' said Bella.

Austen had at last struck upon a reply and the words were coming out whether she wanted them to or not.

'Obviously, I'm not saying the author thinks we can all just do what we want. I'm just saying the author isn't afraid to dwell on the darker side of human nature, seeing through the pretensions and affectations of humans, seeing the frailty of the social contract, how it's all so tenuous and can break down so easily. It's genius, when you think about what Callista's doing here.'

'*Callista*, is it?' Bovis said, an eyebrow rising. 'I wonder what my old friend Stephen would think of your theory? King, that is.' He chuckled at his own joke.

Austen withdrew into silence once again, wanting to kick herself for being goaded. Was she overreacting, getting defensive over nothing? Either way, she felt exposed and stupid.

'I think Austen's raised some very good points,' proclaimed Patti, and it sounded so pointed and like a lifeline thrown to save her from drowning, it made Austen startle and blink in surprise. '*Chosen* couldn't be said to have a single selfless character,' Patti went on. 'There's no good guy. They're all messy and imperfect, like all of us are.'

Austen could feel Patti's sparkling green eyes upon her. She was trying to save her from a book group mauling. All Austen could do was smile thinly, averting her gaze.

'Well,' Bovis grumbled on. 'I never shoved nobody out a fourth-floor window 'cause I caught them going through *my* drawers, that's for sure. But I takes your point, Patti Foley.'

After that, Bella steered the conversation towards the finer details of plot twists and it soon became apparent only Bovis, Mrs Crocombe, Jude and Minty had actually read the whole novel right to the end, and Austen didn't speak again. All the while she hung her head and tried not to shout out loud, *you're getting it wrong. You're missing the point. It's subtler than that, cleverer.* She didn't point out the astute use of motifs of surveillance throughout, or the way the narrator grew increasingly unreliable as the story went on and as the emotional stability of the murderer-slash-stalking-victim broke down.

All Minty cared about was the miscarriage of justice and the police corruption; Mrs C. was obsessed with the breakdown of the marriage and loss of trust between husband and wife, like she was personally offended by it; Izaak was just here for the laughs, and they'd become few and far between; and Bovis had got bored of the whole thing and loaded up on Scotch eggs again. Even the little dog had fallen asleep by the time everyone got so off topic they'd abandoned the book discussion entirely and were debating what to read for next time.

Austen pulled her tote bag over her shoulder at ten to nine and pushed her chair back, giving a quick nod of acknowledgement to Patti, who looked like she was about to yell out for her to stay and save her from the final throes of book club deliberations, but Austen wouldn't be detained any longer.

Patti's a local. She must be used to this kind of thing, thought Austen. These are her people. She came here voluntarily. Not like Austen, brought here by the promise of a free bag of books. How easily she'd been lured. Well played, Jowan.

Yet, the message notification on her phone was enough to put Austen back in her seat for a moment longer. She was surprised to note her hands fumbling in her haste to read the message.

It read, 'At last! I sold my *Prufrock*. They bought also a colouring book.'

'You win! I haven't sold mine yet,' Austen typed back, unaware of the grin transforming her face or Patti's eyes narrowing upon her from across the circle.

Austen had to wait a few seconds for the reply.

'I am counting books all evening. It is very boring. Talk to me? I have wine. Do you?'

This was enough to get Austen back on her feet, shuffling for the door, telling the room she'd better get back to the shop; she had to tidy up.

She'd have raced Up-along, had the function suite's doors not swung open with a loud bang that made everyone's heads snap up.

A woman – no, a shipwreck of a woman – was standing panting and hunched, wrapped in bedsheets, black trails of make-up down her face from crying, her unwashed hair nested at the back. She was holding something in her hands and scanning the room, her wild eyes screwed up in the glare of the pub's strip lights.

'Jasper!' she howled. 'My phone! My phone isn't working. I… my life is inside it. I…' Her chest heaved as she spoke, her voice as weak and faltering as a terrified child.

'Mum!' Jasper sprang to his feet.

'Estée Gold!' shrieked Izaak, his hand thrown dramatically to his chest.

Eyes ping-ponged around the room, not one person understanding what was happening. Izaak seemed to be hyperventilating.

Austen flattened herself against the buffet table to let Jasper past. A chorus of whispers went up.

'Who's Estée Gold when she's at home?' said Bovis.

'Is this who's moved in Up-along?' Mrs Crocombe was asking.

'Jasper Gold?' Sam was saying to herself, her head tipped, like she was straining to remember where she'd heard the name before.

No one in the room but Austen overheard as the young man comforted his mother, taking the phone from her. 'I know, mine too. Come on, let's get you home. It's OK. We'll figure it out.'

He led her from the function suite, lifting the bedsheet behind her so it didn't drag on the ground, like a pageboy lifting a bridal train. Without a word, the mother and son departed into the night, leaving mouths gaping and book club's closing remarks completely forgotten.

As soon as the doors swung closed, Izaak was excitedly filling everyone in between taking great gulps of air. 'Estée Gold is living in Clove Lore! And in our house!'

'I've seen her on the telly.' Mrs Crocombe was nodding, eyes narrowed like this was an episode of *Columbo*.

'Reckons I have as well. On that jungle thing,' Bovis joined in. 'Where they eat the kangaroo's whassits.'

'What? No, forget that rubbish! She must have done that because she was running out of money,' Izaak told them. 'Estée Gold was a star! *Destiny's Peak*. Remember?'

A few *ahh*s of recognition followed.

'Even Leonid watched it in Russia,' he continued. 'It was huge! I never missed an episode. It was *the* show of the Nineties.'

'It was a tacky soap opera,' tolled Minty.

'Well, yes, that's what was so brilliant about it,' Izaak enthused. 'I should have asked her to slap me.'

This silenced the room.

'Uh, the way she slapped Roman Clift? Her onscreen husband? It's iconic. Oh, you people,' Isaak swiped away the incredulous crowd with a wave of his hand. 'I'm heading home to tell Leonid.'

'What do you think's wrong with the woman?' Bovis said bluntly, as Izaak dashed for the door and left. 'Wandering around bedraggled and screaming about a phone?'

Sam, who'd been staring at the spot where Jasper and his unfortunate mother had stood, blinked herself awake now. 'Whatever's wrong, they don't want people knowing. Didn't Jasper just say the worst thing he can think of is invasion of privacy?'

'Quite right,' Minty put in. 'We must exercise discretion if we have a...' she paused, looking a little queasy, 'a celebrity in our midst. We don't want to draw *that* kind of attention to the village.'

'I don't think that's quite what Sam's saying,' put in Jude, bravely. 'Whatever's going on, that woman's in some kind of crisis. We need to rally round, help them out.'

'We must keep calm and carry on as always,' corrected Minty. 'Nothing must change, not because of a TV star.'

'Reckon it's drug addiction,' Bovis concluded. 'All that lot...' he tapped his nose confidentially, 'are on the, whassit called? The co-caine.'

Patti stifled a derisive snort. 'Look, whatever's going on, we have to help them out where we can, but be discreet, OK? You never know what kind of dangerous situations some women are stuck in. Especially ones obviously running away from something.'

From over by the buffet, where Austen was still trying to decide what to do – follow the Golds into the night, or stay and hear the gossip – she felt the mood in the room change from salacious interest to grave seriousness as Patti spoke. It made Austen wonder what Patti knew about women on the run. She was surprised at how much she wanted to stay now, even if she did have the offer of drinking wine and chatting with an uncomplicated digital friend.

However, book club was well and truly over. Drinks tabs were being paid off at the bar, and Austen was soon shouldering the bag of books Jowan had given her and placing her wine order with Finan, the Siren's landlord.

'A bottle of something French please,' she asked, well aware that half the book club were lingering behind her, including Patti, who was giving Aldous a goodnight fuss.

'Big plans?' Finan asked as he took her card payment.

'Just a drink with a friend,' she replied, and the crowd fell quiet behind her.

'Walk you back to your cottage?' Austen turned to ask Patti, her bottle of Merlot in hand.

'OK,' Patti agreed, a little startled, and as they left the Siren together, all eyes followed them.

–

The night was warm and Sahara-scented in the way that only a deep July evening in the South West can be. The very height of summer had arrived, and the sun was never too far below the horizon line. Even the birds were still singing in the gardens as Austen and Patti walked up the slope.

'It wasn't too bad, was it?' Patti asked, trying to walk as slowly as possible. Her cottage was only a few yards away.

'It was definitely more drama than I'd expected.'

'That's Clove Lore for you,' Patti drawled, throwing Austen a quick glance.

'It was nice of you to send me that pen, by the way. You didn't have to, especially not such a nice one.'

'You seem the type who likes nice stationery.'

'You got me!' Austen said, holding her hands out. 'Stationery is the best present.'

Patti stopped. They'd already reached her cottage gate. The tall sunflowers by the door watched on. 'I'm sorry I didn't bring it myself. I could have. I just wasn't sure if you wanted me bothering you.'

Austen seemed to squirm a little but she was smiling, too. Patti read this as a good sign. 'You're not a bother. Come to the shop any time. In fact…' Austen drew out her phone. 'Swap numbers?'

It had been a quick exchange and neither of them went so far as to check they'd entered them correctly by sending a message there and then. That might look too keen, Patti acknowledged, and she still wasn't quite sure what the vibe was. Austen was putting her phone away now, awkwardly juggling the book bag and wine bottle.

'Need a hand with that?' Patti asked.

'I'm good.'

'You told Finan you were meeting a friend. Do you have someone staying?' Patti knew she shouldn't have asked. It was too intrusive. She felt the effect of it immediately.

'No. It's…' Austen shrugged and seemed to be searching for the right words. 'An online thing. I'd better go or they'll be wondering where I've got to.'

'OK, well, see you,' Patti said weakly, watching her go, trying to bite down the words she wanted to call out after her, but they were coming out whether she wanted them to or not. 'It was nice seeing you!'

Austen turned on the slope to call back, 'You too,' thank goodness.

That was their evening over. Patti, who couldn't help feeling disappointed and a little bit silly, slipped her key in the lock, but not before one last glance Up-along to where Austen was still climbing, her head down, fixed on her phone screen once more.

Chapter Fourteen

'I think they must be eccentric, yes?' the message said.

'They're wild! I'm thanking my stars I'm only visiting,' Austen replied, pulling the duvet close around her, knocking the rim of the wine glass against her teeth as she made herself comfy on the big bed at the top of the Borrow-A-Bookshop.

'Your Jowan sounds like my Polonius,' the Parisian told her. 'He comes every day, stays for hours, smoking the Gauloises, speaking poetry in I don't know how many languages. Never buying anything. Always making problems.'

'What kind of problems?'

'With his animals.'

'Animals?'

'Yes. In his pockets. On the string. Cats, mice, homeless dogs he collects. Always feeding them in the bookshop. The mess! The odour!'

'Is he at least a good poet?'

'All poets are good.'

'Are they?'

'Bien sûr. Who is to say *this is bad, this is good*?'

'The reader?'

A silence followed, in which Austen imagined a Gallic harrumph of disapproval.

'How old are you?' Austen typed, taken by a sudden impulse to know more. She wanted to imagine this person more clearly. Right now, the impression she had was of some charming bohemian, sophisticated and self-assured enough not to bother chasing likes and follows on social media; nothing like Austen. Overall, she felt they were decent and kind enough to recognise that Austen was out of her depth with the shop and offer gentle encouragement and advice without being too nosy. They'd already planned their next sunset sale challenge book, Dickens' *Hard Times*. The game was an additional aspect of a growing and very enjoyable friendship; the kind of friendship where, by now, surely, you could ask things like how old someone is?

A long pause in conversation followed. Long enough to alarm her. She sat up, setting down her glass. Had she gone too far? Was this friendship working *because* they knew nothing about one another? Was her question an intrusion?

She typed as fast as she could.

'I'm twenty-five, just so you know.'

If the Parisian had googled her, they'd already have found this out from her scant LinkedIn profile. Not that the Parisian seemed like the type to go hunting for details. They'd be way too cool for that, Austen imagined, thinking how she'd considered looking up the Feint Heart Bookshop herself, just to see what she could discover about the bookseller, but that would be crass and nosy, so she resolved to do no such thing. Probably best not to lean in to the whole sneaking about online thing. This friendship was too nice for that. Too pure and simple. See? Again, she was learning about boundaries and when not to overstep them. Growth!

She typed. 'You don't have to tell me your age, or anything, if you don't want to. Sorry.'

'The Wi-Fi. It glitch in this rat hole,' came the Parisian's reply. 'I am thirty.'

She couldn't account for the thrill this sent through her. Austen's thumbs hovered over the keypad. She held back for as long as it took to weigh up the risk of asking for more.

'I don't know your name,' she typed. 'You know mine. And you know what I look like from my socials. I only saw your hands. At least, I think they were your hands in the video? You were wearing gloves.'

She looked at the words, hesitating over the 'send' arrow. The Parisian wasn't typing.

'God, Austen! Stop forcing things.' She deleted the message without sending it, replacing it with far safer words. 'Tell me about Paris tonight. What is it like?'

The bouncing grey dots that told her they were busy typing pulsed for a long time, long enough for Austen to drain her glass, wondering if the Feint Heart Wi-Fi was playing up again. Eventually, the reply came.

'Tonight Paris is warm. I drink wine on Wednesdays and stay here late. The door is locked. People want to come in all the time, night and day. They *frapper* at the door. *Frapper?* You know? Hitting the door. I ignore. In the tower there is a window. I climb the ladder. I open the window of the tower and I look at the top of the Tower Eiffel. The lights hurt my eyes but even I think they are pretty. No stars tonight. Cloud everywhere and dark, dark blue, except around the moon where the light is perfect silver.'

This made Austen smile. She poured herself another glass, waiting, picturing the scene like an Impressionist painting; a lonely bookseller in a tower, staring out at the night.

'Do you know Paris sounds like bees all night long?' the Parisian continued. 'Like the nests. Alive. Everywhere hot and smoking. On the window sleep the pigeons plus one white dove. I sit here, read, drink wine. Sometimes I sleep here.'

'Are you not lonely?' Austen hadn't hesitated in sending the words.

'Sometimes. Yes. Are you lonely in England?'

'All the time,' she replied, and something tugged sharply at her chest to see the confession sent instantaneously out into the world when she hadn't even realised she had been lonely. She was glad it was only the Parisian who was hearing this stuff.

'Are you lonely now?' they asked.

'No, not now,' Austen replied. It was true. She wasn't a bit lonely talking with this person. She was happy.

The reply that came back turned the glow within her into a tiny flame. It said, 'Me also. I am not lonely when I talk with you.'

They were straying into something a little more than innocent messaging between bookish colleagues, weren't they? The wine was definitely helping in that regard. Austen felt the shift but didn't know how to respond. All she knew was that she wanted to impress this person, so she typed, 'I bought French wine when you invited me to drink with you.'

'Of course.'

Austen laughed out loud and drew the duvet closer around her.

'I wish I was in Paris. You make it sound like poetry,' she told them.

'It *is* poetry. Ah, but I have to work now.'

This jolted Austen. Surely the shop was long since closed? Did they really have to go? They'd only been talking for an hour; long enough to tell all about the bonkers book club, only holding back the truth about the book under discussion and Austen's connection to the author. Why spoil things by getting morose? Not when there was a celebrity and her posh son causing excitement in the village (neither of whom she'd named during their chat), and two elderly lovers dancing around the fact that they were obviously doing more than just selling ice cream together. Then she'd just had to tell her new friend about Aldous and his love of cheese sandwiches and scones, and the haughty lady of the manor, Minty; like a minor royal turned wedding planner.

She hadn't mentioned Patti, of course. There was nothing there she wanted to turn into an entertaining story in the hopes of making her faraway friend send back laugh-crying emojis. Patti was something else entirely. She occupied another sphere for Austen, not at all the same universe that this late-night conversation was taking place in.

Austen didn't want to think about what this signified, the compartmentalising of her encounters with Patti into a separate box to this furtive new acquaintance with the bookseller. She knew it itched at her conscience somehow, but didn't dare examine it.

She was about to type a message telling the bookseller not to go, to please stay five minutes more, when the next message came.

'*Bonne nuit*, Austen.'

Austen watched the screen for a long moment, not wanting to say goodnight, not sure what she wanted to see appearing next. Holding steadfast, she'd force them to speak again.

When the words appeared, they brought a great warm rush that had only a tiny bit to do with the red wine and her thoughts full of a kind stranger sending her messages all the way from the tower window of a Paris bookshop at night.

It read, 'I wish you were in Paris also. *Fais de beaux rêves*. From Delphine. *Bisous.*'

Austen hit 'translate' in an instant. Kisses! *Bisous* means kisses. Thinking she must be glowing with all this energy, she let the phone slip onto the bedcovers, her eyes lifting to the moon outside her window amongst all the bright stars that were obscured for the person on the other end of her phone, no, from a thirty-year-old bookseller called Delphine at the Feint Heart Bookshop in Paris, who felt somehow far closer to Austen than the Fifth Arrondissement now.

She found herself reaching for her notebook and pen by the bedside.

Without blinking, Austen poised her pen at the top of a blank page and disappeared somewhere inside herself. Ink marks formed as if guided by another hand.

She wrote long into the night, lines and lines of poetry, half in her own voice, half in some new style she didn't question in case the flow was somehow cut off.

When dawn broke, her fingers were stiff and she was slumping against the pillows, dozing off, her head still full of words, eventually sleeping right through opening time.

Even as she slept, she was certain she could smell French cigarettes and strong coffee and sweet bakery, and she could hear the distant buzz of motorbikes, the cooing of rooftop pigeons and the engines of busy *bateaux-mouches* criss-crossing the silvery Seine.

Chapter Fifteen

The ballroom at Clove Lore's Big House always looked wonderful in the morning light, and it looked especially lovely today, an event day, with the long tables set out under white linen cloths and freshly cut freesias in simple arrangements sweetening the salty seaside air, mixing with the fresh polish on the floor and a good scent of baking coming from the trays Jude Crawley had only moments ago delivered to the ballroom.

Jude provided all the baking for Big House Weddings, though today the families were taking care of the challah for tonight's meal.

'That's the pierogi for the staff lunches as well as the wedding desserts, Patti,' Jude called in her cheery Borders accent.

Patti was helping the florist manoeuvre the white rose-decked chuppah into position for this afternoon's celebration, and Sam, observing the whole thing from her spot in the corner, was polishing water spots off the silverware. Patti was too absorbed in her task, so Sam had to answer for her.

'Just leave them on those two tables. I'll put them in the fridges.'

'OK, sure,' Jude said, hesitating just enough for Sam to notice.

'Don't worry. Patti can put them away.'

Ever since she'd accidentally fallen on top of Jude and Elliot's wedding cake on her very first day working for Big House Weddings, Sam had been unable to live down her clumsy reputation. Not that many people mentioned it these days, but she'd added the incident to the long list of cringey things she wished she could delete from her memory. She rubbed the cloth along the serving spoons extra hard.

'No, no, I trust you, totally,' Jude was saying. 'See you later.' She beat a hasty retreat, calling to Patti that she'd send her invoice by email.

'No worries,' Patti cried back from across the room, before returning to her conversation with the florist.

It was always like this on event days. A little frantic, but everyone focused on their tasks. And usually, Sam quite enjoyed it, but she'd been up since five doing her mum's laundry rounds. It was getting on for ten now and the navy stewardess-style dress uniform Minty insisted on was already feeling deeply uncomfy.

The washer-dryers at her mum's lock-up a short drive along the headland would be about to finish their cycles. She'd have to make a break for it on her lunch hour to haul everything out of the machines and fold the sheets before stuffing them into delivery bags. If she left it too long they'd come out of the machines creased and she'd have to put them through the big ironing press – a job that required two people.

The sun glinted off the forks she was polishing now, and Sam thought gloomily how boiling it would be at the laundry lock-up today. Clear blue sky and glaring sun might be perfect for a happy chuppah but it's far from ideal for a rushed job in a laundry that's stiflingly hot even on a winter's day.

She moved on to the knives. Back at home, the nurse would be calling in to change her mum's bandages. She should really be there to help make lunch and...

'Ahem!' Someone cleared their throat from the ball-room entrance.

'What do you want?' Sam snapped, fumbling the silver-ware, almost dropping her polishing cloth with the shock of finding Jasper Gold trespassing in the main part of the Big House.

Jasper was in running gear, all white and pristine, although he didn't look like he'd been running. He looked as elegant and shiny as he usually did, only there was a sheepish look on his face. She'd been about to apologise for snapping, but he got in first.

'I was looking for Mrs Clove-Congreve? Uh, Minty?' he said, peering around the ballroom.

'What can I do for you?' Minty said, appearing in the doorway behind him, making him startle. Sam got back to work but trained her ears on their conversation, wishing Patti and the florist weren't talking quite so loudly about the bridal flowers.

'I, um, I'm sorry for the intrusion,' he was saying. 'I wondered if I could possibly...' he faltered.

'Spit it out, dear,' tolled Minty, in what she probably thought was an encouraging way.

'I need a computer to, uh, mail out my CV.'

'Say no more. You can use Jowan's. *Jowan!* Over.' Minty spoke suddenly into the crackling walkie-talkie she insisted on carrying around on event days.

'I's out walking Aldous, Mint. What is it?' came her husband's voice.

There was a long moment's pointed silence while Minty waited for him to stick to the radio protocol she'd drilled into everyone in the Big House.

A deep sigh was followed by Jowan's weary, 'Over.'

At this Samantha sniffed a laugh that drew Jasper's eyes towards her. She'd have been alarmed had he not sneaked her the most surreptitious of smiles that said he too thought Minty was gloriously mad.

'The Gold boy is using your computer, yes?' Minty crowed on, louder than necessary. 'Needs to apply for jobs, you see? Over.'

Jasper wasn't smiling anymore. He probably didn't appreciate his business being broadcast across the estate like this. Sam kept her head turned away to save his feelings. It was clear there was some kind of cash flow problem with the Golds, and, given the state of his mother last night, Mrs Gold wasn't coping all that well.

Jasper had looked pained when he'd offered to pay Austen's book club subs, and Sam was ever so slightly regretting how she'd judged him harshly. *Typical*, she'd thought at the time. *A posh skinflint*. If it hurt him that much to share a measly fiver, which must be nothing to someone like him in all his designer clobber, he really must be as awful as she'd first thought. Now, however, she wasn't sure what the deal with this guy was.

Maybe Bovis was right and Mrs Gold really was one of those celebrity addicts the gossip mags love to troll. Not that Sam had time for reading scandalous stories about ex-TV stars. Still, it made her wonder how Jasper managed to be so calm and collected when his mother was falling to bits up in flat number one.

'Tell the boy to make himself at home, study's all his,' crackled Jowan's voice followed by an exaggerated '*Over*.'

'Roger that, Number Two. Over and out.' Minty smiled graciously for Jasper's benefit. 'Sam will show you where to go. I'm expecting the silent fireworks engineers to arrive in…' she checked her watch, 'three and a half minutes.'

Jasper was trying to thank Minty but she was already on the move, approaching Sam, eyes laser-focused on the sparkling silverware fanned out on the top table before her.

'You're confident you understand the table settings, Samantha? It *is* your first time handling them alone.'

'I've got your diagrams,' Sam said, mortified that Jasper was witnessing this.

'The father of the bride insists on carving from his spot at the top of the table, so he'll need a stack of plates to his right side. He'll serve to his left, and you'll be stationed to his right, assisting. No?' Minty peered through Sam with piercing, expectant eyes.

'Uh, yes?' she hazarded.

'Good-o!' Minty clapped her hands. 'I'll leave you two to it, then. Pip, pip!' And she was gone, out the door at her usual brisk pace. Jasper turned to watch her leave.

'I'll be with you in a minute, Jasper,' Sam said, pretending to be deeply immersed in setting the table, determined to make Jasper wait for her.

Her old head teacher had used the same trick, calling her into his office when she was expecting a telling-off about whatever it was she'd got wrong that week: breaking that stupid chair in the art room that had a wonky leg long before she'd sat on it; or a dressing-down about her scuffed shoes (her mum had told her they'd have to do until the end of summer term; they couldn't afford new ones in May); or there'd be questions about missed lunch money payments and why wasn't Mr Capstan answering calls from the school bursar about it?

The Head would sit there, typing away, ignoring her, even though he'd called her in. She had to stand there suffering until he eventually turned to address her. It had felt awful. Almost as awful as some stranger in designer clothes telling her he was 'too good' for lowly laundry work seconds after meeting her. *Too good for Clove Lore!* She'd show him.

Patti showed the florist from the ballroom, walking her out to her van, only throwing Sam the slightest quizzical look.

In the silence of the ballroom, Sam shifted the cutlery around like she was doing a puzzle, all the time trying to make sense of the sketches Minty had shown her while she was banging on about salad courses and fruit sorbet and the two kinds of fish knives they had and…

'Do you need a hand?' Jasper said, interrupting her very clever plan of putting him in his place.

'From… you?' she blinked.

'Yes, me. Do you think I can't cope with table settings?'

'Hate to say it, but I have my doubts.'

'You're talking to the table setting king, actually. There's not a thing I don't know about it.'

'OK then, what's this?' She held up a big spoon that she was fairly confident was for serving punch.

'That's a tureen ladle, for soup.'

'Oh.'

'Are your guests having a soup course?'

'Uh… no.' Sam brought the ladle down behind her back wishing she hadn't started this game now.

'And you seem to have a cake knife at the head of the table when I assume you're looking for…' Jasper searched the neat rows of implements, selecting one and handing it over. 'A carving knife?'

She took it from him, silently fuming. Of course a posho like him would know all about fine dining. The closest Sam ever got to fancy dinners was the Sunday carvery at the big pub on the other side of the bypass.

'I thought you worked in a laundry?' he said, throwing her completely.

'She does,' came a child's voice from the doorway. Radia was following her aunt Patti into the ballroom. 'Sam's just like Mrs Rabbit.'

'Rads, do your colouring over by the kitchen entrance. OK?' Patti was telling the child. 'Sorry, Sam, I've got her for the next hour. She won't be in the way.'

'Who's Mrs Rabbit?' Jasper asked the child, a delighted gleam in his eyes.

Radia stood stock-still, her face incredulous. 'Everybody knows who she is. She's a rabbit with about one *thrillion* jobs. She works at the aquarium, she flies the rescue helicopter, she puts out fires… you know?' Radia made her eyes goggle like she couldn't believe anyone could be this badly informed. 'On *Peppa Pig*?'

'Ah, OK! Got it,' he said with a serious nod.

'I like Sam,' Radia went on, even though Sam was standing right in front of her. 'She sat on a wedding cake.'

Jasper diplomatically drew his lips together, flashing cautious eyes towards Sam.

'Right, well, that's enough chit-chat, thanks, Rads,' said Patti, pulling her by the sleeve right across the room towards the kitchen.

'But she did!' Radia protested as she went. 'She fell on Jude and Elliot's wedding cake with her bottom and squashed it flat.'

'I'll take her to the kitchens,' Patti called over her shoulder, baring her teeth apologetically before disappearing through the doorway with the little girl, leaving Sam alone with Jasper again, not knowing how to recover.

'Hey, listen,' Sam was already saying. 'We've all been there, upside down in a dessert, haven't we?'

'Have we?'

Sam set down her work. 'I'll show you where the computer is,' she said.

'Jowan's study, yes?' He followed her.

'Don't get ideas about some nice office. That's what they call the basement.' Sam walked him from the room. 'There's not much of their house left for them to have an office...' she began pointedly.

He followed behind her, past the cloakroom in the grand lobby, through a door and down a creaking set of stairs lit by a bare bulb.

'Not now the place has been turned into flats for millionaires.'

'I take your point,' Jasper said, grimly, sweeping cobwebs from the sleeves of his oversized sweater.

'Over there,' said Sam, stopping at the foot of the stairs and pointing to an ancient desktop with a chunky monitor. 'Beggars can't be choosers,' she said with a shrug, having registered the look of horror on his face.

He pulled at the front of his top and flexed his neck like he was warming up for a boxing bout. 'It's fine,' he said. 'This is completely fine.'

Sam left him feeling around the monitor for the 'on' switch, wishing she could keep her hurt feelings in check with this guy. He was a pitch-perfect blend of entitled and patronising – enough to rile her – but there was that curious politeness there too, and the way he'd been with his mum – it was almost enough to ignite her sympathy. Almost.

'Do you know when this thing last ran an update?' he was calling to her in a pained voice as she made it to the top of the stairs.

'Twenty sixteen?' she called back, leaving him to send intern applications to, she imagined, fancy London studios and galleries, where he could escape shabby old Clove Lore with all its inconveniences and girls he was too good for.

'I'll be in the ballroom,' she heard herself saying when she reached the top of the steps. 'If you need anything.' She wasn't sure why she'd said it. He could help himself. These types always could. And yet, even in her stubbornness, she still took care to prop open the basement door, letting a little sunlight reach him.

Chapter Sixteen

That evening, after the singing, and the groom smashing the glass, when fasts were broken and two families had united happily with food and dancing, Patti allowed herself a mug of tea and a few sneaked moments alone on the estate's grand lawns to congratulate herself on another job well done.

Big House Weddings wasn't a terrible place to be. It was certainly better than driving all over the South East like before, working in different venues each time, and not just organising weddings but corporate stuff too. No matter what the event was, she'd taken it on, keeping herself busy, and she'd run herself ragged with it all.

'Ten minutes to launch? Confirm, please. Over.' Unseen, somewhere in the parterre gardens, Minty was bellowing into her walkie-talkie.

Patti listened as the fireworks display engineer broadcast his reply. 'Ten minutes and counting, Commander. Over.'

Commander? Minty was going to love that.

Now that Patti was settled in one place, staging marriage celebrations of all kinds under the one roof, she had time to reflect on life in general. It's amazing what not being stuck in congestion on the A219 on a regular basis can do for a woman. Clove Lore had freed up some headspace, or perhaps more specifically, Clove Lore *and* the arrival of a certain Borrower, had got her thinking about her own plans, and maybe, just possibly, she was entertaining the idea of taking Austen on a sort of date.

Tonight, as the happy couple were leading their families out into the estate gardens, with their eyes turned to the skies, Patti felt she had to risk a message or two and if she was going to do it, it had to be now. She pulled her phone from her pocket and began to type.

–

Austen had had a non-stop day at the Borrow-A-Bookshop. The waves of tourists arriving in their coach-loads had been relentless until, at six, she'd locked the door, turned the sign and posted two hastily filmed videos to her social media account showing the bookshop in its end-of-day disarray and the empty glass domes in the cafe with the stack of unwashed mugs and teapots by the sink.

She added the captions, 'Another busy day done', and 'The reality of bookshop-cafe life. It's 90% tidying up #seasidebookshop'.

She watched the posts loading, thinking only of one follower, wondering if perhaps they'd be on a crowded metro platform, making their way home.

It was hard to imagine Delphine anywhere other than the Feint Heart Bookshop, somehow. Where did she live, even? What did she do outside of bookselling? Maybe that's what they could chat about this evening? If she could steer the conversation that way, she'd be only too glad to tell her all about Levenshulme and her Manchester haunts in return.

She'd try to observe the online etiquette of not asking for more than someone was willing to offer up freely.

Delphine had been so generous with her time, and keeping Austen company when she was alone, she didn't want to scare her away.

Austen's latest posts appeared on her timeline and she didn't have to wait long for the first responses to come in.

Filtering through replies as they popped up, stopping to 'loveheart' those from book lovers and Borrow-A-Bookshop fans across the globe, exclaiming how hers were still 'holiday goals' in spite of the obvious hard work of running a shop and cafe. A few folks were commenting that they'd be there in a flash to help out if only they could – all strangers.

A girl her age, called Emily, who she recognised from her old life in London, sent a 'wow' emoji and the words, 'Still jealous tbh, even with all the cleaning'. Austen recalled Emily starting an unpaid summer stint at one of the big five publishers around the time she was getting into the swing of Callista's strict writing regimen and not finding it quite as wearing as she had at first. Their paths would cross occasionally on the book events circuit. Emily was now head of marketing strategy at one of the big publishing houses, and by the looks of her socials, getting on very nicely in London. It was a tiny reminder of how things might have been for Austen, if she hadn't messed up, but she tried not to dwell on it.

It was nice that people were excited about her bookshop holiday, but all Austen was really hoping for was a word from the Feint Heart Bookshop.

Flopping down in the armchair by the children's book section, she scrolled and waited.

When the text message notification came, Austen flinched at the sound, and seeing it was from Patti, she clicked it open in an instant.

It read, 'Hey! If you're free right now, step outside and look up.'

'*Look up?*' she asked the empty shop, making her way to the door, unlocking it and stepping out into the cool of the courtyard. From this position just off the slope, Austen couldn't see the harbour or the horizon line behind her – it was obscured by the courtyard walls – but she knew the sun would be sinking into the sea in a wash of fiery orange and pinks. The heavens above the Big House and further inland were turning a cool blue and one bright star was already visible.

She typed back. 'What am I looking for?'

'You'll see. Two minutes and counting,' Patti's reply read. 'How was your day?'

'Non-stop. My feet hurt. Yours?'

'Not bad, but it's about to get better, fingers crossed. Can you see the Big House rooftop?'

'Yep.'

'Keep your eyes on that.'

'What are we talking here?' Austen replied. 'On a scale of double rainbow to mushroom cloud?'

'It's definitely more from the rainbow end of the scale. Don't worry.'

In the bookshop courtyard, the strings of lightbulbs overhead flickered into life like they did every night. The sight always put Austen in mind of some Mediterranean taverna, what with the palm tree at the centre of the cobbles and the striking sky blue of the cafe chairs and tables.

Everything was still and serene. Good cooking smells circulated on the gentlest summer evening breeze. It must be the charcoal and seafood from that guy's barbecue stand outside the pub. What was he called? Monty something?

She let her ears tune in to the gentle shushing of the waves Down-along. There was no traffic allowed on the slope and, Austen guessed, the visitor centre car park would be closed for the evening already. Clove Lore once more belonged only to the locals and the lucky tourists who had beds for the night in the holiday cottages or down at the Siren.

'Beautiful,' Austen whispered to herself.

The sky had darkened a shade more – the sun was sinking fast tonight – and Austen peered up at the blinking tail lights from a plane passing high over the turrets of the Big House. There was another one… and another.

'Hold on,' Austen said, pressing her fingertips beneath the frames of her glasses and gently rubbing her tired eyelids. Focusing again on the lights, it all became clear.

Lifting into the sky in formation were fifty, no, more like a hundred, drones, looking very much like something from a sci-fi movie from down here.

'Can you see them?' Patti's message came. 'Big wedding up here today. They booked silent fireworks. First time we've had those in Clove Lore!'

'I see them,' Austen replied, but there was no time for anything else as the hovering machines burst into pink luminescence and, lifting even higher into the darkening sky, formed into two interlinked lovehearts.

Even from this distance, Austen heard applause and the gentle strains of Pachelbel's *Canon in D*.

The lights smoothly changed formation, each one floating equidistant from the next, making Austen wonder how it was done. Now they formed the initials 'A & A', one in gold, one in red, then in seconds they were on the move again, zipping across the sky, breaking into clusters before falling completely dark as though they hadn't been there at all.

Austen blinked, unsure if it was all over, when suddenly a flash of light lit up the sky in a gold shimmering star-burst like a firework exploding from a rocket, only utterly without noise. The lights mimicked fireworks perfectly, right down to their cascading sparks.

This first burst was followed by another, then another. Great crowns of lights in every colour filled the skies above the Big House as the music swelled and the partygoers *oohed* and *ahhed* along.

Austen imagined Patti up there with her pretty green eyes lifted to the heavens. Patti hadn't wanted her to miss this. She'd been thinking about her. She'd reached out.

The little warm glow this ignited inside her all but fizzled out when the phone in her hand started to ring.

Austen rarely answered calls, but this wasn't one she'd allow to go to voicemail.

'Do you like them?' Patti's voice asked down the line. Something about its lovely rich resonance made Austen want to close her eyes and lean back on the shop door frame.

'I really do,' she replied. 'Thanks for mentioning it. I'd have missed them completely stacking the dishwasher or something!'

'No problem.'

'I hope A and A liked it,' Austen said.

'Asher and Amy? Yep, they look pretty happy from where I'm standing. He's draped his suit jacket over her shoulders, and she's all snuggled up under his arm.'

'That's cute.'

There was a pause while the drones blinked into dark-ness once more before burning bright white and forming into a swirling spiral increasing in speed the closer they got to the centre before seeming to disappear one by one like water going down a plughole.

'They're really showing off now,' Austen said.

'And all the dogs and donkeys of Clove Lore are blissfully unaware there's fireworks even happening.'

Austen smiled, thinking of her mum and how she hated noisy pyrotechnics and the kids who set them off in their neighbourhood all autumn long. 'And the chickens,' Austen added. 'My mum says fireworks stop her allotment hens laying.'

'Poor things,' said Patti. 'Hold on, she doesn't eat eggs, does she?'

'Well remembered.' Austen felt the warm glow reigniting within her. 'Dad and I do, and she swaps the rest with her allotment mates for whatever produce they have.'

'That sounds nice,' Patti said dreamily, while the lights formed into a glittering silvery grid, impossibly neat, not a machine out of place. 'I wish we had hens up here at the estate. Your little bit of Manchester must be heavenly.'

'I never said I was from Manchester, did I?' Austen said, her eyes still trained up above.

'Oh, uh…'

'Oh my God, did you look me up?'

'No! At least, not in a weird way,' Patti said laughingly. 'I like your recent TikToks about the bookshop.'

Nothing seemed to bother this woman. She had a kind of poise Austen could only dream of.

'Thanks,' said Austen.

'Did you look *me* up?' Patti asked.

'Umm...' Austen found herself wanting to lie and say that she had for some reason. But she didn't play games. She always got outsmarted.

'Oh! You really didn't? Wow, thanks a lot.' Patti was laughing again.

'I promise I will, right after this,' Austen only half joked. 'I'll go the full Agatha Christie on you, OK?'

It would definitely be intriguing to find out more about Patti's world and what it was like living and working here full time, surrounded by family and friends, but she'd rather get that straight from Patti, and not from her socials.

'Listen,' Patti was saying, suddenly sounding oddly serious. 'I know you're probably busy with the shop and the baking and stuff, but tomorrow is opening night for the cornflower meadows up here at the estate. Minty's calling them the "Golden Hour Wildflower Meadow Walks". They've all been working hard to get it ready and, well, I've had a sneaky look and they're amazing. I wondered if you—'

'I'd like that,' Austen cut in. 'That would be lovely.' There was silence down the line. 'Are you still there?'

'I'm here,' Patti hurried. 'OK, so... I'll see you tomorrow. The gates open at seven thirty.'

'OK then.'

Austen could practically *feel* the way Patti would be smiling. She wished she was up there right now by her side, listening to the music, watching the display. The courtyard was growing quieter and more shadowy as the evening closed in.

'That reminds me,' Patti said over the lilting music. 'I'll see you at four tomorrow anyway.'

'You will?' Austen searched her brain for why that might be.

'For the kids' Storytime? Don't tell me you forgot? Not when there's a storyteller's hat and a cape and everything! Come on!' Patti sounded like she was really enjoying this. She must know Austen was shrinking at the very idea of it.

'You're coming to that?'

'Radia never misses it. I *always* try to miss it.' Another bright burst of laughter came down the line, brighter than anything happening in the sky above them right now, even with the hundred dancing lights. 'But I'll be there tomorrow for yours.'

Austen exaggerated a horrified, '*Ugh!*'

'You'll be great. Only promise me, no pandas in any body of water, please!'

'Got it.' Austen felt as dizzy as the shifting pinpricks of light as they zoomed here and there in their final dazzling finale. 'Maybe I'll try a bit of poetry?'

This idea brought a surprising amount of calm over her. Or was it the thought of Patti being there to console her with her easy, gentle, teasing way?

'That sounds perfect,' Patti said. 'Poetry, then golden hour in the meadow.'

Austen heard her brain saying *it's a date*, like they do in movies, but the words weren't even close to escaping from her mouth. Besides, nobody had said anything about this being a date. Patti was a bookshop volunteer. She was just being helpful. Like Jowan and Izaak. 'Sounds good,' she said instead.

More silence followed, but it didn't need filling with words. The pair stood smiling up at the sky as the drones joined together in one tight ball of incredible multicoloured lights before exploding apart at speed like the Big Bang.

Applause and whoops of appreciation filled the air. Every person in Clove Lore must have been out in their gardens watching the finale too.

A notification pinged right in Austen's ear. 'Oww,' she yelped, pulling the phone away to look at the screen, feeling like she was being dragged back down to earth after some long celestial journey or a lovely dream.

It was Delphine.

'Austen!' it began. 'I have missed you. Tell me about your day. Did you sell our Dickens? I can tell you my customers have been *idiots* and touched every book except the Dickens!'

Austen blinked and stared at the screen, remembering their shared 'before sunset sales challenge'. She wanted to reply right away, telling Delphine she had indeed shifted the copy of *Hard Times* she'd selected for their game, and not only that but the customer had taken a bag full of other classic novels as well.

'Austen?' Patti's voice made its way to her through the odd mix of adrenalin and, was that guilt?

'Oh, God, sorry, I got a message. It can wait, though.'

'No, you go reply. I'll see you tomorrow.' If Patti was annoyed, she wasn't showing it.

'Tomorrow,' she echoed. Austen had her thumb over the red button to cut the call when Patti spoke again.

'And thank you for watching the fireworks with me.'

This stilled Austen, who whipped the phone back to her ear once more. 'No, thank *you* for watching them with me. 'Night, then.'

There was a moment's silence in which Austen was sure she could hear her smiling before Patti hung up.

Turning back to the shop as the very last of the drones descended from the sky and the applause faded, Austen shut herself inside for the evening.

She climbed the staircase to her bedroom, her head bent and face aglow in the light of the phone screen as her thumbs worked busily.

'Have you ever run a children's story hour at the Feint Heart?' Austen asked.

'*Mon Dieu! Non!*'

'I would never.'

'What a question!'

The replies came in spitfire bursts, and Austen laughed all the way to the soft starlit spot on the window seat where she curled up for a long night's conversation, as contented as a cat.

Chapter Seventeen

Samantha had watched the drone display from the estate ticket office near the exit to the big car park and the visitor centre. Izaak had been stationed there for the evening too, on duty to stop walkers entering the estate (which they were usually free to do), only tonight it wasn't safe with the landing and launch zone spread across the dark grass. His husband Leonid had come down to keep him company and they'd watched the whole thing wrapped in each other's arms in the huge jumpers Leonid had recently taken up knitting.

Sam wanted to remark that the two of them made her feel more single than she usually did, but she hadn't wanted them to feel sorry for her or to stop hugging, so she'd fixed her eyes on the sky, occasionally looking over towards the Big House where she could just make out Patti smiling into her phone.

It was nice to see a light on in Apartment One, as well as the glow of the ballroom and lobby. The place was slowly coming back to life after the renovations.

Sam had been stifling yawns all through the afternoon, but now that she was outside in the cooling air, her eyes stung with exhaustion. The effort of following the drone movements had made it worse and, not that she'd admit it, peering at Jasper's window, wondering if that dark shape behind the glass was him or the spooky Mrs Gold, tired her even more. She rubbed at her eyes.

'When can you go home?' Izaak asked, as the drones powered down and the applause from the guests died away.

'Ten,' she said, trying not to sigh.

'We'll walk with you to the house,' said Leonid. 'But I don't mind washing the glassware if you want to leave early.'

'Minty wouldn't like that,' Sam said.

'Try her. She's softer than you think,' said Izaak as they made their way towards the lights of the Big House. 'Don't forget, she's the reason we're together.'

Sam hadn't forgotten the stories. About Izaak pining for his boyfriend living a secret life in Moscow, and how they'd conducted a love affair based on buddy-reading the same books three thousand kilometres apart until, at last, Minty had helped them wangle the work visa, bringing Leonid to the Big House where he'd channelled his academic botanist's expertise into a hands-on head gardener role created especially for him by his new boss. It hadn't been easy, but Minty had been determined to help her pining estates man.

'She's an old romantic, deep down,' Leonid said.

'She's a menace,' Sam said under her breath, trudging towards the last hour of her working day.

'There you are!' came Minty's voice from the doorway.

'When you say the Devil's name…' Izaak whispered, as he and Leonid whisked themselves up the grand staircase to their lodgings.

'Goodnight, you two. Good work,' Minty told them as they went. 'Now, Samantha. You look a fright.'

'Thanks?' Sam said. She'd grown increasingly used to this kind of thing.

'We can't have you scaring the guests. Here.' She held out a plate. 'You can go home after you deliver these pierogis.'

Sam liked the sound of that very much. 'Really? Thank you! Where am I taking them?' Maybe Leonid and Izaak were right; she was an old softie.

'The Golds,' her boss relied. 'And while you're at it,' she said, producing a bundle of mail from under her arm, 'please take their letters. They've been bursting out of their mailbox for days now, but will they empty it? No, they will not...' Minty fell to grumbling, stuffing the letters under Sam's arm, turning away with one last wave of dismissal. 'See you get home immediately afterwards, no?'

'No,' Sam said, absently looking down at the plate and letters. 'I mean, yes!' She shook herself. 'I will. Thanks.'

Now it was her turn to grumble, which she did all the way through the crowds of milling guests showing no signs of wanting to leave, all the way up the grand staircase and along the creepy, dark servants' corridor that led through fire doors to another wing of the house. She was hit immediately by the sharp, clean smell of white emulsion paint. She made her way past all the unoccupied apartments until she reached the end one. There was no sign whatsoever that it was occupied from out here, not even a crack of light under the door.

She stood for a minute, bracing herself.

Eventually, having heard not even a creak of floorboards inside or the hum of a television, she knocked as lightly as she could. If there was no reply, she couldn't be blamed for leaving their mail and leftovers on the mat and making a run for it.

The door was tugged sharply open, only an inch or two, enough to reveal Jasper Gold's fine nose and one startled eye.

'What is it?' he said.

'Minty sent me with these.'

Seeing the plate, he opened the door a crack more and was already reaching a hand out when he spotted the letters under her arm and froze.

'These too,' she said with a shrug, not sure why he'd be so cheesed off to get mail. Sam never got any post.

He relieved her of the plate, keeping one hand on the heavy door to stop it swinging shut.

'Let me, um…' Sam gestured inside the door frame, looking for a table to set the mail down on.

For an overly long moment she witnessed him weighing up what to do, and some stubborn well-brought-up streak within him seemed to do battle with and defeat a darker inclination, and he held the door open a little more. 'You can put them…' he looked into the dark apartment beyond. 'There.'

Sam stepped inside, blinking in the half-light. The whole place was cluttered with dark shapes, crates and boxes, big ghostly lumps covered in sheets. He was pointing to a sofa, absolutely covered in junk. There was a neatly folded bedsheet over its arm with a black silk sleep mask on top.

'Oh!' Sam couldn't help it. Had he really been sleeping on the sofa?

Her hasty glance over the clothing rails and packing crates towards the doorway of the smallest bedroom confirmed there was no possible way through.

Jasper was wincing inside; she could feel it, but he was standing stock-still and straight.

'Right, I'll just…' She placed the letters as neatly as she could on the sofa, noticing there was other unopened mail there. Letters with red print across the top. She knew exactly what those were, but this didn't make any sense.

She'd googled them during her lunch break. The Golds were big money. She'd even figured out why Jasper had seemed familiar to her. She'd discovered sidebar headlines and gossip columns about his dating exploits, of which there'd been plenty. The stories had been illustrated with telephoto shots of him, blond and sleek in a Speedo on the yachts of minor royals and media moguls' daughters, or images of him stumbling out of nightclubs in a white shirt rolled at the sleeves, collar open, with the cast of *Made in Chelsea* or some West End show. There'd been other pictures of Jasper opening the car door for his mother arriving at charity benefit dinners and fancy auctions, all wrapped in black and painfully chic, or at memorial services for dead fashion designers Sam had never heard of.

What would he think of her if he knew she'd cyber-stalked him during her break? Hadn't he said at the book club that the worst crime he could think of was intrusion into a person's privacy? Quite a weird position for an exhibitionist regularly seen stumbling out of clubs with his super-rich mates. Asking for attention! Only now she was in his home, and this person clearly had things going on that they'd rather keep utterly secret.

The massive family portrait against the wall caught her eye as she made to leave. Everyone was poised and elegant, like you'd see in a gallery, only there was something smeared across the smart-suited father's face.

'Is that a…' Sam began.

'Chocolate eclair?' Jasper replied coolly, like this was totally normal. 'Yes, I'd say it was.' He returned her gaze frankly, languid and blinking.

'Seems a waste of a good eclair.'

Jasper only placidly nodded his agreement.

'Did you like the fireworks?' she tried.

'Did I like the fireworks?' he echoed, still holding open the door, watching her occupying his private space, making her feel like some sort of protester making a nuisance of herself.

'They were silent ones. Drones?' she said, pointing a finger in the direction of the lawns. 'They were literally right outside.'

'I must have missed them,' he said in a low voice, throwing a quick glance over his shoulder towards the master bedroom with the look of a man who'd been walking on eggshells all day.

Had she been talking too loudly? Was his mum in bed? Were all the curtains closed for Mrs Gold's sake?

She took one last glance around. That's when Sam realised the figure she'd seen at the window wasn't a person at all, but some sort of grotesque golden animal, a leopard maybe, half in the room, half under the curtain. What a mess! All these expensive-looking things, and they were cluttered up like this was a storage unit.

Sam had seen this place when it was first renovated. All of Clove Lore had. Minty caved under pressure to neighbourly nosiness and arranged for the developers to host an open day so everyone could satisfy their curiosity about the work that had been going on here for months. It was hard to believe this was the same spacious, elegant apartment now.

The master bedroom door was a little ajar and a soft snoring drifted through to them. Jasper picked his way through the obstacles to silently close it.

'Mum,' he said, by way of explanation on his tiptoed return.

'I should go,' Sam said, aware she'd very much over-stayed her less-than-welcoming welcome. 'Enjoy the food.'

'What is it?' he said, his words stopping her. He lifted the foil to look.

'Pierogi. Jude made them for the estate staff. You need to eat them right away. They won't keep.'

As he revealed the glistening dumplings, the delicious aroma hit them both. Sam gulped.

'Have you been working all day, since this morning?' he asked.

Sam knew he was thinking about how she'd shown him to the cellars and Jowan's computer first thing. The flicker at his eyes confirmed it. It had been hard for him to ask for help like that when, by the looks of things, there'd been a time recently when he'd have had rooms full of tech.

'Would you care to join me?' he said, a little grandly, Sam felt.

She wondered if his attitude was a coping mechanism. A way to keep his dignity in the face of all this.

'Um…' She looked around for a dining table or even a safe route to the kitchen. 'Where?'

He returned a defeated stare.

'I know,' she said, suddenly hit with inspiration. 'Can you get away, for a sec?' She tipped her head towards the door of the sleeping Mrs Gold. Sam couldn't be sure of the extent of care his mum needed. From what she'd seen at book club, he might well be doing everything for her.

Jasper, however, didn't take any convincing. He was already reaching for his keycard.

'Better bring a blanket or something,' Sam added. 'And do you have any water, or…'

Jasper scanned the room as though trying to place something. 'Actually!' he said, a finger held aloft. He scurried away and she heard the sound of boxes falling in a landslide, followed by a fridge door opening and what sounded like pill containers rattling. He was back a few moments later with an elegant gold bottle.

'Champagne?' Sam asked doubtfully.

'It's all we have. In fact, it's the last bottle from the old place.'

'I was thinking tap water, but… why not.' She inspected the label more closely. 'Gold?'

'Ah, yes,' he said, pulling a blanket from a jumble of coats behind the door and showing her out into the corridor. 'Dad's winery.' He shrugged like this was a perfectly reasonable thing for your dad to own.

'Course it is. Come on, then,' she said, making haste down the long corridor, through the fire escape door, up clanking metal steps, and through a heavy hatch that it took both of their shoulders to lift, and out onto the flat roof terrace.

Even Jasper looked thrilled. In fact, Sam observed, he looked like he couldn't fill his lungs fast enough with the sweet breeze or his eyes with the glittering constellations.

He hopped up onto the low wall between crenel-lated stone blocks like he owned the place, which, Sam supposed, he partly did, or at least his mum did.

Watching him uncork the bottle felt like a glimpse at this guy's real life. The easy way he moved his hands, the smile, the way his shoulders were dropping from sheer relief. He flicked his smooth hair from his brow as the cork flew over the side of the building.

'You didn't bring glasses,' she told him, still keeping her distance, standing by the hatch.

'I couldn't quite lay my hands on them,' he said, holding the bottle out for her.

'Don't suppose they're *essential*,' she said, stepping up, taking the chilled bottle and bringing it to her lips.

'Careful, little sips, or it'll…'

Pfft! The champagne fizzed up in her mouth and frothed from the bottle as she drank, spilling down her uniform.

'…go everywhere.' He said, drily.

'Thanks,' hiccupped Sam, wiping her mouth and passing the bottle back.

Jasper drank, the night sky a gorgeous sapphire backdrop against the white gold of his hair. He looked like one of the ads in the front pages of the dentist's waiting room's glossy mags.

'Why do you have so much stuff, if you don't mind me asking?' she said, realising she was at risk of being caught staring so she'd better say *something*.

'We've, um, downsized recently.'

'From Buckingham Palace?' An unkind part of her thought of the golden leopard and had wanted to say 'From Trump Tower?' but she figured he couldn't be blamed for his parents' tastes. 'Aren't you meant to downsize all the stuff you own at the same time?'

He took another swig then let the bottle rest on his lap, turning his eyes to the sky. 'I suppose Mum's hoping this is a temporary move.'

'And is it?' Sam hoped she didn't sound too eager to know.

Jasper met her eyes briefly and shook his head, a wry smile forming.

'Well, if you're staying, you can't live like this.'

'None of that stuff's mine. It came from the house. It's Mum's. There's nothing I can do.'

'Is it only called hoarding if you're poor, then?'

Jasper's eyes widened, but he was generous enough to laugh. He hopped off the wall and handed her the bottle, pulling the blanket from where it had been draped over his shoulder.

He spread it on the lead roof and laid the plate down on top. 'Pierogi, Sam? They're very nice,' he said, as though he'd prepared them himself.

Sam tried to lower herself in an elegant way, impossible in the awful pencil skirt of her uniform. To distract him from her struggle with her hemline, she said, 'You need to hold a lawn sale. My uncle Harry had one. Made a fortune.'

Jasper only looked at her, chewing on the first of the dumplings.

Sam went on. 'It's when you lay out everything you want to sell...'

'I know what a lawn sale is.'

'His was mostly mower parts and old tools though,' she added, feeling a little silly again.

Sam wanted to ask what the posh person equivalent of a lawn sale was (a house clearance? An auction?) but the deep crease in Jasper's brow told her not to push it. 'It just seems a shame. That is a seriously nice apartment you've got down there.'

She'd have easily parted with any number of golden statues for her and her mum to live here. Another thought she kept to herself as she chewed her food.

'Mrs Rabbit,' Jasper broke the silence. 'Are you planning on adding life coaching to your list of occupations?'

'Hah!' The Sam of a couple of days ago would have snapped back *at least I have a job*, but this was new territory and there was a new openness in Jasper she didn't want him to close off again.

'I have two jobs because Mum's off work,' she explained. 'She fell on the slope, broke her cheekbone.'

'*Tshh!*' Jasper inhaled sharply. 'Ouch.'

'I know. It looks painful as hell. I'm running her laundry day and night, in between working for Minty.'

'Ah!' Jasper kept eating, but Sam noticed he took only one pierogi to every two Sam took. Probably something they teach you at posh school.

'How did your job emails go today?' she asked.

The question sent Jasper stretching back onto the blanket with a heavy sigh. Propped up on his elbows, his legs straight and very close to Sam's hip, he spoke. 'It was...' he paused, 'not fruitful.'

He'd had only one response, to an email sent to his old friend Tom Faulds-Bowles, the heir of a tennis ball factory fortune and one of the wildest party animals he'd ever encountered. Tom had flown a jet full of his best mates, Jasper included, out to the Maasai Mara for a three-week holiday only that spring.

'Sorry 'bout that,' Sam was saying, passing him the bottle.

'Me too. If I was in London, I'd have better luck. But I'm in exile here.'

That's what Tom had called it when he'd rung Jasper on Jowan's office landline, only minutes after opening his cry for help email this morning.

'Still in exile somewhere in the sticks? What is your dad playing at, mate?' he'd said.

Jasper had known to play it cool. 'I know. He's lost it.'

'I'll ask the old man if there's anything for you here. All right? Can't have my top wingman slumming it by the seaside forever.'

Jasper had mumbled his thanks.

'Oh? What's this? No cheeky comeback? Somebody keeping you there, eh? You haven't got some Devonshire girl chasing after you?' This had been accompanied by a loud horse laugh.

'Nothing serious,' Jasper had said with an attempt at a casual chortle. 'I'm trying my best to get back to London.'

'Try harder, my friend. There's a ton of new girls out already and I can't handle them all by myself.'

Jasper had nodded into the phone. Tom was talking about the debs: rich girls fresh out of college, all pretending not to be interested in forging family alliances that would make them all the richer; girls who were cynical and smart about love.

Jasper picked at the gold label on the bottle. Had that really been his life? It all felt so brainless now, and yet so familiar and easy.

'Exile?' Sam said, snapping him out of it.

'Never mind.' He took a long drink.

Sam sat quietly, chewing. Maybe if she left a silence he'd fill it, too polite not to?

'Dad sells these for two grand a case,' he said at last, passing the bottle back again.

'What? If that's true we've just drunk my mum's mortgage for the month.'

'That's how much *he* sells them for. They're three hundred per unit at Fortnum's.'

'God!' Sam blinked hard. 'How much do they cost to make?'

'Hard to know. A few pounds a bottle?'

'That's not right,' Sam said, shaking her head at the stupidity of the rich. 'That is just not right.'

'Well, that's the last of it. For us anyway.'

He looked so sad Sam didn't know how to act. Her head was woozy from lack of sleep. Still, she sipped. 'That's another quid's worth gone,' she said, just to make him smile again.

'I haven't told her yet,' Jasper said, suddenly, and as if to the night air. 'When I checked the emails today there was one from Mum's acting agent, ditching her.'

'Oh shit!' Even Sam grasped the severity of this. 'I'm so sorry.'

'It's OK,' Jasper said, though both of them knew that was a huge lie.

Silence fell between them and Jasper lowered his shoulders and head onto the blanket, lying flat.

After hesitating, Sam shoved the empty plate aside, lying down too, careful to keep a safe distance; she'd read about Jasper's player behaviour. Not that he'd showed even the tiniest bit of interest in her, of course, but a love rat's a love rat, no matter where they are. She crossed her ankles and focused on the stars.

'This blanket's soft,' she said. 'Cashmere, is it?' She held in the stupid quip about how she was more of a George at ASDA and H&M Home kind of girl than wherever this came from.

'This actually *is* mine,' he told her. 'A birthday present, from Mum. For my twenty-first.'

'Oh yeah, you had that big party.'

'How do you know about... oh, of course.'

She'd seen the pictures online. 'Yeah, sorry.'

'You know, that party cost twenty grand and it only warranted half a page in the *Sun*? And that was only because one of the Jaggers was there, and he only stayed twenty minutes for the photos. Another of Mum's birthday gifts.'

'He was paid to come to your party?' Sam took a quick glance at him in disbelief.

'Of course.'

'Is that… normal?'

'Depends what you mean by normal, I suppose. I've always had a smattering of paid celebrities at my parties. Mum has this idea I'll land some more acting or modelling work if I get enough headlines. I had the entire cast of *Cats* at my fifth birthday party.'

'Jasper, that's insane!'

She felt his wry laugh rumble from his chest through the flat lead roof and into her body. He let his head roll so their eyes met. 'That got me two TV ads and some catalogue work.'

'No way!' Sam propped herself up to better see him. 'You were a child star?'

'That all dried up pretty quickly. We're has-beens.'

'Don't say that.'

'No, it's true. Casting directors wouldn't look at us once Dad started… spending more time away from home, and Mum couldn't get TV work, ended up doing that hateful jungle programme, and I was in the papers for the wrong reasons – most of it made-up crap, by the way, in case you were wondering.' Sam tried to pull a clueless, angelic sort of expression that suggested she hadn't the foggiest idea what he was on about. 'And then…' he went on. 'Then we were forgotten about.'

'I'm sorry,' she said, watching as he turned his face away once more.

'Believe me, it's better to be forgotten these days. I never want another word written about me or my family.'

He shuddered, drawing his legs up.

'You're cold,' she told him. 'We should get inside.'

'No, please. Let's just look up.'

In her exhaustion, Sam couldn't think of any other reason to leave. She fixed her eyes on the deep unending blackness of the summer night and let her body soften against the blanket. The champagne was doing wonders, making the hard roof feel surprisingly comfortable, or maybe it was the week of next to no sleep and non-stop work she'd just had?

'All right,' she told him. 'But just for a minute.'

Down in the harbour, the waves sang their night-time retreat from the shore, growing quieter as they withdrew. The cries of seabirds were replaced by the hooting of two woodland owls, calling and answering one another amongst the estate's monster oaks.

Sam's mind cleared, until she was only aware of Jasper's soft presence beside her. Something about him glowed a warm gold even in the cool of the summer darkness.

Bone tired, her eyes closed softly, and she let herself rest, just for a minute, unexpectedly contented.

Chapter Eighteen

Radia had taken charge as soon as she'd barged into the bookshop near closing time on Friday, dragging a toy fox behind her, saying how much she loved Storytime because it had been her idea in the first place. She set her fox in prime position on a beanbag in front of Austen's storyteller's chair.

'Where's the cape?' Austen whispered to her, while Patti tipped party rings onto a paper plate.

'Cape?' Radia squinted.

'Yeah, and the hat?'

Radia had laughed so delightedly, the penny finally dropped.

Straightening her back to address Patti, who was grinning broadly, her hair falling in especially shiny waves today and with huge red hoop earrings dancing at her jaw. 'There's no storyteller's cape and hat, is there?' Austen accused her.

Patti spread her hands in confession. 'There isn't. Sorry.'

'You don't look very sorry.'

'There *should* be a hat!' Radia had said, suddenly inspired. 'Can I have some of that?' She gestured to the big sheets of paper Austen was holding.

'Sure, just one though. We'll need the rest,' she told the little girl, who summoned the other arrivals, telling them to watch as she set to work with Austen's fresh box of coloured marker pens. Austen didn't pay them much attention after that, working instead on her breathing. She couldn't understand how she was this nervous.

There were only six kids in the end and they were all easily under five foot. Two of them had arrived with a woman who'd introduced herself as Mrs Crocombe's daughter, the head teacher of the local primary school. She'd dropped her golden-haired boy and girl in the children's section and practically begged for a coffee and half an hour's peace in the cafe. Austen had made her what she wanted and left her scrolling on her phone by the counter.

Another woman had arrived a moment later with a younger, boisterous boy in a swimming onesie. She was a teaching assistant at the school, Radia informed Austen, and her name was Mrs Burntisland.

'She'll sit in the cafe as well,' the child said knowingly, and sure enough, the woman retreated to sit with her colleague in the quiet of the back room.

'I'll handle the cafe, OK?' Patti had said at this point, and left Austen to face the kids alone.

The other two children were holidaymakers who happened to be passing at just the right time and who Radia convinced to stay because, 'Austen is going to do something brilliant!' Those parents were currently lost somewhere amongst the shelves browsing at leisure, and hopefully not planning on earwigging.

This was how Storytime began, with Austen turning the sign on the door, dry-mouthed and overheated, wondering why she hadn't just *said* she couldn't do Storytime; she didn't know the first thing about kids.

'Right.' She shook herself, surveying the expectant little faces as they huddled on the beanbags, and Radia handed her a conical paper hat she'd just finished making. It had the letters 'AA' on the front.

'Your initials,' the little girl said.

'Ah! OK.' Austen took the hat knowing there'd be no getting out of wearing the thing. As she put it on her head the kids went mad with applause, totally taking her aback. This was accompanied by a ping from her phone.

'Just treat them like tiny adults,' the text read.

Glancing towards the cafe doorway, Patti was there smiling at her, her phone in her hand and one thumb raised. Then she ducked back into the cafe once more.

Treat them like adults, Austen repeated to herself. Tiny, terrifying adults.

'Um, hello everybody,' she began, not expecting a wall of loud *HELLO*s to hit her back. She adjusted the strap on her grey overalls, realised she was fidgeting nervously, and snapped her hands to her sides. Don't let them see your fear.

'Do you… like poems?' she asked, her tummy turning like a tumble dryer.

'YEEESSS!' the chorus came back.

'You do? Oh, OK. Good.'

'There was an old woman who lived in a shoe…' began the Burntisland boy, showing no signs of stopping until Radia informed him, 'That's a nursery rhyme, not a poem. Don't be so *babyish*.'

The little girl handed the floor back to Austen with an authoritative nod. Was it ridiculous to be relieved that Patti's niece was here to keep things under control? Either way, if things got unruly, she'd be sure to set the six-year-old on any troublemakers.

Austen perched on the Storytime armchair and the little ones leaned closer, waiting for the brilliant part to begin.

'Have you ever written a poem of your own?' Austen asked.

This was met by a quieter chorus of *no*s and *not really*s.

'Shall we try and write one today?'

This idea went down very well with her little audience and Radia took it upon herself to share out the paper and pens.

'How about, have you ever written a *story* before?' Austen asked, still feeling every inch the impostor. There were actual teachers in the next room, probably listening in and judging.

All the children said they had indeed made up stories before. Loads of them.

'I made up one about an old lady who lived in a shooo!' the Burntisland boy sang, noisily rolling his uncapped pens along the floorboards beneath his palm.

'What do you think the difference between a story and a poem is?' Austen asked, hoping that if she pressed on, he'd stop.

Five pairs of eyes gazed up at her. She'd only lost one, and maybe she could get the Burntisland kid back in the game when they put pens to paper.

'Anyone? No? Well, I think the difference is, when you tell stories you can just tell them however you like, yeah?' Nobody looked particularly convinced yet, so she continued. 'Whereas poems are stories told in patterns.' Silence. Austen gulped. 'So, for example, rhyming words are a kind of pattern. Um, how about you?' she tried to recapture the Burntisland boy's attention.

'His name's Barney,' Radia chimed smartly, and Barney gazed up with a dopey look.

'Barney, you told us a famous rhyme a moment ago. Can you remember what it was?'

This was all the encouragement it took to make Barney spring to his feet and recite the nursery rhyme again, and every time he got to the end of a line, Austen wrote down the rhyming words in chunky red marker.

'So, we've got "shoe", "do", "bread" and "bed". The rhyme at the end of each line of the poem gives it a musical, magical, poetry feeling. See?'

'I don't like that old woman,' the Crocombe girl said, and this sparked a loud debate about how it's 'horrid' to whip your children soundly and send them to bed with only broth ('whatever *that* is') to eat, and Austen, sensing they were getting into dangerous territory, way outside of her Storytime remit, steered the group back to poetry.

'There are other kinds of pattern you can use in your poems,' she told them. 'Any sound that you repeat is a pattern. Let's try some now. How about this one.' She raised a finger to her lips and made a 'shh' sound which the group copied.

'It sounds like the sea,' Radia announced, pleased with herself.

'It does, well done,' said Austen, relieved they were going with it. 'What else does *shh* remind you of?'

'Mum shushing baby 'Bastian,' said Barney, really getting into it now.

'Yes! It does sound like a baby being shushed to sleep, nice one, Barney.'

'And it sounds like the wind blowing,' said the Crocombe boy, not wanting to be left out.

'Well done! What does the *shh* sound make you think of?' Austen asked the two holidaymaker kids, realising they hadn't said much yet, and only just twigging that all the others were at school together so these two must feel a bit left out.

'Umm, umm,' the boy said, tipping his head to the side, thinking hard.

'It sounds like a bus when it stops,' his sister said, brightening. 'Or wheels in a puddle!' She was on a roll now. 'Or rain falling on my umbrella!'

Radia was the one to tell her 'well done', and Austen took the opportunity to sketch some tyres splashing through puddles, raindrops hitting a brolly, and all the other things the kids had thought of.

'Wow,' she said when she was done. 'That's a lot of things for one sound, isn't it? What do you think might happen if you wrote a poem with all these shushing sounds in? How might that make your readers *feel*?'

This threw the room back into blanket silence again, and Austen's anxiety, which had settled down for a moment, kicked up a notch.

'Should we… try to write something with lots of the same patterns of sound in? See if we can make a poem that rhymes not just at the ends of the lines but *inside* the lines, too?'

Blank faces stared back.

'Like, how'd you mean?' Radia ventured bravely.

'Well, like this… uh, let's see. The rain slips in sheets from the sky, *shh shh*; The puddles plop and splash, *shh shh*; The, um, the…' Austen faltered, thinking hard. 'The waves whoosh and whirl, *shh shh*; And the mummy swings the baby, go to sleep, *shh shh*. That sort of thing?'

The children exchanged wide-eyed looks and Barney made an impressed 'woah!' like this was some kind of word wizardry. For a moment Austen felt quite proud. 'Now, your turn. Use your pens to write your poems down using words, *or* you can draw the poem with pictures, like my one.'

The Crocombe kids clutched their markers in chubby fists over their blank sheets of paper, but they didn't make a mark.

Seeing their hesitation, and their uneasy glances at one another, Austen said, 'Don't worry, there's no way you can get it wrong. That's the brilliant thing about poetry. It's just having fun with sounds and ideas.'

'But yours was really good,' the girl said. 'What if mine's bad?' Her brother nodded along.

'There is no good or bad poetry,' Austen said, echoing the words Delphine had sent her the other day when they'd strayed onto the topic. She hadn't believed it, of course, and she didn't really believe it now, but she'd be damned if any of these kids were going to leave here today thinking they weren't born poets.

Austen slipped from the chair's edge onto the floor beside the kids, and together they chattered and worked up their ideas until everyone had at least something down on their page. Radia had gone completely quiet and was painstakingly writing lines and lines of verse, the tip of her tongue peeping out.

Looking over the bent heads of the little group, just for a second, Austen let herself revel in the feeling of sharing something good. And, incredibly, she was having fun, not something she'd anticipated from Storytime.

The session was drawing to a close and everyone but Radia, who was still writing, stood up to perform their poems, including Barney Burntisland's energetic take on the assignment which went along the lines of, 'Shh please, it's time to sleep. Bang clash smash crack clang bang,' many times over with only slight variations. Austen pronounced it 'absolutely wonderful' amidst the huge burst of applause from the other kids, and she meant it, too. There was a small squabble between the holidaymaker kids over which sibling had copied the other's idea, and Austen hadn't known how to handle it other than telling them that sometimes two people who know each other very well can be so in tune with each other they'll write similar images. The Crocombe children joined in to say it had to be true because they'd both written about their granny's ice creams in their poems and they'd both had their pages covered up to stop snooping.

As Austen was thanking them for coming and, with some relief, thinking of her evening off ahead, the Crocombe girl turned to ask if Austen was 'a real poet'.

'Anybody who writes poetry is a real poet,' Austen replied, more convinced of this now than before having met these kids.

Radia at last dragged her eyes from her page and peered disconcertingly at Austen. 'Can you read us one of your poems?' she said, and Austen's heart sank instantly. 'Not a made-up, on-the-spot-one, a *real* one.'

'Oh, I don't know about that,' Austen said, packing away the pens and standing, moving the chair back an inch, hoping the subject would be dropped. It didn't work.

'Please!' the Crocombe boy wheedled.

'Poems can be quite private things, you know? Personal,' said Austen.

'Secret?' Radia said, even more intrigued than she was before.

'No, not secret, just hard to share.'

'I shared my poem,' the holidaymaker boy said.

'You mean my poem!' the sister butted in, still cross.

'That's true, you both shared your poetry,' Austen conceded. 'Well, all right, but you mustn't laugh.'

'Unless it's hilarious,' Radia said, not at all comforting Austen's jangling nerves.

With a sharp exhale, Austen drew out her notebook and this set off a chorus of *ooh*s. Austen didn't know whether she wanted to laugh along with her crowd of young fans or for the ground to swallow her up.

The notebook fell open in her hands. It was now filled with her enthusiastically scrawled verses. Looking at them for the first time since the night she'd been transported somewhere far away by the muse that had neglected her for so long, she felt abashed to see these half-cooked things, draft work at best. Her neck was flushing red, she just knew it.

'Get on with it, then,' the Burntisland boy said, hanging upside down on the beanbag, his fringe fanning out so it touched the shop floor.

'Right, sorry,' she said, before wondering why she was apologising. She cleared her throat, flipping through the pages. There'd been some good stuff the other night. Where was it now? 'This will have to do.'

'What's it called?' Radia stopped her just as she'd been about to launch into reciting.

'It doesn't have a name.'

'Ooh, we'll give it a name,' Radia said, puffing out her chest. 'OK. Go.'

Flustering terribly, Austen focused on the page. It didn't help that the holidaymaker kids' parents had chosen this moment to reappear from amongst the stacks, their arms filled with books they wanted to buy, and they were watching her expectantly.

'You and me, in a world of books,' Austen began, forcing her eyes to the lines so she wouldn't see anyone's reactions.

'Under sheets of inky canvas.
I lie on a sheet of white foolscap,
You describe the stars and I translate them.

We are the papyrus eaters
Feint lined, ruled by words.
Between the dust jackets, we sleep.
I trace your lettering as I dream.

I hide in the margins, italics, footnotes.
You rule the page.
Your character scratched from my nib,
Our hands combining.'

Austen raised her head in the strange silence in the room. The children were staring at her, uncertain what they'd just heard, no doubt thinking it wasn't anything near as good as the 'shh shh' poem.

'That's all I have so far,' Austen shrugged.

The two tourist parents clapped politely, if a little stiltedly. The dad attempted an unconvincing, 'Bravo!'

'I said it wasn't very good,' Austen reminded them.

'*You* said there was no good or bad poems!' Radia protested, just as Patti appeared from the cafe to round things up.

'That was wonderful, wasn't it, kids?' she was saying, the teachers appearing now too, just to make Austen's mortification complete. 'Let's all say thank you to the storyteller.'

Patti led the fresh applause until everyone was joining in, and the kids had begun either lying face down on the beanbags or rolling around on the floor after the hard work of sitting still for ages.

The Crocombe boy was saying '*nib*' in a funny voice over and over, quoting Austen's poem, making the others join in and fold over with laughter. 'Scratchy *nib*!'

Patti made her way to Austen's side. Radia had her head bowed again, finishing off her poem.

'You weren't listening in on all of that, were you?' Austen asked Patti, shrinking.

'I only came in at the bit about the nib, but I really liked that bit.'

'Oh my God!' Austen wanted to curl into a ball, but she couldn't help the weak laugh that escaped her lips.

'Honestly, I think you were amazing,' Patti cajoled. 'These kids won't remember *you* specifically anyway, if that makes you feel any better.'

'They won't?' Austen wasn't sure if that did make her feel better after all.

'No, they're little egos on legs. They weren't thinking about you, only themselves. And they'll be going home thinking about rhyme and sounds and all the rest of it, and at least one of them will demand I buy her an arty beret now. Look at her.'

Sure enough, Radia was still absorbed, her pen moving carefully.

Austen laughed again. 'They thought my poem was weird.'

'They're, like, six years old. What do they know?'

'That lot aren't six,' Austen jabbed her head in the direction of the parents.

'I doubt they're on a poetry judging committee. And who cares? You've given their kids a lovely thing. Not everybody *gets* poetry, you know? I definitely didn't. I hated it at school, and I think the teachers hated it too. Then exams squashed any inclination we might have had for it, and,' Patti shrugged, 'that was that. But these kids,' she turned to look at them, 'are absolutely fizzing with it. Look.'

The Crocombe kids were playing some kind of game where one made a noise and the other had to make a second, funnier noise. Forced to see this for what it really was, Austen realised they were having fun with sounds and patterns, and the Burntisland boy was reciting, 'There was an old woman who lived in a ZOO,' making his mother laugh as they gathered their things ready for their late afternoon trip to the beach.

'She had so many PLATYPUSES she didn't know what to do,' he went on, as they reached the door.

'I suppose that is pretty cool,' Austen conceded.

'Thanks again!' the teachers called as they marshalled kids towards the door. 'We'll be sure to spread the word for next week.'

'Next week?' Austen said to herself, while Patti turned the lock for them and set them all free. 'It's weekly?'

'Yep, it is.' Patti's eyes shone delightedly. 'The next one's on Thursday, since there's the open mic event next Friday evening.'

Austen accepted her fate without complaint.

'Come on, Rads, let's drop you at home,' Patti called.

This was enough to snap Radia's attention from her writing. 'Aren't we getting ice cream and throwing sticks off the harbour steps today?'

'Uh, no,' Patti said, collecting the little girl up. 'We only do that at weekends, remember? And we said what happens in stick-throwing club *stays* in stick-throwing club? Don't blab now!' Turning to Austen she added, 'Wanna walk down with us?'

'Oh, uh, sure!' Austen realised they were leaving right this second, and just had time to grab her keycard and wallet.

This made Radia wide-eyed with interest. 'Why's she coming with us?'

Patti laughed before she answered. 'Because, nosy, we're going out somewhere this afternoon.'

'Are you taking Austen for ice cream?' Radia wanted to know as they made their way into the heat of the summer afternoon.

Austen double-checked the door and followed after.

'Nope. Guess again,' the child's aunt said, eyes twinkling wickedly over her head at Austen.

And Radia did guess, all the way down the slope, with increasingly wild and elaborate ideas ('Zip-lining? Donkey rides? An aeroplane to Zanzibar!') until she was safely through the cottage door and Patti's sister, Joy, had appeared briefly to thank Austen for Storytime.

'Have fun, you two,' Joy called behind them as they retreated down the cottage's path dotted with sunflowers at the foot of the slope. 'And please don't be coming home early to do bath and bedtimes and all that stuff, Pats. *Actually* go *out* out... OK?'

Patti waved her sister's words away, 'All right, all right.'

'*Are* we going to fly to Zanzibar?' Austen asked, a little light-headed as they found themselves shoulder to shoulder facing the long trek up the slope. This was the first time they'd really be properly alone together. The prospect scared and excited her equally.

'Minty would tell you her wildflower meadows are way better than that,' Patti said with a laugh. 'Come on. It'll be spectacular, I promise.'

And for a moment, Austen thought Patti was going to take her hand. She even dropped her head to see if she was reaching for her, but she wasn't, and then the moment for taking hands had passed, anyway. A perfect reminder that this was a friendly evening supporting a local event, and with one week almost gone of her bookselling holiday, and Austen anxious to avoid making a fool of herself again, what more could it be, really?

Chapter Nineteen

While Austen had spent her Friday fretting over Storytime, Jasper Gold had a momentous day of his own.

Early that morning, it had taken Jasper a few moments to figure out where he was when he'd woken on the roof under the lightest drizzle of warm, sand-scented rain.

Waking wherever he'd fallen was nothing new to him, but it had been a while since he'd come to with a fuzzy head and a girl in his arms. But with his eyes still gritty and his brain drowsy, he'd not known which girl this could be. Then he'd remembered.

There'd been champagne – a 2012 vintage and easily worth a few hundred quid – and there'd been yet more donated food, and it had tasted so good. Then he'd spilled his guts out about... what? His secret news about his mother's acting agent, his failure to find a job, and, oh no, he'd told her about his unsuccessful modelling career too.

That was when, rubbing his eyelids and wondering if he could stretch his spine without frightening Sam awake, he'd realised how soft and warm she felt, with her head on his chest and her hand flat against his stomach in the most sensational way, and oh God!

He'd frozen, letting the feeling of her warmth sink right into him, awakening his core, making all his nerves flame, and there'd been a split second where she'd sighed in her sleep and nuzzled closer, her fingers spreading with a firm pressure that threatened to make him swoon away entirely, but then she'd frozen too, tensed and jumped away from him, wild-eyed and swearing like a docker.

She'd dashed for the hatch, covering her face for some reason, telling him not to look at her, asking if she'd been drooling, then changing her mind, telling him *not* to answer that, and then she'd fallen to swearing again before disappearing down the ladder and out of his sight.

He'd had to laugh; it was so endearing and just plain unnecessary.

Left alone to clear away the remnants of their rooftop sleepover picnic, the familiar dread of life in the airless apartment below seeped back in.

He wondered what state he'd find his mother in this morning, telling himself he must break the news to her about her acting agent, before chickening out immediately. Not now. He'd do it when she was more robust. There were other, more pressing things to worry about, things he was only just beginning to comprehend, things only he was going to be able to remedy. Nobody was coming to save them.

Crossing the rooftop and peering seaward, he'd been surprised at the sight of the village below, all higgledy-piggledy rooftops and a patchwork of gardens and cobbled pathways, zigzagging all the way down to the harbour. Had it looked this impressive before? He hadn't noticed.

Now, he breathed it all in, basking in the hazy morning light and, with a view that now included Samantha Capstan running at full pelt for the slope, presumably making towards wherever she'd parked her laundry sled, he thought how he'd never seen a finer sight in all his life.

The memory of that strip of paper torn from the advert on the lamp-post back on Sunday evening came to him in a flash. He'd stumbled across her sign after staggering shell-shocked out of the apartment, telling his mother he needed to go for a run when, in truth, he hadn't been able to stand the claustrophobic clutter and his mum flatly refusing to accept that two lorry-loads of clothes and artefacts from their old lives were simply never going to fit in there. She'd kept repeating how she'd make some calls. One of her friends would come through for them. They'd be out of there in hours.

He'd listened as his mum had rung everyone in her contacts list and not one of them answered. He heard the way her voice strained as she left messages saying she needed a 'bolthole, just for a few days, for me and the boy'. There'd been no return calls, of course, and he'd watched his mother grow increasingly immobilised as she tried to hold their new reality at bay.

That evening he'd waited until she'd cried and medicated herself to the point of being unable to stay awake and he'd raced out of the Big House with no idea where the estate paths would take him, barely seeing his way, his head spinning and stomach rumbling.

He'd seen Samantha's sign. 'Help Wanted', it had said. He'd smirked, thinking *this is how they hire people around here?* but as he scoffed and stared he'd been overwhelmed by a sickening sense of inevitability that he couldn't account for. Then out of nowhere, there'd been a girl on the path asking him if he was interested in the job as if she was clairvoyant, like she already knew he and his mum were doomed to rot here forever.

It was the look in her eyes that unnerved him most, the way she could see right through him. She must have known that he was hungry and lost and afraid, and he'd gone and snapped at her. He couldn't recall exactly what he'd said, but he'd bet his life it was stupid and insulting. He remembered the self-righteous feelings blooming within him, and she'd defended herself, told him he'd be useless for any work. She hadn't been wrong about that either.

Except, he still had that phone number from the torn strip that he'd automatically reached out for. A tiny subconscious part of him must have been smart enough to recognise it for what it was: a lifeline.

If he was quick, he'd catch her.

The hatch banged shut behind him as he made a dash for his apartment, then on to find Minty to beg her to let him use her phone. What's the use in pride if it means an empty stomach and a mother needing help today, and not from some notional group of 'friends' who were never coming, the industry turncoats who'd conveniently forgotten all those parties and gifts and favours that Estée Gold had bestowed on them in better times. His dad was out of the question, too; he must know the state they'd be in out here, cut adrift and utterly alone. Seriously, not one person was coming to their rescue.

If it was up to Jasper to fix this, there wasn't a second to lose.

–

'Yes?' Sam answered warily, hoping it wasn't her mum only just realising she hadn't come home last night, or her uncle out looking for her, driving the country lanes, frantic. She'd never stayed out like this before.

'Samantha? It's me. Jasper?'

'Oh!' Sam stopped dead on the slope, the laundry sled threatening to keep sliding Down-along. She hadn't mastered the way her mum had of smoothly running the sled on its ropes in front of her as she sidestepped downhill, stopping at each doorway, gathering up the linens for laundering as she went. 'What do you want?'

She pinched her eyes, scolding herself for being snappy. Nothing had happened last night, nothing he needed to set straight, anyway.

There had, of course, been that moment this morning when she'd woken somehow snuggled up against him. She must have shifted closer as she slept because he'd stayed in the same position the entire night, like he'd been afraid of moving. But he couldn't have known about how she'd been in the nook under his arm. He'd been asleep when she'd jumped away from him, hadn't he?

'I *am* interested, as it happens,' he was saying.

'Huh?'

'In the position.'

It took far too long for her to work it out.

'You want to do laundry?' she scoffed.

'Yes.'

'For fun?'

'Uh, no, I'd prefer it if it might be for money.'

Silence. Sam shook her head, letting this sink in.

'Laundry is really hard work,' she said at last.

'I can imagine.'

'I bet you can imagine it, but can you *do* it?' Sam regretted her tone immediately. This change in him was too sudden. He'd taken some great leap forward and was acting like a decent human all of a sudden and she was still lagging behind. 'Sorry,' she said. 'I'm not a morning person.'

'Do you still need someone?' Jasper didn't sound at all put off.

'Meet me on the slope. Wear something you don't care about.'

This was met with a thoughtful silence down the line. Sam knew he'd be mentally picking his way through his designer wardrobe, discounting all the fancy things he cared about too much to ruin.

'And you'll need grippy shoes,' she added.

'Give me ten minutes.'

'I'll crack on then,' said Sam, bewildered, hanging up.

It was closer to thirty minutes when Sam grew aware of the footsteps behind her. She'd made it to the bottom of the slope and had all the washing bundles gathered in already.

'Oh my God!' It was out before she could stop herself.

Jasper, breathless by the lifeboat launch, was dressed in a pale grey boilersuit, unclasped at the neck, rolled up at the cuffs, and with a pair of white chunky retro high-tops on his feet.

He looked down his body, grinning, and spread his hands to her. He went so far as to lift a heel. 'Like it?'

'Are you a Ghostbuster?'

'It's set wear.'

Sam was none the wiser.

'When I was on set, working with Obsidian Cruz? We were given these.'

'Are you talking about a movie set?'

'I am,' he said proudly, drawing level with Sam, taking the ropes of the sled from her. 'He's only the greatest avant-garde filmmaker of the twenty-twenties. I was a runner.'

'Did you do any actual running?'

'Yep, all over London. Getting the talent their drinks orders, picking up their *prescriptions*.' Jasper lowered invisible shades and raised a meaningful eyebrow. 'I'd rack up miles every day. I was good at it.'

Sam couldn't help getting swept up. 'Is your name in the movie credits?'

'Certainly is.'

'From the movies to the laundries,' Sam quipped, dropping the reins and walking past him, heading Up-along.

Jasper tried hauling the laundry sled after her, but it wouldn't budge.

'Put your back into it,' Sam called over her shoulder.

There was much grunting and straining and when she turned to look down at him, he hadn't moved it at all. 'Not easy, is it?'

'No,' he conceded, running a hand over his brow, pushing his hair aside.

'Would you say you have to be very good at hauling laundry to do this job?'

'I would,' he said, suspicious, eyes narrowing.

'And are you *too good* for it?'

'No.' He let his shoulders fall. 'It would appear that I'm in no way too good for this.'

'And what about me?' Sam couldn't believe she was doing it, but she had her hands pressed to her hips.

Jasper looked up at her. 'I imagine you're very good at this.'

'That's not what I mean. Are you too good for me?'

Jasper seemed to think, before realisation dawned behind his eyes. He held a wrist to his forehead. 'I did say that, didn't I? Listen, that was not what I meant. I mean, maybe it was, at the time, but...' He gave up. 'Please forgive me. I'm not too good for you. Nobody is.'

'Oh.' Sam stepped back down the slope towards him. 'I wasn't expecting you to be so… polite about it. Sorry.'

'Can we start again, from the beginning, please? And I promise not to be all *phnaw phnaw phnaw*!' He mimed a snooty person with their nose in the air being insufferable.

Sam laughed, and with a surge of excitement and camaraderie, she lifted herself to her tiptoes and pressed a kiss to the spot on his cheek where it was pink from the effort of trying to shift the sled.

She was delighted to see he only grinned in response.

'Come on then,' she said, marching Down-along this time, in the direction of the pub.

'Do we *not* have to haul this up the slope, then?' he said, staring after her.

'I was only pretending, to see if you could,' she laughed. 'Finan at the pub has offered to drive it up to the top in his Land Rover. There's a back lane just down there behind the pub. I'm too scared to try bringing the laundry van down it. Too narrow for me.'

'You were tricking me?' he beamed, coming after her, the sled running easily down onto the wide quayside.

'Teaching you a lesson, but I'm done now,' she promised. 'Partners?'

'Partners,' he agreed with a nod as they shared in pulling the sled to the pub door. 'How much exactly does this job pay, by the way?'

'Ah,' Sam said, hoping Jasper was strong enough to shoulder one last shock. 'Well, it's not *loads*…' she began.

Chapter Twenty

Up at the Big House, Estée Gold found herself in a grand ballroom that put her in mind of the one in Joan Rivers' apartment on the Upper East Side where she'd once had a phoney English afternoon tea and they'd laughed like drains talking about sitcom scripts that had come to nothing, only this place was empty and echoing.

Her feet were bare, but she wasn't aware of that fact yet. Her silk pyjamas, a gift from Joan Collins, fabulous woman, back in ninety-nine, were twisted at the waist. She adjusted them now, and clawed her hands through her hair.

'Hello?' she heard someone croak, then realised with dulled horror that the sound had come from her. She gripped her throat and tried to swallow. It felt dry and raw, like she'd flown long haul having swallowed a handful of those pills dear old Dr Bader prescribed on the understanding everyone pretended it was for adult acne. If she had some now, she'd wash them down with... well, anything, actually. The apartment had been entirely empty of spirits, however, and it wouldn't even have crossed her mind to pour some tap water to help with her thirst.

She'd been wandering for what seemed like hours, though she couldn't be sure if she hadn't actually gone in circles, trying doors, walking down endless, twisty corridors and ascending and descending flights of stairs. Where was she? And where was Jasper?

'Mona?' she cried, but her voice was too small to escape the room, like in a nightmare where you finally realise you're helpless.

What would her vocal coach say about this? What was her name again? Tammy? No, Tonya! That's it! Estée wondered vaguely whether she might be able to fit her in for an appointment at short notice. God, it must be years since she'd had a voice consultation. A vague notion about Tonya retiring came to her through the fug in her head. There'd been a farewell party, hadn't there? Then, out of nowhere, there appeared a face, looming round a creaking door, followed by low heels click-clicking on the polished boards.

The woman had a platinum bob, too severe for her face, which with the right contouring could be quite pretty in an English thoroughbred sort of a way.

'Mrs Gold?' the woman was saying, like she knew her. 'What are you doing down here? Are you lost?' She was talking far too loudly.

'I was looking for…' Estée let the sentence float off unfinished. What had she been looking for?

'Come with me. You need a cup of tea,' the woman was saying, a little matronly, but reassuring. She was the sort of solid English nanny type Estée always wanted for little Jasper, but Franklyn insisted on hiring those clueless Californian girls on gap years who he seemed to scare off within days of their arrival, and so another one would be sent for, and another one, and another.

The woman was making her walk through progressively smaller corridors like the house was shrinking. She thought back to playing *Alice* in 1980 at the Theatre Royal, with her grandparents in the audience, and her in the spotlight drinking the shrinking potion. 'A rising star' the local papers had called her. Gran had kept the clippings.

'Curiouser and curiouser,' Estée croaked, her head aching, her feet prickling with pins and needles.

'Come along,' the woman said, guiding her into some kind of time warp kitchen, putting her into an armchair beside an Aga.

It was so warm Estée closed her eyes.

This felt like her granny's little council house scullery back in Scarborough, long, long ago before Estée invented herself. She'd been Jennifer Carpenter back then. Tears were welling behind her eyelids. She wanted to sleep and sob at the same time.

'Let's get you sorted,' the woman said, quieter now, pouring out tea from a proper pot with a crocheted cosy and handing her the cup on a wobbly saucer.

'Who are you?' Estée said, between sniffs.

'You can call me Minty,' the woman said, putting a woollen blanket over her legs and tucking her in. 'We're neighbours.'

Chapter Twenty-one

Patti wasn't all that comfortable with the feeling, but nonetheless it was there. A kind of pride at showing Austen through the gate at the top of the path to the meadows, of having paid for their entry tickets and their plastic flutes of bubbly from Izaak at the kiosk. He'd been discreet enough to say nothing, but he'd winked when he returned her change and told them to have a wonderful time.

Something about guiding Austen down the lane she'd become familiar with over her time in Clove Lore gave Patti the feeling of revealing something special to this woman, and it made her heart swell to see her happy and sipping her drink. Who wouldn't be proud to be taking someone like Austen out?

'You look pretty, by the way,' Patti said, never very shy about these things, but still feeling it was risky this time.

Austen couldn't prevent the smile. 'Thanks. So do you.'

Patti had made a special effort, choosing a long loose dress in deep cherry pink with square pockets. She'd worn her softest white shirt tied over it, unbuttoned to show a silver chain snaking down her breastbone. She'd been sure to roll the sleeves so Austen might catch sight of the star tattoos inside her wrists. When Patti dated she wanted a girl to *know* she was being dated, but so far Austen was staying self-contained and quiet.

'You OK?' Patti asked as they made their way down the field margin between white mayflowers bursting from their buds on a gnarled ancient hedgerow to their right and the estate's now picked-out strawberry field sprawling away to their left.

Austen brought her drink from her lips to say she was fine. 'Just a bit wired after Storytime.'

'Have you done anything like that before?'

'No, couldn't you tell?' Austen laughed like it should be obvious she was a complete faker, or something.

'You've got a natural talent for explaining poetry. If I were you, I'd email your local library back home and offer kids' poetry sessions. Monetise those skills!' Patti's voice bubbled with laughter.

'You think?'

'Yeah, and I'd ask all the bookshops too. And the museums and galleries while you're at it. They love that sort of thing. Public engagement stuff for families.'

Austen seemed to be giving this serious thought. 'I guess I could. I mean, I definitely need to find a job when I get back home.'

'You're not working at the moment?'

Austen shook her head. 'Haven't for a while. I've been volunteering in a thrift shop in the Northern Quarter.'

'Nice.' Patti couldn't help but be impressed, but she could feel the embarrassment coming off Austen. 'That must be amazing… isn't it?'

'It doesn't feel very amazing having your parents pay for everything,' Austen said.

'There are all kinds of ways to give back,' Patti reassured her. 'I bet they don't mind.'

Austen was considering this too. 'They always say they don't. It's just hard, finding book jobs, you know?'

'I don't. Tell me.'

'Well…' Austen sighed heavily. 'I send off CVs, I email on spec. Been doing it for ages, but there's nothing that pays. And so many jobs are in London, and…' she tailed off.

'And it's expensive to live there if you're on an internship or something?' Patti offered.

'Something like that.' Austen was taking another drink, running her fingertips against the leafy hedgerow, setting tiny brown moths fluttering from the branches. 'You like your job, at the Big House?' she asked.

Austen was deflecting, and since Patti had no intention of making her talk about something she wasn't willing to share, she ran with it. 'You know what my favourite part is?' She grinned at Austen, waiting for her to meet her eyes before going on. 'It's when all the guests are in, and the doors are closed, and the celebrant's standing at the front ready to start, and I get to watch the whole thing from the back of the room, knowing it's all gone to plan and we're about to make these people the happiest they've ever been.'

Austen nodded, her eyes back on the dry, cracked earth passing under their feet. 'That sounds satisfying. I've had that kind of feeling when employers' books have launched.'

Patti looked askance at Austen, who was now taking a drink of bubbly. Patti wasn't going to pry into her life. She'd have to let Austen reveal herself in the ways she wanted to.

'It is satisfying,' said Patti. 'Even if working with Minty can be stressful!'

'I can imagine,' Austen laughed, and the sound made Patti want more.

'Plus, I get all the wedding cake I can eat.'

It worked again. This was beginning to feel easier.

They reached the end of the strawberry field and Patti stepped ahead so she could unlatch the gate into the meadow for Austen to pass through.

'Are you ready for this?' Patti asked. 'I reckon we're the first ones here.'

'We are?' The light danced in Austen's eyes. Patti had clocked they were brown the very first time they met, but up here on the promontory as the first rays of sunset were turning the sky pink, her irises shone a golden hazel. Patti resisted the urge to point this out, but she hoped Austen could tell she was getting a little lost in them.

'Hold on,' Austen said, taking her glasses off, and giving the lenses a wipe on the hem of her top that she'd tugged free. She'd definitely noticed.

When she slipped them back on her freckled nose, Patti asked, 'Better?'

'Better,' echoed Austen, and Patti swung open the gate.

She held back for a second, even though she hadn't been down here for days and had only seen Minty's pet project when the seedlings were in bud. She wanted Austen to get the first glimpse.

'Oh my days!' Austen was saying, holding her free hand to the pocket of her overalls like she kept her heart in there.

For the first few moments, all Patti could do was watch from her spot by the gate as Austen walked into the sea of silver foliage and blue starbursts of the cornflower meadow. The summer breeze made the blooms move in waves, mimicking the blue sea in the bay below. Leonid had had the idea of mowing short the grassy paths that criss-crossed the meadow so visitors could walk right in amongst the wildflowers, and Austen had made her way to one of the green entranceways now.

Patti daren't take a picture on her phone, not without asking, so as Austen turned back to face her, delight written across her face, beckoning to her with a hand, Patti committed the moment to memory.

Austen was all in monochrome, with the suggestion of black ink scrolling across her back and shoulders in delicate tracery. The inconspicuously simple greys and black of her clothing made her freckles, light eyes and the auburn hints in her dark waves stand out in shocking contrast as the evening sun kissed them.

'Are you coming?' Austen was laughing, although not quite enough to snap Patti out of this dazed feeling.

Austen was now wading into the meadow, thigh-deep in blue, or at least that's how it looked from here. Patti hurried to join her, plunging in between the rows, immediately hit by the buzz and hum of the hoverflies and bees flitting between the delicate thistle-like flower heads.

'It's beautiful,' Austen said, as Patti caught up.

'Even more than I thought it would be,' said Patti.

'Cornflower blue has to be the best blue. Like, how do you even describe it?' Austen was getting swept up too.

'I've no idea,' Patti said. 'Words are your thing. What have you got?'

Austen laughed and stooped to examine a patch of the raggedy stems, silvery-green, the colour of rosemary leaves, with fat diamond-patterned buds hiding beneath frilled disks of pointed petals layered and rigid like a ballet dancer's tulle tutu, and at their centre, scruffy clusters of stubby, indigo stamens.

'Umm.' Austen considered them closely. 'It's like royal blue? But on a watercolourist's easel? There's a bit of iridescence in there too, maybe, making them sort of glow? I'd love to be a bee seeing these! I bet they give out some kind of amazing light spectrum we can't see.'

'I can kind of see something,' Patti said, leaning nearer, clasping one stem for closer inspection. 'Something that's not quite there?'

'Artists' light?' said Austen.

'Maybe some things are so pretty you can't describe them. Can't even see them properly, if that makes any sense?'

Austen was looking at her now.

'I have no idea what I'm saying, sorry.' Patti laughed, setting the hoverflies zipping back and forth in silent frenzy.

'No, I know what you mean. There's a reason people say 'words fail me'. There's a reason people paint or take pictures.'

'Should we take one now?' Patti risked, but Austen was already there, reaching for her phone in her pocket, but pulling out only her notebook.

'Oh! I must have left my phone at the shop.'

'Don't worry, I'll take it.' Patti set up the shot, angling her arm to get as much of the scenery in as possible. She didn't notice until she was looking at them both mirrored onscreen, but Austen had lost a little of her glow. She snapped the shot and quickly put her phone away again.

'OK?' Patti checked in again.

'I don't like being without my phone for long. Makes me feel a bit lost, you know?'

Patti thought she did but there was some added disappointment for Austen, she could sense it. She thought of Jowan telling her that Austen was forever messaging on her phone, even while serving in the bookshop. 'You like to keep in touch, I get it.'

Austen lifted herself to standing again and Patti sprang up, too.

'I think I see a patch of poppies over there,' she was saying, showing no sign of wanting to leave yet, even if she was missing her phone.

Patti drained her glass and reached for Austen's empty one. 'I'll carry these. Let's go and look for poppies.'

The meadow paths formed a rambling maze and the poppy cluster was right at the centre. The pair wandered up and down the tracks trying to reach them. Some other visitors were entering the field now, couples walking hand in hand, snapping selfies and grinning.

Austen was clearly trying hard to make up for the awkwardness of a moment ago. A good sign she wanted things back on track.

'Tell me about you. How did you end up in Clove Lore?'

'There's not much to tell. My sister and Radia ended up living here, kind of by accident, and I came to visit and I never left.'

'What? You're kidding.'

'I wasn't having the best time in London, I suppose. Or I was ready for a change. And I'd missed my sister, barely seen her in five years, so I jumped at the chance to be closer to her.'

'I can see why it would be hard to leave. It's so pretty here.'

'You should see it in the winter, though. You don't really know a place until you've seen it without any flowers and everything closed up. Some of the cottages have real fires and the chimneys smoke all winter. The whole place smells of coal and wood burning.'

'I bet the Siren's nice on a cold day,' Austen said, and Patti was gratified to hear the dreamy warmth in her voice.

'Oh, it is! When the fire's crackling and there's no tourists.'

'Spoken like a true local.'

'I suppose I am one now.'

'You're going to stay?'

This threw Patti. She'd been asked it before, of course; mainly by Joy, who'd got it into her head that Patti was staying for her sake, and that Clove Lore had been less of a choice and more of a convenience for her. There was the tiniest bit of truth in that, she supposed, but she'd never admit it to her sister. Joy still needed her. And a big part of Patti still needed her big sister, or at least, the daily reassurance that she was safe and happy after all those years not knowing where in the world Joy even was.

'I'll stay a while longer,' Patti said.

'Is there somewhere else you'd like to live, or work?' Austen was really digging now, but rather than discourage her, Patti tried to answer truthfully.

'I haven't given it much thought. There was London for years, and working twenty-four seven, living with flatmates, always out somewhere, always busy. Then there was the dash to Clove Lore when Joy needed me, and then Minty needed someone to get her out of a hole with her business. You'll be surprised to know she's not the best at dealing with suppliers and tradespeople.'

Austen laughed and Patti caught sight of the tiny crinkle lines at the sides of her nose. She should have innocently thought they were cute, but the sight set off a tiny flame in her core. It wasn't just cute.

'You're catching the sun,' Patti said before she could stop herself, and she'd raised her fingertips to Austen's freckled temple with no inhibitions kicking in to stop her.

Austen didn't stop her either, in fact, she brought her own hand up to meet Patti's and they both froze like that, nail tips touching the peachy freckled spot by her eye.

Austen was the first to break the soft, electric connection, looking down with a laugh, blushing.

'What was I saying?' Patti said, joining her in laughing.

'You were telling me if there was somewhere else you'd like to be?'

'Not right this second.'

'No!' Austen, mock annoyed, thumped her arm. It felt beyond amazing. 'For work. Or to live?'

'Right, right,' said Patti. 'I've not really been anywhere. I did always think I'd travel. Didn't even make it to Ayia Napa with my mates.' The space between them wasn't quite so alive with the chemistry crackle of moments ago. Patti's posture softened a little. 'What about you? Are you staying in Manchester?'

'No idea. You are supposed to know, though. People get kind of mad when you don't have it all worked out the closer you get to *thirty*.' Austen said the word in a deep, doom-filled voice and seemed delighted to make Patti laugh again.

'Tell me about it. But you're only twenty-three, twenty-four, right?' Patti said, sweeping away the invisible judgy people making Austen feel inadequate.

'I'm twenty-five.'

'Ach, there's loads of time. I'm two years older than you and I'm happy with my houseplants and my books, and all this...' She gestured to the bands of pink clouds interspersed with tangerine now spreading over the whole panorama of the horizon. The sun was still a complete golden disk, half an hour from sinking, Patti reckoned – and she knew her Clove Lore sunsets.

Deeper into the meadow's centre they progressed, chasing the patch of bobbing red poppies. It didn't matter that there were others around; in fact, it made everything easier, taking the pressure off.

'I wouldn't mind visiting Paris,' Austen said, and it sounded like a confession, so Patti treated it like one.

'Then you should.'

'I might. After this.'

Austen meant after her bookselling holiday, Patti knew. It struck a heavy note. She'd be leaving here in a week. She had dreams of going to Paris alone. Or more specifically, without Patti. Obviously. They barely knew each other.

Still, none of this stopped Patti saying, 'I'd love to see Paris too.'

Austen seemed to let the meaning of this sink in. She must be aware Patti liked her. She wasn't known for her subtlety. In the past, her bluntness had worked in Patti's favour. Many, many times.

'You've never been?' Austen asked.

'Never had anyone to go with. Paris seems like the kind of place you need someone to go with, you know?'

Austen said she did know. 'When did you last have someone?'

'Like a girlfriend?' Patti blew out a breath and scanned the sky. 'Ages ago.'

'Really? Why's that?' Austen was scrunching her nose again, like she couldn't quite believe it. Patti's entire body answered the encouragement.

'Dunno. I always had a girlfriend, all through high school, pretty much, and then college. Long-term stuff. I'm literally still friends with all of them.'

'Oh my God.'

'No, really. Aren't you still friends with your exes?'

'Oh, I've never really had a serious thing.'

Patti nodded. 'I had unserious things too. Quite a lot of them when I first started going out in London. I went a bit overboard with it all, a dating frenzy.'

'Wow!' Austen laughed hard. 'Sounds terrible.'

'Oh it was!'

As they both laughed, Patti decided Austen didn't need to hear about the year of dates or the one-night things that often turned into lovely weekends in bed but never came to anything more (and the next week she'd see the same girl with someone else at the same bar where they'd first got chatting, and the sense of rejection would send her reaching for her apps and the next hook-up). She'd circulated in the same pool for months and eventually got tired of treading water and never finding anywhere to rest. She'd wanted a girlfriend and somehow it wasn't happening. Everyone was too busy enjoying themselves or they were falling hard and breaking up weeks later, over and over again. When she stopped going out nobody really missed her, at least that's how it felt, and she'd been relieved to retreat into work and the peaceful routines of a homebody.

Patti and Austen had reached the centre of the meadow. Patti stopped to pick a red poppy, but when she snapped the stem, the petals fell off and floated to their feet. 'Oh!'

Austen burst into laughter when she presented her with the bare fuzzy stem, its pepper pot head bobbing stupidly between them.

'Thanks a lot,' Austen said.

Patti stooped to lift two red petals, handing one to Austen and slipping the other into her own pocket.

Austen pressed the petal between two blank pages of her notebook before slipping it out of sight once more, neither of them remarking about the poppy after that, but Patti resolved to save the sight of Austen's hand held against the book at her chest alongside her other picture memories of tonight, even if it all came to nothing.

'There were people I liked,' Austen said, suddenly picking up the thread of their conversation again.

Patti didn't move, only planting her feet, facing her, letting her talk.

'There was one girl at school I spent four years pining over. She was my best friend and I never told her how I felt. In the end it was too weird and too late. She ended up going out with one of our other friends. They're still together. Haven't seen her in years. *Argh!* It's so cringe.' Austen brought up her hands to cover her anguished smile, her eyes screwed up in mock shame.

'Not at all. You were kids.'

'Hmm.' Austen seemed to be thinking about saying more, but let her hands drop to her sides, her gaze swinging away across the meadow.

'Shall we sit?' suggested Patti.

Down on the soft mown grass next to the red heart of the meadow, Clove Lore disappeared from view. Patti could only see the sky and they were obscured from the other meadow visitors. She checked Austen was happy with this, not wanting her to get spooked.

'I'm good,' she'd replied.

'Is there, um, anybody now?' Patti asked.

Austen took a while to answer. 'There was… sort of, and there might be something…' She stopped herself. 'No, it's not really a thing… it's complicated.'

'So you're not single?' Patti held her breath. She'd been here plenty of times before and it did not feel good.

'No, I'm single, that's for sure.'

'OK,' Patti exhaled hard and fell silent.

'I always freak people out,' blurted Austen. 'I'm not good at face-to-face stuff, like dates and things. I get things wrong. Misunderstand things. It's kind of my trademark.' She mimed stamping something on her forearm. 'Disaster,' she added, her lips quirking at her joke; her eyes giving away how serious she was. 'Nearly twenty-six and not adulting well.'

'When's your birthday?' Patti steered the subject to a slightly happier place, determined Austen wouldn't be sad tonight.

'November the third.'

'Oh my God, you are *such* a Scorpio!'

Austen laughed, her head bouncing back.

'You are, aren't you?' Patti pressed.

'I don't believe in that sort of thing,' Austen answered primly. 'Mum does, though. She reads my horoscope every night at dinner, and she's always like, "See, the stars said you'd do *such and such a thing* today and you totally did that!" Always looking for meaning in it.'

'I don't really believe in it either,' Patti reassured her. 'But I do believe in Scorpios!'

More laughter. Patti saw the way Austen's shoulders were sinking and her eyes softening.

'What are you?' Austen examined Patti. 'I bet you're a Leo.'

'Taurus.'

'Close.'

'Not really. What would your mum say about Taurus and Scorpio?'

'Well!' Austen seemed to stop herself saying any more, falling to scoffing and eye-rolling. 'I can only imagine.'

Patti knew full well what it meant. They'd be unstoppable together. *If* she believed in that kind of thing. 'Scorpios are creative,' Patti threw in, saving herself from dying of too much blushing. 'I know that much, and they can have laser focus, right?'

'Yep, sounds about right.'

'And they're kind of…'

'Go on, say it.' Austen sat straight up, folding her arms.

'They're kind of…' Patti bared her teeth comically.

'Crazy?' Austen suggested.

'I was thinking… intense.'

'Hmm, OK.' Austen laughed once more.

'I can hardly talk,' Patti hastened to add. 'I'm the original bull in a china shop. I charge before I think, most of the time.'

'And I'm the overthinker. Nice to meet you.' Austen had her hand out for Patti to shake.

After the initial clasp, Patti kept hold of her hand for a moment, amazed to feel Austen's grip tighten into a soft squeeze until it became obvious they weren't letting go.

A fuzzy-bottomed bee passed their noses, drawing their gaze in its wake to where it landed inelegantly on a blue flower head, bending the stem almost to the ground with its weight.

'That is a chonky boy,' Patti said admiringly, still dazed from the soft warmth of holding hands with this woman in the middle of a summer meadow.

'A total bomb of a bee!' Austen joined in. 'I wonder if the word "bee" relates to bomb somehow. Big buzzing bombastic bees.'

'The wordsmith Scorpio can't help finding poetry in everything.'

The way Austen's attention shifted from the bee to Patti made all the buzzing in the meadow stop entirely. The sun lit the seaward side of their faces, washing them in an apricot glow. It was Austen who shifted closer first. It had to be. Patti wasn't going to be the one to make the move. She wanted to have no regrets from pushing Austen too far or too fast.

'I'm glad you chose the bookshop holiday thing,' Patti said, as Austen drew her curled legs against Patti's, setting every nerve in her body alive.

'Me too,' Austen said, as their hands loosened their grip, instead travelling up the other's bare summer-warmed arms.

Patti didn't try to hide the fact she could barely breathe. She closed the last inches between them to brush her lips over Austen's, taking away her smile and replacing it with helpless parted lips, and in one tortuous press closer, they were at last locked in a summer sunset kiss Patti would never recover from.

'I like you,' Patti told her in a sigh, and Austen kissed her back all the harder.

Chapter Twenty-two

Sam had been pleasantly surprised to find that Jasper was not completely hopeless in what she'd still insisted was only a trial role, and for a temporary job, at that.

'So, do I get the position?' he'd asked after hefting the clean, folded sheets, still warm from the machines, into the back of the laundry van ready for delivering first thing the next day.

His cheeks had been pink from the effort but his hair still fell annoyingly perfectly. Sam, on the other hand, regretted being seen all hot and sticky at the end of the shift.

She'd been the one who invited him back to her house to collect his wages, and he'd climbed into the van without protest, but it was Mrs Capstan who'd insisted he stay for sausages and mash since it was Sam's afternoon off from the Big House and they both looked fit to drop.

The rescue cats had bounded into the hallway to inspect the newcomer, and the oldest of the lot, an overfed ginger tom, slumped onto his side against Jasper's high-tops, giving him his lazy, swishing-tailed seal of approval, even if Jasper didn't stoop to pet him, instead standing awkwardly, staring at the circling band of felines.

He should really have left to see how his own mum was getting on, plus he wasn't all that keen on cats, or any animals, really. Yet, catching the smell of gravy from the kitchen had been enough for Jasper to fold, and he'd asked if he could be of any help.

After lunch, Caroline Capstan, her face still bruised and bandaged from her fall like she'd had a nose job, set down her cutlery and asked, 'How many hours did you do today, Jasper?'

'Seven till twelve,' Sam put in. Weirdly, the laundry had taken way longer with the two of them than it would have taken Sam on her own. She put it down to him holding her back and the need to thoroughly show him the ropes, but it was actually because they'd spent the entire time talking about their favourite *Schitt's Creek* and *Friends* episodes over the noise of the machines running, and they'd stopped in at the visitor centre for cans of Pepsi which they drank standing in the deserted smokers' shelter.

'Let's get that settled, then,' Mrs Capstan said. 'Pass me my bag, Sam.'

She fished out her purse and counted notes and coins onto the table. Jasper averted his eyes, choosing to stare at the goldfish tank in its alcove by the telly.

'I make it fifty pounds and... nine pence,' she told him, sliding the money across the table.

Sam might have imagined Jasper would put up some resistance for the sake of his pride, saying it was too much – it wasn't; it was minimum wage – or pretending that he didn't mind helping out, just for show, or maybe he'd take the notes and ignore the coppers. But he didn't hesitate in sweeping up all the cash after holding out his hand in a solemn shake like they had sealed some big deal. The money was slotted neatly inside his wallet and stowed safely in his back pocket in seconds.

When Caroline rose to clear the empty plates, insisting the two of them stay put, she could serve custard without help, Jasper whispered to Sam, 'Does she always pay in cash?' and Sam told him she doesn't usually pay at all.

'Shall we split it?' Jasper asked earnestly.

'Don't be daft. That's all yours.'

He thought for a moment, then stood, excusing himself like this was a ballroom in *Bridgerton* and not an early Nineties new-build off the A39.

Sam heard him asking Caroline if he might use the landline to call home, but she didn't get to hear the actual conversation. He'd taken the phone into the back yard while her mum got the sticky toffee pudding out of the microwave, but she could imagine what he was saying, telling his mother how he'd found his way to some honest cash and she wasn't to worry, he was taking care of her.

When he returned to the table, bringing the teapot that Caroline had put into his hand, Sam thought he looked ethereal, like he could just as easily have floated in.

'Everything all right?' she asked.

'I think so.' He ran a hand through his hair as he sat. 'It was Jowan who answered.'

'OK?' Sam waited.

'He said Mum had lunch with them today, and now Minty's up in our apartment with her. What do you think it means?'

Sam was relieved Mrs Gold was back in the land of the living and that she'd eaten (and eaten well, if Minty had anything to do with it). 'It means Minty's got herself *involved.*'

'Is that a good thing?' Jasper didn't look too sure.

'I'd say so,' said Caroline, placing a steaming bowl of glistening, golden cake drowned in hot custard in front of him. 'Minty knows what she's doing. She may just have discovered she and your mother have more in common than she realised.'

Reassured by this, Jasper fell to eating with an inward smile. Sam watched him working his spoon, scraping up every drop of her mum's go-to comfort pudding.

When Sam threw an amused glance at her mum she knew she'd interpret it like some kind of admission. An admission that she'd been too quick to judge this guy. An admission that she probably fancied him quite a bit, actually.

Her mother hid her chuckle in her bowl but for the first time in a long time, and for all three of them, there was a sense of something new and happy and really rather special happening.

'Cup of tea, Jasper?' Caroline asked, and he sprang up immediately to fill their cups himself.

After dessert, as Sam was stretching her legs out under the table, her mum prompted, innocently, 'I think you two should go to the cinema tonight,' and she reached once more for her purse.

–

Jasper had clearly determined not to complain, even though it had felt more than a bit strange, drying her hair while Jasper showered in the little bathroom at the top of the stairs, and he was now stoically wearing a promotional 'Orangina' t-shirt from 1998 that had been left behind by her dad. Sam determined not to give away how much she was enjoying all this.

Stifling yawns, and with Jasper's hair still wet and shoved back so he might have passed for a lad from the local college, they both climbed into the van while

Caroline waved from the doorway. 'And make sure you get some popcorn!' she called after them.

It was seven o'clock and a fine evening. Caroline stood a while on the steps watching them go.

None of them noticed the figure in the grey car at the end of the cul-de-sac with the camera raised to his eye, taking shot after intrusive shot. Sam and Jasper were too busy talking and laughing as the van banged and sputtered away from the privacy of the Capstans' home.

–

It was funny how Sam hadn't realised the movie theatre in Barnton had seen far, far better days until she saw it through Jasper's eyes. All those times her mum had driven her along the coast as a kid, excited for *Toy Story* movies, *Up* and *Wall-E*.

Tonight, even as they pulled to a stop in the car park round the back, the place looked provincial and shabby. The rain had stopped on the ride over but the sky was grey and the tarmac black and wet. The open back doors of the chippies and kebab shops, the wheelie bins and litter had never looked this drab before. What must Jasper be thinking?

She winced as they walked inside to find literally nothing in the foyer had changed in as long as she could remember. Sam paid for the tickets at the old-fashioned booth – these, however, were surprisingly expensive – while Jasper took it upon himself to buy the popcorn, Sprite and a big bag of Revels.

He seemed excited to be here, so maybe it wasn't too mortifying, but when they walked into Screen One (of two) she cringed at the old red velveteen seats that were worn and stained to a degree it was best not to think too much about. She put her energy into willing the house lights to go down so he didn't look too closely. Their footprints crackled on the sticky flooring as they found their spot in the centre of an empty row, right in the middle of the theatre, but Jasper still said, 'This place is great.'

Sam looked around doubtingly. 'How many red-carpet premieres have you been to again?'

He considered this carefully. 'Not that many. Only Cannes a few times, and Mum took me to the Globes when I was six, and...'

'The *Globes*? The Golden Globes? Oh my God!' Sam flicked some popcorn at him.

'I just love cinema,' he shrugged, picking the popcorn from his top and eating it. 'It always took me away from everything – au pairs, exams, Mum and Dad fighting, and everything else.'

'I can appreciate that,' Sam said. Jasper probably had an insider's insight into the movie world from working on sets and stuff. He probably loved all those clever, arty films she thought looked tedious.

'What's your favourite movie?' she asked, and his eyes lit up.

'Easy. *Jaws*.'

'You're kidding? Why *Jaws*?'

'It's like this movie that by rights should never have been made. The whole production was beset with problems and arguments and things going wrong. Spielberg had to think on his feet, you know? Innovating as he went along. I could watch it every day for a week and not get tired of it.'

'I thought you were going to say some clever documentary about the environment or something.'

Jasper shrugged and whipped popcorn into his mouth. 'What's your favourite?'

'Honestly? *Die Hard*.'

She waited for him to laugh out loud, to mock her and say he expected her to say *Love Actually* or *Harry Potter* (both of which she absolutely loved as well, but he didn't need to know this right now). Instead, he bobbed his head, seemingly impressed. 'Best Eighties bromance, hands down.'

'Exactly!' she turned in her chair to face him, making the rickety arms strain and creak. 'Mum makes me watch it every Christmas. She likes it more than I do. And Alan Rickman's genius in it.'

'Hans Gruber! Yes! And the score! And the incidental music, have you ever noticed it? Amazing! They take the whole film to a whole other level.'

'We should watch it together.' Her heart seemed to stop. It was out. Too late to take it back.

Jasper met her eyes just before the cinema fell dark. 'We should.'

As the first of the trailers ran, Sam grew aware of how close they were, and how empty the theatre was. The seats were packed in tight and if she let herself slump in this uncomfy chair like she wanted to, they'd definitely touch thighs. This led her to worry about munching popcorn next to his ear or burping from the Sprite. She'd have to lay off it. She was about to cross her leg away from him, attempting the impossible feat of squashing herself into the corner of the small seat, when she grew aware that Jasper had leaned a little closer, his face turned to hers. He'd opened his palm. She looked down at it as he whispered, 'Is this OK?'

In answer, she slipped her hand into his. The feeling lit up her face in a blooming smile she couldn't hide as they both turned to the fanfare of the movie titles on the big screen.

Just like that, they were on a proper date – Sam's first ever date – and it felt amazing.

Chapter Twenty-three

On Saturday, Austen had made one of everything: the granola slices, the lemon-lime pie and a tall, frosted courgette cake, following a recipe that Izaak had insisted she try. He'd gone so far as to bring the cream cheese and spices himself (and of course a box of courgettes from the estate gardens), but he hadn't stayed to help in the kitchen, telling her that he and Patti were dealing with a sudden change of plan for the evening event, but she wasn't to worry about it. It would be fine. He'd been emphatic about that. And since it wasn't Austen's own event, rather one that was taking place in her holiday home, she didn't worry.

She had unboxed the books by Simon Graeme Bloom, multiple copies of *The Fallen Proud* sent by his publisher, and she'd arranged them in the windows, keeping a pile by the till for him to sign when he arrived. He sounded nice, from his author bio on the flyleaf.

> Simon Graeme Bloom writes books in a precarious garret in his (partially) restored Northumberland castle folly with views over Lindisfarne, where he has lived all his life. He is servant to two Manx cats and a rambunctious rescue tortoise named Benjamin, purported to be twenty years

old and planning on outliving the author despite Bloom's daily shoreside observational rambles and his devotion to healthful living and foraging, which he writes about in his popular weekly *Guardian* column, 'Bloom in Britain'. *The Fallen Proud* is Bloom's fifth novel for Penguin and winner of this year's Coffee Shop Book Prize.

Austen hoped he'd arrive with his own people. It had been a long time since she'd been a helper at an author appearance and she didn't fancy falling into the role again, even for one evening. She'd work the till and be the bookshop caretaker. That was her job, keeping quiet and inconspicuous in the background.

Besides, she didn't want to be too preoccupied with the event. There was Delphine to correspond with and, despite her protestations that she wasn't upset, Austen had a niggling sense the Parisian was nursing hurt feelings after last night.

She hadn't realised anything was amiss after the corn-flower field visit with Patti, who'd walked her back down the slope, stopping to hug her and tell her she'd had a lovely evening, and then she'd left, walking on down to her cottage without even asking if she could come inside or anything.

Austen had watched her go, obscured by the same hydrangea bush the pair of them had crouched behind to observe Radia only six days ago when they'd first met. She hadn't been able to stop herself smiling at the sight of Patti retreating, the cool of the evening descending fast, as she replayed the kiss – their only kiss of the evening – and the way they'd laid down in the spot by the poppies to watch the sky changing colour, toying with each other's fingers, stroking wrists and circling thumbs in smiling silence. It had been enough to make Austen bite her lip and fight the impulse to roll on top of Patti there and then, kissing her for the whole night, but they'd quickly been beset by other golden hour guests.

Patti had been the one to suggest they should probably call it a night, and they'd walked as slowly as they could Down-along, talking nonsense about fantasy travel plans, all safely noncommittal, not promising the other anything, but trying hard to make the other laugh out loud, which they did, a lot.

Patti had left Austen holding the bare stem of the poppy she'd presented her with in the meadow and, twirling it in her fingers, Austen had floated in through the door of the dark bookshop and upstairs to bed where she'd slept the whole night in peace.

This morning had brought the notifications as soon as she switched her phone on.

'*Bonsoir*. Shall we look at the stars? I have cooked us some *moules*. Not that you can taste them, but you must imagine them. The recipe is from this book.'

This was accompanied by a photograph of a nineteenth-century gastronomy, all words, no pictures, and there were greasy smears and marks on the page. Austen didn't have time to wonder if they were Delphine's spills or historical ones as there were more unanswered messages from her.

'Are you cooking tonight? Tell me what you are eating.'

'Austen? Are you there?'

'The *moules* is a joke. I know you are vegetarian.'

'Should I worry? Are you with the book club people again?'

'Austen? It's late. You worry me.'

The last one had been sent a little before two this morning and had made Austen's cheeks burn coming to realise the anxiety she'd caused.

'I will not sleep. I do not know if you are alive or dead. Respond, please. I miss you.'

Austen had typed her reply that morning with flying thumbs, sending back words to say she was fine, she'd been out walking then gone straight to bed, she'd been so tired. No need to tell Delphine she'd been with Patti; that felt wrong somehow.

'I'm so sorry,' she'd told her friend in Paris.

There'd been silence until after lunchtime when the shop had been loud and busy with browsers forced indoors by a rain shower. Today was a day for shopping and sitting in cafes sipping coffee, not for paddling on the beach or exploring the estate gardens. Austen heard the ping as she was ringing up a bundle of Ordnance Survey maps and a dictionary of humorous English idioms for a customer.

It read, 'I forgive you.'

Austen had taken a while to think about this. Had she really done something so wrong that it warranted forgiveness? Was this just Delphine's wry, Gallic way, or was she in earnest?

Austen composed and deleted various replies until she struck upon, 'Good. I don't want you to be upset.'

'Also, perhaps I overreacted? Please don't disappear again. I wanted to phone the English police but how to explain where you may be?'

'I doubt they'd have come looking for me,' Austen replied, even with a shop full of customers wanting her attention. 'You need to be missing for twenty-four hours before you can file a missing persons report. Or maybe that's just what happens on TV?'

There'd been more silence after that and Austen had cajoled Delphine with silly bookshop anecdotes for a couple of hours, sending GIFs from the TV show *Black Books* of the grumpy, drunken bookseller throwing tantrums in his shambolic shop. She'd titled them things like, 'Me right now if someone asks another stupid question'.

There'd been smiley reactions, eventually, followed by a few comments about how the Feint Heart was particularly tiresome today. At four, Austen shut the shop and climbed the stairs so they could talk properly.

'I wrote a poem, actually,' Austen had typed, partly because it was true and she wanted to let Delphine know she was responsible for getting her writing again; and partly because she wanted to smooth over any lingering tensions between them, and this felt likely to tempt her into talking.

'Austen Archer writes poetry??' the reply came.

'I do, actually. Or rather, I haven't for a long time but you helped me pick up my pen again.'

'Let me hear some,' Delphine asked.

Seeing the words made Austen quail until Delphine followed them with a naff animated GIF of a bouquet of cartoon flowers and the bouncing words '*s'il vous plait*', not at all like her, but Austen took this as a sign they were making better progress than she'd supposed.

Within moments she was sharing the poem she'd read aloud to the unimpressed kids yesterday at Storytime.

She hit 'send' after every stanza, ensuring it was too late to take them back.

When she'd finished, there was a painful wait for a reply, so she'd typed, 'That's it. I told you it's possible to write bad poetry. Say something. I'm dying here.'

'"You and me, in a world of books"?' came the response, as Delphine quoted her opening line back to her. 'Who is it about?'

Austen stared at the words. Who, not what. Who was it about? How did she answer that without looking crazy?

Austen took a breath, reminded herself out loud that she had barely any dignity left to lose, so why not? She told the truth.

'It's inspired by you and our conversations.'

She watched the grey dots bounce on the screen for an age until the reply arrived at last.

'It is *incroyable*! Beautiful! You have written a wonderful thing. A story of us! Thank you!'

Austen let out a breath, astonished. 'You're not weirded out?' she asked.

'Why would it be weird? You and I have an exceptional thing.'

Austen looked at the screen. It was true. They had a connection she'd never felt before, certainly not with a stranger. Except, Delphine didn't feel all that much like a stranger anymore.

'I think *ink drinker* would be better than "we are the papyrus eaters", no?' Delphine was saying. 'We are the ink drinkers'.

Austen scrolled back to look again at her verses. Delphine's way was a better fit.

'Not as obscure?' Delphine insisted.

'Right,' Austen typed back. 'We are the ink drinkers. How did you come up with that? I love it!'

226

'*Buveur d'encre* is a saying typical of France for greedy readers. Like your English book eater?'

'Ah! Bookworm, you mean?' said Austen.

No reply, and no bouncing lines appeared. In the lull, Austen typed, 'The poem says that I create you, because I sort of have to.' She hit send before worrying she wasn't making sense. 'Because there are things about you that I don't know,' she added. 'Gaps I have to fill in for myself. Like, where are you from? Do you have someone special in your life? Do you live alone? There's stuff I'd love to know.'

She'd waded in so deep now she was in danger of drowning. She clicked the camera icon and snapped a selfie of herself making a peace sign beside her eyes, smiling, and before she could hesitate, she sent it.

'This is me,' she wrote. 'Are we doing this? Are we filling in the blanks for each other?'

Worst-case scenario, Delphine asks her to respect her privacy and they go on as before, keeping one another company. Yet, that felt almost impossible now that they'd had the strange breakthrough of Delphine staying up into the night, terrified for Austen's safety. Delphine's messages this morning had felt something like a tiff, and now here was Austen willingly sharing the poetry Delphine had inspired, and it wasn't scary at all. It was easy, actually.

The reply came immediately. 'You're very pretty, Austen. I will send you a photograph tomorrow when I have slept. I was awake all night afraid you were disappeared. I look bad.'

'I won't mind what you look like. I bet you look great,' Austen told her.

There was another ping.

For a second, Austen thought Delphine had capitulated, but the image that appeared on her screen was of some French actress from a black and white movie with a lit cigarette in a long holder. 'This is what I look like most days,' Delphine joked, adding a laugh-crying emoji.

Delphine must have known this was a cop-out because she kept typing.

'Please accept the following. To fill the gaps, as you ask: I was not born in Paris, but in St Etienne. My parents sent me to school in Paris and I did not spend much time at home after that. They are not like your English parents, like Mary Poppins. They are cold.'

Austen held off responding, and the messages kept coming.

'After school, I worked in Paris and I studied English. I was a waitress for ten years. Ten years of emptying ashtrays and drying the water circles under glasses, yes? Can you comprehend how bad this was for me? All my friends are married, or live in the country and Paris is so expensive. *Par conséquent*, I am alone.'

This made Austen's heart ache.

'Does this answer your questions?' Delphine went on. 'I should have told you before, but I was ashamed. It is unhappy to be alone and without family or many friends. Not pleasant. And I wanted you to like me and not pity me.'

'I'm sorry,' Austen replied, 'I shouldn't have pushed you. But you've got Polonius, haven't you?' she added to lighten the mood. 'He's your friend.'

'??' came Delphine's reply.

'The stray pets guy? Sorry, I was trying to be funny.'

'Let us not say sorry again. We are beyond sorrys. Austen, tell me more poetry please. I want to close the shop and take my phone to the tower. It's raining here.'

'It's raining here too.'

While the drops grew heavier on her bedroom window and the afternoon sky darkened with clouds rolling in off the Atlantic, Austen typed her verses and sent them to the woman who had unlocked them.

She tried not to think of the blank looks that the grown-ups had given her at Storytime yesterday, or the suspicion that Patti had listened as she recited her poem about her Parisian counterpart. Austen had got the strange feeling Patti hadn't liked it, the same way Callista hadn't liked her writing, but she put all of this to the back of her mind and tried to accept Delphine's praise, even though the poems looked so thin and underdeveloped on her screen. Delphine seemed to love them and they'd talked for a long time after.

The bang at the shop door at half six made Austen start up from the bed, dropping her phone. 'The book event!' she shrieked.

Even in her panic, and despite her horror of ever being late for anything, she still grabbed her phone and let Delphine know that she was needed in the shop for the next couple of hours, but she'd be back by nine and they could pick up where they'd left off.

'Don't worry. I'll be back. I promise.'

Delphine assured her she'd be there waiting and signed off with 'xoxo' before Austen dashed downstairs, cursing the events programme for interrupting her conversations with Delphine and hearing more funny, heart-rending revelations about her life.

They'd only just discovered some shared tastes in music, and they admired the same artists and a few film-makers. They'd even shared similar experiences in school (Delphine had loved art classes and abhorred maths, just like Austen).

They'd been inching closer to sharing their experiences of dating, and Austen had been on the point of telling her about her best friend back in sixth form and how she'd adored her in secret for years and could never tell her. She'd wanted to go into even more detail than she had with Patti the night before. She could tell Delphine anything and not worry, somehow.

She was going to tell her how the whole thing had crushed her confidence at seventeen, confirming her worst fears about herself, that she wasn't suited to rela-tionships, destined always to mess them up. She'd tell her the whole thing later tonight, spill it all out, risk-free, but now there was work to do.

Austen hauled the shop door open without lifting the blind. *Patti will not be impressed when she sees the place isn't ready…*

…but there on the step with her hand raised to knock again was not Patti Foley, prepped for hosting tonight's book event, but her old boss, Callista Flyte.

Chapter Twenty-four

For the first time since arriving in Clove Lore, Jasper was smiling. His second laundry shift had been even harder than the first, what with Saturday being the big changeover day and so many more cottages requiring fresh bedding and towels, but despite the hard work there was some new kind of exciting tension vibrating between him and Sam since their cinema date the night before.

She'd driven him home to the Big House after the film, dropping him off, and he'd foolishly hopped out the van thinking she'd get out too, but she'd stayed in her seat, the engine running, so there'd been no goodnight kiss. Not that he necessarily *expected* her to want to kiss him, but he'd hoped.

For the first time in his life, he was coming to see the significance of first kisses. Up till now he hadn't given it much thought. Kisses just sort of happened to him, and frequently, too. Club kisses, and Uber kisses, and penthouse kisses. Things that probably hadn't meant much to the girls, he was fairly sure of that, because they hadn't really meant that much to him, he was coming to realise. Not now he had the idea of kissing Samantha Capstan in his head and making this first move suddenly seemed like a huge deal.

She'd put her lips to his cheek, down on the slope when he'd offered himself up as her laundry helper, and it had set off firecrackers under his skin, but it had felt impossible to make it happen again. Maybe, he was figuring out, this kind of thing was *supposed* to feel momentous and a bit firecracker-y? One thing was for sure, if an actual first kiss did happen, he wanted it to be as amazing as he imagined it would be.

Today it hadn't felt like the right time, since they were working and the laundry was sweaty and stuffy in spite of the rain and just not the right place. Even when there'd been so many moments when it felt like it might happen as they'd squeezed past the open machine doors or lifted the bundles together into the van.

In the end there'd been a great deal of awkward laughter, awkward in a sort of exhilarating way, and the whole shift had flown by, and somehow it was over and she was handing him the envelope with his name on it, in Mrs Capstan's handwriting.

He'd walked back to the Big House afterwards, via the convenience store at the visitor centre where he'd blown his pay packet on two big bags of groceries, all the while giving himself a stern talking-to about how that was precisely not the correct way to part from Samantha for the rest of the day. A cheery 'See you, then,' hadn't sent the right message at all.

He was like this around her, he was learning. Like a different person. A nicer one, but also cowardly. He should have said something smooth and confident, flashed his grin, all the stuff that had worked on the Chelsea girls. But at work, when Sam was observing him, wide-eyed and without an ounce of wile or pretence, impressing girls didn't feel quite so much like a game. There was something at stake with her. For the first time in his life he was afraid of messing up. This meant something.

And yet, all these thoughts were obliterated by the sight that met him when he struggled with his shopping through the door of Apartment One.

He'd expected a repeat of last night when he'd returned from his cinema date; Minty and his mum sorting through boxes, imposing order, and his mum telling the stories of each object or garment.

'This? Oh, I wore this dress to a Chelsea Clinton benefit in Yonkers. It was for, I want to say… sea lions? Or was it teen drug recovery centres? I forget. *But* I do know I paired it with my Birkin 25 and the Gucci pump.'

Minty had been banging on about how if you 'buy cheap, you buy twice' and instructing Estée on the correct way to store her cashmere.

'Mind you, I don't buy *at all* these days,' she'd been saying while she worked. 'The curse of the Big House dweller, I'm afraid. Pin money always ends up directed towards the latest leak or rustiest thing. But when I did shop, long ago, I bought quality, and you see…' She'd held out her arms to indicate the twin set that looked laundered, lavendered and pressed a million times. 'I take care of them, and they last. Aquascutum, dear. Style over fashion.'

Estée had evidently approved of this, and the pair had chatted on, sharing stories from the different sides of the waspish world they occupied.

But as he opened the door today, tired after a hard morning's work, it took a while for Jasper's eyes to adjust to the unexpected darkness. The curtains were once again drawn. Everything was worryingly silent.

'Mum?' Jasper asked into the shadows.

Estée was hunched in front of their gilt coffee table in the dark, her arms clasping her legs, her chin to her knees.

'What's happened?' He flew to her side.

She pushed the newspapers on the table towards him. 'It's out,' she said.

There it was. The awful thing they'd been waiting for: the notice in the *Gazette*, announcing the bankruptcy of Mrs Estée Gold, with the notice to her creditors to contact her old lawyer to arrange recovery of outstanding debts.

'OK,' Jasper said, taking a deep breath. 'I'm glad. It's done, isn't it? We don't have to wait for it to come anymore.'

'Jasper…' his mother began, but he was cut short by the knocking at the door.

'This can't be bailiffs? If we're insolvent, all our debts are written off, right?' he asked, making for the door.

'Jasper!' his mum yelped again, staggering to her feet, reaching for a second paper beneath the first, but it was too late. He'd opened the door.

There stood Samantha Capstan, white as a sheet, holding out a local paper. She was panting like she'd run all the way up here.

'Well?' Sam said, letting him see the front page and the headline, 'Gold Playboy Hides Out in Devon', with a photo of himself in a borrowed Orangina promotional t-shirt and damp hair, climbing into a battered laundry van with Samantha in the driver's seat. The photographer had caught her grinning at Jasper.

'Oh!' Jasper's shoulders fell.

'There's this too,' Estée said, approaching the pair, showing him the folded-open pages of the *Sun*. The same picture, only smaller and accompanied by a telephoto shot of Estée being walked across the Big House lawn wrapped in her bedsheets, Jasper's arm around her on the night of the book club. 'They've been watching us, waiting for the announcement, I suppose,' Estée said, handing him the paper.

'Jasper, you didn't tell me you were waiting for big news to break,' Sam said. 'Didn't mention the fact we'd all be front-page news either. You could have told me. I could have helped.'

'I, uh…' Jasper's mouth continued to move, but in his exasperation, no words came out. How was he supposed to tell her that the waiting had been torture? That he'd known every case of bankruptcy in the country was announced in the *Gazette* for every journo across the world to sleaze over? How do you tell someone you don't know, but you really actually properly fancy, that your life up to this point has been controlled by a father who, it turns out, could up and leave without even saying goodbye, running off with a Croatian model only a couple of years older than Jasper himself? How did he admit to being cut off by the man who'd cosseted and protected them all this time, and now they were screwed by a clever prenup and laws written in complicated legalese by men just like his father, designed especially to let them get out of family obligations without so much as a backward glance? It had been bad enough finding themselves evicted and exiled to the countryside. Did he have to tell nice, genuine people who he'd only just met his sob story too?

'I could have been prepared, at least. I could have warned Mum!' she went on, tearing the paper from Jasper's hand. 'Slumming it by the seaside,' she read the subheading out loud. 'Notorious playboy Jasper Gold is rumoured to be dating a laundry worker, Samantha Capstan (20), a sign of the hard times the London-based love rat has fallen on.'

The article went on to list the double-barrelled names of transatlantic heiresses he'd been photographed with in recent years and, to really hammer home their fall in fortunes, they'd dredged up a collage of yacht shots and pool parties, benefits and awards ceremonies where Jasper and Estée stood polished and poised for the cameras they clearly used to love.

She kept reading. 'A trusted source close to the family told us of their surprise at the twenty-one-year-old socialite consorting with commoners, saying that Jasper claimed the washerwoman was "a bit of fun" to distract from the family's downfall. "Knowing Jas, he'll be back on his feet and on the scene before the season's over," our source commented.'

'Oh my God,' Jasper snatched the paper and his mother broke into fresh tears behind him. 'Oh my God,' he said again.

Sam watched on, still catching her breath, her eyes welling with tears.

'Did you say that? That I was a bit of fun?'

'No, of course not! I, uh…' Then it hit him. 'Bloody Tom Faulds-Bowles!' What had he said? When Tom was fishing for info about the local girls? He couldn't recall exactly but whatever he'd told him, he'd have been trying to be discreet about his whole situation here.

Had Tom been crowing about their phone call to the rest of the gang in some club? Had someone overheard, one of the guys' hangers-on maybe, and rung the papers with a titbit of gossip, looking to make some cash?

Estée drifted back to the sofa and melted down into it. Jasper's eyes followed his mother.

'Did you say that?' Sam said again, taking a step back, her arms dropping to her sides, her face pained.

'I wouldn't have used those words exactly,' Jasper began, but Sam cut him off with a cry of her own and her hand thrown to her mouth. 'I'm sorry, listen…' he called out, but Sam was already running down the corridor.

'It's over,' Estée sobbed from the couch, shaking uncontrollably now. 'We're finished. Jasper, get me my pills. Quick, I can't stand it!'

The familiar feeling of being trapped once more washed over him as he saw Sam turning the corner and disappeared out of sight.

'Quickly! And my sleep mask!' Estée howled, snapping her fingers.

Jasper slowly closed the door and turned to face the darkness.

Chapter Twenty-five

'It's you,' Callista said as the rain fell in the courtyard around her and she closed a black umbrella.

Austen automatically stepped aside, letting her into the bookshop, but no words came to her. Callista was soundlessly snapping her fingers and squinting.

Oh, no. She couldn't remember her name.

'It's Austen.'

'Of course, of course,' blustered the author. 'You work here now?'

'It's a working holiday,' was all Austen could manage before Patti bounded into the shop.

'Ah, good! You've met. Simon Graeme Bloom was stuck in…' She paused. 'Where's he stuck?'

'Frankfurt,' Callista chimed. 'Air traffic control strike.'

'That's it, Frankfurt… And Ms Flyte shares an agent with Simon, and ta-dah! She kindly accepted his invitation to come and help us out. Isn't that amazing?'

'It is amazing,' Austen said, not quite believing what she was hearing.

Callista was scanning the shelves like a hawk.

'We don't have any of your books in,' Austen said, pre-empting her. 'I mean, I've sold the ones we had. We're all out.'

'Not to worry.' Callista swept a hand. 'Jasmine's bringing the boxes now.' At the door appeared – as if conjured by her boss – a tall girl with shiny black hair to her waist and an eager-to-please expression that Austen recognised as the one she used to wear.

'Where should I put them?' the PA asked, and it took Austen a moment to remember her manners. 'On the desk is fine, thanks. I'll put some in the windows, but we'll have to be fast.'

Patti, who'd had her eyes fixed on Austen all this time, jolted into action and made for the cafe to gather chairs.

'Do you need anything?' Austen asked Callista, falling right back into her old role. 'Water? Something to eat?'

Callista, however, was burrowing in the big pocket of her white linen jacket and pulling out a pearl-chambered vape. The sight of it set off something within Austen like nostalgia.

Callista excused herself and Austen turned to gather a bundle of books from Jasmine.

'How's the latest release selling?' Austen asked, examining the hardbacks.

Jasmine seemed shocked at her bluntness but didn't say anything at all.

'Sorry, it's just... Never mind.' Austen supposed she had no right to ask, but a prickling possessiveness washed over her all the same. She wanted to say, 'I used to be you' and fought the urge to ask, 'Does she call you in the middle of the night too?'

Jasmine was beautiful with huge soft eyes and a quiet, elegant way of moving. She was younger than Austen by quite a few years, by the looks of her. A recent under-graduate, she reckoned. She'd already set out the book-plates and Callista's special book-signing pen with the little cloth to rest her hand on to prevent smudges. Now she was producing from a bag the kombucha Callista had been devoted to for years.

'She still drinks that stuff then?' Austen said, hoping her smile didn't look as pained as her heart felt.

Jasmine shot her a look. 'Still?'

'I worked with Callista, a long time ago.' *With, not for.* Austen knew she wasn't being as welcoming as she should. She hated this about herself.

Did Callista ever take Jasmine to her private members' club for lunch, or let her use her day spa pass like she had Austen? Did she upgrade her to business class when they flew, or was she stuck in economy on her own? She wasn't going to ask. She had a tiny bit of pride left.

'I'm Austen,' she yielded. Jasmine showed no sign of recognising the name. 'She probably hasn't mentioned me much.'

Jasmine shook her head. 'Not at all,' she said, and it felt defensive.

Patti came back into the shop now, hefting a stack of chairs. She was watching them.

'Can I get you a cup of tea?' Patti asked.

'No thanks,' Austen said, before realising she'd meant Jasmine. 'Oh, sorry. I'll just…' She pointed her way to the window shelves, giving herself a hard mental kick and telling herself to stop being weird.

Through the glass, Callista was pacing the courtyard, drawing on her vape as though it was life support. She looked exactly the same, Austen thought. Just as austere and glamorous as always, and kind of ageless too. Nobody knew how old she really was, and no interviewer dared ask. Austen suspected she was in her mid-fifties by now but couldn't be sure. She took her time replacing the

Bloom titles in the window display with Callista's books, keeping her eyes fixed on her.

'Do you want to do something after?' came Patti's voice at her shoulder.

'Oh! Um...' Austen flinched then tried to recover herself, remembering her promise to Delphine. 'I might be busy afterwards, sorry. I agreed to... this thing, and...'

'Right, of course, no worries.' Patti backed away.

'It's not that I don't want to, only I promised someone and...'

'Don't worry about it.' Patti sounded firmer this time, so Austen let it go.

How could she tell the woman she kissed only last night that she was secretly looking forward to spending the evening talking via an app with someone she'd never even met? If she hadn't promised her time to Delphine, she'd go anywhere Patti wanted to go.

Patti had withdrawn, unboxing wine glasses across the room now, and she'd said it was fine, so it probably was, right?

Austen recognised the sinking feeling. It meant she was messing up on all fronts, yet again, and she didn't know how to make everybody happy at the same time. And now Callista was here.

She peered at her. She'd want to talk as well, wouldn't she? She'd want to catch up, tell her all her book news? And there was still this thing unresolved between them. This was Austen's chance to get it out in the open, to talk about that kiss and all the awful stuff that came after it.

'Who am I giving this to?' Jasmine asked, holding some printed notes, Callista's biography for the start of the event.

At that moment it dawned on Austen that Jasmine's t-shirt, worn under a blazer and with black shorts, read 'Boulder County' and there was a picture of a buffalo and the words, 'Where the Rocky Mountains meet the plains'.

'Boulder's in Colorado, isn't it?' she heard herself saying.

Jasmine didn't respond.

'And Colorado's where Callista's ranch is.'

'Who's going to introduce her?' Jasmine said, ignoring the question and looking a little pleadingly between Austen and Patti.

'It's Patti's event,' Austen said, keeping her eyes fixed on Jasmine.

'Yeah, but it's your bookshop. You can do it if you want,' called Patti, who was busy tidying a corner of the bookshop that really didn't need tidying right now.

Austen should have said, 'No, not on your life,' and run straight out the door all the way back to Manchester, but the absolute worst parts of herself were clamouring for attention and healing. 'I'll do it,' she said. 'But I don't need notes.'

'You don't?' the two women chimed at the same time, and Patti and Austen exchanged brief glances, Austen's shamefaced and Patti's straight-up confused.

Jasmine left the papers in Austen's hands anyway and pulled the door open, calling out into the courtyard, 'Make-up time, Callista,' and it was so informal and easy, the way she summoned her. Austen would never have dared do that, but there was Callista switching off the vape right away and walking directly inside.

'Can we go somewhere private?' Jasmine asked, holding up a cosmetics bag, a new one, not the one Austen had carted around for two years.

Patti answered for her. 'There's a small bedroom by the stairs there. You're not using it, are you, Austen?'

Austen shook her head and drifted into the kitchen to think, that stupid Boulder t-shirt still in front of her eyes.

She ran through the options. Callista had brought it home as a souvenir for Jasmine. *Very* out of character. She'd never given Austen gifts from her travels. Or it belonged to Callista, and Jasmine was wearing it. Again, the very idea of sharing anything with Callista, touching or borrowing her stuff, seemed outrageous, and she wasn't a t-shirt sort of woman anyway. Or, and she liked this possibility the least, Callista had taken Jasmine out to the ranch.

Bella from the Siren called in then with the chilled white wine and orange juice, but Austen struggled to hold a conversation with her, she was so agitated. Patti said something about 'stage fright' and how Austen was going to do the introductions tonight. Bella smiled in sympathy and then was gone.

Austen pottered in the stacks after that, telling herself she was making the place tidy, all the while eyeing the door to the bedroom, which remained closed.

The audience filed in and Patti welcomed them, ticking their names off her list. Most of the book club arrived too, even though some hadn't bought tickets for the original event; they'd only decided to come when they heard it was Callista Flyte making an appearance tonight.

Mrs Crocombe and Izaak sat together, and Jowan appeared with Aldous, closely followed by Bovis and then Jude, who'd brought her tall, long-haired husband, Elliot, with her. They all seemed very eager for a glimpse of the superstar author.

'Much more exciting than Simon Russell Gloom or whatever he was called,' Mrs C. announced loudly, and Jude discreetly corrected her, saying, 'It's Graeme Bloom.'

As the time drew nearer to seven and the chatter in the shop reached its peak, Patti cornered Austen at the far end of the Lifestyle and Gardening section.

'Are you OK? You've gone a funny colour. I can introduce Callista, if you want. That was the plan anyway.'

'I have to tell you something.' Austen panted like she'd run a race. Folding over, she held her hands to her knees.

'Are you sick? What's the matter?'

'It's Callista.'

Patti only listened.

'When I said it was complicated with somebody and I messed up...'

Patti looked down the shelves to the door by the stairs. 'It was her?'

Austen nodded, holding her stomach.

'Oh!'

'I was her assistant.'

'I thought you were going to say *girlfriend*.' Patti tried to laugh, but seeing Austen struggling to compose herself, she stopped. 'What is an author's assistant? Like a PA?'

'Not exactly,' said Austen. 'I mean, there wasn't really a job description as such. I responded to her ad in *The Bookseller* looking for an author's companion.'

'A companion?'

'I know, I know. It was unusual.'

Austen recalled her dad remarking that it sounded worryingly like a mad old duchess in some Victorian novel looking for someone to fan her and chaperone her to church, and that was precisely why Austen applied. It was intriguing and like an adventure into a world she'd never had access to.

'She wanted someone to manage her diary, book her appointments and taxis, keep her company when she was in the thick of writing, that sort of thing.'

Patti was squinting, suspicious. 'Still sounds a bit weird.'

'It was my dream job. Everywhere she went, I went. I kept her home stocked up with groceries and stationery supplies. I dealt with the fan mail so she could concentrate on writing. She'd be at her desk from nine till five every day, like she worked in an office, you know?'

'Really?'

'I guess that's how you write fifty-three novels and umpteen screenplay adaptations.'

'It's not how I imagined writing would be. It's not very romantic.'

'Oh, but it was!' Austen blurted. 'In a way.'

Austen saw Patti absorb this with a little flinch. 'Is that how it went wrong?' she asked, and Austen could only nod, feeling ridiculous.

'I'm sorry for being like this. I wanted you to think I was cool and not a complete mess.'

'I think you're very cool,' said Patti. 'Only, maybe not when you're hiding in your own bookshop. Go on, get out of here. I'll do the intro.'

'Are you sure?'

Patti sent her on her way with a kiss on her cheek and a hug Austen didn't want to stop, but with a groan she made her way to the cafe.

All evening, Austen listened from her perch on the cafe countertop. Patti read Jasmine's pre-agreed introduction notes, and the room burst into applause when Callista revealed herself, stepping from the little bedroom into the spot in front of the cash desk apologising for the 'let down' but she was 'dear Simon's stand-in' this evening. She'd stayed on her feet the whole time, pacing slowly back and forth, doing her usual routine, telling the same stories Austen had heard many times before, her audience predictably laughing along, just as charmed as everyone always was. Austen didn't need to see it to know exactly how it looked.

Then the Q&A began after what seemed like forever, and Mrs Crocombe was the first to speak up.

'I want to know just how you do it. Writing big house-bricks of books every year...' This got a laugh, none louder than Callista's delighted hoot. 'And you write for the telly, and you travel all over. How do you do it?'

Austen hopped off the countertop and came to the cafe door, remaining hidden, turning her ear to the room. 'Don't say it,' she whispered.

'It's all down to having the perfect assistant, isn't it?' Callista began. 'Jasmine, here, take a bow. Jasmine keeps me in check, runs my whole life for me, and all I have to do is sit down and type. I couldn't do any of it without her.'

Just like she'd praised her own dear indispensable Austen.

Austen took off her glasses and softly pinched her scrunched eyelids. Did she really deserve this? Had she been so disruptive and unkind to Callista that the universe was repaying her with this hideous cosmic coincidence?

'I'm wonderin' what your 'usband thinks of all this?' Bovis butted in. He obviously hadn't put his hand up.

An ominous sort of silence fell. Austen knew what was coming next. The brush-off. Something along the lines of, her husband helped by taking care of their ranch, and they reunited as often as possible. Wasn't she fortunate to have such an accommodating man in her life? She blessed the day she met him, etcetera, etcetera.

But instead Callista said, rather coolly, 'Well, it's not common knowledge yet, nor does it really need to be, but the fact of the matter is, we're separated as of last year, and...'

Austen emerged from the cafe so she could see it for herself. What exactly did Callista look like when she was finally telling the truth?

'And that's that!' the author said, with a nod towards Patti to let her know the questions had better move on.

'Anyone else?' Patti asked, nervously, throwing a glance to where Austen was standing open-mouthed behind the rows of chairs. 'No? OK, let's begin the signing then, shall we?' she added quickly, ignoring Izaak with his hand raised.

Austen worked the till while Callista met her public, smiling for photos and asking them to kindly spell their names for her because she'd hate to make a mistake. When the last books were rung up and the customers had left the courtyard it was nine o'clock already.

Delphine would be waiting.

Patti, Jude and Elliot were removing the chairs and Jasmine waited at the shop door with Callista's bags and coat, a picture of efficiency.

'Jazzy, go and wait in the car. I'll walk up the hill myself,' Callista announced. Jasmine gave Austen one hard look before she left.

'Shall we step outside?' said Callista, clutching her bottle of kombucha and a wine glass and, without waiting for Austen to answer, she walked out into the courtyard and pulled up a chair. Austen followed right behind her.

'What's going on in your head?' she said, no sooner had Austen perched across the table from her. 'You've worn that thunderous, haunted expression since you opened the door to me. Out with it.'

Austen immediately dismissed about a hundred things she didn't have the right to ask her former employer. Jasmine, her divorce... none of that was open for discussion, she knew that, so she tried to settle on the few things she needed clarity on.

Jude skipped past with her husband. 'We'll be off then, night-night,' she said.

Then Patti followed. 'What should I do?' she asked, plainly.

Austen suppressed a desperate urge to hug her. 'You should go and put your feet up. I'll do the last bits of tidying up. Let's do something tomorrow, yeah?' She hoped Patti understood this meant she'd explain all the rest tomorrow.

There was no goodnight kiss this time, but Patti still asked if she was sure she'd be OK. It was supposed to sound meaningful, Austen knew.

'I will be,' she replied, and nodding, Patti walked away, her eyes on the cobbles, setting off the sickening sense in Austen of simply not knowing how to keep everybody happy and that she must be seriously testing Patti's patience.

–

'What about your job?' Callista's coolness stung more than if she'd still been angry with her. 'Austen, I have room service and a bubble bath waiting for me somewhere near Bristol airport, can you please help me out here. What is it you're trying to say?'

Austen tried again. Maybe she wasn't being clear enough, but directness was never her strong suit. 'It's just, I've often wondered about how it ended.'

Callista was shaking her head like she could barely recollect it. 'I'm not following.'

'You do remember, don't you? At your book party?'

Callista grew still, her lips thinning.

'Please don't say you don't know what I'm on about. This is hard enough. You and me. We...' Austen had no idea why she was lowering her voice, there was nobody around. 'We kissed,' she whispered.

'No.'

'No?'

'You kissed me if I remember correctly,' said Callista flatly.

Austen drew upon all her strength. 'I'm not sure that is how it happened. There'd been so many... moments before that. When it felt like it was going to happen. Please don't pretend I imagined it all. I really don't think I did, and I thought, I still think, that we might have had something, if we'd done something about it.'

Callista looked tired. She exhaled a long breath before carefully picking her words. 'Austen, I was aware that you admired me.'

'You were?'

'It's my job to be aware of feelings, even those implied or unsaid, and you were, well, you were very easy to read.'

Austen's heart picked up in its rhythm. This was excruciating.

'But you didn't *like* me,' Callista went on. 'Not in that way. You only think you did. You saw in me what you wanted for yourself and you confused it for attraction.

That's what I mean when I say you admired me.' Callista shrugged. 'It happens.'

'I can't believe you're saying that. You know you kissed me first, and when I kissed back, you didn't stop me.'

Callista sighed. 'Perhaps I did. I'm sorry. I shouldn't have done that.'

'You didn't like me at all, then?'

'You were a very efficient assistant.'

'You know what I'm asking. Please, help me here.'

'Then I'm sorry. No. I didn't have feelings for you. You're a very sweet person, but I wasn't interested in anything more than work. Look, I do have to go. Jasmine's waiting.'

Austen felt the words cued on her tongue. *Is Jasmine more than work? Do you like her admiring you? Or do you actually like her back?* But she didn't say any of that.

Callista pushed her chair back.

Desperation gripped Austen. She'd never get another chance to understand what happened if she didn't push through the shame and feeling utterly stupid and just tell her how much all of this had impacted her.

'I felt like you cut me off from everything, just when I was getting started. You ditched me.'

'How could we continue to work together? It was unprofessional...'

'You told me I wasn't a good writer.'

This made Callista stop. She fixed Austen with a concerned look. 'I'd never say that to anyone.'

'You did. I showed you my poems and you said...'

'That they were still your immature work? That all poets go through their juvenile phase before they find their voice?'

'Words to that effect, yes.'

'And you believe I was wrong?'

This swiped the air from her lungs. 'Well, yes… No. I don't know.'

'When you asked for feedback were you expecting only compliments?'

Another direct hit.

'How old are you?' Callista was looking at her now like a puzzle to crack.

'Twenty-five.'

'*Hmm.*'

'What does that mean? *Hmm?*' Austen mimicked the sound.

'You are too old to be this lost.'

'Hah!' Austen gasped.

How was this going so badly? Callista was supposed to be confessing she'd had feelings for her, admitting she'd been unfair, unkind, dismissive. She wasn't even willing to admit she'd been hurtful and now she was calling her immature?

'I'm sorry, but it's true.' Callista went on. 'I merely commented on how you hadn't found your voice yet. You'd barely found your feet! And it looks like you haven't done much searching since then. Please, Austen, don't use me as the reason you stopped your writing journey. Poets aren't born. I hate to break it to you, but they're not. They make themselves. There is no muse. There's bum-in-seat word-catching. There's soul-searching. There's hard graft and working on your craft. That's it.'

Callista searched Austen's face for understanding, growing exasperated. 'You always used to look at me just the way you're looking at me now, like I was this special creature. You had stars in your eyes then too, but I worked for all of this, cultivated myself.' She pointed a finger to her own chest. 'It's called self-discovery.'

Austen's insides crumpled like paper in a fist. It hurt because there was truth in it.

'I never once lied to you, Austen, or to myself, in all the time I knew you. I loved my husband. I did not want a relationship with you. I was sorry to lose you as my PA, but that's all that happened there.'

'You were cruel. You said I was more paper and ink than flesh and blood to you.'

Callista really had had enough now. She'd taken her first few steps towards the passageway onto the slope, but this stopped her.

She turned, looked into Austen's eyes and said with a firmness blended with blunt compassion, 'And I meant it.'

Austen let her go, listening to the scuff of her sandals on the cobbles until it got lost in the rustle of night air through the courtyard palm tree.

Chapter Twenty-six

On Sunday morning, down at the foot of the slope, in the kitchen of the old fisherman's cottage with the sunflowers by the door, Joy Foley was pouring two mugs of tea, one for her, one for her sister, while Radia dipped toast soldiers into a boiled egg, pretending she wasn't listening in.

'So, you left her talking things over with her ex?' said Joy.

'When you put it like that it sounds a lot worse than it actually is,' Patti replied, still in pyjama shirt and shorts, and emptying the dishwasher.

'But you said she's still hung up on this woman? This older, powerful, glamorous woman?'

'I didn't say any of that,' Patti protested, noisily throwing the cutlery into their plastic compartments in the drawer. Annoyingly, everything her sister had surmised about the situation was true.

'I don't like it,' Joy persisted. 'I'm sure Austen's a lovely girl, but if she's messing around with other people you need to steer well clear.'

'There's such a thing as giving someone the benefit of the doubt,' Patti said, eyeing Radia, who was theatrically peering at her iPad, both eyebrows raised in sham interest over *CBeebies*.

Patti lowered her voice. 'I'm pretty sure that Callista was abusing her power over Austen, exploiting the fact that she has all these younger women fawning over her, starstruck.'

Joy poured milk into the steaming mugs and indicated with a jolt of her head they should move out of earshot of the six-year-old, who let out a disappointed '*aww*' as they moved through to the little den. 'Can you at least speak up a bit?' Radia shouted after them.

'No!' chorused the sisters, and Joy laughed.

Joy laughed a lot more these days; she was transformed, really. Everybody remarked on it. Even her posture was different. She stood tall and open, and everything about her had softened. But etched in her brain was the memory of running away from a bad man, and that she'd never shake.

'If it feels even the tiniest bit *off*, you should stop things now, before she draws you in any further,' Joy warned, standing by the fireplace, which was full of dried flowers.

Patti curled up on the low couch, cradling her mug. 'She likes me,' she shrugged.

'Does she? Has she called you since your date? Isn't it her turn?'

'Turn? Have you read a rule book for dating or something? There's no turns.' Patti knew she sounded like a defensive teen. Deep down, she felt it really was Austen's turn to bring something to the table.

'You've done all the chasing...' Joy went on.

'I've never chased anyone in my life. Look, it's just fun. A holiday thing. She'll be leaving in six days, anyway.' With every word Patti's heart sank lower. She wasn't fooling anyone.

'Just be careful, please. It's good that you're dating again, but I don't want you getting hurt by someone not into you enough to understand that her spending the night with her ex isn't a nice thing to do when she's just started seeing you, and…'

The doorbell rang, stopping Joy before she could spiral further.

'I'll get it!' yelled Radia, accompanied by chair legs scraping on flagstones.

'You sound like Mum,' Patti hissed to her sister.

She wanted to point out that nobody knew for sure whether Austen had spent the night with that awful author woman, and that one casual wildflower meadow date didn't constitute 'seeing' someone, but Patti had to admit she'd struggled to sleep last night wondering if Austen was falling back into old bad habits with Callista Flyte. Did Austen have the will to resist her if she tried it on? Would Austen even want to resist? Ugh! It was maddening how Joy could read the situation like this.

Joy was still talking. 'Mum was smart enough to warn me about… him.' She let her voice fall to a whisper. They tried not to talk about Radia's father within the child's hearing. 'And so were you, once. And I should have listened to you guys. Just promise me you won't throw your heart at someone who isn't going to be good for you. Someone who isn't making you happy.'

'Austen *is* making me happy!' Patti all but yelled, just as Radia appeared, dragging a surprised-looking Austen behind her.

Patti sprang to her feet.

'*You've* got a visitor,' Radia beamed, looking between her aunt and the blushing bookseller.

'Uh, hi, everyone,' mumbled Austen, taking in the whole room with a weak wave. She seemed to realise nobody was going to say anything and that Patti was simply watching her expectantly, her eyes shining, so she added, 'I, uh, wondered if you wanted to come out with me today?'

Patti shot her sister a meaningful look, while Radia broke into a little dance, jiggling Austen's arm.

'Are you going on *a date*?' the little girl sang.

'I don't know,' Austen said, waiting for Patti to answer. 'Are we?'

'I'll get changed,' Patti said, grinning, and pointedly handing Joy her mug. Making for the stairs, she added, 'Come with me, Austen, if you like?' and the pair of them climbed up, Joy making a grab for Radia who'd been innocently set on following them.

'I was worried that woman might have killed you,' Patti said, hurriedly brushing her teeth, while Austen sat down on Patti's unmade bed, watching her through the en suite door. They'd been in her bedroom for precisely thirty seconds and Patti was wasting no time in getting ready for their date.

'Did you think she looked angry with me?'

'*Hmm*, not angry as such. But she was pretty scary.'

'I never thought so. I guess I always found her... impressive.'

'I'd gathered that much,' Patti said wryly, before rinsing her mouth and drying her face.

She emerged from the bathroom, ruffling Austen's hair as she passed. Austen pretended to be bothered by it, scrunching her curls to fix them.

Patti pulled open the wardrobe doors. 'Are you OK? Seriously now.'

Austen inhaled deeply and blew the breath out hard. 'Well, I didn't die.'

'But you got some stuff out in the open?'

Patti was unbuttoning her pyjama shirt. Austen turned her back and fixed her eyes on the floor, trying to control the flush of heat across her face. Where did Patti get all this confidence from? Austen would have got changed behind the locked bathroom door and still been embarrassed.

'I did,' she said, forcing her brain to stay on topic. 'It wasn't great, to be honest, and she gave me some tough stuff to think about.'

'*Hmm*, well, I hope she's thinking about things too. I didn't like her,' Patti said, punctuated by the soft rustle of getting dressed. 'I'm sorry, but there it is. I don't think Callista is as nice as she wants everyone to believe.'

Austen accidentally turned her head at this and found Patti pulling what would once upon a time have been a bright red Kate Bush t-shirt over her head. 'Say what you really mean,' she said, averting her eyes only after catching the tiniest glimpse of her soft, beautiful belly.

Patti then pulled her hair back into the smallest messy knot, curls falling round her face and tendrilling down her neck, confirming that everything, even looking amazing, came so easily to her.

'If I was saying how I really felt, I'd have said that I think that woman's an exploitative dickhead, but I politely kept that to myself.' That grin again. Austen couldn't help smiling, even though she was tired and her head hurt from staying up late again.

Delphine still hadn't replied to her message apologising for the event running over. Not strictly true, the overrunning thing, but she'd wanted to wait for their next proper conversation to tell her everything about Callista.

All she'd told Delphine was that she'd had the strangest night and asked if she was still up, but Delphine hadn't responded. No amount of refreshing the chat summoned her, so she'd gone down to the little bedroom at the foot of the stairs, at first just to see the place where Callista and Jasmine had prepared for the event. She hadn't been sure what she'd been looking for: signs of some heated tryst, maybe? A sense of Callista somehow left behind? Her aura?

There'd been nothing there but an empty Evian bottle, which she'd thrown into the wastepaper basket. Austen had laughed at how ridiculous she'd become, standing in the little room, repeating aloud the words, 'I'm too old to be this lost.'

Callista hadn't been wrong about that. But it wasn't strictly true that she hadn't done any growing at all. There'd been a whole bunch of new experiences these last few days. She'd made progress since coming to Clove Lore, hadn't she?

'Wakey, wakey!' Patti was saying through Austen's thoughts, coming to sit beside her on the bed, making the mattress bounce. 'Did you sleep at all last night?'

'I look that good, huh?' Austen tried to joke, but Patti wasn't going to be put off. There was a touch of concern in her gaze.

'I… kind of stayed up writing most of the night,' Austen confessed. 'Poetry.'

Patti nodded, slow and careful.

'I was trying to write the other day when you found me on the harbour, and I couldn't.'

Patti just listened. She'd clamped her mouth shut so her lips turned pale.

'But then after seeing Callista again, it turned out, I had lots to say. So I wrote it all out.'

'Let me hear some then.' Patti turned her body to face her. 'And don't give me all the protesting that it's no good and stuff, just read it. I'm nice. I listen.' She pressed her hands together like an angel and pulled what was supposedly an innocent pout of some kind.

'I don't know, it's so amateurish…'

'Ah–ah!' Patti raised a warning finger, silencing her, and something gave way inside Austen. She handed over her notebook with a doleful look, but she didn't feel anywhere near as bad as she'd expected.

Patti turned the pages, coming to a stop in the middle of Austen's messy scrawlings.

'A kiss that should not have happened?' she said, reading one of the titles. 'That's not about us, is it?'

'No, of course not.'

'Can I read it?'

'Knock yourself out,' Austen said, all bravado.

'Pupils tightened to two black dots,' read Patti.

'You're reading it *out loud*?' Austen interrupted.

Patti laughed and carried on.

'Pupils tightened to two black dots,
her hand swipes over cursing lips.
She retreats in fury and wanting.'

Patti lifted her eyes. 'Wow! That's intense, Austen.'

'I was feeling intense when I wrote it, I guess. I was trying to remember the moment I started gaslighting myself about Callista. She fired me because we kissed.' Austen let this information hang in the air for a moment. 'And I know she wanted to kiss me. I could see it, and I could feel it. So, I wrote out what I actually saw. She admitted kissing me back, last night, but she maintains it was a mistake. She apologised, actually.'

Patti took this in.

'I'm starting to think that maybe it wasn't the healthiest of working relationships,' Austen continued, smiling wryly. 'We both made mistakes. Probably should have ended a lot sooner than it did, for both our sakes.'

Patti nodded, closing the notebook, shutting in all the things Austen had agonised over all night when she'd been trying to make sense of the things Callista had told her.

'OK,' Patti said, decisively. 'So, Callista stole last night and, from what you're saying, quite a big chunk of the last few years for you. Can we at least salvage today for us?' Her lips curled into a smile. 'You said you were taking me out somewhere? I'm ready if you are?'

Chapter Twenty-seven

All the way up the slope, Austen refused to tell Patti where they were going.

After the rainfall of yesterday the air was clear and the day full of promise, as though everything had been washed and all the bad stuff taken away on the tide.

Austen inhaled the freshness as they climbed, up past the cottages and onto the path to the visitor centre.

'Did it help? Seeing her again?' Patti asked at last, as they passed the touristy fudge concession and the convenience store.

'She told me I didn't want to be *with* her; I wanted to *be* her. That I admired her too much.'

Patti let her eyes flit to Austen's. 'And what do you think of that?'

'I didn't agree. Not at first, anyway. But I thought about it all night. She said I was starry-eyed about her. I think that's probably true.'

They crossed the big car park at the visitor centre where the Sunday day-trip coaches were parked up and the cars were still spilling in off the main road.

Patti had been quietly thinking, but said, eventually, 'That woman fancied you, Austen. Make no mistake.'

Austen dismissed this with a wry laugh, but she nevertheless hoped Patti would go on.

'She must have had her own stuff going on too,' Patti said. 'I'm thinking she might not be perfect after all.'

'Oh no, I knew that,' Austen agreed. 'Or, at least, I figured it out last night.'

'The husband stuff?' Patti guessed.

'Yeah. I always thought she was in denial about her feelings for me, or for women in general, maybe? But now I'm thinking she really did love that guy, whoever he was. Whatever it was, I'm hoping that now, maybe, she's in a happier place.'

'With Jasmine?' Patti was kind enough not to look at her now.

Austen sighed and shrugged. 'Who knows? Maybe. Or maybe she's just as stuck as she always was, and she's doing the same thing with her as she did with me. Whatever's going on there, it's private. But I reckon she likes her in ways she didn't like me. I believe that much is true.'

Austen stopped now in front of a little stone cottage at the far side of the car park. There were hanging baskets frothing with pink flowers. Austen wasn't so lost in intro-spection that she didn't notice how the colours, against Patti's t-shirt, made the pink of her lips pop.

'Must sting a bit though?' Patti's voice was gentle.

'It's just a bit strange. Maybe a bit sad. I...' Austen stopped herself.

'Go on, you should say it out loud.'

Austen blew out a big breath first. 'I stopped writing because she said I was in my juvenile phase. And, I think... she was right. There! I said it. She was right, and I took it to heart like it was some big insult and I got totally blocked. Last night she said I wasn't growing like I ought to be.'

Patti gave a sceptical frown. 'From what you've told me, she's not one to talk about growing. Kissing assistants isn't exactly mature, is it? Or ethical?'

Austen took this in. Callista was far from perfect, but it had been Austen putting her on a pedestal and admiring her out of all proportion, and yes, she *had* wanted to be just like her.

'I've lost years of writing time when I should have been practising and improving.'

Patti was having none of this. 'You're still so young. There's plenty of time. And I don't know if anybody's told you this before, but you're allowed to be a bit crap in your twenties when you're still figuring stuff out.'

'Thank you! That's the nicest thing anyone's said to me,' Austen mugged, her hand to her heart, but her smile soon fell again. 'Callista said I was too old to be this messed up.'

'I think you're doing fine. What would she say about *me*? Living in some random seaside village, looking after my sister's kid more than I need to, as a distraction. I should be making plans, being intentional.'

Austen took Patti's wrist. 'Maybe we're both finding our way.'

'And that's OK,' Patti said, smiling again. 'The all-seeing superstar Callista doesn't get to have the last word on you,' she added.

This, however, sent Austen's brain back down the rabbit hole of last night, and hidden deep down there were Callista's last words from yesterday telling her yet again that she hadn't felt alive to her in the ways Austen wished she was.

'Patti?' Austen said suddenly, looking into her green eyes. 'I'm flesh and blood.'

'Uh, I know that.'

'OK, good.' Austen stepped closer. Patti's smirk turned into something more serious, and she tipped her head in response to Austen leaning in until their lips met.

When they kissed this time, Patti wasn't as reverent as she'd been at the cornflower meadow when she'd clearly been holding back. This time, she brought her hands to Austen's face, running her thumbs softly over her cheekbones as she kissed her deeper, not hiding how her breathing was turning shaky the longer they touched.

Austen let her hands rest on Patti's arms where her muscle moved softly. The feeling weakened Austen's core, turning her soft, making her sigh into the space between Patti's lips.

This was kissing. Not a desperate, painful thing, stolen at a boozy book party, tasting of vapes and regret.

When they moved apart, Austen's vision was hazy. Patti was blinking like the sun was suddenly too bright.

They both laughed at nothing.

'So,' Austen cleared her throat. 'This is what we're doing today.' She jerked her head, indicating the cottage behind her.

Patti took a moment to read the sign by the door. 'A paper-making workshop?'

'Is it stupid?' Austen contorted her face.

'No! It's perfect, actually.'

They looked at each other in a new, delighted, exhilarated way before pushing through the door and Austen told the craftsperson inside that they were their eleven o'clock appointment.

Chapter Twenty-eight

Patti had no idea the art of making your own paper was so messy, or came with quite so many opportunities for getting closer to your paper-making partner. Even though that's exactly what the textile expert, Morwenna, said she'd intended when setting up 'Pulpitations Paper Dates'.

The estates cottage, once an eighteenth-century milking parlour, now an historical oasis on the tarmac shore of the vast visitor centre car park, was low-ceilinged and entirely whitewashed, decorated with strings of bunting and twiggy mobiles. Seaglass suncatchers sparkled in the two low windows. Morwenna's grey-white hair was wrapped many times and piled up on her head, bound inside a colourful batik cloth. She wore a floor-length kaftan and a lot of big jewellery.

'This is like the bookshop's twin,' Austen said, while the owner gave them a quick tour of the equipment, which looked more like a hippiefied kitchen than an art workshop, set out as it was with an ancient butcher's block table cut with deep grooves from decades of use and multicoloured with seeped-in dyes tinting the old oak.

'Blender, basin, drying area. OK?' the woman said, pointing to everything. 'And over here,' she added with a flourish, pulling open the doors of a shabby French press closet, 'is my textile store.'

She proudly stood aside to let them look inside.

'Wow!' Patti reached in to touch the neatly cut squares of fabric in every colour and texture.

'We'll be using recycled textiles in our paper today,' Morwenna said. 'Pick one.'

Austen had insisted Patti choose and she dismissed all the scraps of shot silk and towelling, hemp and wool, choosing instead a simple patch of faded blue with white cottony rips and stray strands.

'Denim,' the woman said. 'Good choice. You'll be repurposing scrap remnants of the most polluting garment on the planet, jeans, into artisanal paper. OK, pop that scrap in the blender.'

'Really?' Patti wasn't sure what was going on.

'It needs breaking down into its individual threads. Austen, you add some water.'

The gentle strains of whale song and gongs emanating from hidden speakers was broken by the loud grinding of the jug blender as it tore the scrap to threads.

It didn't look great, but Morwenna seemed pleased with the end result. 'Perfect. And now, into the pulp.'

The sloppy mess of old shredded newspapers and paper packaging they'd helped tear up when they arrived had been sitting in a big cauldron by the bare brick fireplace looking increasingly like gloopy wallpaper paste the longer it soaked.

The instructor passed Patti a basin to fill with pulp. 'Dunk it in – you want it two thirds full. Good, now drop in your threads, and mix.'

'Mix how?' Patti asked.

The woman held up her hands and wriggled her silver-ringed fingers delightedly. 'Go on, both of you. Get your hands in.'

The pair exchanged smiling glances. The pulp was cool and surprisingly silky when Patti plunged in up to her wrists. Austen poured in the sloppy mess of shredded denim, then sank her own hands under the surface.

'Give it a good mix. And when the threads are distributed you can add some petals, if you like.' Morwenna produced a tray of small clay bowls, each one filled with different coloured petals. 'I've got dried rose buds, orange nasturtium, sunshine-yellow calendula, white pansies, violets…' she reeled off.

'Cornflowers, please,' Patti and Austen chimed at once, spotting the delicate blue blades.

'Don't be shy then,' the woman said, and even though Austen's hands were messy, she picked out the bowl and sprinkled the cornflower confetti into the pulp.

'And mix?' Patti guessed.

The tutor nodded her encouragement, stepping further off to allow them to concentrate on swirling their hands in the basin.

At first Patti tried to avoid Austen's fingers under the opaque shallows, but Austen reached for her fingertips. A quick glance told Patti it wasn't accidental; Austen's smile said as much.

Patti let her fingers roam across the smooth backs of Austen's hands, feeling all the way to her wrists which she enclosed in a gentle grip.

A new focus came over her. Patti knew Austen could feel the sudden shift too. This was no longer innocent paper-making but something fiendishly sensuous and soft. Patti wanted to lean her forehead against Austen's and explore hands underwater all afternoon.

'Time to turn the mash into paper,' Morwenna said delicately.

Austen, who'd been high-spirited and laughing before, was quiet now, her eyes alight.

The teacher wordlessly demonstrated the last stage in the process, showing them what looked like a picture frame with a taut cloth stretched across the aperture.

They both lifted their dripping hands from the basin while the woman lowered the frame in, keeping it level, then after a quick submersion in the goop, raised it again. The liquid strained through the cloth mesh.

'And what's left of the pulp, fabric threads and petals has formed a really rather beautiful leaf of paper.'

The next bit didn't look quite so easy. Morwenna transferred the frame to the drying area where some cloths were laid out flat, and she quickly flipped the frame over, leaving the thin, wet sheet deposited on the cloth.

'That will be dry by tomorrow morning,' she assured them.

'Ready for you to write poems on,' Patti intoned for Austen's ears only.

Austen's smile bloomed pink like her heart was swelling with happiness.

'Now, I'll leave you two alone,' Morwenna announced. 'Make as many sheets as you wish. The studio is yours for the next hour.'

'You're leaving us?' Patti tried not to sound too pleased.

The woman only smiled a twinkling smile. 'If you want to leave before then, just pull the door shut. I have my keys.'

She was gone in moments. Patti watched her through the low window, climbing onto a bike and cycling away across the car park.

'Is she working for Mrs Crocombe?' asked Austen.

'Maybe she's got money on us?'

Austen cocked her head.

'Nobody's told you about Mrs C.'s betting book?' Patti said, lifting the paper-making frame again. 'She runs a book on who's going to get together in the village.'

'Shut up!'

'It's true. They're all in on it. Izaak especially, he's the worst. And Minty.'

'No!' Austen was laughing, but she still clutched her elbow in a self-hug. 'You think there's bets on whether we'll get together?'

'I heard there was an early bet on you and Kit, the new chef at the Siren.'

'What!'

'Don't worry. I've been in that book for a whole year with my name beside literally every woman travelling through.'

Austen eyed her, not sure if she was enjoying this anymore. 'Nobody's won any money off you?'

'You have to get together with someone. I never did. Not even close.'

'Yet.' Austen said, before pulling her lips closed.

Patti tried not to react, for Austen's sake. A hint of worry had crept in around her eyes again, and she wanted to wipe it all away and get back to the easy joy of messing around with the gloop.

'Come on,' she gestured with a nod. 'We've only got an hour.'

They moved back over the basin again, sinking the frame together, lifting it and letting the excess liquid drip through.

'You think Mrs C.'s money's safe?' asked Austen in a quiet voice, and Patti leaned her head against hers as they watched the paper form inside the frame.

Before they could lift it to the drying table, a notification buzzed from Austen's tote hanging on the back of the workshop door.

The way she pulled her head away felt oddly jarring for Patti, who was suddenly alone with her hands dripping over the bowl.

'I'll switch that off,' Austen said as she went.

But having wiped her hands on her apron and retrieved her phone, Austen spent a few moments by the door, reading the screen.

'Everything OK?' Patti asked across the room, suddenly aware it was a little chilly in here with all the stone and hard flags underfoot. She hadn't felt it until now.

Austen kept her back turned, her head down. 'Uh-huh,' she was saying, distractedly. She was typing.

When Austen returned, Patti could see the light from her phone glowing through her apron pocket. She hadn't turned it off after all.

'Sorry. I'd been waiting for a reply,' said Austen.

'Friend from home?' Patti asked, moving across the room and turning the paper out onto the cloth to dry. She handed the empty frame to Austen. 'You can do this one.'

'Not exactly,' Austen said, cagily, Patti thought. She dipped the frame and pulled a new sheet from the pulp, letting it drip. 'It's someone I met online, actually. We've been chatting a bit.' There was a blush across Austen's cheeks. Patti much preferred when it had been her that put it there. She tried to squash down the little jealous streak that was taking her entirely by surprise. This wasn't like her at all.

'That's nice?' Patti hadn't meant it to sound like a question.

'They've been super nice to me,' Austen replied, not meeting her eyes. 'It was her who got me writing poetry again.' Austen turned out the sheet onto the cloth. It didn't go as well as Patti's efforts, slipping into one side of the frame as it came out, getting crunched up. 'Aw, I spoiled that one.'

'Do one together?' Patti suggested.

Austen nodded, a little of her earlier enthusiasm gone, Patti sensed. As they held the frame together another message arrived on her phone. Austen reached for it immediately.

'Sorry, it's just, they've been ill overnight,' she said, sheepishly. 'They're a bookseller, in Paris, actually.'

Patti didn't say anything.

'I can reply later. Sorry.'

Patti could feel Austen's agitation. She wanted to talk to this person in Paris more than she wanted to do this. This called for some acting. 'No, no,' Patti said. 'You'd better take it. Sick friend, and everything.'

'You sure?' Austen was squirming.

'Hundred per cent.' Patti did her best to look unbothered, even shooing Austen with dripping hands.

'I'll only be a minute.' Austen took her phone right outside the workshop door, leaving Patti to turn out the last sheets of paper alone.

–

'Thank you for coming with me today,' Austen said again as they walked back down the hill.

Patti had been a bit too quiet for comfort and they'd left the workshop before the Pulpitations lady came back.

'Thanks for organising it.'

Austen nodded, feeling a little desperate again. She'd only stepped outside for five minutes, not even that; just long enough to be sure Delphine was OK. She wanted to make Patti understand, but somehow showing her their exchange felt like rubbing her nose in something she shouldn't.

The Parisian's first message had been characteristically effusive.

'I have a terrible fever and nobody is looking after me. I slept through your messages last night. Nightmares and sweats. Horrible!'

Austen had asked if she could get out and see a doctor, or at the very least find someone to help nurse her better, but Delphine confessed she had nobody.

'I closed the Feint Heart. I am in my apartment alone eating chicken noodle soup. It is depressing!'

'I wish I could be there to help, you poor thing.'

'Don't feel sorry for me, I'll weep. This is the worst thing about being alone in a city.'

'What can I do to help?'

'Keep me company?'

'I will later. Right now, I'm out.'

'You are not at the borrowing bookshop?'

'I'm paper-making with Patti, one of the shop volunteers.'

'You're on a date?'

Austen hadn't known quite how to reply without making Delphine feel more alone, so she fudged it and replied, 'Just getting to know each other.'

It had taken an oddly long time for the reply to come through, and when it did Austen had exhaled in relief.

'I only want you to be happy, Austen.'

'Me too. I want you to be happy, and feeling well again. You should rest.'

'I should. I am very sick indeed. If I'm dead by morning please tell Polonius not to bring his animals to my funeral.'

Austen had laughed, then glancing back into the work-shop window to check Patti wasn't watching, she told Delphine she'd be in touch later, signing off with, 'Get some sleep. I'm thinking of you.'

Austen knew now she'd made a mistake, leaving the date she'd dragged Patti to. It was supposed to be her way of thanking her for all her help with the events, and her concern over Callista, and for the golden hour meadow date.

'Are we OK?' Austen asked now as they trudged Down-along.

'Course we are.' They were almost back at the book-shop. 'But I should get on with some work.'

'Really? You don't want to get some food, or…'

'Thanks, but I have a bunch of emails waiting. I'll see you at the Storytime on Thursday.'

'Oh, OK.' Austen had blown it. 'And I can't tempt you to a drink at the Siren?'

Patti appeared to be thinking about it, but the notific-ation sound from Austen's phone made her come to a halt by the turning for the shop passageway.

'Who is she? This person in your DMs?' Patti asked, the sparkle gone from her eyes.

'Just a bookseller friend, in Paris.' Austen added a small shrug.

'But you talk all the time?'

'Kind of. They get me. I get them.'

'Do they own their own bookshop?'

'Uh, actually, I don't know.' They hadn't talked about the ins and outs of it all, and Austen had simply assumed Delphine was a kind of shop caretaker, working alone, all hours of the day and night.

'How did you find them?'

Austen felt her temperature rising.

'They just messaged me when I arrived here,' she said, attempting another shrug. 'They liked one of my TikToks.'

'Do you...' Patti inhaled deeply, like she hated asking. 'Know what she looks like? I mean, not that it matters or anything, only...'

Austen didn't want to say no, for some reason, so she interrupted with, 'They were going to send a photo today, but they got sick.'

Patti fell silent, considering this.

'Oh no. What does that face mean?' Austen wanted to know, suddenly feeling embarrassed and defensive.

She could tell by Patti's body language that she was trying not to say something, but just couldn't stop herself. 'Nothing. It's just... what do you actually *know* about this person?' Patti fixed her eyes on the cobbles.

Austen knew immediately what she was driving at. She replied as reassuringly as she could under the circumstances, but she couldn't deny the heat rising across her chest. This was humiliating. 'They're not some weird scammer, if that's what you're thinking.'

'I didn't say they were. You just have to be careful. My sister — who's the smartest person I've ever met — like, we're talking genius level — got taken in by this guy. He was super nice at first, then he turned demanding, wanted all Joy's time and attention, and eventually he isolated her from me and from Mum and Dad. He stole all her money…'

Austen tried to keep calm, but this riled her. 'I'm not stupid, and I've only been chatting with Delphine *online* for a week. And they haven't asked me for a thing, or even once told me what to do.'

Austen, however, couldn't help searching her brain for instances where Delphine might have done those things. She couldn't pinpoint any exactly, but there was a growing unease in her belly.

'Well… that's good,' Patti was saying. 'Just beware of any red flags, OK?'

Austen couldn't reply. She fixed her eyes on the slope.

'It's just…' Patti was clearly trying to squeeze some lightness into her voice. 'I get the tiniest impression you might not always be the best judge of character.' She even gave Austen the gentlest nudge with her elbow, as if to prove this was all still banter. 'I mean that in the nicest way. You want to overlook people's flaws, seeing only the good in them. It's not a bad thing.'

'Are you talking about Callista?' Austen felt herself shrinking.

Another ping came from her phone. It was maddening to feel this torn and this stupid.

'All I'm saying is get a photo,' Patti said. 'Some proof that they are who they say they are. It shouldn't be hard.'

Austen wanted to defend herself. She knew stuff about Delphine. She'd seen their hands in a video filmed in a bookshop. She'd heard their life story, sort of. They were messaging from the bookshop's own account. They'd even sent pictures of books they were selling, and that one of the rainy street outside the shop. There'd been a few lunch pictures of whatever she was eating that day. How could

Delphine do any of that if they were lying about who they were? They're obviously genuine. Why wouldn't they be? Why would anyone waste hours of their life lying to a stranger online?

The fragments of pride that Austen had worked hard to rebuild in the past few days stopped her saying any of this. Instead, she nodded like she was taking on board Patti's advice. 'I'll see you at Storytime, then?' she said, standing still, feeling small, as Patti turned Down-along.

'Of course. Thanks again for the paper-making. I loved it.'

'You're sure we're OK?' Austen called stupidly after her, while messages from Paris chimed on her phone.

She couldn't help looking at the latest message.

Are you still on your date? D, x

Chapter Twenty-nine

'Hey. How are you feeling now?' typed Austen, later that evening.

'Terrible. *J'ai fait* a small *sieste*, and now I drink espresso.'

'Should you drink coffee when you're ill?'

'I don't understand this question.'

'OK, well, just keep resting.'

'Talk to me. I will read your messages and rest. Tell me about the date. Who are they?'

'You sure you want to know?'

'Talk!'

'Well, her name's Patti and she's an event planner.'

'Attractive?'

Austen hovered her thumbs over the letters. Telling the truth felt wrong somehow but she wouldn't lie about Patti.

'She's very pretty, yes. Curly hair, green eyes, and she always wears bright red or pink clothes, like the total opposite of me.'

'You prefer the black and grey. Classic. Me also.'

Austen thought how she hadn't always dressed this way; years ago she'd been a kind of muted rainbow dresser, but that stopped with Callista. Austen had, she realised, chosen monochromes to complement the author's all-white linen look that she was as famous for as Jackie Collins was for leopard print.

'I've been thinking recently I should wear brighter things,' Austen typed.

Lately, meaning *since meeting Patti*, she realised. Was she really as suggestible as Callista had implied? She guessed so.

'But black is very chic,' Delphine told her.

'I thought you wanted me to do all the typing?'

'That is true. I am dying. Go on.'

'When she walks into a room she makes it come alive. You know? Like she's pure sunshine. And we've been on a couple of really nice dates.'

'She likes you a lot.'

'Maybe not so much now.'

'What did she do? Must I come to England to fight her?'

Austen laughed against her will. It hurt, but she did it.

'It was silly, really. But it was about you. She said I'm naive for not asking for some proof about who you are. I know. It's ridiculous. And that's what I told her, and I think she ran out of patience with me.'

Austen didn't add that her constant messaging with Delphine had been the thing that initially tested Patti's patience. The disagreement was simply the last straw. Austen's eyes teared up, making it hard to read Delphine's reply.

'What proof does she need?'

'I know. It's offensive, right?'

'*Non.* I think it is sensible. Do you trust *everyone* you meet online?'

Austen's shoulders settled now, the muscles relaxing. She hadn't even known they were hunched up.

Delphine was typing again. Austen made a secret wish she was sending a hasty selfie so that all this suspicion could be put to bed immediately. Austen would never admit it would be reassuring for her too. But the reply, when it came, wasn't what she'd hoped.

'I am tired again, Austen. I will return to bed. Will you sleep? Or will you worry all night about this Patti?'

'I'll sleep,' Austen replied. 'I'm sorry if that made you feel awkward. I don't want it to, especially when you're ill. But I wanted to explain what was happening. Anyway, I really, really like talking with you. You've been such a good friend to me here.'

'Me also. I like talking with you very much. You don't understand how special you are to me. *À demain*, D.'

But Austen wasn't done yet, and the lack of a kiss at the end of Delphine's sign-off made her panic. Was she upset with her too? Was there no one Austen couldn't piss off this week? So she typed some more.

'I really would love a photo, just so I can picture you, nothing more, x.'

Austen sent her message, the last of the evening, it turned out. The little check mark appeared. Delphine had read it. There wasn't much more Austen could do now.

More exhausted than she'd realised after the last few roller-coaster days, Austen solemnly pulled the covers over herself and thought of her mum drawing three tarot cards of three lovers, all turned on their heads. Austen knew every reading was open to interpretation and relied on context and character. She also knew to be cautious about attaching significance to random, meaningless things, only right now, she felt especially superstitious.

At the back of Austen's brain as she tried to sleep, she couldn't help but wish life would offer her a simpler hand, but she knew, even deeper down, that she could have played this so much smarter than she had. She should have listened to the warnings for what they were. Now nobody was happy, and it was all her fault.

Chapter Thirty

A blustery Monday morning had shoved any clouds far inland, leaving Clove Lore utterly awash in a painterly blue. Up at the Big House, the wind was making the windows rattle. Jasper, however, didn't notice any of that.

Peering down from his spot behind the curtains of the big bedroom in Apartment One, he was scanning the estate's hedgerows and field margins looking for telltale telephoto lenses reflecting the late July glare.

'I still think you ought to visit the poor girl,' Estée Gold said from behind her very last Baume De Rose facial sheet mask.

Jasper couldn't understand how she'd woken up so chipper. He'd expected at least a month of her hiding under her bedclothes weeping and dribbling incoherently. Now here she was, chivvying him along with relationship advice while dealing with her long-neglected skincare regimen and her correspondence at the same time.

'I've got nothing to give her,' Jasper said, coming to sit cross-legged on his mum's bed, which she had made all by herself long before he'd even woken up, something he didn't know his mum was capable of.

Maybe it had something to do with their discovery that she'd finally run out of appetite suppressants and quaaludes from that quack in Myrtle Beach? Was this what she was like when she wasn't self-medicating? It had been so long he couldn't quite remember. Whatever this change was, it was weirdly unnerving. She'd cried, of course, for most of the day before, and thrown herself around dramatically until she'd worn herself out, and she'd slept for a long time, but after that, she'd emerged serene and calm.

'She was a nice girl,' Estée pressed.

No one was disputing the fact that Sam was nice. She was perfect.

'Didn't you see the look on her face, Mum? She couldn't have had any idea what it's like to be splashed all over the internet and the tabloids. She's from a totally different world. And you know they wouldn't leave her alone if we were seen out together again.'

He shuddered at the idea of the pair of them being surreptitiously snapped by shelf-stackers at the super-market and their pictures being flogged to some tacky website for the sake of clicks, and all to raise more ad revenue for a bunch of creepy news magnates whose parties his mum probably used to beg to get into, back in the day.

'They got what they came for, Jasper,' Estée said resign-edly, still opening letters at her dressing table. 'We're not interesting enough now for them to come back.'

Jasper didn't believe her.

'Sam thought we were normal people, like I could actually be a normal… boyfriend.'

He remembered the taste of that sausage and mash in its pool of gravy, and the custard and steamed sponge pudding, and how happy they'd been in that cosy little kitchen with Sam's mum treating him the way family were probably supposed to treat one another.

'I've got nothing to offer her, nothing but trouble, anyway,' he went on, in full retreat now. 'I couldn't even pay for her cinema ticket, and now I don't even have a job!'

In his hand he still clasped the note his mother had found on the mat this morning with Sam's careful cursive lettering telling him Mrs Capstan was recovered enough to come back to work, so he wouldn't be needed anymore. He couldn't see how that was true when she'd still looked so fragile the other day, but he'd accepted this as Sam's last word on his employment status.

'You can achieve anything you set your mind to, Jasper,' Estée remonstrated. 'I was very proud of you for finding that job. You'll find another.'

This morning had brought a new kind of resolve for Estée, as though she'd accepted that she had nothing, and she expected nothing.

Jasper had been astonished to observe that the letters she'd just opened from her acting agent and literary agent – unceremoniously dumping her – had solicited nothing more than a wry acknowledgement, and she'd simply carried on working her way through the pile.

'See! Here's my residuals for this year,' she said, passing him a letter with an old-fashioned cheque attached. 'One hundred and seventy-five dollars. The insolvency people will enjoy absorbing that.'

She laughed at the absurdity of it all. She'd been lead actress in *Destiny's Peak* for pretty much the whole of the Nineties, and this was how they paid her for reruns on obscure streaming channels. 'There's a certain freedom that comes with losing everything, I'm realising,' said Estée. 'And the receivers *are* allowing us our monthly pocket money, remember? If we're very good, we'll be able to eat.'

He'd read the paperwork too. They were afforded a tiny sum every month to cover basic living costs on the understanding they couldn't run up credit of any kind anywhere, while the debt relief order meant their seized assets would cover everything they owed, wiping it all away, and they had nothing further to pay in future.

A van was coming on Tuesday morning for the leopard statues and the jewellery and a fair number of Estée's purses and paintings. She'd already roped in Minty to help with the inventory.

His mum seemed to be looking forward to it. It was absurd. She'd assured him he was allowed to keep his watches and monogrammed luggage. It didn't seem much to show for a life, he'd thought, and he was still wallowing in this stark realisation now.

Last night, he'd watched Estée standing over the waste disposal unit, discovering it couldn't actually destroy credit cards, and he'd tried and failed to take the plumbing apart underneath to fish them out again. Jowan had to come up with his wrench and sort it out for them in the end.

Estée had laughed then too, a little maniacally, cutting the rescued cards in half with Minty's dressmaking shears while Jowan watched on, unsure what to do.

This new attitude was all very unexpected, but she really did seem lighter now the initial shock had passed.

'Be a good boy and run down to ask Minty for some coffee,' she said, still focused on the letters. 'Ah, here's a business association asking me to cut the ribbon on a new bank in Scarborough. The irony, *hmm*?'

Bewildered, Jasper made for the door. He had no idea where Scarborough was, even though it was his mother's home town, let alone how they'd get themselves to a bank opening, having no money and no car.

He didn't interpret Estée's new, accepting attitude as testament to the fact that his mum had, once upon a time, been the penniless Jennifer Carpenter. Her dad had been a barber in Woolworths, while her mum mopped the floors at the Scarborough General, and they'd survived some very lean times, so losing almost everything all over again was not quite so unimaginably catastrophic for her as it was for Jasper, who'd been born at The Portland and had his first *People* magazine photoshoot twelve hours later.

Estée talked on. 'Take those dishes back down too, darling. I've washed them. Tell her thank you.'

Sure enough, by the door was a stack of Minty's clean plates on a tray, the result of days' worth of donated food. 'What have you done with my mother?' Jasper said, bewildered. 'I didn't know you could wash dishes.'

Estée chuckled and waved him away without lifting her head. 'And go talk to that poor laundry girl!'

Jasper, however, was going to do everything he could to avoid Sam from now on, to prevent leading the press to her door ever again, even if he did have her number in his wallet next to the cinema ticket stub he'd been sure to keep, a reminder of the short time he'd fooled himself that a simple, happy, private life was possible.

Chapter Thirty-one

The Borrow-A-Bookshop was constructed on some obscure date in the eighteenth century specifically to withstand the onshore winds that can hammer the North Devon coast at this time of year. Its stonework bows out around its middle like a sponge cake hot from the oven, and it sits with its pointed roof pulled down over its squat little body like a gnome's hat, its shoulders turned against the sea, its high-walled courtyard sheltered from the worst of the weather.

It was the perfect place for Austen to hide away from the Atlantic gusts and, other than the whistling noises in the chimney, which she was too distracted to pay much attention to, she had no idea how blowy it really was out there. It was the kind of morning where if you so much as attempted the slope, you'd be sunburned in minutes and blown all the way to Barnstaple.

Not daring to venture too far, the tourists stuck to the visitor centre and donkey sanctuary, and Austen's shop doorbell barely rang all day long. When it did, she'd sprung up, hoping it was Patti. It never was, of course.

Austen had created a kind of nest in the armchair dragged into the space behind the counter, where there were empty tea mugs dotted around. She sat hunched under a blanket, a tense overheated lump, refreshing her screen way too many times to be healthy.

'Gah!' She shook the phone, but it didn't help. There'd been no word whatsoever from Delphine since last night when Austen had confessed Patti's suspicions and (almost) totally unrelated, she'd asked for a photo of her. Now she was beginning to see that had been a huge mistake. She'd offended her, and now she was nursing hurt feelings in her bookshop, and she was ill! It was too awful.

'Please let me know you're OK,' she typed, sending her message into what had become a desperate one-sided conversation, all in blue, every one of her posts going unread.

'I just need to know you're all right. I won't bother you again if you don't want me to. Just send one word. Please.'

She sent communications on into the early afternoon, her mind racing, her heart cracking. She'd really hurt her friend.

'I'm so sorry if it sounded like I doubted you.'

But there came not one word in response and no evidence Delphine was reading her messages.

It hadn't taken long for the tiny misgivings seeded by Patti to sprout like triffids. She'd made the even bigger mistake, in her frustration, of sending a message that would leave Delphine in no doubt about that fact.

'You have to understand, you gave me so little information to go on.'

She hadn't fully understood how harmful this might be until she saw it appear in their chat thread and she'd read it as through Delphine's eyes, imagining her reaction.

She held her thumb on it, hoping the app offered a way to delete messages. In her panic she couldn't work out how to do it, and the doubts only put out larger tendrils.

The bookshop camaraderie? Was it some kind of fantasy-spinning trap? Were they even really a bookseller?

Racking her brain, she'd concluded Delphine hadn't fully answered her questions about how to go about pricing the second-hand stock, and they didn't seem to have any industry insiders' solutions to that problem, come to think of it.

Polonius, the troublesome customer coming in with his stray animals on strings? Was he a figment of someone's imagination? The 'before sunset' book challenge? Had there really been two specially displayed copies of *Prufrock* or *Hard Times* simultaneously on sale in Devon and in Paris? How could any of that be fake?

There'd been so much that felt utterly real. The whole thing had! The little exchanges about their daily lives, the way they shared their triumphs and irritations about shop life. The way Austen had wanted to blab all her secrets, yet Delphine, when she thought about it, hadn't spilled a great deal. But wasn't she just being aloof and, well, a bit French?

Austen's heart constricted when she reminded herself that she didn't know her surname, or where exactly in Paris they lived.

The shop was real though. It had to be.

She opened Google Earth and searched for the Feint Heart Bookshop. Instantly the map zoned in on a pin in the Fifth Arrondissement.

'It definitely exists.'

She allowed herself to fume for a moment, now that she was safely assured she hadn't been taken for a fool so completely as to believe in a place that wasn't even real. Patti had made her doubt even this.

She zoomed in, choosing the 'street view' of the shop, and watching as the screen reorientated and her view fell to earth, the topography becoming a satellite image of the area.

There it was, next to the statue of Voltaire in his frock coat and curly wig, the Feint Heart. It was even prettier than she'd imagined with its wide, shadowy windows hinting at the bookstacks inside, and a desk by the glass. There were window boxes of red blooms, and a bicycle chained by the door with books piled in its basket and a sign where the saddle would be with the word '*Ouverte*' written on it. Panning up the building, tilting the street scene with her fingertips, feeling every inch a voyeur and not liking it one bit, she scowled in triumph.

'See, Patti, there's the tower. It's all true. It has to be.'

From the grey rooftop sprouted a fairy-tale turret with a narrow window in the stonework. She zoomed in on the window now, hoping to see a face behind the glass but finding only the huddled white shape of a nesting dove on the sill. Hadn't Delphine mentioned the pigeons?

She panned even further around the scene, completing a 180-degree turn until she spotted it, the top of the Eiffel Tower, just visible, just as Delphine had described. Again, all proof that the Parisian was telling the truth and Austen had offended them horribly. How could Patti make her doubt her new friend like this?

Any number of things could be preventing Delphine from replying now. There could be a problem at the shop, a power cut or something making her stay away. Though it might be nice if Delphine could message her and let her know. Maybe she can't because she's grown more ill? Or she's had an accident? Where was she messaging from yesterday; home, wasn't it? Had she dragged herself in to the shop?

That ladder to the tower sounded precarious, and Delphine said she'd drink wine and climb up there sometimes to sleep. Could she have done that and fallen? Was she lying there hurt, right this second, with the shop door deadlocked and nobody aware she needed help? Maybe she couldn't reach her phone, or it's out of battery!

Austen sprang to her feet, then sat down again just as fast. She had to do something. A few clicks on her phone screen took her to the shop's phone number, one more click made the number connect after some hissing silence.

'Pick up, pick up, pick up, please.'

But the tone rang on and on, no voicemail clicking into life, no way of shouting down the line so if there was someone in the shop they'd hear her and know she was trying to summon help.

After some minutes of desperately listening to the ringtone, she knew she needed another plan. Could she call a neighbouring shop?

Back to Street View she fled, only to discover the buildings on either side of the shop where helpful neighbours might conveniently be waiting to spring into action, seemed only to be flats or lock-ups and not businesses at all. There was no way of calling them.

She made the little avatar walk down Delphine's street, unable to make out the names of any of the stores. By now she was already asking herself how she might phone the French police from England.

Which number did she ring? She googled it and found there was something called the Police Nationale, as well as the Gendarmerie Nationale, and something called the Paris Police Prefecture. So, did she ring one of those? How do you even report an accident that might not have happened to a person who *some people* think doesn't even exist? Would they even understand what she was trying to say if she got through? *Dammit*, why hadn't she taken the opportunity to try out her French on Delphine? She might have brushed up her language skills a bit, or she might have been able to glean whether Delphine was really French.

There it was, another vine of doubt wrapping around her.

She hated the idea that her Delphine could be some kid in the States, or some lonely old man in the Hebrides, or somebody she used to know or had met once and somehow irritated or enticed, making them cruelly set out to trick her.

All those French words and phrases dropped here and there in the chat? How authentic had they been? Or were they clunking great red herrings only a fool would fall for?

But why would Delphine – why would anyone – lie like that?

Patti had hinted about Delphine being a con man enquiring about banking or passwords, and she'd been cross and told her of course she hadn't.

And yet, she searched her brain now, hadn't Delphine asked her if she was in charge of everything, including the shop money? *No.* Austen shook her head, it had been said in admiration, or to fully grasp the Borrow-A-Bookshop concept. They hadn't wheedled or asked questions like scammers do – *what's your mother's maiden name?* Or *what's the name of your first pet?* – in the hopes of gathering enough information to guess your passwords.

Anyway, this was the Borrow-A-Bookshop they'd been talking about. How could Austen have given away secrets about codes and passwords that she didn't even have?

She recalled Delphine asking one evening when her birthday was, but that was just ordinary conversation and not at all the kind of stuff hackers need to gain access to, say, someone else's social media accounts.

Delphine had said hers was on Christmas Day. That seems a strange thing for someone to make up. Or was it another intriguing fact, designed to draw Austen in more, make her marvel and exclaim at how interesting Delphine's life was? Or had they picked it simply because it was the easiest date to remember? Liars need to keep things straight.

Austen found herself wondering, now that she was consumed by her doubts, if the Feint Heart account had been hacked, allowing someone to pose as a bookshop employee? She searched across Instagram, TikTok and Facebook, looking for evidence of other active accounts in the shop's name that were being updated regularly by Delphine, or by someone else – some other, genuine Feint Heart bookseller. But there was nothing, only the original account she'd followed six months ago, and they'd still only posted that one video and nothing else. It was a relief and a frustration at the same time, bringing her no closer to finding an answer.

She'd message again, every hour, until she got some kind of response, even if it was a hurt and disappointed Delphine telling her to stop bothering her. At least then she'd know.

So that's what she did; the whole day through and right past bedtime and after dark.

Only at gone eleven that night did something change and Austen sat bolt upright in bed, blinking her tired eyes in disbelief.

The screen had turned suddenly white in her hands. The entire chat history was gone, replaced only by an app message: 'We are sorry, something appears to have gone wrong.'

She refreshed the app and searched for the Feint Heart account so that she could start again with her messaging, apologise afresh, telling Delphine there was some glitch in their messages, but it was all gone.

'No results,' the screen told her.

She searched again, and two more times, until it was impossible to avoid reaching the sickening conclusion that someone had deleted the Feint Heart Bookshop account and she had no way of ever reaching Delphine or finding out if she had cut Austen off because she was offended and hurt by her accusation, or because she was some kind of catfishing con artist, or a fantasist and flatterer who'd realised they couldn't go on any longer without being rumbled.

A cold stillness settled over Austen as she lay awake trying to reconstruct the conversations they'd had, searching for answers and, on each path she followed, she'd draw another blank and have to chase some other avenue until all she could hear was Callista telling her, quite correctly, that she was too old to be this lost.

Chapter Thirty-two

It had been Mrs Crocombe who noticed it first, the dying away of the electric buzz that accompanies all our lives to such an extent some of us barely notice it anymore.

Mrs C., of course, notices everything, and as soon as the power went down on Tuesday morning, she'd initiated the Emergency Ice Cream Protocol, invented after the great flood of two Christmases ago.

The stuff in the deep freezers out the back would be fine for twenty-four hours so long as no one opened the doors, but that morning's freshly made containers in her ice cream kitchen hadn't set properly yet and needed to be shifted fast. The Big House had its own generator and catering-sized freezer. They'd be able to help.

Mr Bovis swept into action, loading the tubs onto the Ice Cream Cottage's branded pink sled, hauling them up the slope with the help of three hardy tourists from the Netherlands who really got into the swing of the whole emergency response procedure and looked to be having a great time. One of them filmed the whole thing on an 'Insta Live', whatever that was, and Mrs C. promised them each a triple scoop from the display fridges as soon as they got back down to the shop, hopefully before all those lovely flavours melted into a milky soup.

It was easy going up the slope because of the wind direction bearing them upward from behind. Everyone remarked how it was like being shoved on a ski lift, and the sun beat down on them through it all until, panting and laughing, they arrived at the Big House, which had new solar panels and enough power to turn the freshly made ice cream solid and keep it that way for at least twelve hours. Mrs C. fought the stubborn streak inside herself telling her to reach for her betting book and ask if the Dutch boys were staying long and how many of them happened to be single. The new part of her that shied away from interfering with love in every way possible, won out and the men remained happily unbothered by Clove Lore's Cupid.

Once her ices were safely in the Big House fridges, she'd sent them back down the slope with Bovis with instructions to 'let them have anything they fancy from the parlour, double waffle cones, strawberry sauce, the lot!'

Mrs Crocombe and Minty had been making plans for an Earl Grey and a gossip by the Aga when they were stalled by the sight of Sam Capstan and her mum, still bruised and bandaged over her face, in the lobby, looking like they'd had a fright.

'Come into the kitchen, quick sharp. What on earth's going on? Is it a tree down?' Minty tried to ferry them further inside, but they wouldn't be detained.

'We're in a right pickle,' Mrs Capstan told the older women. 'The electric's off up at the laundry lock-up and...'

Minty's walkie-talkie crackled into life, cutting her off.

'This is Number Two, over,' said Jowan, somewhere blustery, with Aldous in the background yapping and howling into the wind like a wolf.

'Receiving, over,' said Minty, and everyone acted like this was all perfectly normal, only Sam gave her mum a quick glance that made Mrs Capstan sniff a laugh that she had to hide. 'What's going on out there? Over.'

'I'm with the fella from the power company. 'Lectric lines' blown down between the promontory and the village. Says it's an easy enough job to fix but they're waiting for more men to arrive to do it. Reckons it'll be 'bout five before power's restored.'

'Well, that's no good, you see,' Sam butted in before Minty could do her sign-off. 'We've just hauled five loads of clean bedding out the washers, the power's gone off and now we can't get it dry.'

'Is that all?' Mrs C. said, hobbling off to the kitchen. 'You can dry it at five, can't you?'

'We need everything done and delivered by noon,' Sam explained.

Minty didn't think she quite saw the problem. 'They can be late this once, I'm sure.'

'No,' said Mrs Capstan. 'Even if we get the power back by five, it'll take an hour's tumbling to dry them all, then there's the folding and bagging up, and the delivery takes a good hour, hauling the sled. It'll be getting on for bedtime by the time the holidaymakers get their linens.'

Again, Minty seemed unfazed, and Mrs Crocombe looked like if she didn't get to a pot of tea soon she might expire.

Now it was Sam's turn to make them see the urgency of their situation. 'It's just, the holiday let landlords haven't been very happy with me being slow at the laundry this last week. A few of them have rung Mum to say they're considering shifting to that big company that does most of the coast.'

'I see,' said Minty, stepping closer.

'Things picked up a bit when Jasper was helping, but now he's… not working with us,' Mrs Capstan said delicately, 'I've stepped in again as of yesterday, but the last thing we need is a day of delays and fifty angry landlords and families ready for bed with no sheets.'

'So, can we use your machine, please, Minty? And we can drive along to our house, the electric might be on at home, and get a load on there.'

'Well, yes, of course,' Minty said. 'But we've only a small dryer. It takes about three hours to dry one load.'

'But yours is the only working machine in Clove Lore and we've five machines full,' said Sam.

'And those are massive thirty-five-pound commercial washer loads,' Mrs Capstan added.

Sam was already accepting defeat. She turned to her mum. 'If those landlords put in calls to the Speedy Laundry company at Bideford today, they'll never switch back to you. It'll be the end of the business, won't it?'

'Oh, however did we manage before machines?' Mrs Crocombe commiserated, her hands on her hips and brows knitting tight.

Minty, however, was smirking and shaking her head like a woman with all the answers. 'Samantha, knock on every door in the house, won't you? We'll need all hands on deck. Well? Hop to it, girl.'

'Oh! Right!' Sam scurried off, looking none too pleased, in the direction of Apartment One, while Minty raised her walkie-talkie to her mouth, switching frequency as she did so, and looking more than a little high on her own authority.

'This is Commander One, calling all units. Come in, all units. Assemble at the Capstan laundry with your largest wash baskets. I repeat, bring the big baskets. We have a Code Amber situation.'

–

'She's barmy,' Kit, the chef from the Siren, was saying, and Finan, the pub landlord had to agree, as they stood at the back of the crowd at the laundry lock-up with Minty inside the unit's doorway ready to address them all, her platinum bob blowing back in the wind, which was by now, thankfully, dropping as the sun blazed in the cloudless sky.

Mrs Crocombe, Sam and her mum, Izaak and Leonid, Jude Crawley and her husband Elliot, Jowan and Aldous (asleep inside his master's jacket), made up the rest of the assembly, while Mrs Gold and a tortured-looking Jasper were only just arriving.

Mrs Gold loudly announced she'd had to change into 'something more suitable' and, to Izaak and Leonid's delight, she'd settled upon wearing a gold lurex jump-suit with actual tasselled epaulettes and what she probably thought passed as a suitable (only four-inch) stiletto heel for tramping up and down the Clove Lore estate in.

Izaak mimed an appreciative claw action at her, and she winked back her thanks.

'If we're all quite ready?' Minty said, her patience wearing thin. 'Our friends' business is at stake today, and we have precisely two hours to dry these sopping linens.' She turned to indicate the machines' open hatches inside the lock-up behind her.

'She thinks she's bleedin' Evita,' Finan said *sotto voce* to Kit, who smothered a laugh.

'In the days before drying machines the washerfolk hung their linens over the hedges all across this estate.

We're talking over a century ago when drying lanes were commonplace. In fact, it was a tradition across the entire country, worldwide even! We are fortunate in Clove Lore to have retained much of our prized ancient hedgerow, some of it dating back to the sixteen hundreds! That is why we have a great many songbirds. The rest of the country hasn't fared so well. In fact, I spoke at the commission for rural affairs South West women's chapter only last month on this very topic, and, do you know, we have lost over *fifty per cent* of our ancient hedgerow habitats since the war, and…'

Jowan cleared his throat, pointedly.

'Ah, yes, quite right. Time is of the essence,' she said. 'Volunteers, please fill your baskets and drape the Capstans' sheets over every hedgerow along the length of the Big House estate perimeter. That's at least eight hundred yards of prime drying space. I reckon with this baking sun and the winds holding steady at twenty knots, we can expect to be folding by noon. Best of luck, everyone. The incoming holidaymakers of Clove Lore, and the Capstans, are depending on you.'

'Surprised she didn't salute,' Finan grumbled, as he and Kit queued up for their bundle of soggy sheets.

'Thank you, Minty,' Caroline was saying, but Minty had her eyes to the sky.

'Don't thank me yet. Let's roll out!' and she marched off with her filled basket on her hip like a sergeant major on wash day, and she had never looked happier.

At Mrs Crocombe's insistence, Isaak and Leonid were grouped with Estée Gold, who'd 'need to be shown the ropes', she told them, and Mrs Gold had tutted and said she'd often helped her mother with washing as a child. Yet, she still let the men lift the baskets and teetered off behind them, kicking grit from her open-toed shoes as she went.

'You two, work together,' Mrs C. told Sam and a reluctant Jasper, who was still hanging back, hoping not to be noticed. 'Take a load between you to the top of the cornflower meadow, it's bound to be blustery out there.'

'Mum!' Sam had said through gritted teeth, her back turned upon Jasper.

'Off you two go,' Caroline Capstan insisted. 'I can't very well haul sheets over hedges with this.' She pointed to her bruised face. 'I'll keep an eye on things from up here. Go on. Shoo!'

Sam's shoulders dropped as she sullenly lifted a filled basket and turned for the meadow. 'Come on then, if you're coming.'

Chapter Thirty-three

'Look, if we've got to do this, we should try to be civil,' Jasper said, as they wafted the first of the sheets up into the air like they were making a bed, only they both let go of one end and inelegantly flung the damp linen over the hawthorn hedge, which was almost as tall as Sam herself.

The sheet snagged on the branches and Sam inhaled like a woman on the brink of a short cry and a long nap.

'Let's try again,' she said. 'I mean with the sheet.'

Jasper tugged and adjusted it until the hedge was draped over on both sides with one sheet. He was sweating already in spite of the steady breeze whipping up and over the promontory.

The air smelled of washing powder, earth and sea salt. Behind Sam, the sea of cornflower heads bobbed and bent, growing raggedy in the wind.

Jasper tugged a white duvet free from his wet bundle and Sam took her two corners. 'On three,' he said, counting down for the throw.

They worked like this for a while, Sam looking forlorn, and Jasper increasingly pained.

'I don't really want to be civil with you,' she said at last, and the sound of the wind nearly whipped the words away without him hearing.

'I get it,' he said, and they moved along the hedge pulling their baskets with them.

A blackbird burst from the mossy stone bank at the hedgerow's roots, crying in alarm and flying away furiously. 'Oops.' Sam watched it go. 'Hope it comes back.'

Jasper hadn't a clue what it was planning on doing, he told her weakly, hoping she'd smile. She didn't.

'I'm sorry,' he said, letting the next sheet ball up in his hands with frustration. 'You've no idea what it's been like since the papers broke our story, and…'

'I do know, actually. I've been visited by three reporters since then, all knocking at our door. I told all of them to get knotted, you needn't look so worried. All your secrets are safe. But I had the entire queue at the post office gawping at me and whispering yesterday when I went for Mum's lotto ticket. And then some girl I haven't seen since school called in at the laundry to ask if I fancied a coffee and a catch-up one day soon, because I guess *suddenly* I'm not just boring, dumpy, works-all-day Samantha Capstan, I'm Jasper Gold's slumming-it girl, and I'm interesting!'

'I'm so sorry.'

'Are you? Because during all that, you were hiding in your castle full of fancy crap with your mother, and I was dealing with it all by myself.'

'I'm sorry,' he said again. Sam sniffed hard and rubbed the corner of her damp sheet against her forehead where it was growing hot. Her cheeks were red.

Jasper usually avoided big emotional scenes with girls like the plague. He had no idea if she was going to sit down and sob or start screeching like his mum when she's overdue for one of her retreats.

Sam went on. 'Why didn't you tell me you were bankrupt? Why didn't you tell me the paparazzi follow you about? I felt such an idiot seeing it in the papers like that.'

'I don't know… I liked feeling *normal* with you. It wasn't something I've ever had before.' He swallowed. Would she ever understand? How could she?

'And that's why you were slumming it with me? So you could pretend to be like us poor people, like Marie Antoinette playing with her pigs on her farm?'

'Uh?' Jasper had no idea what she was on about with the Marie Antoinette's pigs thing, but he got the gist from the blazing fire in her eyes that she was livid.

'I was never *playing* anything,' he tried. 'I was trying to keep Mum from going under. I was trying to be the man for once. And I needed a job. And I liked you. It all seemed to just land at my feet. I couldn't believe my luck, and I was really, really happy for once.'

Sam's expression shifted, only a little, but he felt her yielding.

'I knew it was all about to come crashing down as soon as the announcement hit the papers, but I'd no idea the press would follow us here, honestly. I thought we'd found somewhere private. Remote, even.'

'It's North Devon, not Grand Cayman. You can't hide here. Real people, people like me and Mum, are just trying to survive. Trying to be part of something. You wouldn't understand that.'

Jasper let the words sink in, lifting his gaze from Sam's tearful eyes to the field margins beyond. All the way up to the Big House every inch of gnarled old hawthorn, blackthorn, hazel, rowan and holly was now draped in white.

Sam followed his eyes and for a moment the pair of them stood gazing at the blue cornflowers under the blue sky contrasted with the white snow-like cotton as far as the estate stretched.

'I *am* part of something,' Jasper said, as if to himself, but Sam heard too, and she looked back at him.

'What were you thinking, shutting me out? I wanted to help you,' she said, her voice cracking.

Jasper shrugged. 'I thought you'd be better off without me bringing all that unwanted attention to you. Privacy is so precious, and you don't know that unless you've never had it. I wanted you to keep your world, keep all this, for yourself, and stop it getting ruined. It's awful being watched all the time, picked apart, lied about! And you can't do anything about it because you need people looking at you to bring in acting jobs and money, and Mum needs it, you know? Like she really, *really* needs it. If a director called her right now, she'd be on a jet before you could say *ciao, darling*.' He managed a smile, even though he didn't feel like smiling at all. 'And I thought Mum was going to collapse again, like she has before, like she did when Dad cheated the first time and, actually, all the times. I thought she'd end up back in the Priory, or whatever the free version of the Priory's called, but she seems kind of fine, actually. It's weird.'

'Maybe she's more resilient than you think she is. Maybe she likes it here.'

He shook his head, thinking hard.

Sam moved back to her basket and handed him a fresh sheet. They worked quietly for a while, listening to the breeze and the birds and the tide coming in way down in the windblown harbour.

'I don't care if people talk about me, Jasper,' she said, calmer now.

'You should. It's awful. The things they say! The things they make up about you. I never minded for myself, but Mum, she was mauled in public over and over.'

'But she had you. You looked after her. And I'm guessing she was proud to be providing for you. She must have wanted to do it.' She watched him for a moment, her expression softening entirely. 'You're not the only one with a runaway dad, you know? I haven't seen mine in years, nobody knows where he is. Last we heard he was with some woman in Bodmin and they were having a baby together. There's a little brother or sister out there who I've never even met.'

Jasper grew even more still, his eyes fixed upon her. 'Jesus! You're right. I'm so sorry.'

They'd both read the papers. It was out there now – the fact that Jasper's dad was going to become a father again at the age of sixty-one.

'It's grim, huh?' Sam said.

'It sure is. I knew when dad cut us off, it was coming. Hiding out here was just the calm before the storm. The lawyers warned us that all cases of bankruptcy and insolvency are printed in the official public record, and ours would appear there too, as though our family life was some business going under. As though Mum had somehow failed to keep us afloat, when in fact Dad stitched her up with a vicious prenup way back in the Nineties.'

That's what happens though, Jasper supposed, if you're a stunningly beautiful, vivacious (and utterly penniless) soap actress scooped up by one of the most cut-throat financial advisors to the mega rich in the business.

'Years ago, as soon as some of the terms of the prenup expired and Dad knew his money was safe, he stopped hiding the affairs. That rumbled on for a while, making everybody miserable. Then, out of nowhere, he was saying he had to get divorced and remarried to protect some new Croatian assets.'

'Ugh!' said Sam. 'His new family?'

'Yep,' Jasper said, drily. They hadn't had a clue how catastrophic that transference of his father's protection from them to his new family would be.

'There'd been enough of Mum's personal savings to keep us in Chelsea for a while after the divorce went through, but he cut us off from any of his funds, and Mum's cash ran out pretty quickly. Mum had been gagged from making any money through selling her divorce story to the press, not that she'd ever dream of doing that. Then we were turfed out of our house. Dad said he'd found us the perfect place to stay in Devon, and we believed him. Didn't take us long to realise he meant it was the perfect place for him, keeping us well out of the way.'

'And you've been living with that all hidden inside you for weeks now?' Sam said.

'You've had it so much harder than me,' he said, gripping a hand to his stomach where his gut clenched. Only now was he realising the only difference between his situation and Sam's was that he'd lost access to a fortune, whereas Sam had never had that privilege in the first place.

'We've had it kind of the same,' Sam said, taking one tiny step closer. 'The good thing was, you had your mum and I had mine. We weren't alone.'

This came as a revelation to him. 'I guess so.' He even sniffed a laugh.

Sam's basket was empty now, and the whole length of the far meadow hedge they were responsible for was covered in laundry. Jasper threw his last sheet over the hawthorn all by himself and stooped to lift his empty basket.

'What do we do now?' he said, genuinely at a loss, thinking of the mess he'd made of everything. 'Me and Mum will always be in the newspapers as long as it means somebody's making money from us. They'll never leave us alone.'

Sam swiped the back of her hand across her forehead.

'Jasper, I wouldn't care if the *Daily Mail* slept in my wheelie bin every night for the rest of my life, trawling through my rubbish, watching all my comings and goings, so long as I'm not on my own.' She fixed him with a look. 'So, it's up to you, really. What do *you* want to do now?'

'I know exactly what I want,' he said, knowing that all he longed for was to take Samantha Capstan in his arms and kiss her for the first time; and not some stumbling-out-of-a-nightclub or in-the-back-of-a-cab-at-three-a.m. kind of a kiss, but a sunlit, breezy-day-with-the-girl-you're-falling-for kind of a kiss, but he was too frozen with fear to move.

He dropped the basket to the ground.

'We're a mess, Sam,' he told her quietly. 'Me and Mum. Our life, it's a big mess. His eyes fell to her mouth, his will weakening.'

'Life is messy,' she said with a shrug. 'What matters is not being too afraid to live it.' The grin on her face swept away the last of his reservations with the summer breeze, and his heart told his feet to move without his head knowing anything about it. He was closing the gap between them, and she was responding, bringing her body closer until his arms were somehow tight around her. The feel of her almost drew a whimper from deep inside him.

Lowering his mouth to hers, he felt her body lifting. She was on tiptoe, her eyes closing softly and he was kissing her the way he'd wanted to since the day he first saw her, when he hadn't understood at the time that she was going to be the best thing to ever happen to him.

—

Up at the Big House, where every one of the low cropped box, yew and privet hedges were draped in white, Minty whipped her binoculars from her eyes and turned to the women assembled by her side in the sunshine, mugs of tea in their hands.

'Well?' Caroline Capstan said.

'I think we can leave them to it now, ladies,' she replied, the picture of discretion.

Mrs Gold smiled softly, while Mrs Crocombe rummaged in a pocket for her matchmaking book, then, thinking better of it, raised her mug in a toast.

'To a good drying day,' she said instead, and all the women agreed it was indeed a perfect day.

Chapter Thirty-four

Having stayed hidden away, oblivious, in her bedroom all through the laundry dilemma, Austen woke up on Wednesday morning knowing she couldn't go on like this for another day. She'd annoyed nobody more than herself. This was supposed to be her bookshop holiday. She had three nights of it left, and she'd wasted so much precious time.

First, she swept all the sand out the door, stopping to wonder vaguely where all the broken twigs, blown leaves and a white pillowcase in the courtyard could have come from.

Then she set her book swap box on a table just outside the door with a sign. 'Take a book, leave a book. I am your little free library,' it read.

Pleased with that, she'd been inspired to go on and create a 'pick a poem' mood board, which she stationed by the till point – the plan was that visitors would pick a word that resonated with them from her board and Austen would recommend a suitable poem.

So far two customers had tried it – the first person had picked the word 'fame', and Austen had gone to the shelves and found them a book which she passed to them open at Percy Shelley's 'Ozymandias'. Their eyes had lit up with recognition and happiness the way she'd witnessed when her mum read her aunties' cards favourably, filling them with the sense of having been seen.

She'd left them to read the sonnet while she made their takeaway flat whites. They'd been charmed with the whole thing and even decided to buy the book.

Yet, the retired couple on a coach trip who'd chosen the word 'advice', hadn't been at all pleased when Austen presented them with Philip Larkin's wonderfully sweary 'This Be The Verse' and they'd left without buying anything.

She didn't let this worry her. Larkin's not for everyone, and the new Austen had promised herself she wouldn't let her fear of other people's impressions of her hold her back, especially people who didn't really know her.

If she was going to sort herself out, it had to be herself driving it. She knew she had to be doing it primarily for herself too, and not to impress anyone, not to placate anyone, and not because she'd eaten up what a person had said about her and made it her entire personality. This was the beginning of the new age of Austen. This was maturity. Still, she'd have liked it very much if Patti had replied to her apology yesterday.

She'd kept it short:

> I'm sorry I answered messages on our lovely date, and I'm sorry I got defensive about Delphine when you were just worried about me. I hope you will forgive me. A x

All Wednesday, she baked and she sold books and refreshments and whenever she felt wistful she'd go and stand in the 'Self-Improvement' section, taking any title down off the shelf to read a page or two.

So far, she'd learned that 'self-actualisation' was the thing adults should be working towards, and not to punish herself for setbacks, and that she was worthy of 'unconditional self-regard', even if other people had put conditions on their love for her. All of which she'd found extremely enlightening.

She'd also, less helpfully, read that if she didn't get a full eight hours' sleep every night (which she almost never did) she'd lose 'brain elasticity', and even though she didn't know what that meant, it only served to make her feel anxious about not sleeping, and then she'd read that to help herself sleep she must stop consuming coffee, wine, tea, chocolate, sugar and soft drinks immediately, which she felt was unlikely, and that only made her more anxious. Then she'd pulled down a huge tome called *How Anxiety is Taking Years Off Your Life* and she'd wanted to yell in the stacks and had to have another cup of tea and a slice of pie to calm down.

Progress and healing, she was beginning to realise, wasn't going to be linear. She was allowed to feel overwhelmed by it all too.

Then she'd asked herself whether she couldn't come up with a recipe of her own for the last few days at the cafe, and not something her mum lived off, or her dad adored, or a recipe for courgette cake that Izaak had used to get rid of the last of his veggies. What did *she* want to sell in her own cafe?

It struck her that what she really loved eating when she visited coffee shops were enormous fat scones. So she'd gone to the source (Nadiya Hussain, of course) and baked two batches following her recipe from off the bookshelf; scones she intended to serve with the strawberry jam and big tubs of clotted cream that had been in the kitchen when she arrived. She ate one straight away with a big pot of tea and felt very satisfied.

Amidst all this introspection, she'd made time to put together another poetry session for Thursday, remembering how happy she'd felt when Patti suggested she could do something like that for a living. Though, she'd been careful to remind herself she had to choose her own way in life. Still, Patti might well have struck upon something, and she wasn't the type to say things she didn't mean, so it couldn't have been empty flattery.

She'd decided to give herself a proper chance to test if she really did have the required skills in this area, and, fortunately, there were books on the shelves about teaching creative writing and she'd skimmed her way through those, taking notes in a brand-new book from the stationery display. Come Thursday, she would be ready to unveil the fledgling Austen to the most astute audience of them all – kids.

The fact that Patti would be bringing Radia had only a little to do with the energy she put into sorting herself out as best she could in the short time left to her in Clove Lore. She'd hurt Patti and driven her away when she was already unsure of Austen. She was going to have to make amends, so she pinned all of her hopes on Thursday at four o'clock when she'd see her again.

Chapter Thirty-five

As she propped open the doors at four o'clock to welcome the little poets inside, Austen's whole body bristled with nerves.

The kids filed in, holding hands with eager parents. The head teacher of the primary school arrived, saying she hoped she didn't mind but she'd sent a message to local families about today's special session since the last one had been so interesting. Austen only gulped and said she'd do her best this time round.

The visitors just kept coming, everyone expectant and smiling, and very, very noisy. The children were taking seats and flopping down on beanbags and scurrying this way and that in the stacks, everyone keen to get a cup of squash and half a jammy, creamy scone.

Finally, Austen caught sight of Radia skipping into the courtyard, dragging her toy fox, with a large notepad under her arm.

The old Austen would have ducked behind the shelves, taking care to pretend she hadn't been caught looking out for Patti, but Austen was tired of all that stuff, so she stayed on the steps peering out.

'She's not coming,' Radia said as she bounced inside, and Austen only then recognised that the woman following behind her with Monty the barbecue guy was Patti's sister.

'Rads!' Joy warned. 'Sorry,' she said to Austen, stepping inside, looking embarrassed.

'Is Patti at work, then?' Austen asked. 'I thought she was coming here today?'

'Oh, yes, that's right, she's at work,' Joy said, finding a seat right at the front nearest the door.

Radia returned to say, 'No, she isn't. She's in bed watching *Dr Pimple Popper*, like she has been for *ages*.'

'Radia!' Joy hissed, and Monty seemed to be hiding an awkward smile.

'Well, it's true. You said if she eats any more raspberry ice cream she'll throw up.'

'Is she sick?' Austen asked the little girl, who pulled an incredulous *adults are so stupid* face. 'She's sad, silly!'

'Oh! Hearing that makes me a bit sad too,' Austen told her, glancing at the open door as though she might run straight through it.

'What are we doing today?' Radia asked, shoving her way through the kids sprawled on the floor so she could sit in the same spot as she had last week.

It was too late to run to Patti. Austen had a Storytime session to give and, by the looks of things, a completely full house, so she closed the door and, with a heavier heart than before, she began.

'Today, kids and grown-ups, we're going to find our writing voice. Any ideas what that means?'

'*Aheh-ahem.*' Radia got her attention at the front. 'The hat.' She pointed to the cone of paper with 'AA' on the front.

Breaking into a smile, Austen placed it immediately on her head. 'Thank you, Rads. Can't forget the special hat, can we? Right, everyone, grab a pen. Let's begin.'

Chapter Thirty-six

Her rucksack and tote bag – almost completely packed – lay by the side of the bed, which Austen would sleep in tonight for the last time. She had one last Friday of book-selling to get right, and the open mic event to host this evening, then it would all be over. She had a cab booked for ten o'clock on Saturday from the visitor centre, and if there were no delays, she'd be back in Manchester by five.

But first, there were things left unresolved that she had to fix today if she was ever going to call herself a grown-up.

She was still figuring out how exactly she was going to go about it as she turned the sign on the shop door for the last time. She pulled the handle, letting in the still summer morning air and, unusually, the laughter of a whole group of people in high spirits.

The sound drew her out across the courtyard to the end of the passageway where she was met by the sight of Minty wearing a sundress, gripping Jowan's arm, while their little dog trotted smartly by their side. They were followed by the glamorous Mrs Gold in the widest, floppiest-brimmed hat she'd ever seen and a huge pair of dark shades. She'd also opted for some sort of catwalk tuxedo, even though it was only nine in the morning and still very much flip-flops and shorts weather. She was talking loudly into a phone asking if someone was 'sure the champagne's on ice?' Behind her was her son and – Austen couldn't quite believe what she was seeing – he was wearing white trousers and a t-shirt with the words 'Capstan's Holiday Laundry' across the back. He was walking Down-along with the rest of them, and holding hands with Sam, who for the first time this fortnight didn't look as though she had the weight of the world on her shoulders.

Spotting Austen, Sam called out as they passed, 'Come and see this!'

Austen, giving in to her curiosity, ran back to lock the shop door before shuffling down the steep slope to catch up with them.

She didn't have to go very far before they all drew to a halt and Minty separated from the group, letting herself in through the little white gate of the Ice Cream Cottage and knocking on the door.

Everyone was giggling and whispering and standing up on tiptoes to look over heads into the shop. Austen stayed at the back, totally at a loss about what was going on.

Mrs Crocombe came to the door, a picture of confusion, her hair still in the curlers she had slept in.

'There you are, Mrs C.!' cawed Minty.

'What's going on 'ere then? You're all grinnin' like scarecrows,' the woman replied, suspiciously.

'We've a surprise for you, Letitia,' said Jowan, Aldous twirling at his feet evidently hoping all this excitement meant he might be getting a cone or a little tub of vanilla.

'What you on about?' she said, but Mrs Gold was advancing upon her now, holding up a vanity case with the look of a gunpowder plotter about her.

'You, Mrs Crocombe, are going out to brunch,' she said, and hastened the woman back inside and right up the stairs, Minty and Sam following behind. The door banged shut behind them.

'What is going on?' Austen asked, once the women had disappeared inside, leaving her standing with Jowan, Jasper and a very disappointed Aldous.

''Twas Mint's idea,' Jowan replied, 'and you may have heard that when Mint gets an idea, resistance is futile.'

'Mum's giving Mrs C. a makeover,' added Jasper. 'She'll come down those stairs looking like Gal Gadot.'

This seemed unlikely. 'I'd better stick around then.'

Just then, a voice reached them from down the slope. 'Have I missed it?'

Austen knew, even before she'd whipped her head round, who it was. 'Patti!' Her name flew from her mouth.

'Hey,' she replied, looking like she might not have come if she'd known Austen was going to be here. Still, she drew closer and came to a stop in front of the Ice Cream Cottage.

Jowan and Jasper exchanged a glance, and the younger man suggested they head Down-along to make sure 'everything's set up'.

Austen was still none the wiser about what these locals were up to. Right now, though, all she cared about was checking if Patti was OK. She was paler than before, and tired-looking.

'Did you get my message?' she asked. The men had gone now, leaving them in the quiet morning with the sound of gulls calling from the rooftops.

'I did.' Patti jammed her hands inside the pockets of her cropped red baseball jacket, which looked so adorable it set off a pain in Austen's chest.

'I meant it,' Austen pressed. 'I'm really sorry. I was stuck in my own world, being all self-obsessed.'

'Forget about it. It's fine.' Patti didn't look fine. None of this was fine.

'Can we talk, or…'

'I'm doing this.' Patti pointed to Mrs C.'s door like that explained anything.

'Tonight, then? At the open mic night. You're coming, aren't you?'

'I've got to work there. It's my event.'

'Of course. Yes, duh!' Austen pointed to her own head like she was firing a bullet. Then, stopping herself goofing about, she whipped her hand down. 'Listen, I wasn't lying when I said I really liked you.'

'Did you say that?' Patti blinked, her face expressionless.

'Well, if I didn't, I meant to.'

They fell silent. Patti looked at the ground while Austen searched her brain for something winning to say. Something that could fix all this. But it was Patti who spoke first.

'How's Delphine?'

'Uh, well… you might have been right about all that. I probed a bit, asked a few questions and… they just disappeared.'

Patti's face fell. 'Shit, Austen…'

'Here she is!' They were stopped from saying any more by Minty leading Mrs Crocombe out of the ice cream parlour like she was the mother of a young bride. Estée Gold followed behind, looking extremely proud of herself.

'Bloody hell!' Patti gasped, as Mrs Crocombe, fully made up with a lined Nineties red lip, her face powdered to a translucent matt finish, and a set of amazing black lashes, reminiscent of Estée Gold in her TV star heyday, stepped onto the slope. 'You look epic, Mrs C.' She beamed, and Austen was glad to see her acting more like her former self, only wishing she would turn those smiling eyes on her.

Mrs Crocombe swished a chiffon lilac sundress and showed off ballet shoe-pink fingernails. She'd put on her wedding day pearls, too, and her mother's silver bracelet. 'Is anyone going to tell me what all this is in aid of?' she was asking, slipping a pink basketweave handbag over her forearm.

'You'll see,' chirped Sam from the back, and Minty led the way, slow and stately Down-along, where it was plain to see from Austen's viewpoint what was about to happen.

Mrs C., who hadn't been able to fit her specs on without knocking her lashes skew-whiff so had left them at home, couldn't see a thing.

'You coming?' Patti said, as the party moved off.

'I'll get back to the shop,' said Austen. 'There's some stuff I need to work on.'

Patti hadn't hung around to ask what that meant, trudging down the slope after the women, her hands still shoved in her pockets.

Austen stayed fixed to the spot, watching them as they made their way down past the sunflowers in Patti's garden. She waited while they passed out of sight, obscured by the roofs of the lifeboat launch and the lime kiln, before they emerged again into the sunshine out on the harbour wall. Her eyes followed the figure of Patti passing the whitewashed front of the Siren's Tail and out onto the long arm of ancient boulders that formed the old cob.

The whole group stopped, and Mrs Crocombe hadn't appeared to understand what to do, until Mr Bovis, her colleague and admirer, way out at the end of the wall by the harbour lantern, rose from a white-clothed table set for two with a bottle of bubbly peeping out of a ice bucket.

Austen could make out that Bovis was wearing a rather smart morning suit and a dapper hat with a white band – his outfit had Minty and Estée written all over it (that duo were in danger of become Clove Lore's own prime interferers at this rate).

Bovis walked along the sea wall towards Mrs C., holding out a bouquet of pink blooms, and tipping her head to one side in dawning recognition, at last, the matchmaker made her way towards him.

When they met, he crooked an arm for her to take and she planted a kiss on his cheek, making the little gang gathered on the wall burst into applause. With a sweep of his arm, Bovis showed his brunch date to their table.

At a signal from Bella, now standing in the pub doorway in her strawberry frock, Monty Bickleigh and head chef Kit filed outside with trays laden with food for Bovis and his matchmaker-turned-perfect-match and the romantic quayside brunch they'd been ambushed into by their friends.

The others, still keeping a respectful distance, clapped and whooped.

Austen might have heard Minty remarking at the top of her voice, 'And about time too!' had she not been rushing up the hill to her bookshop, even more determined than before to prove to Patti that she wasn't the shambles she'd let her believe she was.

Chapter Thirty-seven

Austen tapped the mic and the little speaker at the back of the room boomed. 'Can't have open mic night without an actual mic. Thanks, Finan, that's perfect,' she said.

'You're welcome,' the pub landlord replied, before taking his seat right in the middle of the bookshop, which was all set out with chairs.

'You're staying?' Austen asked over the PA system.

'I reckon everyone in the village'll be turning out to support your last night here,' he said.

'Why? Why would they do that?' Austen, who'd already felt nervous, was totally alarmed now.

'Because you're our Borrower,' he told her with a smile.

Austen wished everyone felt the same way, but so far she'd had a hard time drawing any conversation from Patti Foley.

She'd arrived half an hour ago and seen to the drinks. Then she'd escorted their special VIP guest inside. All of that had kept the two apart. Still, Austen had a plan and she wasn't going to be put off.

'And I'll just do a bit of an intro an' read one of my poems, then, shall I?' she'd heard Meg Rawlings asking Patti with her strong West Country accent. Austen had once upon a time thought the poet put the accent on for the telly but, it turned out, she was the real deal down-to-earth Meg Rawlings in private too. Seeing her making herself at home in the Borrow-A-Bookshop now, she was nothing like the cerebral, pacing, restless Callista Flyte. She was small and mousy with a wry twinkly smile that said she'd been doing this for so long literally nothing could faze her. 'Do you need a room?' Patti was asking. 'Or can we get you anything to eat?'

Meg had drawn foil-wrapped sandwiches from her bag and taken a seat right in the front row. 'A glass of white to wash down my butties would be nice, please.'

The poet had stayed there at the front welcoming everyone as they filed inside, even signing a few of her latest books before the evening had properly begun for people eager to get their copies. 'Beat the crowds,' she joked, posing for selfies and generally being what Austen thought of as a safe pair of hands at an event like this.

'She's fantastic,' Austen remarked to Patti when they found themselves alone together in the cafe.

'Let's not do this,' Patti said. 'Pretending everything's fine. I feel silly enough as it is without pretending.'

'I don't want that either,' Austen told her, trying to detain her by standing in front of the cafe door, the sound of people arriving and milling around growing louder behind her. 'Listen, I know you've got work to do,' Austen pleaded. 'But I have to tell you, I've done a lot of learning since I turned up here. And a lot of that's down to you making me wake up, and yes, some of it was down to Callista, and maybe even Delphine, or whoever that was. You all showed me some things about myself that I needed to see. It's been kind of sucky, to be honest, but I've really dug deep, and I've been trying to work out who I am, and who I'm not, and...'

'And what did you conclude?' Patti cut her off.

'I figured out that I might not know all the things I am yet, but I definitely know what I don't want to be, and I don't want to be the kind of person who meets an amazing woman and hurts her. No, not just an amazing woman – an actual once-in-a-lifetime kind of woman who is so incredibly kind and funny and sexy, and did I say amazing?' Patti almost smiled at this, and it was enough to make Austen hope. She went on. 'I was distracted and thoughtless and confused, and because of that, you're sad.'

'I am sad,' Patti agreed, her eyes on the ground.

'See! And you're the kind of person who just straight up says what they mean. You don't pretend at all. You say it how it is all the time.'

Patti shrugged. 'Because I'm not worrying what people are going to think of me all the time. I just trust that some people will like me for who I am, and the rest don't matter.'

'Exactly.' Austen was nodding. 'That's exactly it. I want to live like that.'

'It takes practice.'

'I'm working on it.'

An alarm on Patti's phone chimed. 'I have to get started,' she said.

'Talk after?' Austen didn't care how pleading she sounded.

Patti held her gaze for a second, seeming to think. 'Sure.'

When Austen followed her through to the bookshop, after some deep breaths and having given herself a stern talking-to about sticking to the plan, Patti was in front of the mic, and every seat was taken.

Minty had just arrived, announcing loudly like a town crier that she'd have got here sooner but she'd just been interviewed on the telephone for an article on historic hedge preservation and her one-woman revival of the ancient tradition of washday hedge drying. The reporter had assured her it would be a hit with the readers of *The Lady*, who were interested in countryside customs and sustainability. There'd been a smattering of applause at this, led by Meg Rawlings herself, and Minty had taken her seat, delighted.

All the locals were in, including the volunteers and the new residents of the Big House. Sam was stationed behind the table with the wine glasses, but she had doe eyes fixed on Jasper in the crowd, who was gazing back at her. They could have been at a Harry Styles concert and wouldn't have taken their eyes off each other.

The only villagers missing, Austen realised, were Mrs Crocombe and Bovis. As Austen scooched into the last seat (sharing it with Aldous who, apparently, got his own chair at these things), she asked Jowan where they were. 'Didn't their brunch surprise go well after all?'

'Oh, uh…' Jowan didn't know quite how to put it. 'They've been AWOL since noon.'

'Oh? Oh!' Austen's eyes bulged and she fought the impulse to clap her hands. 'They're probably making ice cream.'

'Yes, I imagine that's what it is.' Jowan's soft, slightly blushing smile made her think of her arrival, two weeks ago, and how she'd been so keen to convince Jowan she was a good person she'd been in her usual agonies, making sure to arrive on the dot of five, wondering what he thought of her, trying not to be rude or strange, tying herself in knots. She'd been acting, instead of just enjoying being herself.

'Thank you,' she said to him now.

'For what?' he whispered as the room hushed.

'For letting me borrow your shop. I get it now.'

He looked at her in surprise and delight like she'd at last worked out some secret cipher the rest of the world was in on. 'I knew you would, lass. Good for you.'

Patti, in front of the mic, raised her hand and magically gained the room's attention. As she welcomed everyone, little Aldous clambered onto Austen's lap and, after frisking her blazer pockets for snacks and finding none, he promptly fell asleep.

'Please welcome our V.V.V.V. I. P. guest, Devon's own poet laureate, Meg Rawlings,' Patti said, smiling into the mic with not a hint of nerves or self-consciousness about her. Everyone was cheering and clapping as Meg bounded up to Patti, shaking breadcrumbs from her jumper.

Austen could feel the warmth of the audience for her already. They loved her and she hadn't said a word.

Patti perched on the cash desk facing the audience just off to the side of the performance space. Austen tried not to stare at her and found herself wondering why she was all in black tonight, like a stagehand. It suited her, of course. She'd look beautiful in anything. Yet, Austen hoped her dress didn't reflect her mood. She'd give anything to see her laughing and joking around in bright scarlet and pink just one more time.

'Good evening, everyone,' Meg began. 'It's delightful to be back in Clove Lore and to see so many old friends again. I was thrilled to be invited to introduce your open mic event and to launch my new collection, *Not Averse to Love*. It's only eight ninety-nine.' This got a laugh from the crowd. 'And it contains all my smash hits including your favourite, and mine, "I Wandered Lonely Around

Stroud", and my latest poem "I Should'a Listened to My Mammy".'

Austen caught Patti glance at her then with a tiny flash of humour in her eyes that asked, 'What is going on?' Austen had to look down in case she spoiled things by laughing out loud.

'Before I hand over the floor to you younger ones, I thought I'd share a poem about *my* first open mic night, back in 1976 which, many years later, I shared on the Parky show, and I know he loved it! See what you thinks of it, me dears.'

She narrowed her eyes a little, and although she held her book open, she never once looked at it. She spoke slowly and with a kind of cunning delight that the audience couldn't help smiling at.

'The thing about open mic night is, anyone can do it.
They even lets me take a turn,
And to think I almost blew it!
I stared into the spotlight. Oh! My knees did tremble,
And when I started to recite, all that came out... was
    mumbles.
Speak up! the jazzy poet said, from under his black
    beret.
She makes no sense! the MC cried. I think she's lost
    her marbles.

But I had my little poem, see? The first one I had
    written.
An' I'd worked ever so 'ard on it, the rhymin' bug had
    bitten.
An' I was the one on stage just then, an' weren't about
    to weaken.

So what if it's not Shakespeare? I'm a poet just for
    speakin'!
So, I fixed them with a glassy stare, and let 'em 'ave my
    composition,
And even though nobody clapped, I'd made the right
    decision.'

She ended her poem with a cheeky smile that prompted
applause, and there was some genuine laughter from
Minty, who was clearly a fan, and some confused, disbe-
lieving chortles from Izaak and Leonid, who'd never heard
light entertainment poetry before and were obviously
thinking British people were madder than they'd realised.

After some words of encouragement from Meg, and
another round of applause while she took her seat, Patti
opened the floor to the local poets who came up one by
one to perform, and all of them were received warmly and
in the spirit of the evening.

Austen, however, held off right until the end to speak
up. By then her hands were clammy and her heart
thumping impossibly hard.

Patti was asking if there were any last writers wishing
to perform.

She was looking towards Austen with a hint of fading
hope when she raised her hand and said, shakily, 'I'll read,
if nobody minds.'

Every head in the place turned to watch Austen deposit
a snoring Aldous onto Jowan's lap before walking slowly
to the spot in front of the mic.

Austen planted her feet to stop the room spinning
dizzily. She clasped the mic to steady herself, broadcasting
a loud gulping swallow over the PA system.

Austen was suddenly aware that Patti was on the move, scurrying into the audience and taking what had been Austen's seat next to Jowan. As she passed by, she'd whispered a quick, 'you can do it.'

Austen, adrenalin spiking, fixed her eyes on Patti over the heads of all these staring, expectant people waiting to be entertained and impressed.

'I've um… Oh my!' She flinched at the sound of her voice booming from the speaker. 'Sorry. I've, um, chucked a lot of poems in the bin on this holiday…' This elicited a nervy, scattered laugh from the crowd, giving Austen time to fix her specs and swallow again.

'But I wrote this,' she went on, 'after leading a workshop for kids on finding your voice, and after receiving some encouragement in that regard from someone I met while holidaying here in Clove Lore, Patti Foley, who never seems to have trouble just being herself.'

More laughter followed, and heads turned briefly towards the smiling Patti. Austen felt even more of her inhibitions fall away. She looked down at the notebook in her hand.

'This really felt like *me* writing something for once, if you see what I mean? I wasn't trying to sound like someone else, or impress anybody, and I wasn't trying to hide myself either.'

'What's it called, me dear?' Meg asked from the front row, seeing Austen faltering once again. There really were an awful lot of people watching her right now.

'A title?' said Austen. 'Uh, OK. How about… "How I realised I was more than paper and ink, that I'm an actual, loveable human with feelings and everything and it's *me* who gets to decide who I am and where I end up, so I should stop being afraid of real-life flesh and blood people and just use my voice and say what it is that I need?"'

Patti, now practically bouncing in her seat, whooped loudly and clapped in the fresh silence.

'It's a bit long,' Meg said, making the room laugh, 'but I likes it fine. Go on, then, you can do it.'

Austen had never heard silence like this before. This was what expectation sounds like, a great big void you have to fill with your talent – at the risk of disappointing everyone.

Austen had rehearsed late into the night, picturing this very moment, and she wasn't about to disappoint herself.

'OK, here goes nothing,' she said. So she began, slow and clear, into the mic, her eyes fixed on Patti for strength.

'I was spiral bound up in you. And others before and
    after you.
Admiring everyone except myself.
Confusing my voice with yours, hers, anyone's.
Abridged. Translated. And left unreadable.

But my own small voice is still here inside,
along with my pulse, my vision, my touch, my nerves,
    my sinew.
I take a deep breath all of my own, I open my mouth,
and I speak myself anew.'

At first nobody in the room seemed to know she'd finished, and Austen had to take a step back and nod that it was OK to clap now if they wanted, which everyone did. Even though it felt a bit slow and lukewarm, Austen didn't care because Patti was on her feet, applauding hard, her own personal standing ovation.

Meg stood too and said into the microphone, 'And now… wine!' which made the room relax into instantaneous chatter. The event was over.

Austen knew she had to work fast before Patti fell into work mode again. She reached down behind the till and grabbed the gift she'd prepared for this moment.

Crossing the shop, dodging all the people who were starting to mill about and talk in groups, she took Patti by the hand and pulled her out into the courtyard where the first stars were showing in the summer twilight.

'You were amazing,' Patti said, when they came to a stop.

'Thank you, I tried, and that's what matters. I think it's the first honest flesh-and-blood poetry I've written in years.'

'Good, well, don't stop. Keep speaking yourself. I like this Austen.'

'I'm learning to like her,' Austen agreed. 'She's not perfect though.'

'Good!'

Patti noticed the gift concealed behind Austen's back. 'And you're also a thief, it looks like?'

Austen presented her with the big bunch of cornflowers.

'Did you take these from the meadow?' Patti was smiling.

'With help from Leonid and Izaak. They said Minty wouldn't mind, if she knew I was giving them to you.'

Patti took the flowers in her hands, their bobbing blue heads dancing and drooping in a dense, raggedy cloud. 'They're beautiful. Thank you.'

'I need you to know I'm grateful for everything you've done for me,' Austen began. 'And that I hate seeing you sad. You're all in black tonight. It doesn't feel like you.'

'I don't know,' Patti said, the toe of her boot scraping the cobbles. 'I guess I wanted to be like you for a while.'

'*You're* copying *me?*'

'Well, you do look very cool.' Patti freed a hand from the flowers to touch one of the shoulder straps of Austen's overalls where they formed a bow. She slipped her hand around it, holding on, her eyes fixed there. 'Why wouldn't I want to be like you?'

'Because I was a mess. Because I'm only just learning who I am.'

'You already know the foundational stuff. And I like all of it. You're good people, Austen Archer. And a shit-hot poet in the making.' They couldn't help laughing at this. Some of the apprehension was floating away.

Patti shifted her flowers aside so she could draw Austen into a one-armed hug. 'I wish you could have figured some of this stuff out before you got here. We could have had the best two weeks,' she said, smiling regretfully as she released her again.

'I know,' Austen conceded sadly.

Patti had more to say. 'My sister came here and found a way of breaking old habits. She ended up staying. She was kind of hard work before that. Kind of a mess.'

'But you guys worked it out, and now you live with her.' Austen didn't care that she sounded hopeful and eager. She wanted Patti to know she couldn't bear to leave without her knowing how much she'd wanted her, if only she hadn't been too lost in herself to fully recognise it at the time.

'That's true,' Patti laughed, and this time it was Austen reaching for her. She put an arm around her shoulder and pulled her close.

'I'm going to miss you so much.'

'Your holiday's almost over, huh?'

Austen nodded, her head pressed against Patti's.

'By my calculations, it's not over for another... like, twelve hours?' said Patti, pulling away so she could meet her eyes.

Austen grinned at this.

'And I'm not sleepy at all,' Patti added. 'Are you?'

What seemed like a long moment of silence passed, during which the pair took in each other's shifting expressions and Patti most definitely bit at her bottom lip in the most devastating way.

'How quickly can you get that lot out of my book-shop?' Austen blurted.

They turned to look at the chattering crowds still inside, loud bursts of laughter spilling through the open door and into the night.

'If we start moving chairs about in a persuasive way, I reckon we could chase them off in twenty-five minutes,' Patti said decidedly. 'Fifteen if we bang the corks back into the wine bottles.'

'You lock the door after the last person leaves,' Austen said, pushing back imaginary sleeves.

'Meet me upstairs?' said Patti.

'Let's do this.'

Austen and Patti marched back into the party.

Chapter Thirty-eight

Kissing Patti all night long had been the easiest thing she'd ever done.

Austen hadn't felt the need to hide or act or fake any aspect of herself. They hadn't even bothered with the leftover wine for courage, hadn't needed it, and that would have wasted precious minutes anyway.

Austen had found Patti upstairs, sitting inside the window seat waiting for her, ignoring the beautiful moon outside, seemingly preferring to watch Austen stepping inside the bedroom and sliding the door closed.

'Has everyone gone home?' Patti asked.

'Yep.' Austen clambered onto the bed on her knees, making her way to Patti inside the recess in the stones above the headboard. 'You look amazing sitting there,' Austen said, not feeling shy, wondering at this daring person she was becoming.

She kneeled at Patti's feet on the bed, tracing the ivy leaf tattoo around her ankle with a finger. Patti leaned forward to watch Austen lift the loose fabric of her black trousers higher to the point mid-calf where the leaves grew tiny and the leafy tendrils stopped.

'That is such a cute tattoo,' Austen said, wanting to do nothing but praise this woman all night.

'What about yours?' Patti said, her hand on Austen's shoulder.

Austen leaned forward now so her arms rested across Patti's thighs. 'It's Sappho.'

'Lines of poetry?'

'What else?'

'I can't read it,' Patti said, and Austen didn't hesitate to untie the straps at her shoulders, pulling at the vest underneath and turning her body so Patti could read the words on her back in the night-glow from the window, her fingertips tracing the ink under Austen's skin. 'Come now, luxuriant Graces, and beautiful-haired Muses. I shall sing these songs beautifully.'

When she fell silent, Austen turned to face her again, lifting onto her knees so she could hold Patti in her spot on the window seat cushions.

'That's how I'm going to live, beautifully, not just how I want to write,' Austen told her, as she lifted her lips to Patti's throat, kissing her as softly as she could, making her way along her jawline and up to her bottom lip. All the while Patti ran her fingers over Austen's arms and back, drawing her closer until they were locked in a kiss neither wanted to break.

Austen was sure they'd only fallen onto the bed to sleep just after dawn, so they'd only slept for an hour or two at most.

She could barely open her eyes when the sunrise came, so she dozed on, the warmth of Patti beside her, naked under the white sheet, keeping last night's soft memories alive in her sleepy brain – visions of Patti sitting in the window seat while Austen let her mouth trail down the centre of her chest, over her belly and down to where Patti held her softly, leaning back against the glass, coming apart entirely while Austen took her time with her mouth and the flat of her tongue, telling her afterwards she didn't expect anything in return, that she was only happy that Patti was happy, and Patti had laughed and pushed her down onto the bed, telling her in a devilish tone that she wasn't leaving Clove Lore without tasting her too.

Austen's body still thrilled at the memory of Patti's touch as she stretched out on the cool sheets now, in the bright morning light, thinking she must have dozed off yet again. It really must be time to get up.

Her hand travelled across the covers, searching for the warmth of Patti's body once more. The bed was empty.

Austen sprang awake, looking around the room. Nine o'clock, and no sign of Patti.

She looked on the floor. No clothes. She listened for her. Not a sound. Pulling on a t-shirt, she padded down the metal spiral and across the empty shop to the cafe. If she knew Patti at all, she'd be making her breakfast and coffee, but no, there was no one here.

Austen poured a glass of water and made herself drink the whole thing.

'Don't panic,' she told herself. 'She'll be around somewhere. Just get dressed and don't leap to conclusions.'

She went back upstairs, showered, dressed and was lugging her bag downstairs, burningly aware her taxi was leaving in twenty minutes from the visitor centre and that if she was going to allow herself to think the worst, this might be the time to start doing it.

Patti's blue cornflowers were in a vase on the table by the door. The table where Austen was supposed to have organised some kind of display at the end of her stay. In the rush of last night she'd forgotten all about it and now there was no time to do it.

She checked her phone for only the third time, which seemed like a reasonable number of times, and not overanxious or obsessive, just the normal amount of concern that you'd feel if the woman you'd had the best night of your life with had done a runner while you slept and she isn't here now to say goodbye to you before a journey of hundreds of miles.

There were no missed calls and no messages. This couldn't be good.

And yet still Austen didn't want to catastrophise. 'She'll be here,' she told herself, sitting down behind the till. 'She wouldn't leave without saying goodbye. No way.' She held herself in a hug and hunkered down. She wasn't going anywhere without finding out what was going on.

The minutes ticked closer to ten. She was going to have to get that taxi now, or the driver would be leaving without her. Was her holiday really ending like this? It couldn't be?

She left the keycard on the shop counter, checked she had her notebook in her pocket, and as calmly as she could, made her way to the door where she'd forgotten to turn the sign to 'closed' last night.

She flipped it over now, thinking of how it all began, filming herself turning the sign on her first day, and how there'd been a message from a friendly stranger to say hello, she'd never know who, even though she'd burned to know, and she'd got lost in a dreamy fantasy of connection across the miles, of collegiality, and well, she had to admit it, romantic feelings for some airy person who dematerialised into nothing as though they hadn't shared a thing.

There was no way Patti was doing the same thing now; disappearing. It simply wasn't possible. They'd had something bigger than mere love letters on a screen. Right?

Austen crossed the shop again to close the door to the little bedroom. The room where Callista had hidden from her public with Jasmine, the new girl she was probably infatuated with. She thought of the staleness of her feelings for Callista now, how bitter and cold the entire thing had been, nothing like the wild, writhing, breathless heat of Patti holding her, making her call out her name, kissing her hard, pressing her to the bed. That was real. That was worth all the pain of the last few days and any that was yet to come. She'd take it all for Patti Foley.

Austen shouldered her tote bag, now full to the top and jagged with books, and she made for the door. She'd come a long way in the last two weeks, she knew, and one thing was for sure: she wasn't leaving without telling Patti exactly how she felt.

Hurriedly now, she reached for the latch and, as she gripped it, it turned in her hand, the door pushed inward almost knocking her back into the cash desk.

'Oh my God,' Patti cried. 'I thought I was going to be too late! Were you leaving?' She was helplessly out of breath, her arms full of... were those picture frames?

'I was coming to find you. What's all this?' Austen's heart thumped hard.

'They're yours. Well, they're for the shop. But they're yours.' Patti lifted a forearm to wipe her brow. She was wittering now. Not something Austen was used to seeing from her.

She lowered the things in her arms onto the display table where the cornflowers stood in their vase.

Austen lifted one of the frames to inspect it. There were words handwritten inside, and if she wasn't mistaken, they were on the handmade paper from their workshop date.

Pupils tightened to two black dots.
A hand swipes over cursing lips:
She retreats in fury and wanting.

'You framed my poems?' Austen asked in amazement.

'I did!' Patti said. 'And it took me way longer to copy them out than I thought it would. Turns out calligraphy isn't my thing.' Patti was still panting but she laughed through it. 'Do you like them?'

'I do. I mean, some of these poems aren't very good. You took them while I was sleeping?'

'That I did.' Patti seemed delighted with her ingenuity. 'And I think they're *all* good, actually. Even ones about accidentally kissing some horrid bat. A poet's work is supposed to reflect them at every age. I can't wait to read the ones you write next, and the ones you'll write this winter, and next year, and when we're little old ladies!'

'Hah!' Austen watched as Patti opened out the stands behind the frames and propped them up on the display table. 'Wait a minute, what are you doing?' she said.

'Well, you know how Jowan always makes Borrowers leave a display here, to show their reading tastes for the next lot to arrive?'

'O-kay?' Austen waited.

'This reflects my taste. And you should be really proud of yourself. I'm proud of you.'

Austen felt herself fold. She stepped into Patti's arms and held her close. 'Thank you. That's the nicest thing anyone's ever done for me. I don't even know how I'm supposed to leave now you've done all this, and after last night, and...' Austen stopped. 'See? I knew you wouldn't have done a runner!'

'As if!'

'What do we do now?' Austen said.

'Do you want to go home?' Patti asked, blunt as always.

'I mean, not directly.'

'What does that mean?'

'It means I was just getting into the summer holidays and I'm not done yet.'

Patti smiled, her shoulders settling, pulling Austen in for another kiss.

'Patti?' Austen asked eventually, pulling away only a little. 'Do you *want* to stay here? In Clove Lore, I mean? You said a few times you weren't quite sure if it was home or if it was just somewhere you kind of ended up by accident?'

'It feels a lot more like home with you in it.'

'But there are other places you want to see? With me?' Austen risked asking.

They drew apart, considering one another, two slow grins spreading as their eyes grew wide at the possibilities.

Chapter Thirty-nine

Patti had been due some annual leave, she'd told everyone, as they'd stuffed backpacks with everything they could think of, and Joy had made them unpack it all because they'd been wildly unrealistic about how much they could carry, and of course she'd been right.

Backpacking through Rome and along the Rhine and on to Switzerland would have been impossible with all the books Austen had thought she might need for the journey.

They'd packed so much adventure into August, and arrived in September with suntans, blistered feet, battered hiking boots and a million delicious summer memories.

Their postcards were currently stuck on fridge doors from Clove Lore to Levenshulme. They'd preferred writing home the old-fashioned way, especially now Austen was on a tech detox. She couldn't bring herself to look at her cell phone anymore, and Patti hadn't questioned it. She understood.

There was a distinct hint of early autumn in the air as they got off the train on the very last leg of their journey before they returned to England.

The metro station was cool and quiet out in the Fifth Arrondissement, and even though Patti would have killed for a croissant and a hot chocolate, she had an inkling if they didn't make this their first port of call in the city of light, Austen might not be able to enjoy their week of Parisian hostelling.

'Statue of Voltaire,' Austen said, walking hand in hand with Patti, pointing out landmarks she seemed to expect, even though she'd never been here before, her steps growing slower and smaller, nothing like the bubbling, joyful Austen of Barcelona and Cadiz.

She was growing quieter, and had been for the last few hours as they'd approached Paris by coach and then by rail, travelling as cheaply as they possibly could.

'There it is.' Austen halted on the other side of the road from the Feint Heart Bookshop.

It was a dull morning and the lights were on inside, even in the tower where the little slit window glowed.

The window boxes were planted with yellow autumn dahlias. Someone was placing a book in the window display, just a shadowy figure Patti couldn't make out clearly.

She bit her tongue, not wanting to say anything to spook the already deliberating Austen, who had let go of her hand and taken a step closer to the kerbside as the motorbikes zipped past. She was scanning the street now, standing like a lost child, holding herself.

Patti didn't like the possessive spark that fired within her now and she dampened it down, imagining how poor Austen felt facing the confusion and doubt she still lived with.

Patti knew she still wondered about Delphine. It troubled her that she might have been toyed with almost as much as it troubled her that she'd hurt someone she'd cared for, or that something really had happened to her and she was all alone now without family or friends.

She'd watched Austen reading books on catfishing and ghosting, trying to make sense of it all, asking herself if that's what had happened to her, trying to deal with the feelings of being entirely convinced of one reality when something quite different may have been playing out.

'What the heck is that?' Patti said, making Austen look too, far down the street to where a man in a trench coat was walking tiny bouncing things on slender leads like strings.

They watched as he slowly grew nearer until it was apparent to them both he was walking seven tiny chihuahua pups, tumbling all over the place, all while smoking a long white cigarette.

'It's all very French,' Patti remarked, before falling silent again.

After watching an internal battle wage within her, written in the unfamiliar way her girlfriend held her body, Patti observed Austen stepping out, dodging the traffic.

She let her go, seeing Austen grow smaller as she made her way to the other side in safety, before stopping, frozen, looking first down at her feet, then to her right and up at the rooftops.

The change took all of a second. 'Look, Patti!' Austen shouted over the road, beckoning Patti to come and join her.

Patti darted through the traffic, not wanting to look in the windows of the bookshop, instead following the point where Austen's sparkling eyes were fixed.

'It's the Eiffel Tower,' she was saying, looking like she might cry. 'Oh my days!' Austen seemed to be re-thinking her plans.

Patti smiled to see it, but said nothing. If Austen was going to walk away from ever knowing the truth about

Delphine, she'd absolutely have to be the one to make that decision.

'Come on,' Austen said, taking her hand and holding it fast. 'They say it's the most beautiful sight in Paris from up at the top.' And she moved off, not looking back for traces of phantom booksellers, her steps growing in intention as they walked away from the Feint Heart.

'You definitely don't want to go in?' Patti checked.

Austen didn't even have to think. 'Nah, not really. I thought I might, but I don't.'

Patti brought their joined hands to her lips and kissed the soft skin of Austen's fingers as they walked away.

'To the Eiffel Tower, then?' said Patti, with a flush of enthusiasm for the rest of their travels.

'Yes!' Austen agreed, picking up the pace and grinning at her girlfriend, taking in her green eyes and her wide smile. 'Although I'm definitely already looking at the most beautiful sight in all of Paris.'

The women ran on, laughing and gripping hands tightly as golden leaves fell from the trees and swirled around them in the autumn breeze.

Epilogue

Autumn in Clove Lore is a time of plenty, and nowhere more so than up at the Big House where the whole estate basks in the golden glow from the surrounding woods, the trees are burnished orange and red, and the low sun over the Atlantic lights the mellow mists in the estate gardens.

Minty and Leonid's pumpkins are growing fat in the field, a good two weeks off prime picking time when, with any luck, half the county will queue up to wander amongst them with a cup of hot chocolate and one of Jude Crawley's reasonably priced pumpkin spice gingerbreads.

Any pumpkin patch profits are already earmarked for growing Minty's latest venture which, with the help of her formidable sidekick, Estée Gold, has come swiftly to fruition.

Izaak's ticket booth at the entrance to the estate was requisitioned by the lady of the manor weeks ago and it is now transformed with home-made bunting, wooden benches and racks of all sizes, each one laid out with boxes upon boxes of new season apples and plums from the estate's heritage orchard and jars of Minty's preserves, made on her trusty Aga.

The farmers from the adjoining fields over the promontory had been paid a visit by the two women and pressed into donating a few potatoes and, come

December, some Brussels sprouts. One farmer, particularly taken with Estée, had pledged a sack of carrots every week from now until January, should she be around to collect them from him, and Minty had been swift to accept his generous offer before Estée could object.

Every school and Girl Guide group in the district were currently collecting harvest offerings of cans, dry pasta, rice and trick-or-treat lollies and chocolates, whatever their neighbours could spare, all for the sake of the Clove Lore Community Surplus Food Pantry.

It had been Izaak and Leonid's bumper crop of summer courgettes that did it, giving Minty the idea for a food bank and produce-swapping service where anyone going short of something was welcome to stock up, and anyone with a glut was free to exchange damsons for chillies, or pears for bulbs of garlic.

Minty hadn't stopped there, and the big supermarket along the bypass had received an unannounced visit from her entire entourage, including Jowan and Aldous. Estée and Minty led the delegation, cornering the manager by the cold meats. They'd been so insistent that he could be doing good with his short-dated items instead of chucking them in the skip out the back that he'd found himself nodding in bewildered agreement. They'd cajoled and persuaded until the poor man had regretted not making a run for it when he first saw them marching in, and he'd agreed to a daily delivery of perishables if only they promised not to come back.

The local papers and radio stations had got wind of the project soon enough and there'd been no stopping its momentum until today, when Estée was preparing to cut the red ribbon on it. (As Minty has been heard to remark, 'Where's the point in having our very own global icon if she can't help us rustle up a few dented cans and a bit of charity veg?')

The TV star had graciously gone along with the whole thing, giving all the reporters a quote for their articles and promising that anyone stopping by would be welcome to an autograph.

Now the moment has come and the press and local schoolchildren, the whole congregation of the church, and they weren't sure how many Scout troops are waiting for her to step out from the food store.

Inside the shed, Izaak and Leonid, wearing the same branded apron as Estée who'd also opted for a khaki jumpsuit (and a pair of gold wellingtons – her contribution to the Food Pantry's uniform design) were pumping her for yet more *Destiny's Peak* gossip.

'Can I ask just one more thing?' Leonid said in his gruff Moscow accent.

'The press is waiting, darlings,' she said with an indulgent eye roll, perfectly content to make the reporters wait out there a little longer.

'Please! You know we watched it a hundred times between us,' Isaak begged.

'Oh, go on then,' she caved, not so secretly loving every second of their attention.

'In the third season,' Izaak began, 'when Coral is pushed through the glass table and it shatters and her wig comes off?'

'Yes?' Estée said, as though that didn't sound insane.

'Was that really Fenella Lansbury doing her own stunts?'

'Oh darlings,' she told the rapt husbands hanging on her every word. 'Fenella couldn't even fall convincingly onto a mattress. No, that was her stunt double, but I,

346

on the other hand, was the one taking that twenty-foot dive from the balcony in season five while I was trying to escape the cocktail party snake charmer who was actually Coral's husband Tandy back from the dead and out for revenge!'

'I *knew* that was really you!' Leonid said, hands pressed together.

'Well, thank you, darling,' sparkled Estée Gold, wiping a clod of muck off a King Edward spud and placing it back in its crate. 'You can't hide talent.' Her own personal fan club burst into agreement.

'Go on, do it one more time, the slap,' Izaak said.

'Just not so hard this time!' Leonid looked half nervous, half ecstatic, offering up his face to the actress.

'If you insist,' said Estée, squaring up to Leonid. 'You, Mackauley Dustin Forester, are a cad!' And she mimed stripping off an evening glove, poising her hand dramatically in the air, while Izaak clapped and hooted in approval.

'Ahem!' Minty interrupted from the hut door. 'We're ready.'

'Sorry, darling, I'll have to slap you later. I need to get on with the show.' Estée followed Minty out into the waiting crowd like she was arriving at the foot of the stairs at the Met Gala.

A cheer of approval went up as the camera flashes flared, carrying right across the estate to the quiet spot in the parterre borders where Sam and Jasper were hiding away behind the box hedges, tired and grubby from a day of hefting food crates into the store.

'Sounds like Mum's hit her mark,' Jasper said, lifting an ear to the applause.

'She'll be loving that!' Sam agreed, snuggling closer to Jasper in his big black padded coat. He could always be counted on to keep her warm, she was finding. 'Do you reckon she'll be happy, shifting veggies at a food bank?' Sam had her doubts.

'I dunno. She's loved being wanted, that's for sure. And she's the sort of person who needs to keep busy, until the next job comes in.'

'And Minty'll make sure she's busy! Hah!' Sam laughed. 'I heard her talking about planting a Christmas tree farm the other day. Woman's nuts!'

Jasper only smiled and pulled her closer.

'Shouldn't we go back? Show some support?' Sam asked, not in the least wanting to move from their cosy spot amongst the grey stone planters and leafless rose-bushes.

'Nobody will notice we're not there. They'll all be looking at Mum,' he said, before bringing his mouth to Sam's in a soft kiss, nuzzling his nose to hers, making her smile.

Things had been like this for weeks, easy and simple, the way it should be when two young people find each other. There'd been some let-up for Sam at the laundry now Caroline Capstan had the all clear from the doctor and she was back at work, and Sam was free to concentrate on assisting Patti Foley with the winter event planning, now she and her devoted girlfriend, Austen, were on their way back from Paris, having had the time of their lives apparently.

There'd been talk of Austen commuting back and forward from Manchester for a while, now that she had some poetry workshops booked in up North at local youth clubs and libraries, as well as an upcoming regular spot at the Clove Lore primary school (thanks to Radia petitioning the head teacher until she'd simply given in and cleared an hour a week off every year group's timetable for learning the rudiments of creative writing).

The autumn was shaping up to be a very gentle one indeed.

'And you?' Sam asked now. 'Are you going to be OK now Estée doesn't need looking after? Is working at the laundry really going to be enough for you?'

Jasper kept her close, speaking softly in between kisses at her temple. 'Once I get Minty on board with my Clove Lore community cinema plan, I reckon I'll have more than enough.'

Sam and Mrs Capstan had helped him write the proposal with proper costings and a profit forecast and everything (and if they knew Minty like they thought they did, she loved any talk of profits – anything to keep her beloved estate not just afloat but thriving). All they needed was the projector and speaker system and no, it wasn't going to be cheap, and it'd need to be shipped over from the manufacturer, and that would cost an arm and a leg, and there'd be licences to procure and agreements to sign with the council and no end of risk assessments and red tape. But come the lighter days, Jasper predicted he could seat up to one hundred paying ticket holders at any one outdoor movie showing on the lawn while the film rolled on the grey stonework of the windowless east wing end wall of the Big House. Not quite the silver screen, but close enough, and Jasper was convinced it would draw audiences of locals and holidaymakers from all corners of Devon for a night out under the stars.

'I have this idea of having our red-carpet premiere on Valentine's night,' he told Sam. 'What do you think? Will you be my date?'

'Won't you be in the film booth doing all the techy stuff?'

'Yes, with any luck. And you'll have the best seat in the house right next to me.'

'Oh, VIP section, is it?' Sam said, before pressing her lips to Jasper's once more. 'If you're buying the popcorn, I'm in,' she told him, and the pair sank into another kiss, dreaming of the cold days ahead and all the plans being made across Clove Lore where the latest residents, Jasper, Estée, Patti and Austen, were intent on making themselves thoroughly happy and at home here.

A Letter from Kiley

There's always so many people to thank, and this time I'll begin with my wee family, I'm so proud of us and I love you so much. Thank you Nic for all the kind things that you do, and for fixing my laptop when I sprayed it with water from the hose when I was 5,000 words from the end of this manuscript and it all stopped working. Michael is the most caring person I've ever met and you taught me, amongst many other things, about being intentional. Thank you for Meg Rawlings' titles in this story. They really made me chuckle.

I am learning all the time and trying to grow just like Austen in this story. Attending a Fiona Lucas book plotting workshop in early 2023 was where I came up with the outline for this story. Thank you for being so clever and inspiring, Fiona. I'm so grateful for that day.

Vicky and Mary Jayne are not only wonderful writers but lovely friends. Thank you for everything.

Thank you, lovely Dream Team as well. I'd be lost without you.

Thank you, Keshini and everyone at Hera Books for this, our tenth book together. What a team! And I'm so grateful to Diane Meacham for yet more perfect cover art. Thank you for giving me cornflowers! Jenny Page corrected the proofs of this story. Thank you so much.

I really want to show some love to the booksellers and their customers who have gone out of their way to support me in recent years. First of all, my local bookshop, **Nantwich Bookshop and Coffee**. You are all lovely! Thank you for everything including two amazing book launch events.

Haygates Book Shop! Why are you such legends? Thank you so much.

For **Tealeaves and Reads**, thank you for your love and support! You deserve all the good things. Your book boxes are gorgeous and I have loved our Christmas book party nights!

The Unplugged Book Box were stellar last year, supporting me with a special limited subscribers' edition hardback of *The Borrow a Bookshop Holiday*. It was gorgeous! Thank you so much.

The Happily Ever After Book Box are also extremely lovely folk who donate to local animal rescue organisations with every book box order. Check them out.

Chris, David and the team at Blackwell's Bookshop, Manchester are beyond amazing, helping a girl out time and again. Thank you so much! Red Newsom, Lead Bookseller, wrote an amazing 'Behind the Shelves Bookseller Stories' article for *Books Are My Bag* which helped inspire Austen's childhood love of the library summer reading challenge and her joy at suggesting just the right book (or in this case, poem) for her customers.

I'd be utterly lost without booksellers all over the globe stocking my stories. Thank you all so much for your support.

Finally, thank you, lovely readers, reviewers, bloggers and book friends who have encouraged and supported me hugely with this series. I am beyond grateful for everything.

I'll be back very soon with the fifth instalment of the Borrow a Bookshop series, which will be another love song to booksellers and book lovers everywhere. Please come and meet me once again at the Borrow-A-Bookshop for Valentine's Day, 2025.

Until then, come find me on Instagram @kileydunba-rauthor or on the 'Kiley Dunbar Author Facebook Page'.

Love, Kiley x